Quinton spent the next few hours examining and appraising the contents of a French vitrine, but even the Sèvres figurines failed to claim his undivided attention. When Justine wasn't foremost on his mind, he found himself struggling with a sharp sense of guilt. Why should he hide his attraction to Justine from Helene Haymes? He was attracted to Justine as he had never been to another woman. Why would the old woman object to that—or to him? Yet Justine had been so adamant about Helene not knowing about them. Still, Helene was paying his salary, and he did not really know Justine . . . did he?

THE APPRAISER

JACK MAYFIELD

ace books

A Division of Charter Communications Inc.
A GROSSET & DUNLAP COMPANY
51 Madison Avenue
New York, New York 10010

THE APPRAISER

An Ace Original

First Printing: June 1981
Published simultaneously in Canada

2 4 6 8 0 9 7 5 3 1
Manufactured in the United States of America

*For my Key West friends,
especially Margaret Foresman,
Janet Hayes Padron and
Peggy Tufford Hillmer*

PART I

Chapter One

Quinton Armstrong opened the iron gates of an address on Simonton Street and stepped into the courtyard. "Christ!" he murmured in awe, and drew in his breath. "Unbelievable!"

He felt as if he had been transported into another time, a past era. The house, a rambling three-story mansion, looked like something conceived by a 1930s Hollywood set designer; great white columns in the tradition of the antebellum South rose from the ground to the peak of a sloped roof, supporting balconies above and sheltering porches below. The great windows were all fixed with shutters, the paint chipping away; all except those at the front door were securely closed. Above the door was a transom window in the shape of an open fan, the small panes beveled and cut of the finest crystal; he recognized the work immediately as from Tiffany and Company, and mentally dated it as from the turn of the century.

Standing inside the gate, Quinton took a handkerchief from the breast pocket of his suit coat and wiped at the perspiration on his brow. It had been the middle of winter in New York, windy and bitterly cold, and now, four hours after boarding a flight at LaGuardia airport

he found himself in the hot, humid, tropical climate of
Key West, Florida. He was reminded briefly of Viet-
nam, but pushed that comparison away immediately.
The gardens surrounding the house were filled with
lush vegetation. Untended, plants stretched their ten-
drils across the walkway and entwined the lower columns of the house. The word *decadent* came into Quinton's mind, and he was reminded of the garden used in
the movie of Tennessee Williams' *Suddenly Last Summer*. He stuffed his handkerchief, the linen limp with
sweat, back into his pocket, and continued to stare at
the house.

The railings of the second and third floor balconies
were ornamented with gingerbread carvings, the sort
seamen had been noted for whittling when circumstances kept them in port. He remembered reading
in a brochure he had bought on Key West that no two
seamen executed the same design; no plagiarists the old
men of the sea.

Quinton pushed his sunglasses back on the bridge of
his nose and lowered his gaze.

The front porch sloped toward the yard. The planks
had been freshly painted a dull grey, but years of
accumulated paint failed to hide sections that looked
dangerously worn and scarcely capable of sustaining a
man's weight. His attention was drawn to the far corner
of the porch. He had not heard the click, click, clicking
of the swing. He heard it now and saw a young Negro
woman lolling back and forth. She saw with her eyes
closed, her hands folded peacefully in her lap, her
shoeless feet rhythmically propelling the swing to and
fro. He had the impression she was sleeping and the
movement of her feet was as automatic as breathing. He
started to move up the walkway when a Doberman,
hidden from view by the ferns growing along the base

of the porch, sprang to its feet and bared its fangs with a threatening growl.

"Quiet, Lucifer!" the young woman commanded without opening her eyes. "You Misser Armstrong?" Before he could reply, she added, "If you ain't, I'm not supposed to hold this here dog back."

"I'm definitely Mr. Armstrong," Quinton assured her.

The young woman opened her eyes as she sat forward. She laced her thin fingers through the chain collar about the Doberman's neck. "You're safe to go to the door now," she said. She smiled, revealing even white teeth. "You sure turned pale when Lucifer stood up," she told Quinton with amusement.

Quinton said nothing. She had obviously been watching him through lowered lashes and had been enjoying the fright the dog had given him. He climbed the steps and moved to the door, an eye kept warily on the Doberman. If the bitch could get a charge out of frightening him, what were her limits? He imagined his terror should she suddenly release the Doberman's restraining collar.

Quinton pressed the doorbell and heard muffled chimes inside the house.

"You gotta press longer than that," the young woman told him. "Mama's in the back and she don't hear so good. Miss Helene, she don't answer the door."

Quinton smiled a thank you, and put his finger back on the bell.

An auspicious arrival, he thought.

The prolonged sound of the door chimes excited the Doberman. The animal strained forward, almost yanking the young woman out of the porch swing. Quinton recoiled, not caring if the fear on his face amused her.

She shouted the dog's name, yanked at its collar, and cuffed it alongside the head. The dog immediately quieted and lay down at her feet, its head on his forepaws, its eyes fixed on Quinton.

Quinton hadn't heard the door open. When he turned back from the Doberman he found himself confronting a very large Negro woman in a white apron and kerchief. His nerves must have caused him to flinch, because the woman smiled, leaned out through the door and shouted, "Betty Sue, you teasin' people with that Dober again?"

"No, Mama," came the meek reply.

"Likes to have her fun with that dog," the woman explained to Quinton. "You Mr. Armstrong?"

Quinton nodded. His throat was constricted and he didn't trust his voice to reply.

"Miss Helene's expectin' you," the woman said, and stepped back for him to enter.

The interior coolness struck Quinton as he entered, and he sighed his relief.

"A hot day," the housekeeper noted. "Awful hot for November." She pointed toward closed double doors near the center of the entryway. "You can wait in there, Mr. Armstrong. Miss Helene, she's napping. I'll see if she's up yet." She glanced at her wristwatch as if to confirm the time of a regular schedule, shook her head doubtfully, and started climbing the spiral staircase with an ease that was incredible for a woman of her massive size.

Quinton remained where he stood and watched her retreat along the second floor landing. Before moving to the doors she had indicated, he took a moment to glance about the entryway. It did not meet his expectations. Aside from the crystal chandelier, which was French, early eighteen-hundreds, and a small boulle console table that might or might not have been a reproduction, there was little of value. The matching pair of chairs on either side of the front door were copies of early Queen Anne, worth at auction about one hundred dollars a piece, and the oriental carpet, because of the gigantic size of the entryway, looked like a scatter rug and was a Danish imitation of the Chinese original. All this Quinton took in with the expert eye of a practiced appraiser. Then he marched into the study to wait for his audience with the famous—or infamous—Helene Haymes.

Quinton's disappointment with the entryway was somewhat alleviated by the furnishings in the study. He dropped his briefcase onto the sofa and crossed the room to examine a boulle armoire that stood against the opposite wall. Even in the dim light coming through the cracks in the closed shutters he could tell it was an original. Excitement surged up inside his chest. He ran his hands carefully along the armoire's surface, feeling for cracks in the tortoise shell and brass inlays. His hand moved uninterrupted and he detected no repairs or missing pieces. He had never seen an antique in such excellent condition and he had an impulse to disassemble the doors in search of a signature. If the armoire had been signed by Boulle himself, it would be worth a fortune. Contemplating the possibility, he moved back to the sofa and sat down.

The study was furnished like a museum. Because of this, and because of the coolness, Quinton would not object to a long wait should Helene Haymes be slow in receiving him. He expected slowness; the woman was, after all, he reasoned, close to seventy. He loosened his necktie, ran his index finger around the collar, and let his gaze travel about the room.

His reflection was thrown back at him from a gilt cheval mirror.

Quinton Armstrong was a man of thirty-five. Even

sitting, his height was obvious, six-foot-one in his stocking feet, with broad shoulders, narrow waist and slim buttocks. His face was finely featured, although seen as a whole it gave a rugged appearance, with a square jaw, cleft chin, deep-set blue eyes and a high forehead over which his dark hair now spilled damply, clinging to olive-complexioned flesh.

Quinton looked like anything but what he was—an expert in antiquities. As a secondary profession, a profession that paid him a regular salary and kept him in the present instead of burying him in the past, he was manager and part owner of a New York public relations firm, Coleman and Armstrong. He did, or thought he did, look like a typical Madison Avenuer, a man in the grey flannel suit.

Although the suit he was now wearing was not grey flannel, as he looked at his reflection in the full-length mirror, he realized how out of place the suit made him. During the taxi ride from the airport, a quick cruise down the main street, Duval, he had not seen one man wearing a suit. A few, those who clung to tradition despite the stifling weather, wore neckties, their shirts short-sleeved. Quinton lamented not having packed sports clothes in his weekender.

He wondered vaguely if his mode of dress would impress Helene Haymes. From her letters, he would judge her to be a woman with very decided tastes and definite ideas as to how a business should be operated. He cast his mind back to the previous week when her first letter had come in to Coleman and Webster. It had been addressed to his attention, *Mr. Quinton Armstrong, Appraiser,* and had informed him that she, an extensive collector of antiques, wished to hold an auction of her priceless treasures. She had made reference to the Rothschild auction in England and to an article he had written in the *New York Times* reporting the event.

Quinton had found the letter amusing. The very idea that a collector in the United States, especially in a small town like Key West, Florida, would compare her collection to the Rothschild's was enough to make him laugh. The letter had requested him to fly to Key West to discuss arrangements for such an auction. He had tossed the letter into the wastebasket as he had left the office for lunch.

Quinton's lunch companion that afternoon had been Hal Crimmons. Hal was a free-lance writer. Once steadily employed by a Washington, D.C. newspaper, he had resigned to write the great American novel, had bombed out with bad reviews and a less than respectable acceptance by the public, and was now selling most of his material to a new magazine patterned after *Vogue* and *Town and Country*. Somewhere between martinis and Amaretto, Quinton had mentioned the funny letter he had received from some crazy dame in Florida. He had only mentioned the letter because Hal had been bemoaning the false leads a reporter had to sort through to get a story and he had wanted to impress on him that other businessmen also had their share of kooks and crazy requests to weed out. He didn't know why he remembered the woman's name, perhaps because of the two *Hs*. He had always had a memory for names where the initials of the first and last were the same. It gave the names a kind of theatrical rhyme that was easy to remember; like Helen Hayes, Claudette Colbert, Deanna Durbin and Robert Redford. He had mentioned that to Hal after he had recited the letter and said, "Signed, 'Cordially, Helene Haymes.' "

Hal had almost choked on his Amaretto. "Not *the* Helene Haymes?"

Quinton had never heard of *a* Helene Haymes, certainly not *the* Helene Haymes. Not one to conceal his ignorance of celebrities, he had asked, "Who is she? Some old actress?"

Hal contemplated him with surprise. "She made a few movies in France and England," he had answered, "but movies weren't the source of her fame. Her infamy." He had stared at Quinton over the rim of his glass, his mind ticking away behind tired, grey eyes. "I guess you're too young to remember her," he had said. "Helene Haymes was as famous an American woman abroad as Isadora Duncan or, coming up to your era, Grace Kelly. She was a hotter item in the press than Elizabeth Taylor or Jacqueline Onassis were at their peaks. One reason was her fanatical evasion of the press. I don't know of one reporter, myself included, who ever managed to get an interview with her. I was egotistical enough and young enough to think I had a chance, but . . ." he shrugged his shoulders. "When I managed to get into her hotel room in Paris after the war she threw a string of abuses and several vases at me and had me thrown out on my ass. It was when I was a reporter with an army newssheet. I thought I was hot shit. I'd interviewed Edith Piaf and Marlene Dietrich. Even the G.I.'s pinup, Rita Hayworth, by telephone. I thought I was a pro and ready to tackle Helene Haymes." Hal had smiled, remembering.

"And why," Quinton had pressed when the reporter had fallen silent, "did you want to interview her?" His thoughts had half been on the conversation and half on the letter sitting in his wastebasket.

"Aside from the fact that she was probably the most beautiful woman of the century," Hal had answered, "she had developed quite a name for herself because of the men she attracted. As young as she was when she left this country, she listed an American diplomat, France's most famous actor, a member of the Krupp family, and even a king as her lovers. Her name was linked with several European scandals. She was even reputed to have been seen on Hitler's arm at a formal function in Berlin, although that was never corroborated during a later investigation.'' Hal had drained his glass, still smiling from past memories, and ordered another round.

''For your added information, Helene Haymes spent the entire war years in Europe. That in itself would have made a story. Later she became very verbal over the division of Berlin, but her statements always reached the press through letters to the editors. She would not consent to an interview. She evaded reporters and dodged photographers with the skill of a spy whose life depended on photographic anonymity. Incidentally, she was also accused of being a spy.

''As I told you, she was the beauty of the century. But she was more also. She was a woman who didn't hesitate speaking her mind even if it was in the form of letters and telephone calls. She should have been made the figurehead of the women's liberation movement.''

''Isn't that a bit of an exaggeration?'' Quinton had mused.

''You wouldn't think so if you'd seen her,'' Hal had told him. ''She was Dietrich, Garbo and Eva Perón in one package.'' The fresh drinks had arrived and Hal had paused to satisfy his thirst. As long as Quinton had known him, he had never known Hal to react with such interest as he had to the subject of Helene Haymes.

''In the early fifties,'' Hal continued, ''Helene Haymes developed a low profile. Rumor had it she had moved into a liaison with an English lord of questionable character and political convictions. During the Joe

McCarthy era, that scourge on our country, old Joe tried to have the lady brought back to America to face his committee, but that failed miserably.

"I understand the English ignored his requests for extradition, which added fuel to the story of a love affair with an English lord of high rank.

"In the late fifties, the gentleman in question died of a massive coronary during a pleasure cruise to Monaco. The last photograph I recall seeing of Helene Haymes was taken by a photographer who had been tipped off and met the Englishman's yacht as it sailed into the harbor. Helene Haymes came ashore with the body. It had been raining, but even through that moisture on her face the tears were distinguishable. The photograph reminded me of that great shot taken of the Duchess of Windsor through a palace window after the death of the Duke.

"After that Helene Haymes simply vanished. Other ladies claimed the notoriety. Ingrid Bergman, Marilyn Monroe. The mysterious Helene Haymes was allowed to fade into the press oblivion she had claimed she wanted. And now, out of the blue, you get a letter from Helene Haymes and you call her a crazy and throw the letter into a trash can!" Hal had laughed with gallows humor, chiding Quinton.

"It's probably not even the same Helene Haymes," Quinton had told him in retaliation.

"More than likely it is," Hal had said. "She came from Florida. From Key West, as a matter of fact. I remember the press once referred to her as a *Key West Conch*."

"A what?"

"Conch is what's locally known as a five or six generation resident," Hal had explained. "The lady's ancestors were probably salvagers, a big business in those days, or sponge fishermen. Have you ever been to Key West?''

Quinton had said he had not.

"A tropical paradise," Hal had told him. "You should go. Especially now that you have an opportunity."

Quinton had left the luncheon feeling captivated by Hal's stories of Helene Haymes. He had returned to the office, dug the woman's letter out of the wastebasket, and read it over again. The idea that she, Helene Haymes or not, could compare her antique collection to that of the Rothschild's still amused him. How many millions had the Rothschild's auction brought in? More than he cared to think about. Now this lady was planning a comparable event. Even Hal, Quinton had thought, should see the humor in that.

Quinton had attended the Rothschild auction.

He had taken two Frederic Remington bronzes belonging to a client to Sothebys in London, an all-expense paid trip, and had happened to be in the country at the time of the auction.

The auction had been skillfully planned, even down to publication of an elaborate illustrated brochure of the collection that had sold for several English pounds. The brochure alone was now a collector's item. The collectors, the wealthy, the investors—all had gathered from the four corners of the globe. A large Arabic contingency had been evident. They came by plane, helicopter, boat and limousine; they came and were caught up in the madness of buying. Items had been bought by antique dealers and sold immediately before sold tags had been placed on them, deals had been consummated, money exchanging hands, sometimes even before the auctioneer's gavel had terminated the bidding. Furniture, grantedly pieces of the best periods of French and English production, but in sad states of disrepair, had sold for exorbitant prices. A representative from Christie's who had sat beside Quinton had kept scratching his head in disbelief, muttering, "Unbelievable! Unbelievable!"

Now Helene Haymes hoped to hold a comparative auction! The old dame was probably dotty enough to believe her lifetime of collecting could compare to the Rothschild's generations of accumulation.

Quinton had still been holding Helene Haymes' letter in his hand when Hal had telephoned.

"Listen, Quint. How would you like to make yourself an easy five thousand dollars? A bonus, so to speak?"

Quinton had not been overly enthusiastic in his affirmative reply. He had known Hal Crimmons for a long while, if not well, and he had assumed that Hal had been making him the brunt of another of his jokes or the extra Amarettos at lunch had finally reached his grey cells. At fifty-five, Hal's body had begun to react to the daily doses of alcohol poured into his system under the guise of "relaxers."

"What do I have to do to earn this five thousand?" Quinton had played along. "Who do I kill? Your publisher?"

"Not my publisher, old man! He's a real sweetheart!"

"Yesterday you hated his guts," Quinton had reminded him.

"That was yesterday. Today he's a sweetheart. Does the five thousand interest you?"

Interest him? Quinton had thought with dour amusement. Who wouldn't be interested in five thousand dollars? There was that exquisite *biscuit de Sèvres* figure he wanted at Parke-Bernet. Then, time

permitting—and finances—the vacation brochure he
had picked up on Martinque came to mind. "What do I
have to do for this windfall?" he had repeated.

"Do what I couldn't," Hal had answered evenly.
"Do an interview. With Helene Haymes." Before
Quinton could respond, Hal had added hurriedly, "I've
already cleared it with my sweetheart of a publisher.
With all the publicity of those *What-ever-happened-to?*
pieces, he feels an interview with Helene Haymes
would be lead article material. He's even talking cover
treatment. Do you know what that means, old man?
Instant fame as a writer."

"I'm not a writer of personality pieces," Quinton
had stated.

"But you're a writer," Hal had argued. "You do an
occasional piece for the *Times,* not to mention all those
stuffy articles for antique magazines. Besides, you
once confessed under the influence that you wanted to
become another Hemingway when you were younger.
Old man, there's a personality interviewer inside you
hoping to burst out, believe it. And it's a natural.
You've got an in. Helene Haymes needn't even know
you're doing an interview. You've been invited to Key
West for another reason. She wouldn't even suspect."

Quinton had said he'd think about it merely to escape
Hal's persistence, but he had already determined to
decline the offer. Although adding the *biscuit de Sèvres*
to his collection would have elated him and a vacation
away from New York would have quieted his nerves
and made him forget about Joanna and their divorce
proceedings, he liked to think of himself as an up-front
person and tricking an old lady into an interview that
intruded into her private life went against him.

After work, Quinton had walked up to Parke-Bernet
and reexamined the figure he coveted. He reconsid-

ered the offer to write an article on Helene Haymes, but once again dismissed it. He knew himself, and if he traveled to Key West to discuss the old woman's desired antique auction, he knew he would take one look at her collection and tell her the truth, that comparing it to the Rothschild's was pure fantasy or foolishness, or both. The end of the auction and the end of the interview.

The following day's mail had produced a second letter from Helene Haymes. It stated simply that she had failed to include necessary remuneration to cover the expenses for his trip to Key West. A check for one thousand dollars had been enclosed. He had stared at the check drawn on Barclay's Bank in Manhattan and examined the signature like a handwriting analyst trying to visualize the personality who had used the pen. Oddly, there had been no quavering lines or wobbling loops, no indication that the signature belonged to a woman who must now be close to seventy. The signature had been cold, flowing, and gave the impression of self-assured youth.

Quinton had struggled with his options most of the morning. At eleven-thirty, Joanna had telephoned. Her attorney had not yet worked out the property settlement to her satisfaction. She had naturally wanted more, Quinton had naturally wanted to give less. The conversation had deteriorated into name-calling and sundry obscenities. He had left the office for lunch in a foul mood, hating the world and every rotten son-of-a-bitch in it. He had not had a luncheon date with Hal Crimmons, but the reporter had showed up at Moriarty's, a local hangout, still enthused over the possibility of an article on the illusive Helene Haymes. He rushed over to Quinton's table.

"Christ, Quint!" he had moaned. "I'd love to write

it myself. But I haven't got an invitation to Key West, and I'm too fucking old to have Helene Haymes toss me out on my ass again. It would cause my swollen prostate to explode like a balloon.''

Hal had reached into his pocket and withdrawn a one-page contract with his magazine and a check made out to Quinton W. Armstrong in the amount of twenty-five hundred dollars. "Half now, half when you finish the interview,'' Hal had told him and dropped the check on the tablecloth in front of Quinton.

Quinton had sat staring at the check, saying nothing, noting the way the sweat from his martini glass had been soaking the corner and spreading rapidly down to obliterate the inked amount.

"Think of it, Quint. You're a gay divorcee now. Pardon that expression. But consider all the strange ass you can buy for five thousand big ones.''

Quinton had seen no point in telling Hal that in ten years of marriage he had not had a strange piece of ass, that now that he was on the market again he hadn't yet managed not to equate a piece of ass with an involvement—and he intended to avoid involvement at any cost. Nor had he, when he had been a bachelor, ever found it necessary to pay for a piece of ass. The possibility that now, at thirty-five, anyone, even Hal, might think it necessary for him to shell out hard earned money for sex shattered him. Like the vain schoolboy, he had left the table and gone into the men's room to cast a reassuring glance at his reflection.

When he had returned, Hal had ordered another round of drinks although Quinton's had been half full, or half empty, depending on one's attitude.

"There'll be an extra thousand in it for you if you manage to get a recent photograph of Helene Haymes,'' Hal had said.

Perhaps it had been the drinks, perhaps Joanna's telephone call and the obscenities still echoing inside his skull, perhaps it had even been his near-obsession to own the Parke-Bernet *biscuit de Sèvres*—whatever the reason, he had the magazine's check stuffed into his coat pocket.

"Good man," Hal had congratulated.

Quinton did not feel like a "good man" now. Sitting in Helene Haymes' study, aware that in all the furnishings he had seen there was only one exceptional piece, the boulle armoire, he felt more like a damned soul about to sell out his integrity for the almighty buck. At home in his Gramercy Park apartment the *biscuit de Sèvres* figurine already occupied an optimum space in his curio cabinet, and he had requested his travel agent send him additional brochures on Martinque. The advance from Hal's magazine had, in fact, already been dispersed. If he did not string Helene Haymes along in estimating her antique collection long enough to come out with an acceptable interview, well, the *biscuit de Sèvres* would have to be sacrificed at a loss and he would have to make up the difference in refunding the magazine's advance. With the liquid cash Joanna was intent on leaving him, that would be no easy feat.

Quinton was silently cursing himself when the study door opened. He turned, expecting the housekeeper, but found it was her daughter. The young woman stepped quietly into the room, closed the door without a sound, and crossed to a chair to plop down with familiarity. Fixing him with her dark eyes, she stared at him with an appraising smile.

"Tired of your killer companion, are you?" Quinton said.

She giggled. "Lucifer ain't no killer," she said.

"People just thinks he's a killer, and Miss Helene she likes 'em to think so. Thataway there's less chance someone's goin' to try to break in and steal somethin'."

It was the longest speech Quinton had heard her make and there was some quality in her voice that made him regard her more closely. She was, by her development, in her late teens. Yet there was the attitude of a much younger person about her.

"You from New York," she said. "I heard Mama talkin' to Miss Helene."

Quinton nodded. "You ever been to New York? What was it? Betty?"

"Hmm. No, ain't been. Don't wanta go," she answered. "I don't wanta go to no Yankee place."

Many of you Southerners still feel that way, do you? Quinton was about to ask, but then, something in the expression in her dark eyes clued him that she was autistic. He smiled at her, and silently forgave her for scaring the hell out of him with the Doberman.

The double doors opened and the housekeeper's bulky frame appeared. "Betty Sue, what you doin' in here?" she asked angrily. "You know you ain't allowed." She stepped aside to allow her daughter to flee past her into the entryway. A door opened and slammed closed. "Hope she didn't bother you none," the housekeeper said. "She don't mean no harm."

"None done," Quinton assured her.

"Miss Helene, she'll see you now," the housekeeper announced in a nuance that made the statement sound practiced for his benefit. "But you gotta go up to her. She ain't up to comin' down."

"That will be fine." Quinton rose and gathered up his briefcase. "Where do I go?"

"I'll show you," the housekeeper said with no obvious objection to again tackling the stairs. "It's all the
way to the top."

What better place to hide away? Quinton thought as
he followed the slow-moving housekeeper up the spiral
staircase.

Chapter Two

As Quinton approached the third floor landing, he hesitated from necessity. Despite the housekeeper's age and bulk, the woman appeared unaffected by the climb while his breathing was labored, the rapidity of his heartbeat escalated to the point of threatening to burst through his rib cage. With each flight of stairs the temperature had increased until now the air was as sultry, if not more so, as it had been outside. His legs felt positively wobbly. Evidence, he told himself, of too many cigarettes and the abandonment of his bi-weekly workouts at the gym, a routine he had ended the day Joanna had announced her intention of divorcing him.

Leaning against the banister, Quinton glanced down and found himself staring at the top of the great chandelier. The oriental carpet beneath the chandelier had lost its pattern to the height and had become a mere splash of muted colors.

Quinton experienced a rush of vertigo, a malady that had plagued him since youth, and he clutched tightly to the railing, forcing his gaze away.

The housekeeper had stopped, realizing he was not following her, and was watching him curiously. For an instant she looked as if she was going to come back to assist him.

Quinton felt a flush of embarrassment at his weakened condition, and envy of her stamina. He pushed himself away from the banister. "I can now understand why Miss Haymes didn't feel up to coming downstairs," he said lightly.

"She seldom does," the housekeeper told him. "Mostly I bring her what she needs. She don't have visitors." She turned away and moved down the passageway, stopping before an ornately carved door to wait for him before knocking.

Quinton didn't detect a response from inside the room, but obviously the housekeeper did. As she opened the door, she said, "Mr. Armstrong's here, Miss Helene," and she stepped aside for Quinton to enter.

Quinton stepped over the threshold into a darkened room.

The exterior shutters had been drawn and sheer curtains on the insides of the windows filtered what precious little light penetrated the slats. The housekeeper closed the door behind him, and he stood blinking to accustom his eyes to the darkness.

He could sense that the room was expansive and he could detect varying shapes of furniture: a fourposter bed, bureau, armoire, groupings of chairs and loveseats. A heavy feminine fragrance permeated the room and he recognized it immediately as Joanna's favorite.

"Forgive the absence of light, Mr. Armstrong, but I'm suffering from an eye ailment. I'm Helene Haymes. I'm in front of the fireplace to your right." Her voice had a pleasing, youthful resonance.

Quinton distinguished a pair of bergère chairs, and in the one facing him a figure in a pale dressing gown. He squinted to discern more, but the attempt was futile.

Carefully, he picked his way toward Helene Haymes'
end of the room and stopped behind the empty chair.

"Welcome to Key West, Mr. Armstrong. And to my
home. Please be seated." Definitely a no-nonsense
attitude.

"Thank you, Miss Haymes." Quinton moved awkwardly around the chair and slipped onto the down-
filled cushion, depositing his briefcase at his feet.

"If the darkness makes you uncomfortable, I could
possibly endure a candle," the woman said with acquiescence.

"It won't be necessary," Quinton assured her. His
discomfort was complete; the heat and the darkness and
the legendary, unseen woman sitting across from
him—a very minor relief a candle would give.

"Good," Helene Haymes said. "I believe too much
importance is placed on physical appearances. To discuss business, what difference does it make what color
my eyes are or that my skin is wrinkled? Would it
change anything if you could see that my hair is tinted
or my dressing gown is of silver-grey silk?"

"No, none whatsoever." Quinton had attempted to
make his voice reflect amusement, but to his own ears it
was hollow. Damn! If it had been just any old woman
sitting across from him in a cocoon of silk and darkness, he would have said, *Hell, yes, it makes a difference. I like to see whom I'm talking to.* But it wasn't
just any old woman. It was Helene Haymes, a woman
he had never heard of a week ago, but who, after Hal
Crimmons' indoctrination, demanded respect and, he
had to admit, reduced him to awe. Quinton had met few
celebrities in his lifetime, and for the effect it was
having on him, he could have been having an audience
with a queen. His reaction disturbed him. He had always considered himself more sophisticated, less im-

pressionable, and this added to his discomfort. Then,
too, there was the constantly rising question of his
integrity. The question of his integrity had nagged him
since the afternoon he had taken the magazine's check
and thereby agreed to write the old woman's unau-
thorized biography. His sense of guilt was even more
acute now that he was actually in the woman's presence. He was suddenly grateful for the darkness as he
imagined Helene Haymes' eyes probing his.

"But as appearances go, Mr. Armstrong," the
woman said, "yours is impressive. You are much
younger and more handsome than I anticipated. I usually found men who deal in antiquities to be stooped
and shriveled and rather careless about their images.
You are certainly none of those."

Quinton was startled. The darkness was evidently
her friend but not his. He was at a disadvantage while
she sat watching him with the eyes of a cat. He shifted
his position uncomfortably. Anger began to well up
inside him, but he was frustrated for lack of easily
directing or unleashing it. At whom was he angry? At
the old woman because of her fantasizing a fortune to
be made from an auction of her antiques? At Hal Crimmons, because without Hal's cajoling he would not be
here? At himself for his gullibility, for having put his
integrity on the line? The only image he easily equated
with anger was Joanna. He quickly pushed her from his
thoughts. He focused again on the blur that was Helene
Haymes and realized his eyes were adjusting to the dim
lighting. He could distinguish, or imagined he could
distinguish, the shape of the woman's head, then the
body tucked into the curve of the chair. She was a
woman of small stature. Her features, although veiled
by the darkness, appeared refined. She had a high
forehead. Her perfectly coiffured hair was the color of

her dressing gown, a silvery gray. Her lips were thin and heart-shaped. There were hollows at her cheeks that the deeper shadows would not abandon. Her eyes continued to be hidden, but he could sense the power of her gaze. Her arms rested on the arms of the chair, her hands, pale and skeletal, hanging limply over the dark carvings.

Quinton could see, yet could not see clearly. The lighting made it difficult to differentiate between visual realities and the possible illusions of his mind's eye.

Helene Haymes gave the illusion of youth. Yet he knew from Hal Crimmons that she must be near seventy. Her head he expected to see drooping from the burden of the years. Yet the untrustworthy lighting gave her chin the poised defiance of agelessness.

"I hope your trip was pleasant, Mr. Armstrong."

"Yes, I enjoyed the view from . . . "

"I found your article on the Rothschild auction most informative."

So much for the exchange of pleasantries, Quinton thought. "Is the article what prompted you to write to me?" he inquired.

"Not entirely. You were recommended to me by a friend. He felt the marriage of my antique collection and your abilities as an appraiser and public relations executive would be advantageous. To both of us. Anyway, he convinced me of such. You'll forgive me, Mr. Armstrong, but I detect a diffidence from you. Is it for your ability or my collection? You have apparently judged my collection by the few pieces you have seen in the rooms below."

Quinton said nothing, his silence as affirmative as if he had spoken.

"Ah, you have then," she murmured. She leaned slightly forward in her chair, her silvery hair catching a small shaft of dim light from the shutter slats. "There, of course, was the boulle armoire in Papa's study. If you had the opportunity, you no doubt would have removed the doors and checked for signatures. I assure you you would have found one, Mr. Armstrong." She leaned back away from the shaft of light. "Each piece of ormolu is also signed. The armoire is one of the rare pieces still in existence created by the master of tortoiseshell himself."

Quinton felt the rush of excitement, but he quickly smothered it. A few important pieces did not a good auction make, he thought, and realized how pompous that would have sounded had he voiced it. "In your letter your reference to an auction on a par with the Rothschild's was, well, was . . ."

"Then there was the chandelier," she interrupted. "That actually came out of the palace at Versailles. The chandelier, like so many of my other pieces, was removed from the palace prior to the invasion of the Nazis during the war and was hidden in a monastery for protection. How I came by such items is another story."

A story I'd like to hear, Quinton thought, remembering Hal had told him Helene Haymes had been seen on Hitler's arm at a Berlin social function.

"You should not have been hasty in your appraisal of my collection, Mr. Armstrong. There are eighteen rooms in this house. The only items of value placed on the first floor are those that cannot easily be carried away." Leaning to her right, the woman fumbled in the drawer of a side table, removed something that jangled, and extended a ring of keys toward Quinton. From the shadow of her chair, she said, "I believe a preview of what you will be working with is in order before we talk further."

Quinton reached for the extended ring of keys, thinking it would be best to tell her now that a choice piece like the boulle armoire and a few other objects he might find scattered about the rambling old mansion would not merit an auction of the sort she envisioned. It would be better to have them carted off to New York or London, entrusted to Parke-Bernet, Christie's or Sotheby's. He urged himself to express his opinion and then get the hell out of this sultry darkness, return to New York, refund the magazine's advance money, sell the *biscuit de Sèvres*—and plead with Joanna to leave him enough in her divorce demands to prevent his credit from being ruined.

"Turn to your right as you leave this room," Helene Haymes instructed. "Go to the last door at the rear of the house. The key with the fleur-de-lys stamped on it opens the lock. After you have examined the contents of the room, I suspect our conversation will then reflect more enthusiasm on your part." She relinquished the keys with hesitation. "No one has been in that room except myself since my return from Europe," she explained, an odd quaver in her voice. "I regret I must share the contents with you and not be present to observe your appreciation."

Clutching the keys, Quinton rose.

"You do like antiques, don't you, Mr. Armstrong?" the old woman inquired. "You're not one of those unappreciative scoundrels who look at a work of art and see only dollar signs? God, how I hated dealing with those ghouls. But deal with them I did, and as you will see, I dealt successfully."

Quinton understood her dislike of many antique dealers. Few who came to him for appraisals actually appreciated the workmanship and beauty of the objects they bartered over. "I assure you I appreciate antiques," he said.

"Then you will see much to appreciate, Mr.

Armstrong. When you return you may ask questions of any piece that fascinates you. I know every item in my collection. Their histories are stored away in my head.'' She touched her temple with a pale finger. ''I may be an old woman and can't remember things that happened only yesterday, but I remember my treasures.''

Quinton moved to the door and opened it, glancing back at her in hope of catching her in the shaft of light from the passageway, but she had extended a hand before her face to shield her ailing eyes from the glare. He stepped quickly into the passageway to spare her the pain.

Outside the room, he heard singing from below, possibly the housekeeper's voice traveling up the stairwell. He smelled the aroma of food cooking, and realized he was hungry. He hadn't eaten since early that morning and it was now mid-afternoon. He hoped Helene Haymes intended to serve him lunch; if not, the grumbling of his stomach would punctuate their conversation.

Quinton did not anticipate that their next conversation would be a long one. After a polite viewing of her treasures, he could smoke a cigarette to add courtesy to the time away from her; then he would go back into her darkened chamber and recommend a notable auction house. If she couldn't handle the truth about her collection, well, he mustn't concern himself with her disappointment. As for Hal Crimmons and his magazine, Old Hal would have to live with the fact that Helene Haymes would remain a mystery woman. And surely Joanna, after ten years of marriage, could be made to see reason. ''Look, darling, I made a mistake. I sold out my integrity for a twenty-five hundred dollar advance and now I have to pay it back.'' Her imagined laugh of derision echoed through the nooks and crannies ot the old mansion.

The last door at the rear of the house was carved of heavy, polished mahogany. Into the face of the panel was a fleur-de-lys in relief that matched the design on the key the old woman had given him. Quinton glanced at the ring of keys and then at the surrounding doors. He was amused to discover each door had a carved symbol corresponding to a symbol on a key. He inserted the proper key into the lock and pushed open the door.

A musty odor rushed out to assault his nostrils. Grimacing, he reached around the door frame and sought a light switch. I'll have no cigarette in there, he determined. A quick glance inside and he'd loll around in the passageway long enough to appear polite. He located the switch plate and flicked the knob. The room was flooded by light.

Quinton caught his breath.

The room was packed from floor to ceiling. Only narrow passageways had been left between objects. It did not take an expert appraiser, as Quinton considered himself, to be struck by the beauty and the value of the objects in the room. Forgetting the unpleasant odor, he stepped quickly inside and closed the door. He felt like a child being given carte blanche in a candy store, not knowing which way to turn first, what to touch, to examine, to admire or want.

His gaze was caught by an eight-foot-high vitrine inlaid with malachite and lapis lazuli. He recognized it immediately as the work of one of the leading master furniture makers for the court of Louis XV. The beveled glass doors were coated with dust and grime, evidence that the housekeeper had never been allowed inside the room. He used his damp handkerchief to wipe the dust away, and then caught his breath with

surprise. The shelves of the vitrine were crammed with
porcelain figurines. His hands trembled as he opened
the doors and found himself confronting a collection of
Sèvres and *Dresden* and early *Wedgwood*. He gingerly
took pieces down, examined them, and found them in
faultless condition. He checked manufacturers' marks
and mentally began dating and evaluating. He suddenly
wished he had the magnifying glass he had left in his
briefcase in the old lady's room, having been convinced it would not be needed.

Quinton turned from the Louis XV vitrine. He
dropped to his knees to examine a bureau plate with
large ormolu cupids on the four corners. He had seen
such a desk go at the Rothschild auction for in excess of
sixty thousand dollars. This one was in better condition. Excitedly, he turned from one direction to
another, his eyes greedily exploring one object and
moving hurriedly on to another. His amazement periodically escaped him in the form of pleasured gasps. He
had never visited an antique store in this country or
Europe with an inventory to equal that in the room; few
museums could boast of so many original pieces. Moving down each aisle, he became like one caught in a
dream as one piece surpassed another.

Finally, he fled back into the hallway, his sight
satiated, his mind reeling. He lit a cigarette, not to
politely waste time, but to consider what he had discovered. The old woman had intimated this was but one of
many rooms housing her treasures. Impossible, he
mused. Even forty or fifty years ago when she had
presumably started her collection of fantastic antiques,
it would have taken millions of dollars to acquire so
many important pieces.

Quinton was still standing in the hallway outside the
room, his cigarette burning unsmoked between his fin-

gers, when the housekeeper appeared on the landing. She looked at him curiously. Going into a small utility room, she emerged with an ashtray. "Here," she said stiffly. "Miss Helene don't take to smokers. Her papa made a fortune in tobacco but never smoked hisself. No Haymes had ever smoked until Miss Justine, and she, she does it out of defiance."

Quinton pulled himself from his thoughts. He had scarcely heard the housekeeper. He noted the ashtray and stuffed out his cigarette with an apology. He walked back to Miss Haymes' door, rapped lightly, and let himself inside.

Again, his eyes needed to become accustomed to the darkness, but he forged ahead toward the bergère chairs without mishap. As he seated himself, he had the distinct sensation that Helene Haymes was smiling at him from the dark cocoon of her chair. "You said a preview of what I would be working with," he murmured. "How many rooms house your collection?"

"Ah, now you are impressed," the woman said with amusement. Her voice turned immediately serious. There are twelve rooms. Three are furnished livably with choice pieces such as this room. The other nine are used for storage much like the one you viewed. Then, of course, there is the attic. I haven't been there myself in ten years, but the inventory is here."

He noted the large book now lying across her lap.

Scarcely above a whisper, he said, "The quality of treasures in the other rooms is . . . "

"Comparable to what you've seen," she anticipated.

"How could you have possibly collected so much? So many priceless pieces?"

Helene Haymes did not answer for several moments. Then, quietly, she said, "What do you know of me,

Mr. Armstrong? Of my past? Pardon me for asking, but you're very young. The name Helene Haymes may mean nothing to you.''

"I have heard stories," Quinton admitted.

"Ah, then the stories are still circulating," she mused sadly. "The price of infamy has been my seclusion here in this house for more years than I care to remember. I am a prisoner of my own past. As a Key West Conch, my privacy is locally respected. Oh, I suppose I am still occasionally mentioned at cocktail parties to amuse and entertain visitors, but there are so many active characters on this island that one as retiring as myself concedes major importance. Maria, my housekeeper, tells me there is now a rumor that I have died and been quietly buried. When this is so I suspect the stories will flourish again for a short time. Maybe one of the local authors, Tennessee Williams perhaps, will immortalize me. It amuses me to think I might become one of his famous lady characters. But until my death nothing will be written about me. I forbid it.''

Again, Quinton was grateful for the room's darkness. He felt the vellicating muscle at the corner of his mouth react to her statement and casually raised his hand to conceal it.

"I have been called many things, Mr. Armstrong. Courtesan, mistress, whore. But I've always thought of myself as a collector of antiquities. Collecting had been my true passion in life. Wherever the circumstance found me I always managed to seek out the choicest antiques. I always shipped them home to Key West. This house, my parents' house and grandparents' house and their parents' house, has been added to and reinforced merely to hold my antiques without collapsing. Before my father died he was rumored to have said that I had become a cornucopia of antiques and would bury him under his own roof unless I ceased shipping my treasures from Europe. How long, he once wrote me, before you drain Europe of all its relics? It was an obsession with me, my collecting. If a man was inclined to present me with a gift, and there were many who did, they knew the greatest way to please me would be to present me with a choice piece of boulle furniture, an old master's painting, any work of art that had survived the ages. I was not interested in jewelry, although I've boxes filled with it. Those, too, are mostly antiques. I've a necklace that once draped the ill-fated neck of Marie Antoinette and an emerald ring inscribed to the syphilitic Madame de Pompadour.''

Quinton sat enthralled. The woman's voice had gained power as she talked, her subject taking possession of both her listener and herself.

"Where possible I obtained documents of authenticity for those pieces in my collection,'' she went on. "I hounded historians and dealers of antiquities throughout Europe. I once flew to Eygpt because I learned a man at the Cairo museum was an expert on pre-Elizabethan jewelry. He identified a ring in my possession as belonging to Sir Henry Bedingfeld, who had been entrusted by Mary Tudor with the custody of the future Queen Elizabeth. I was noted for my tireless devotion to authenticating antiquities. It was part of my passion.

But when the scandals began my fame turned to other areas. I could no longer move with freedom from antique shop to shop, from museum to museum without dodging reporters and photographers. It became impossible to attend auctions. Then came the war and what wasn't destroyed was hidden away or confiscated by the German bastards.''

When she paused, Quinton, remembering Hal's

curiosity, dared insert "Where did you sit out the war in Europe, Miss Haymes?"

"Sit out?" she echoed. "One doesn't sit out a war like that one, Mr. Armstrong."

Quinton waited in silence, thinking she was mentally formulating an explanation. Instead, she sighed wearily. One pale hand came away from the chair arm to sooth her brow. Scarcely above a whisper, she said, "I never thought I'd see my beautiful possessions. I didn't buy them for speculation as I was often accused. In the beginning, I bought to keep things away from the unappreciative antique ghouls. Then I bought simply because I couldn't help myself. Now they must go, all of them. So sad, like dying twice."

Quinton cleared his throat. "Your collection is astounding. I can understand your pain at being forced to sell. I must ask you, Miss Haymes, if you've considered the possibility of selling through a New York or London auction house? Key West is, after all, rather out of the way. I'm not certain how many buyers an auction would draw here."

Quinton saw the pale fingers of her hand tighten. "New York or London are out of the question," she said firmly. "Did they suggest to Rothschild that his antiques be put through an auction house? If such a suggestion was made to him, he was wise to have ignored it."

"But, Miss Haymes," he swallowed and found his throat constricted, "you are not a Rothschild, and Key West is not in England where the European and Arabian buyers find easy access."

"I'm aware of my lineage, Mr. Armstrong," the old woman answered stiffly. "I am also schooled in geography. I'm not senile. I know Key West is in the United States, that it is the southernmost city in the United

States. I'm also aware that it has an adequate airport, a connecting highway to the mainland, and ample harboring for yachts. It is, after all, a resort, called, by some, the last resort, and has an abundance of hotels and motels and guest houses. If the proper brochure is sent to the right people, the aficionados of antique collecting will most certainly come to Key West. They would travel to far less accessible places. I did. The question that must be settled between you and me is, Are you capable and willing to handle such an undertaking?''

Quinton shifted his weight uncomfortably. ''You want me to manage the entire auction and everything related to it?'' he murmured.

''I do,'' she answered. ''You will be responsible for the appraisals, supervising the brochures, hiring the auctioneer, handling publicity. To the point, everything connected with the disposal of my treasures. For this you will be handsomely paid.''

''Why?''

''Why you? Because you were recommended by a man whose judgment I respect.''

''Not why me,'' Quinton corrected her. ''Why the auction in the first place? Forgive me for being blunt, Miss Haymes, but you've lived with these treasures most of your life. You have admitted they are an obsession with you. Why, in your declining years, do you wish to dispose of them? If it's financial, a few select pieces would surely suffice in keeping you splendidly for the balance . . . for several years.''

Quinton could detect her shadowy form stiffen. Then, as if by forced control, she relaxed. Her hand moved absently over the carving of the chair arm, the slender fingers tracing the intricate design.

''The truth is, Mr. Armstrong, that these are not my

declining years,'' she answered quietly. ''These, if not this, are my final years. I am incurably ill. My doctors give me eighteen months, two years at the outside.''

''I'm sorry,'' Quinton managed.

''I've got one heir,'' the woman continued. ''A niece named Justine. She's twenty-eight. Unmarried. The Haymes lineage ends with Justine, since I doubt she'll ever marry, ever have children. She displays no interest toward the opposite sex. Not that she's a lesbian, she isn't. Justine is, I think, an asexual person. A rarity, but there it is. She is interested in two things only. Her art and the theater. She calls my antiques old furniture. My priceless porcelains she refers to as knickknacks. My museum quality jewelry is old-fashioned.'' Helene Haymes' voice was drained of power. Sighing, she added, ''But I love her. She's a sweet, dear person. If I left the legacy of my collection to her, she would be forced to do as you suggest, send everything off to a big city auction house. Oh, they'd dispose of the collection and Justine would receive enough to support herself handsomely, but she'd still be cheated just by the very nature of auction houses.''

''But you realize, of course, that no auction guarantees full value for merchandise sold,'' Quinton told her. ''It's the possibility of bargains on a grand scale that attracts most buyers to auctions.''

''Yes, I realize that,'' Helene Haymes assured him. ''I also realize something further, Mr. Armstrong. Tell me, have you ever seen sharks at sea?''

''Sharks at . . . No,'' Quinton answered. ''Only in aquariums.''

''I'd like to tell you a story, Mr. Armstrong. I was quite young and just learning to sail. I was pleading with my father for my first boat. He was a pampering parent, I a spoiled child. He argued against the boat and kept telling me the sea was dangerous. I argued that the sea was my friend. The sea, he told me, is no one's friend. He took me out on his yacht one afternoon. He anchored near the Dry Tortugas. It was a hot, sultry day. I dove off the yacht and swam to cool myself. When I climbed back on board he asked me if my friend the sea had been refreshing. I knew then he meant to teach me a lesson. The crewmen stood on deck, and I saw they held chunks of bloody meat. My father signalled for them to throw the meat overboard. Almost immediately the water churned with sharks. 'This is your peaceful, friendly sea,' my father said. He took a shotgun and fired at one of the larger sharks. Its blood instantly spread in the water, but it continued to attack the pieces of meat being thrown from the yacht. It wasn't even aware in its greed that the other sharks were attacking him, tearing at his flesh as he tore at the chunks of bait. I had never seen such a frenzy. I was horrified. I learned my lesson.

"I also learned another lesson, Mr. Armstrong. It applies to this auction. I want you to create a frenzy among the buyers just as my father created a frenzy among those sharks. I'll supply the bait, my collection. I want you to use your skills as an appraiser and public relations man to drive those bastards into a frenzy of bidding. If I must part with my treasures, if they must go to the ghouls of the world, let them go for top value."

Quinton stared at her shadowy form, aghast.

He was not a man of passion. He was by nature somewhat staid, or, as Joanna accused, a man lacking gusto. He had considered that statement more relative to a beer commercial, but he had not debated the issue. Now, listening to the fervor in Helene Haymes' voice, he felt lacking because his own inclination was to rise to the occasion, and he could not.

"Of course, I shan't expect an answer from you until

you've had time to consider and have inspected the entire collection,'' the old woman said, her voice regaining composure. "As for now, Mr. Armstrong . . ."

"Please call me Quinton. Or Quint,'' he told her.

"As for now, Quinton, I am fatigued,'' she murmured. "I have made arrangements for your accommodations at *The Pier House*. I understand it's a nice place, one a young man would enjoy. It's also within easy walking distance of my home. I'll have my niece direct you.''

Quinton had expected to be staying in the old mansion, a guest while he examined her collection. Somewhat disappointed, he rose and retrieved his briefcase.

"You may take my inventory book with you,'' Helene Haymes told him. "In the event you find the part of my collection you have viewed keeping you awake, some of the items might interest you.'' Although the book was heavy, she extended it toward him without effort. "We'll meet again tomorrow. Around noon. Thank you for coming, Mr. . . . Quinton. If you'll wait below in the study, I'll have Maria send Justine to you.''

Quinton left Helene Haymes and descended the spiral staircase.

He felt odd in a manner he could not discern. The old woman had impressed him, but then, he reasoned, he had been predetermined to be impressed. The preview of her collection, however, was something entirely different. He had anticipated a few choice pieces amidst a hodgepodge of paraphernalia of the sort old women were prone to accumulate. Not so in the case of Helene Haymes. If the quality of her entire collection was equal to what he had previewed, he had stumbled into a gold mine of antiquities. The responsibility of apprais-

ing and cataloguing each item was in itself a formidable
task. Add to this the charge of arranging an auction of
the type she demanded and the mind boggled. He did
not know if he was qualified for such an undertaking.

As he approached the entryway, Quinton's attention
was drawn from his thoughts to the young Negro girl
Betty Sue. She was standing behind a hall tree peering
around at him like one engaged in a game of hide-and-
seek. When he looked at her, she giggled and covered
her mouth with her hand. She mumbled something
through her splayed fingers and he was forced to ask her
to repeat herself. She pulled her hand away. "I know
somethin' you don't," she chanted twice. Fleeing her
hiding place, she dashed off through a side door.

Through the Tiffany panes of the front door, Quinton
could see his luggage where he had left it just inside the
front gate. He had been in such awe of the old mansion
and then fright of the Doberman that he had forgotten it
entirely. The Doberman had found it, and was now
lying with its paws stretched protectively over the worn
leather.

If it's up to me to retrieve it, you can keep it, old boy,
Quinton thought.

He strolled into the study to wait for Helene Haymes'
niece.

The lower rooms of the house were warming up now,
with the tropical afternoon sun beating against the
closed shutters. Quinton noticed the ceiling fan, sought
the switch, and turned it on. The fan's blades whirred
and began pushing about the sultry air. He reached into
his pocket for his handkerchief to wipe his brow, noted
the grime from the vitrine he had dusted, and stuffed the
handkerchief back into his pocket. He looked forward
to the moment he could strip away his northern, winter
clothing and stand naked in front of an air conditioner.

He hoped *The Pier House* was modern, air-conditioned, and that he would not be boxed into an oven-like room.

He wiped his brow with his naked hand.

As his hand fell away, the study door opened.

He turned to the woman who stood in the frame and stared at her with pleasant surprise.

She was in her late twenties, of medium height, with long auburn hair and beautiful eyes a startling shade of green with an intelligent expression. Her cheekbones were high and created a natural hollow of her cheeks. Her hair was worn brushed straight back from her face, but the severe style only tended to soften the planes of her face. She wore a white loose-fitting dress that emphasized her tanned flesh, and white sandals with laces that crisscrossed about her ankles and lower legs. A gold pendant hung about her slender neck; the astrological sign of Gemini, he saw, with diamonds and emeralds set around the symbol of the twins. The pendant was an antique, or a copy of one. The pendant was not flattering to her features which, like her aunt's, were small and refined.

"Since there is seldom a man in my aunt's study," she said with a captivating smile, "I assume you're Quinton Armstrong. I'm Justine Haymes. I'm to be your guide to *The Pier House*." There was the same husky resonance in her voice as in her aunt's, the same hint of an accent common in people who spoke many languages and had thus lost their ease with any one in particular, even their native tongue. Stepping forward with a youthful stride, Justine Haymes extended her sun-darkened hand. "Please call me Justine," she instructed. "I'm sick to death of being called *Miss*. May I call you Quinton?"

"Please," he told her. He reached for her hand and

with contact experienced a current that surged up his arm and settled in his chest. He had not felt such physical attraction since the day he had met Joanna.

Justine Haymes, with a laugh and a flutter of dark lashes, gently pulled her hand from Quinton's. "That," she said, indicating the ceiling fan, "is taboo in Aunt Helene's house. It might damage her precious antiques." She stepped to the wall and switched off the fan, smiling back at him. "Are you ready, Quinton?"

"Ready," he said.

Chapter Three

When Quinton and Justine emerged from the house, the Doberman sprang away from Quinton's luggage and bared its fangs. Seeing Justine, the animal underwent a transformation. Whining, stubbed tail between its legs, the dog dashed away around the side of the house.

Justine gave no notice to the animal's behavior, and Quinton did not question it.

Moving down the walkway, Justine stooped, retrieved Quinton's suitcase, and handed it to him. "Not planning a very long visit," she said after judging the suitcase's weight. "Oh, well, you can buy more. Once my aunt has managed to get you here, she'll not easily allow you to get away. She'll want to relish all your 'ahs' and 'ohs' of appreciation and tell you stories relating to each and every item in her collection." The statement was not made with criticism, more as a matter of fact announcement.

"You don't like antiques, I take it," Quinton said.

"Not particularly."

"But still you wear an antique pendant."

Justine's hand instinctively touched the pendant.

"It's beautiful," he said. "Late nineteenth century,

I'd say. Russian, possibly Faberge. The zodiac sign of Gemini.'' He had said all this to impress her, and they both knew it.

''A gift from my aunt,'' she said, laughing suddenly. ''You'll find it on your inventory list, and it is Faberge. It's the only one of her *treasures* I've known her to part with.'' She had unlatched the gate and now pushed it open to step out onto the sidewalk.

As Quinton followed her from the yard, he asked, ''Do you believe in astrology?'' He noted she was wearing the same fragrance, Joanna's and her aunt's scent, and he searched his memory for its name.

Justine turned and eyed him thoughtfully. Slightly theatrical, he thought, the way she cocked her head to one side and lowered her dark lashes to contemplate him. ''Astrology is perhaps one of the only things I do believe in,'' she answered seriously. Reaching around him, she pushed the gate closed.

''I understand you also believe in art,'' he said.

She threw back her lovely head and laughed. Two young men peddling by on bicycles turned and looked at her approvingly and at him with envy. ''So my aunt has been discussing me already,'' she said. Mimicking her aunt's voice, she said, '' 'Justine is interested in only two things, art and the theater.' Correct?''

''Something like that,'' he admitted.

''I paint,'' she said in a nuance that was indiscernible. She turned and started to walk away from the house, Quinton following. Suddenly in a carefree voice, she said, *''The Gingerbread Gallery* carries my work. If my aunt doesn't monopolize all your time, I'll take you by to see my paintings. As for the theater, I scandalized my family by running away to New York at age nineteen. Naughty of me, but I did get away. I auditioned for over a hundred shows and ended up with a two-line walk-on in a Greenwich Village production. In other words, my theatrical career ended by popular demand. Now I content myself with local theater. I like to think I'm good, and the local critic on the *Key West Citizen* agrees with me. Of course, that could be because I'm Justine Haymes, a wealthy Conch girl.'' She glanced at Quinton. ''Do you know what Conch means?''

''I've been told,'' he answered.

''You'll hear the expression often here,'' she told him.

He could not tell if she was being critical, sarcastic, or merely stating a fact. He wondered if she was bitter about returning home from New York a theatrical failure, but didn't dare ask. ''It's beautiful here,'' he said in an attempt to feel her out.

''Beautiful? Yes, it is beautiful. Some call it a tropical paradise. It's also hot as hell. Quinton, you needn't stand on formality with me. Why don't you remove your coat and loosen your necktie? The mode of dress in paradise is casual. Comfort first. What else did my aunt tell you about me?''

The question, tacked on to the end of her comment about the local mode of dress, took Quinton by surprise. He was in the process of removing his coat, and almost blurted out Helene Haymes' confidence that she felt her niece was asexual. He caught himself just in time, mumbling, ''Nothing more as I recall. We were more taken up by discussing her collection.''

''Are you certain she didn't work in her 'end of the Haymes bloodline' routine?'' Reverting back to mimicry, she said, '' 'Justine's a rarity. She's not interested in men, not a lesbian either. She's asexual, my niece. Such a pity.' '' She turned and observed him through lowered lashes. ''Correct again?''

Lying had never been one of Quinton's accomplishments. When he formulated a lie his countenance underwent an obvious change before he could voice it. Either his right or left eyebrow arched, his jaw tightened and, according to Joanna, he stuttered dreadfully. He had not been personally aware of any of these alterations in his appearance until they had been repeatedly called to his attention by the suspicious women he had known, Joanna in particular, and by then it had been too late in life to correct them. "Well . . ."

"I assure you I'm not asexual," Justine told him, "despite what my aunt might have told you. I'm not a lesbian either, there she was correct. You look shocked, Quinton. Don't tell me you're from one of those eastern puritanical families that blush at the mention of sex? Dear, dear, I'll have to watch my vocabulary."

"Neither you nor your aunt seem to have any compunction about discussing intimate family affairs," he said uncomfortably.

"Affairs?" Justine laughed. "It's the lack of affairs, *my* affairs, that troubles my worldly aunt." There was definitely a tone of bitterness in her voice with that statement. "Because at my age she had already been through numerous lovers, she looks on my aloofness with men as an affliction." Justine, who had increased her pace during their conversation, slowed. "But enough of me," she said. "Tell me about Quinton Armstrong, appraiser."

Quinton was slightly taken aback. He had never been proficient in giving a capsuled accounting of himself. "Where do I begin?" he said.

"Begin where you like." She stepped closer to him and ran her arm through his. "Are you married, Quinton Armstrong? Did you leave a Mrs. Armstrong back in New York you're anxious to return to?''

"I'm in the process of a divorce," Quinton answered.

"Oh, that can be nasty business."

"Can be, and is," he said.

"Then let's not discuss it," she said lightly. "It doesn't exist, not for us, not at this particular space and time in our lives. Did she discover you had a mistress?''

"No," Quinton laughed.

"Then you discovered she had a lover?"

"No. I thought you said we wouldn't discuss it, that it didn't exist."

"I just wanted to clear up the point of your having a mistress," she said, suddenly serious again. "Most men are such sexual fanatics. One woman is seldom enough for them. I think it comes from an insecurity with their masculinity. They need more than one woman to prove to themselves that they're virile and desirable." She tightened her hold on his arm. "I didn't take you for one of those men, Quinton, but your sex is often devious and mysterious."

"I thought it was the feminine gender that was supposed to be mysterious," he said teasingly.

"See how misinformed you are?"

"Your aunt is certainly a woman of mystery," he said.

There was a hesitancy in her step that was scarcely perceivable. He would not have noted it if he had not been looking for a reaction.

"Oh, you found her mysterious, did you? What's your wife's name, Quinton?"

"My . . . her name is Joanna. You're not very subtle in changing conversations."

"I don't want to talk about my aunt now," Justine

said. "You see, I don't find her mysterious. What's your wife's astrological sign?"

"I really don't want to talk about my wife any more than you want to talk about your aunt," he said pleasantly.

"Which means you're covering up because you can't remember her astrological sign. All right, Quinton. We'll forget your soon-to-be ex-wife and my aunt." She pointed to a building they were passing. "The Rose Tattoo. It's an excellent restaurant. And down there at the end of the street you can see the docks where the tour boats tie up. If my aunt and I allow you the time, you should go out on the glass bottom boat. We have a beautiful reef here. Not, I understand, as spectacular as Australia, but beautiful. To the right of the dock is *The Pier House,* your home away from home while you're in Key West. They also have a good restaurant." She stopped walking and looked up at him, her green eyes meeting his. "Speaking of restaurants, did my aunt arrange for you to dine with her this evening?"

"No. My next appointment is tomorrow at noon." He had almost said *audience.* Her mention of dining reminded him of his hunger.

"Then would you consider it forward of me to invite you to dinner tonight?" Justine said, the smile returning to her lovely face.

"Forward, shocking, and perfectly wonderful," Quinton told her.

"A date then," she said. "At eight o'clock. I'll meet you at *The Pier House.* There's no reason to confuse my aunt's asexuality theory, so we won't tell her." She reached for his hand and held it as they continued walking toward the lobby of *The Pier House.* Outside the glass doors, she stopped. "Tell me, Quinton. Is my aunt's antique collection as valuable as she estimates?"

"I'm not aware of her estimation," Quinton answered, "but judging from what I've seen, it's exceedingly valuable."

Justine's eyes probed his. "Did she explain to you why she's suddenly chosen to dispose of the collection? There's her age, of course, but Haymes women have a history of longevity, usually living well past ninety."

Another confidence Quinton could not, would not reveal.

"Well, eight o'clock then," Justine said when she saw he was not going to respond. She stood on tiptoes and gave him a quick kiss on the cheek. "Until then," she said, and turned and walked away.

Quinton, the touch of her lips still burning on his cheek, pushed open the glass doors and walked into the lobby. He felt almost light-headed, whether from the heat or Justine Haymes he could not determine.

Quinton peeled his clothes away, took a cold shower and vigorously toweled himself dry. Almost immediately perspiration beaded on his body. He moved back into the bedroom, turned the air conditioner on high and stood so that his body received the full blast of cold air.

Recalling how the two flights of stairs at Helene Haymes' had had him huffing and puffing like an old man, he turned and examined his reflection in the full-length mirror on the back of the bathroom door. His body was still solid, muscular, and for that he paused a moment to thank Joanna; she had been the one to insist on his weekly workouts at the gym. She had not, she had told him, wanted to be married to a man who went to seed at forty. He had five years before reaching that traumatic age for a man and except for a slight spread about his middle there was no evidence that his discontinuation of the weekly gym routine would reduce him to seed. He had found grey salting the dark hair at his temples and, more disturbing, grey in the mat of hair on his chest and pubic area, but hell, his father had been completely grey all over at fifty. You couldn't fight heredity.

He remembered what Justine had said about a man needing reassurance of his virility and desirability, and he turned away from the mirror, wondering, despite himself, if she found him desirable. He certainly found her so. She also disturbed him in a vague, unclear manner, as did her aunt. His gaze stole back to the mirror to reexamine the slight spreading about his waist that he would have preferred to ignore, and he tried to see himself as he imagined Justine would see him. That was enough to send him plowing through his suitcase for the swim trunks Hal Crimmons had reminded him to bring.

He strode to the window and looked out. The tiny beach area for *The Pier House* was below and to the left of his window. The sand was dotted by lounges and brightly umbrella-ed tables. Tanned, for the most part youthful, bodies sprawled on the lounges and stretched on the sand near the water's edge. The men wore scant bikinis for maximum exposure to the sun, the elastic fabrics scarcely concealing their genitals. The women wore even less it seemed. As his eyes scanned the crowd, he saw that several women wore no tops, their sun-darkened breasts no objects for concentrated attention. He wondered why only women with unattractive breasts were so eager to expose themselves.

On the beach, Quinton ordered a piña colada, defeating the purpose of swimming. Despite the hunger gnawing at him, he decided not to order food. He clung to the shade of an umbrella until he finished the caloric

drink. There was only one other couple with skin as
pale as his; they, too, obviously new arrivals. The man,
a paunchy fifty, apparently made the same judgment,
because he glanced at Quinton and gave an uncomfortable smile. For the most part, the sun-worshippers were
friendly. One of the young, topless women winked at
Quinton and ran her tongue suggestively around her
lips. She could not have been out of her teens but had
already affected the aura of a hardened woman of forty.
When he failed to respond to her blatant flirtations, she
scowled at him, extended her middle finger, and turned
her attentions elsewhere. Her next conquest was the
fifty-year-old newcomer who had smiled at Quinton.
Sitting beside his wife, sipping a planter's punch, the
man's pale face blushed at the girl's antics until it
seemed to compete with his drink for the most vivid
shade of pink.

Smiling, Quinton finally trotted to the water's edge
for his swim. The Gulf of Mexico's waters were
chilled, invigorating. He made it to the raft a few yards
out where a young man and woman were sunning
themselves, and pulled himself up on the edge. His
chest was heaving with the exertion of the short swim.
He vowed to cut down on his smoking.

There were several small boats moored beyond the
raft. A large fishing boat passing in the channel sent the
boats and the raft into movement. The young couple
who had been holding hands as they slept sat up. The
woman looked at Quinton and he felt like an intruder.
He slipped into the water and swam back and forth
between the raft and the beach several times. Then,
panting but refreshed, he stretched out on a lounge until
the searing sun drove him back to his room.

He still had time to waste. Sitting on the bed, he
opened Helene Haymes' inventory book. The entries

were made in a childish scrawl, each item numbered. His gaze moved down the pages picking out entries at random.

Cloisonne Jewelry Casket, Chinese, 17th Century.

Pietra dura table top, c. 1620, belonging to Ferdinando II de Medici (authenticated).

Cabinet w/mirror, signed Jackson and Graham, exhibited Paris Exhibition of 1885, awarded Medal of Honor, (medal in file with documentation).

Faberge egg, gold, pearls, diamonds, presented to the Dowager Empress Marie Feodorovna by Nicholas II, c. 1897, (authenticated).

Quinton's eyes skipped down the pages until locating the armoire he had seen in the old woman's study:

Armoire, French, tortoiseshell and brass, signed A.-C. Boulle, thought to have been kept in Louis XV's bed chamber.

The more Quinton read the greater his amazement. Helene Haymes' collection would rival the best museums. Also, the more he examined the inventory, the greater his apprehensions. In all honesty, he did not feel himself qualified for the assignment for which she wanted to engage him. He had handled numerous estate sales, appraised a great number of collections for insurance purposes, but never had he encountered a collection as extensive as Helene Haymes'. He closed her inventory book and tossed it beside him on the bed. The traveling, the Key West heat and the swimming had exhausted him. Within moments, he was asleep.

And then he began to dream.

Helene Haymes' voice intruded on his unconscious. Her husky, resonant voice—like a voice-over on a television show. The scene was a yacht at anchor, bobbing peacefully, romantically on the blue Gulf waters, islands visible on the distant horizon. As Quinton drew closer he realized there were several people on deck. He recognized Justine, her dark hair tied back from her laughing face and cascading over her tanned, naked shoulders. She was speaking excitedly to the shadowy shape of a woman he instinctively knew was her aunt. He could not discern her words, only visualize the movements of her heart-shaped lips. Then a man emerged from the cabin. He was tall with a mane of white hair and intense green eyes. He held a shotgun in his right hand and carried the bloody stump of a carcass in his left. The peacefulness of Quinton's dream vanished with the appearance of the man. Stepping forward, the man flung the carcass into the blue water. Sharks began to appear from nowhere, fighting each other for the offering, tearing at each other's flesh until blue was tinted red. Then, with horror that caused him to cry out in his dream, Quinton saw himself bound and lashed at the aft of the yacht. He instinctively understood that as soon as the sharks had reached a frenzy he was to be thrown overboard. While he screamed and pleaded for mercy, the shadowy form that was Helene Haymes left the comfort of her deck chair and approached him. The shadows moved with her as if she were permanently encased in darkness and repelled light. "Why do you cry and bellow?" she asked sharply. "You failed me. The price of failure is death." Then Justine appeared over the old woman's shoulder. Although she spoke, her voice was deadened by the wind and the turmoil in the water alongside the yacht. He knew she was pleading for his life, but he had the impression she was doing so in the mimicking manner she had when relating to her aunt. There was an odd smile on her lips. The man pushed past the women and unlashed Quinton. He was an old man with heavily creased lines about cold, green eyes. But his age was not reflected in the strength of his arms. He pulled Quinton to his feet and hauled him screaming to the side, forcing his head down until he could see the razor-like teeth of the creatures to whom he was to be sacrificed. Behind him the women were shouting, their voices mingling in confusion. "Push him!" "No!" "He failed!" "He tried!" "He's not desirable." "He's not virile." "He tried!" "He failed!" "Feed the sharks!" "No!" Then Quinton felt himself being lifted as if he were weightless. He was raised so high he could no longer see the yacht, only the blue sky and the distant islands. He was seized by vertigo that mingled with his terror. Hurled into space, he felt himself falling and glimpsed the water rising to accept him. Beneath the surface a glimmer of greyness streaked toward him with open mouth.

Awakened by his own scream, Quinton sat bolt upright in bed. His body was drenched with perspiration despite the air conditioner. He swung his legs over the side of the bed and sat with his head cupped in his hands while he returned from the netherworld of the nightmare. Even though he understood the dream, that he had taken Helene Haymes' story of being on her father's yacht, combined it with other bits of conversation, and then added a measure of his own insecurities, it did not lessen the effect on him. He had not had a nightmare since—when?—since he had been a very young boy.

When his trembling subsided, he rose, showered again, and dressed and escaped the room. It was not yet five o'clock and he did not want to remain in his room until Justine arrived at eight. Alone, he might sleep again, dream again.

Outside, dark clouds had obscured the bright sun. A cooling breeze was blowing across the island from off the Gulf, stirring the palm trees and creating white caps on the water. The temperature had dropped considerably. Paradise as paradise should be, he thought. Knowing literally nothing of Key West, he followed the flow of tourists. When he found himself outside the Chamber of Commerce building, he went inside and was given a brochure on the island by a pleasant middle-aged woman. It listed points of interest and a smattering of early island history. There was a fold-out map that told him he was in Old Town. Outside again, he ambled about aimlessly, avoiding the many gift and souvenir shops. Consulting the brochure, he walked up Whitehead Street. On one side of the street were buildings, one, now a restaurant called *The Pigeon House,* the brochure told him had been the original Pan Am headquarters. The opposite side of the street was walled off, a Navy base during the second World War, now abandoned but still retained by the U. S. Government. Inside the gate, he had a glimpse of the Little White House where Harry Truman had resided during his frequent visits.

Quinton was about to turn back when he noticed the Ernest Hemingway House listed on the brochure. He decided the effort to visit Hemingway's Key West home was a must. Hemingway had been his idol during the days when he had thought to become a novelist— that was before the antique bug had bitten him. He still considered *For Whom the Bells Toll* and *The Old Man and the Sea* two of the greatest American novels. He loathed what posthumous biographers had done with Hemingway's life.

The Pulitzer Prize-winning novelist's Key West home had been bought and turned into a museum. Quinton didn't bother to veil his disappointment. The house had been allowed to deteriorate. As a commercial venture, it was apparently successful. The tidbits of information thrown out to the visitors were without enthusiasm, the old woman who recited them stifling a yawn. Quinton left the group and wandered around on his own. He peered into the upstairs studio where the novelist was reputed to have stood up to type his novels, examined the salt water pool, noted the multitude of lazing cats, and then headed for the gate. The white-haired man who had collected the tour fees sat with his head bowed over his chest. He was old enough, Quinton thought, to have been Hemingway's father. The old man looked up, nodded.

On impulse, Quinton stopped. "You'd think they'd spend more money on restoring the house," he said.

"Not my concern," the old man said, and lowered his head again.

Quinton returned to *The Pier House,* went into the bar and had two martinis. Fortified, he returned to his room and propped himself up in bed again with Helene Haymes' inventory book.

At precisely eight o'clock, the telephone awakened him.

"I'm in the lobby," Justine announced. "I'd come up, but everyone here knows me and the scandal of my going to a man's room would spead through Key West before I kicked off my shoes."

Quinton blinked away the cobwebs from his skull. "It's still light out," he murmured, glancing toward the windows.

"Only barely," she said, and laughed. "You're apparently one of those men who retires early. Do you want to forego dinner?" Her voice sounded as if it was of no concern one way or another.

"No, no. I'll be right down." He hung up, went into the bathroom and splashed his face As he brushed his teeth, he thought of Joanna. Leaning into the mirror, toothpaste splattering the surface, he said aloud, "So I'm a staid son-of-a-bitch, am I? We'll see!"

She was wearing a long gown of cool cotton, white as her afternoon dress had been. It was cut in what Joanna had called "the empire line," the material gathered beneath the breasts and then flowing free, accentuating the hips when they were in movement.

She stood just outside the glass doors of the lobby, speaking to a young man. She was attentive, laughing, reaching out occasionally to touch his arm with familiarity. The young man was tall, about Quinton's height, with a suntan that matched hers, teeth that flashed white when he smiled, and a stance that said he was aware of his handsomeness, his attraction for women. He wore a pale blue sports shirt, muscular biceps straining at the fabric of the short sleeves, and white trousers that were tight and revealing.

Quinton hung back, watching, experiencing a sensation ridiculously like jealousy. What right had he to feel jealous? To Justine Haymes, he was a stranger, an appraiser called in by her aunt. It was probably only out of kindness that she had offered to have dinner with him. Regardless, envy welled in him. No woman, with the exception of Joanna when they had first met, had ever looked at him as Justine was now looking at the young man. He fought an instinct to turn and retreat to his room.

Then the young man gave a gesture of farewell, turned and walked away. Justine glanced through the glass doors, saw him in the lobby, and waved him outside.

To his surprise, she raised herself on tiptoes and kissed his cheek when he joined her. "That will start a tiny rumor,'' she said. She slipped her arm through his. "Do you like French food?''

"Hmm.'' He could still feel the warmth of her lips on his cheeks. There was a fluttering inside his chest. *Damn! What's happening to you?*

"Then we'll eat at *Chez Emile*,'' she told him. "It's near, and the food's as good as the best French restaurants in New York.'' She started leading him away from *The Pier House*.

"Who was the Adonis?'' he asked, wishing he had bitten his tongue instead of voicing the question.

"Who? Oh. That was Aaron. He is an Adonis. Isn't he beautiful?''

"Very handsome,'' he conceded. "An old friend?''

"No. A new friend,'' she answered. Turning, she stared up at him. The sun was now setting, the light expiring golden on her beautiful face. "Why Quinton, you almost sound like a jealous lover,'' she teased.

"Nonsense,'' he scoffed, and tried to laugh. "I scarcely know you.''

"Then it isn't love at first sight? When you met me nothing inside cried out, 'Justine Haymes is my soulmate?' ''

"Don't make fun of me,'' he said, irritated.

"I didn't mean to,'' she said, and increased the pressure of her hand on his arm. "In any case, you wouldn't have cause to be jealous of Aaron. He may be an Adonis, but there's no Aphrodite in his life. He's gay.''

"He's . . .''

"Gay,'' she repeated. "Homosexual. You mean you couldn't tell?''

"No,'' he admitted. "It never occurred to me.''

Laughing, Justine said, "You're the sophisticated New Yorker and I'm the smalltown Conch girl, and I have to point out obvious deviations. You're apparently a naive fellow, Quinton Armstrong.'' She leaned her cheek against his arm. ''Don't change though. I like you as you are.'' They crossed the street in silence. She stopped before a staircase in an old brick building. A sign beside the archway read *Chez Emile*. ''Before we go up,'' she said, ''there's something I want to say to you. I didn't come up to your room because I wanted to avoid a scandal, but by the time we finish dinner it's going to be very dark. There's not even going to be a moon tonight because the clouds are gathering for the storm that's predicted for morning. I live in the guest cottage behind my aunt's house. No one's going to see us if I take you home with me. I hope that appeals to you, Quinton, because I want very badly to sleep with you.''

Chapter Four

"Did you enjoy your dinner?" Justine asked.

Quinton told her he had, but, in truth, because of her expressed desire to sleep with him, he had scarcely tasted the food. Now as she led him in the direction of Simonton Street and the guest house she occupied behind her aunt's home, he found himself already aroused by anticipation. Jesus! he thought. I'm like a horny schoolboy! He felt the pressure of her as she leaned against the curve of his body, smelled the fragrance of her perfume and her hair, and if he had been capable of such abandonment, would have stopped and kissed her passionately there on the street. Instead, he contented himself with her nearness and with expectation of what was to follow.

It was a dark night, moonless, as she had said it would be, the only light the occasional arch of a street-lamp. There was a gentle wind, cool and refreshing, promising the predicted storm by morning. Music drifted from the windows of houses they passed, that, too, gentle, soothing, and he was reminded of something Joanna's mother had said at a dinner party following one of their monthly nights at the movies. Joanna had been arguing the story's merits and her mother had said without the background musical score she would have found it a total bore. "Life would be enhanced,

my dear,'' she had said, ''if each of us had a personal
built-in musical score in some obscure pocket of our
skulls to influence our responses.'' Joanna had looked
at her mother, thinking her intoxicated on her one
gimlet, and had said peevishly, ''Mother, sometimes
you sound like a Pavlovist!'' 'Whatever,' her mother
had said, winking at Quinton. Well, Quinton now
thought, he had his background musical score, and it
did enhance his mood. He felt contented; no, exhila-
rated. He slipped his arm tightly about Justine's shoulders. ''I love your hometown,'' he told her.

''Do you?'' she said. ''Then you'll appreciate your
stay here. Arranging my aunt's auction isn't going to be
a hasty procedure.''

His mood instantly fled. He had already made a
decision concerning her aunt's request, and that was
that he was not qualified. He thought it unfair not to tell
Justine, so he said, ''I'm afraid I won't be arranging
your aunt's auction.''

''Oh,'' she murmured indifferently. ''I suspected as
much. They walked a short distance; she seemed to be
thinking about what he said. Then she asked, ''Did she
intimidate you? Or was it the collection?''

His reaction to her perception was a mere contraction
of his stomach muscles. *Both*, he would have replied if
he had been inclined to be truthful. He said, ''It's just
that I'm not convinced such an auction is possible here
in the U. S., in Key West. This isn't England. It's a
long way from Europe, from the monied collectors and
investors. They'd have to cross the Atlantic, not the
English Channel. Even if that didn't prove a deterrent,
there's the consideration that Key West is not a major
city. That creates other unfavorable aspects.''

Justine stepped away from him suddenly. ''Well,''
she said, ''you would be the best judge.'' He detected a

sting of acidity in her voice. "Here we are." She unlatched the gate and swung it open. The hinges creaked, but she seemed to have no thought of disturbing her aunt.

Quinton followed her into the yard. There were no visible lights inside the house. Because of the dense foliage and the gathering storm, the grounds within the wall were as black as a pit.

"Take my hand," she told him. Her hand found his, and he followed her.

"You must be able to see in the dark," he murmured; as for himself, he could scarcely see the blur of her white dress and she was directly in front of him. It seemed to effect his equilibrium. Or was that his anticipation? As they rounded the side of the porch, he heard the low, threatening growl of the Doberman and realized the creature was standing on the porch, less than two feet away, and on a level with his face. A vision flashed through his mind of the dog springing, fangs bared, for his throat. "Jesus Christ!"

"Lucifer!" Justine snapped.

The Doberman, recognizing her voice, whined; his nails scraped the porch planks as he retreated.

"I should have gotten rid of that dog after . . ." She let the sentence remain hanging, which disturbed Quinton all the more. After what? After it had torn out an intruder's throat? Chewed up the postman? Disfigured a child?

"No matter how hot I was for your body, I don't think I'd come a-calling on my own," he said, shuddering.

"He's part of the burglar-proofing for my aunt's collection," Justine said out of the darkness.

They rounded the back corner of the house, and there was a lighted window near its center that cast a wedge of illumination across the veranda. Quinton sighed his relief; regardless of the Doberman's apparent fear of Justine, he had continued to imagine it leaping at him from the darkness.

"Maria and Betty's room," Justine said, indicating the window. She had lowered her voice to a mere whisper. A shadow passed inside the frame of light, and giggling softly, she pulled him quickly behind the trunk of a tree. Like two housebreakers, they peered around the trunk.

As Quinton watched, Maria, the housekeeper, moved in front of the open window. She lifted a hair-brush from a bureau and raked it through her grey hair; then she began unbuttoning the front of her soiled uniform. Turning to someone in the room behind her, she said, "You don't question your mama, girl. You just do as I say, and keep your mouth shut. I ain't wantin' to be driven away from here with you. Who'd take us in? A fat, old nigger mama and her crazy girl?"

Justine tugged at Quinton's arm. "Come on," she whispered. "Maria's problems aren't any of our business."

The grass carpeted their footsteps as they dashed across the yard to the door of a small cottage. Justine opened the door—it hadn't been locked—and they hurried inside. After closing the door, Justine said, "My honor is protected from gossip." Laughing, she moved into his arms, clutched at his neck and pulled his head down to receive her kiss. Her lips were moist and warm, her tongue probing inside his mouth. She pressed her body to his and he felt the response in his loins.

But then, as quickly as she had clung to him, she pulled away. Crossing the room, she drew the draperies and switched on a dim lamp. "What do you think of my cottage?" she asked, smiling back at him.

"A stunner," he said, meaning it. "But then you Haymes women seem to make a practice of stunning me." He let his gaze sweep the interior, hoping the effort to veil his distaste was not futile.

The entire cottage was decorated in Art Nouveau and Art Deco, his two least favorite styles. Two walls had been painted acid green, one a deep purple, the fourth a crimson red. A sofa designed in the shape of lips dominated one wall, its red velvet upholstery clashing with the purple behind it; he recognized it as a copy of a Salvador Dali, but that didn't make him appreciate it any the more; even Dali had designed some grotesque pieces. Chrome framed chairs were scattered indiscriminately about the rest of the room, with mirrored side tables, these cluttered with Deco vases and lamps and bronze and marble statues of dancing, leaping, contortedly posed women. Even the draperies were printed with Deco designs of flowers and coyly posed women peeping from behind entwined vines, the stylized arabesques of their hair blending into the hues of the leaves and flowers. The carpet was tufted, geometric designs in splashes of color. The overall effect was, to Quinton, unsettling. It looked like a nightmare conception of a madhouse. So this, he thought, is where all Helene Haymes' junk found a home. The only thing out of context with the rest of the room were the paintings staggered at odd angles along the walls. They were of tropical birds and vegetation and a couple of interesting scenes of the sea; common in all of them were the storm clouds in the sky backgrounds. "Are the paintings your work?" he asked.

She nodded. "But not my best. The best have been sold, or are hanging at a local gallery. I don't really consider myself a painter, so you needn't compliment them."

"I think they're very good."

"Do you? Perhaps you're easily pleased because they're mine and you're going to sleep with me. I wish you'd been around when I thought of myself as an actress. I could have used the praise. Would you like a drink? I only have wine." Without waiting for him to accept or decline, she crossed to a standing screen—more ethereal Art Nouveau ladies painted in a setting of formalized flowers—and pushed back one panel to reveal a wet bar.

"Wine will do nicely," he said, although he had no wish for anything alcoholic; he was not always his most virile under the influence.

She dropped ice cubes into two glasses and splashed white wine over them.

Avoiding the lip-shaped sofa, Quinton seated himself on a large footstool, perching on one corner to allow her space to join him, which she did.

"You don't like the cottage," she said. "I could see it in your face. You're not a difficult man to read, Quinton." She sipped her wine, her green eyes staring at him over the rim of the glass. "I guess your taste runs more along the lines of my aunt's. Oh, well, to each his own."

"I guess," he said, and made no effort to deny he disliked the decor of the cottage. As always when she mentioned her aunt, he had the distinct impression of thinly disguised animosity in her voice. He debated as to whether he should question it, but, upon consideration, decided there was no purpose. When he had reached the decision not to handle the old woman's auction, that had also concluded his writing the magazine article. He had no need to know of the relationship between aunt and niece, except to satisfy his own curiosity. And that could wait. He set his wine glass aside, the contents untouched, and leaned his head into the curve of her neck. He tasted the salt on her flesh and felt with his lips the pulse of blood surging through her slender neck.

She stretched to set aside her wine. When her hand returned, it settled on his thigh and slid upward to his groin. She felt his hardness, and he moaned softly with the pressure. "So eager," she murmured. "So hungry." She lifted his chin with her free hand and stared into his eyes. "Will you be kind?" she whispered. "Will you be gentle?" Before he could answer, she said, "But not too gentle." She lowered his head and kissed each of his eyelids. "Not here. In the bedroom. In a soft, cushioning bed." She released him and rose. Reaching for his hand, she lead him into the cottage's only other room.

A dim bulb was burning within a multi-colored glass shade, casting prisms of colors across a white silk-draped bed. The wall behind the bed was paneled in mirrors set at slight angles that reflected numerous images of Quintons and Justines as they undressed.

Her body was exquisite, the ribbons of flesh, untouched by the sun, as white and smooth as the finest marble. Her breasts were full, firm, the rosettes large and the nipples erect. She brushed a hand teasingly across his genitals as she passed him to stretch out on the white silk. He reached for the lamp switch, but she said, "No. Leave it on. I want to see you as I make love to you." And she lifted her arms to receive him.

He fell on her without restraint and would have entered her had she not rolled to prevent it.

"There's no reason to hurry," she whispered. "We've all night, my love. We should savor this. I *must* savor this, because there are so few men I'd make love with." She laced her fingers through his hair and drew his mouth to her breasts.

When she had reached a fever pitch, she urged him

from her onto his back. Bending over him, her tongue trailed saliva from nipple to nipple and then down to his navel, then still further until the touch of her tongue and engulfing warmth of her mouth caused him to cry out with abandon. Joanna had never done that, would never do that, take him into her mouth, and the sensation was new to him. His body quivered near the crest of stimulation, and she withdrew, sliding back up his muscle-tensed body to stretch out on top of him.

"You're like a tightly coiled spring," she whispered into his ear. "What woman wound you so tightly, my darling, without teaching you to let up to prolong and cherish the utmost moment?"

His thoughts cried, *Joanna! She wanted it over and done with! She called me staid, boring, but to her sex was dull, a tedious wifely duty to be executed with bother and haste. She made me dull, and then divorced me for being as she made me.* But he said nothing, only moaned and embraced her and told himself he had never been with a woman as exciting, as lovable, as concerned for his enjoyment. Because of this, he took an initiative Joanna had never allowed him; he pushed Justine onto her back as she had pushed him, and he made love to her body with his mouth. Then when she was wet and groaning with pleasure, he entered her. They rose together through levels of sensation that Quinton had not traveled before, and at the pinnacle they climaxed with the simultaneousness of longtime, practiced lovers.

After, he lay on top of her, a dead weight, satiated, until she urged him to grant her freedom. He rolled onto his side and she snuggled against him, pulling his arm around her and cradling his hand between her breasts.

He thought he heard her whimper, and then definitely felt a spasm along her back. "What is it?" he asked. "Was I so bad that I made you cry?"

"You were wonderful," she mumbled. "We were wonderful together. That's why I'm crying. I finally found a man sex was good with, and our time together will be so short."

Quinton felt a rush of confusion and guilt. He also, now that she had voiced it, felt her anguish. The loss would not entirely be hers. He had never had sex with another woman, not even prior to Joanna, where he had felt satiated and fulfilled as a man.

"How many days before you leave?" she asked, controlling her emotions.

"I don't know," he admitted. "Two, maybe three." He couldn't afford more, financially or in time.

"Well, at least we'll have those," she murmured. She lifted his hand to her lips and kissed his fingers. "Now sleep, my darling."

"Are you sure you don't want me to go?" he asked, remembering the Doberman and dreading the prospect of stealing across the darkened yard. "What if your aunt comes to the cottage? Or Maria? I don't want to compromise you."

"No one comes to the cottage," she told him sleepily. "My aunt hates the way I've decorated it, and Maria's too busy with the main house. So sleep, Quinton. You can slip out in the morning before anyone's up and about." She snuggled more tightly against him, sighing with exhaustion and contentment at having him hold her.

But Quinton could not sleep.

He lay in the ugly Art Nouveau room with the prisms of light through the colored glass shade illuminating the objects around him, and he listened to Justine's steady breathing. In the distance, he could hear the rumble of thunder as the storm approached and an occasional flash of lightning managed to penetrate even the heavy draperies, emphasizing the large lidless eyes of the

ethereal Nouveau women trapped forever in their maze
of vines and formalized flowers.

It was dawn when the storm struck.

He drifted into a troubled sleep with the rain pound-
ing against the roof and a shutter from the main house
banging back and forth in its frame.

While he slept with the disturbing sounds, Justine
awakened.

She removed herself from beneath his arm, turned
over and stared into his face, smiling a smile without
mirth or obvious reason.

Chapter Five

The eye of the storm had passed over the island and was now over the gulf. The rain continued, but with less intensity. Along the distant horizon an end could be seen to the dark masses of clouds: a patch of blue sky widening noticeably.

Quinton had the desk clerk call him a cab. He had been drenched once today already, when Justine had awakened him, kissed him good-bye, and sent him off with a dainty umbrella that kept collapsing in the wind. His clothes now hung like shapeless rags in a carwash over the shower door; her umbrella rested in the waste-can waiting for a maid to dispose of it, the spine broken.

Unlike New York, where the first raindrops signaled a mass flashing of ''Off Duty'' and ''Occupied'' signs, the cab arrived almost immediately. Quinton rode in a solemness that matched the weather to Helene Haymes' Simonton Street address. He was about to disembark and make a dash for the house when he spotted the Doberman through the iron gate on the porch. The fierce-looking animal rose from its haunches and came to the edge of the curtain of rain, barking and baring its fangs. Quinton did not have Justine's way with the beast, so he sat back in the cab and asked the driver to blow his horn until someone came out of the house to see to the Doberman.

"I don't blame you," the driver told him. "Them dogs are killers."

The door opened and Maria emerged. She grabbed the Doberman by the collar and motioned to Quinton that it was safe to enter.

He hurried through the gate and rushed to the dryness of the porch. Brushing the rain from his shoulders, he said, "Good morning, Maria. How are you today? And Betty?"

"We're as good as the Lord intends us to be," the housekeeper said dully. "And it ain't morning. It's twelve-thirty. Miss Helene's been expectin' you, and she ain't one to be kept waitin'. You'd better go up." She tugged at the Doberman's collar to silence him. "Hush, Lucifer! Hush, or I'll thrash the livin' daylights out of you!"

Quinton would not liked to have bet on Maria's chances in a confrontation with Lucifer.

A dampness had settled inside the house to mingle with the musty odor Quinton remembered from his first visit. He climbed the two flights of stairs and knocked on Helene Haymes' door.

A muffled voice instructed him to, "Enter." The room, as yesterday, was cloaked in semi-darkness, perhaps even darker today because the outside greyness did not penetrate the slats of the closed shutters. "I'm here, same as before," the old woman told him. "Come, sit down, Mr. . . . Quinton." As he crossed toward her, she murmured, "Punctuality is a virtue, Quinton. I disapprove of people who are habitually late. I hope the storm is your excuse today and that it is not one of your traits." There was a slight edge to her voice, but not the tone of heavy criticism. "Would you like tea? coffee? perhaps a toddy? I can ring for Maria."

"No, nothing, thank you." A toddy would have perhaps helped to revitalize him after last night's sleeplessness, but he detected an impatience in her voice. He opened his briefcase and removed her inventory book, placing it on the table at her elbow.

"You were, I trust, impressed," she said.

"Most impressed," he assured her. "However, Miss Haymes, I . . . "

A pale hand rose from the chair arm and gestured toward some far point in the room. "I've something to show you," she said. She rose from the chair, surprising him; he had assumed that as well as an eye ailment, she had the common infirmity of the aged that made walking difficult. "This way, please." She was also taller than he had judged while she sat in the chair. As he followed her across the room, she said, "I read an article of yours in an antique magazine. I often pore through old issues when insomnia strikes. It seems you have two weaknesses in collecting. Sèvres figurines and English miniature paintings." She stopped before a long table, a mere shadow in the darkness. "There's an intensity lamp at the far corner. Please turn it on."

Quinton located the lamp and depressed its switch. A light illuminated a large Adams table, its entire surface covered with miniature paintings. He glanced toward Helene Haymes, but she had raised a hand to shield her eyes from the sudden, painful glare, and was stepping back away from the arch of light. Quinton turned back to the display, sighing his approval.

"The great painters of miniatures are all represented there," the old woman told him. "Hans Holbein, Susan Penelope Rosse, Lawrence Cross, and my favorite, Samuel Cooper. They date from the fifteen hundreds to the beginning of this century."

Quinton lifted a miniature portrait closer to the lamp.

He experienced a rush of excitement as he recognized the portrait as Anne of Cleves, signed by Hans Holbein. Holbein had been the first English-born miniaturist of note. Holbein had worked for a time at the court of Henry VIII. It had been the King who had commissioned the artist to paint Anne of Cleves, whom he had been considering for his fourth wife. Quinton's hand shook, realizing the antiquity he held, that Henry VIII and Anne of Cleves, themselves, had probably handled the portrait. Still holding the Holbein portrait, his eyes scanned the remaining miniatures.

"I take it from that coveting look on your face that the Holbein is your favorite," the old woman said from the shadows. "Take it. It's yours. A gift from me."

"I . . . couldn't . . . possibly," he stammered at her generosity.

"You could, and will," she said flatly. "It's to show you that I can be generous. That I will be most generous with you if you and I manage to pull off this auction. Now turn off that infernal light. I've used medicine in my eyes and it attacks them like ground glass." Without waiting for him, she turned and started back across the room. "I'll have the miniatures moved to another room where you can examine them at your leisure."

Again seated across from the remarkable old woman, Quinton said, "I must confess, Miss Haymes, that until this morning I had determined not to handle your auction."

"Oh, " she said sharply. "Then you must have been doubting your ability. Certainly it wasn't the collection."

"That's correct," he admitted. "Partly."

"And what changed your mind?" she demanded.

Quinton had rehearsed the answer to that question. "I couldn't come up with anyone in this country any more capable than myself," he said. It was only partially a lie; she needn't know of the influence of her niece on his decision.

"From self-doubt to self-assurance in one morning," she said with amusement. "Very well, then. It's settled. You'll handle the auction. We've only the details to discuss. Frankly, I prefer to discuss business arrangements over a stiff drink." Rising, she moved to the wall behind her chair, a vision in pale silk that appeared to float more than walk, and pulled a bell cord. As she returned to her chair, she said, "You were seen with Justine last night, Quinton."

Quinton's breath caught in his throat. Christ, he thought. Had the old woman been standing at her window in the dead of night, her cat's eyes peering down into the garden as they had fled across the lawn to the cottage? Or this morning in the rain?

"Key West is a small island, Quinton. A friend telephoned this morning to ask who the handsome stranger was she had seen dining with my niece at *Chez Emile*."

He relaxed. "Your niece was kind enough to dine with me," he said.

"Kind? Justine? Well, she must have impressed you, Quinton. Good. I'm glad. I hope you'll see more of one another."

So do I, Quinton thought. It was, after all, the primary reason he had decided to accept the challenge of the auction.

"We will be working closely together, Quinton. Isn't this so?" the old woman asked.

He nodded affirmatively; then, thinking she could not see him clearly, said, "Yes, quite closely for several months."

"Then, personalities proving agreeable, we should become friends."

"I sincerely hope so," Quinton told her.

Neither spoke for a time; then Helene said, "Quinton, will you please indulge me? Would you open the shutters across the room? This confounded medicine the doctors are giving me makes my senses so acute, especially my eyes, but it's a grey day and the light should be bearable."

Quinton obediently rose, crossed the room and slid the window open. The shutters swung out in the wind and a cool breeze blew into the room and lost itself to the musty odor. He returned to his chair, aware as he seated himself that the dull light gave him his first definitive view of Helene Haymes. She did not look her age; indeed, she appeared ageless, a legendary figure swathed in silver grey silk, her hair tinted a matching shade. The light was still not sufficient for him to discern her eyes, but he thought them to be a cunning green, similar to Justine's. Her cheekbones were high, the shadows emphasizing the hollows beneath. Her eyebrows were arched, penciled in in the fashion of the forties; her nose was small, defiantly tilted at the end. He wondered how many times that famous face had gone under a plastic surgeon's knife to retain its youthfulness.

"If we are to be friends," she said, "there are certain things I feel you should be told. As I said, Key West is a small island. Gossip here is a way of life. You might hear gossip, rumor or Conch legend concerning my family and not be capable of distinguishing it from reality. The scandalmongers can be cruel. What they don't know for fact they invent. I've heard some of these inventions, and they're vicious. God knows I've spent a great deal of my life fighting malicious fictions about myself. I suppose you've already heard some of them." She paused as if expecting him to confirm her suspicion.

"I have heard rumors," he admitted. "Only in New York, not here."

"What have you heard?" she asked bluntly.

Quinton hesitated, then said, "That you were Hitler's mistress."

"Ah, yes, that one," she scoffed. "It's true that I met the maniac. An officer of importance in the Nazi army introduced us at a party. I was even photographed on his arm, but I was far from becoming his mistress. The very scrubbed, Aryan Eva was present. Her jealousy was boundless. To relieve her sense of competition with me, I uttered something about not even finding the Führer attractive. The bitch rushed to him to confide my statement, no doubt adding adjectives of her choice. Had my officer friend not gotten me away from the party and out of Berlin, I should no doubt have joined the Jews who were disappearing daily."

Quinton could imagine Hal Crimmons' excitement at having heard her story; he also imagined how Hal would have pressed, questioned, satisfied his reporter's mind. But Quinton said nothing; it was not yet his time to question.

"But that's all past history," the old woman said with a weary sigh. "It's not typical of what's expected of an old woman, but I dislike talking about the past. It's gone, done with. It's the present that concerns me, the effects my past have on Justine. That's the unfairness of it. I should very much like to talk to you, Quinton. About Justine. But not now. I'm much too weary." She passed a hand over her brow, sighing again. "Perhaps tonight, if you'll be so kind as to have dinner with me."

Quinton hesitated. He had anticipated another evening with Justine. The mere thought of another evening such as last night's and he felt his pulse quicken. Still, he could not refuse the aunt's invitation; she had become his employer from the moment he had agreed to arrange her auction. "I would be happy to have dinner with you, Miss Haymes," he said.

"I believe you can dispense with the *Miss* Haymes business," the old woman said with an impatient gesture of her hands. "It will be difficult enough to relate personal matters we must speak about without having to battle formalities. Refer to me as Helene. It will also make me feel less old, a handsome gentleman calling me by my Christian name. Around eight, then. I suppose you'll want to spend the rest of the day examining the other rooms housing my collection?"

A gentle knock on the door prevented Quinton from answering.

Maria entered. The silver tray in her hands gave evidence of her ability to anticipate her mistress' wants. "Scotch and soda, Miss Helene." It was a statement. "And you, Mr. Armstrong?"

"Scotch and soda will be fine," Quinton told the housekeeper.

Maria fixed their drinks, glancing at the open shutters with a questioning expression. "The storm's almost over," she said to her employer. "The sun will be out soon. You want me to close them before I go?"

"I suppose it will be necessary," the old woman answered.

Maria closed the shutters and then shuffled from the room.

Quinton sipped his scotch and soda and wished he had been demanding enough to ask for a Bloody Mary. The effects of last night's sleeplessness was telling on him; he felt as if he had a hangover.

Helene seemed less inclined to conversation with the darkness settling back in around them. She listened

aptly as Quinton told her of the necessity to return to
New York to make arrangements for a photographer,
printer and firm to do the color separations for the
catalogue.

"I'll also have to bring in an auctioneer and an
assistant to help me with blurbs and editing the text of
the catalogue. The expense, Miss . . . Helene is going
to be considerable. Then, we should have someone
reliable to act as liaison among local innkeepers, restaurants and the like and those who'll be attending the
auction. It'll save confusion and let the bidders reserve
their frustrations for the battle over the items. Your
Chamber of Commerce will, no doubt, be of considerable aid, but a privately employed . . . "

"Yes, yes," the old woman interrupted. "All these
details I'll leave to you. Have your statements sent
here. To Justine. I'll appeal to her to hand the financial
matters. She's a good head on her shoulders, that girl,
even if she sometimes refuses to put it to use. Now,
Quinton, my energy's waning. I'll leave you to your
tasks and expect you tonight at eight." She reached into
the drawer of the side table at her elbow and handed him
the keys he had used yesterday. "Please make certain
each room is locked when you leave it," she said.
"With Lucifer, Maria and Betty keeping guard, rob-
bery is unlikely, but I'm told my sleepy little island of
Key West has changed drastically in the past ten years.
Justine tells me we have more than our share of young
drifters, most of them on drugs and not adverse to
robbing an old woman to afford their addictions."

Quinton could not refrain from saying, "Do you
mean, Helene, that you've spent the past ten years shut
away in this house?"

"Except for visits to a clinic in North Carolina. Oh,
don't fret, Quinton. I've been happy here, living

among my treasures. I'd grown weary of people long
ago.''

"But not to even go out, to visit your friends
and . . .''

"I gave up most of my friends the day I decided to
live the life I chose. Most of my contemporaries are
dead anyway, or senile. When I first returned to Key
West my brother was alive. He and a very young
Justine were my only companions. Then he was killed
in a boating accident and I had only Justine. She would
have been enough of a contact with the outside world
for me, but maturity and the fact that she somehow
blames me for my brother's death have altered her
attitude toward me. Sometimes I go days without seeing her. I can't remember when last we had a quiet
dinner together. Do you find Justine beautiful, Quinton?''

The suddenness of the question, thrown at the end of
her complaints about her niece's neglect, took Quinton
aback. "I . . . well, yes, I do. She's . . . very
lovely.''

There were several moments of silence before the old
woman, with the ambience of a warning, said, "She's a
strange young woman, Quinton. Complex beyond my
understanding. I would hate to see . . . ah, but we
shall have our discussion tonight at dinner. Would you
pull the bell cord for Maria as you leave?''

His appetite to learn any details the old woman might
give him of her niece stimulated, Quinton rose reluctantly. "Until tonight then,'' he said. He gave a gentle
tug on the bell cord to summon Maria to do the old
woman's bidding, and let himself out into the hallway.

The storm past, the air was heavy with humidity. He
made a mental note to not immerse himself in his work
beyond the time the shops would close; thanks to the

power of credit cards, he would purchase cool cotton clothing. He removed his jacket and rolled up his shirt sleeves. As he let himself into the first of the rooms housing Helene Haymes' remarkable collection he heard Maria ascending the spiral staircase.

The room in which Quinton worked, the door and key marked with the emblem of the Napoleonic bee—the emperor's choice to replace the pre-revolutionary fleur-de-lys of France's royal family— was situated next to Helene Haymes' self-imposed prison. As he was clearing an Empire writing desk on which to spread out his appraising parapher-nalia, he heard Maria open the woman's door. Her voice was muffled by the dividing wall and he dis-cerned only scattered words: '' . . . foolishness I tell . . . no better sense than my Betty Sue . . . it ain't goin' . . . '' He wondered what Helene Haymes had done to merit her housekeeper's anger; perhaps in-dulged in another scotch and soda against doctor's orders. Helene said something, and the voices dissi-pated to whispers.

The ''Bee'' room, as he came to refer to each by its emblem, like the ''Fleur-de-Lys'' room, was filled to capacity, only narrow aisles left to allow movement from front to rear. In the rear, a shuttered window cast a dull glow from the outside. The room was stuffy and odorous from months or years of not being opened. He used his handkerchief to wipe the dust from the top of the writing desk and that mingled in the air to increase his discomfort. Well, Helen Haymes might be adverse to light and fresh air, but he was not. He edged his way down the nearest aisle, pausing to admire a carved font with inlaid malachite and lapis, and reached the win-dow to find the latch totally rusted. When he turned it, it snapped between his fingers. Damn—he'd suffocate if he didn't have air. Determined, he gripped the remaining fragment of the latch and twisted until he felt it turn.

The window creaked up in its frame and he half-expected Maria to suddenly materialize at her employer's request and demand he again block off the gentle breeze of fresh air whistling softly through the slats of the shutters. He waited in anticipation, but when he heard no footsteps, became bold enough to also unlatch the shutters and push them open. He blinked into the glare of sunlight and inhaled with appreciation the air cleansed by the storm. The breeze instantly began to dry the perspiration on his forehead; he undid the top buttons of his shirt so his chest might also benefit against the room's oppression.

The window overlooked the back yard with its lush, unkept vegetation. Tall bamboo palms cloistered along the outer perimeters, not quite concealing the crumbling condition of the limestone walls. Red hibiscuses, untended, had entwined themselves parasitically through the palms, their showy flowers, made brilliant by the rain, resembling scattered drops of blood against the backdrop of greenery. Beyond the wall, Quinton had a clear view of the neighboring houses, most small and unassuming, what the brochure from The Chamber of Commerce referred to as cigar houses built by the employees of the island's once flourishing tobacco industry. A noise directly below the window brought his attention back to the yard. He saw Betty Sue playing with the Doberman; the girl tossed a good-sized stone to the far side of the yard. As it disappeared into the vegetation, she shouted, "Fetch, Lucifer!" The large dog bound across the yard and reappeared with his black and brown fur glistening, the stone between his powerful jaws. That dog plays with heavy stones as if they were near-weightless rubber balls, Quinton thought, and shuddered. He was about to retreat back into the room when the sound of an opening door drew his attention to the side of the house.

Justine emerged from the back door and started across the wet grass toward her cottage. Her dark hair was combed straight back from her face and twisted into a tight bun at the nape of her slender neck. She wore a silk dressing gown that opened with each step to reveal a glimpse of naked leg. Inhaling on a cigarette, she flung the butt to the ground with an irascible movement, interrupting her gait to step on it and grind it into the wet grass.

Sight of Justine caused a fluttering within Quinton's chest. He leaned from the window with the intention of calling out to her, but the sudden appearance of a man from around the side of the house caused her name to die in his throat. Shielding his eyes against the glare of the sunlight, he studied the man intently. He was tall, darkly tanned, with dark brown hair. He wore a white tank top that flattered his muscular body. Lucifer, seeing the man at the same time as Quinton, bared his teeth and strained at the leash Betty was fastening to his collar.

"Quiet, Lucifer!" Betty commanded.

The man glanced toward the dog and Quinton was afforded a clearer view of his face. It was Aaron, the man he had seen Justine talking with last night outside *The Pier House*. Quinton felt the jealousy that had quickly blossomed inside him ebbing. Aaron, Justine had confided in him, was a homosexual. There was no reason for jealousy, not that he had a right to that emotion in any event, he reminded himself.

Justine, also turning at the sound of the dog's barking, saw Aaron approaching. She halted, turned, and Quinton thought he detected a stiffening of her body.

She glanced toward the main house, said something Quinton could not hear, and turned and hurried on to the cottage, Aaron quickly closing the gap between them. He caught up with her on the cottage steps. Seizing her arm, he turned her away from the door.

Because of Lucifer's barking, Quinton could not hear their conversation, but he had the distinct impression they were arguing. Curiosity gave way to protectiveness. He came away from the window and hurried down the aisle so quickly he almost upset the font on his way to the door. He took the stairs two at a time, and reaching the entryway, turned toward the unfamiliar back of the house. He hurried through a maze of rooms and finally burst into the kitchen. Maria turned from the sink, her eyes widening with surprise.

"What is it, Mr. Armstrong?" the housekeeper demanded, a note of alarm creeping into her voice. No doubt she thought something had happened to her employer.

Quinton brought himself up short. Through the panes of the kitchen door, he saw Aaron turn away from the cottage, his face set and angry, and stride off in the direction from which he had appeared. The cottage door closed behind Justine.

"What is it?" Maria repeated. She stood, wide-eyed, clutching the knife she had just picked up to shred a head of lettuce.

Quinton was flooded by a sense of foolishness. He had acted like some buffoon of a knight charging to the protection of his lady in distress; *his lady and imagined distress*. He felt color flush his face. The upset he had caused the housekeeper only made his foolishness more intent. "I was just stepping out for some air," he murmured unconvincingly and moved on across the kitchen and through the door.

The Doberman commenced barking again at his sudden appearance in the back yard. He gave one reassuring glance to see if Betty still restrained the dog, and then crossed the yard and knocked on the cottage door.

He heard Justine approaching the door, and tried to compose himself. He was fumbling to redo the buttons on his shirt when she opened the door.

He immediately noted the anger in her green eyes.

"Aaron, I told you I can't . . . oh, Quinton." Her anger fled behind a welcoming smile. She stepped back. "Come in." Glancing toward the main house, she said, "I hope my aunt didn't see you. I don't want to dispel her theories of my asexuality. What would she talk about without her end-of-the-Haymes-bloodline narrative?" She closed the door behind him, turned and leaned against it to confront him, the smile still hovering about her lips. "You shouldn't surprise a woman like this. Especially before she has time to put on her makeup." She pushed away from the door. Standing on tiptoes, she kissed the cleft in his chin, and then quickly stepped away before his eager arms could encircle her.

Quinton lowered his half-raised arms, acutely aware of the lingering scents of her perfume and the heavier odor of cleansing cream. His mouth felt suddenly dry. "I happened to be watching from an upstairs window," he said, "when you were arguing with your gay friend."

Justine's steps faltered on the way to the Dali sofa. "Happened to be watching?" she said accusingly without turning. She moved on to settle herself on the red velvet Dali had so outrageously designed to resemble a woman's lipsticked mouth. Her smile returned but was belied by the cold expression in her green eyes.

"I wasn't spying," Quinton told her, although now

he himself felt as though he had been, had stationed
himself at the window for the express purpose of watching for her. "Those upstairs rooms haven't been aired
in God knows when," he murmured, and told himself
he sounded like a boy compounding one lie with
another. Why did she make him feel that way? So
blamable, so vulnerable?

The expression in Justine's eyes softened; her smile
became genuine. "I don't really object if you were
spying on me, Quinton. In fact, it would make me feel
more important to you, less temporary." Before he
could respond, she deftly changed the subject. "Poor
Aaron. He's having lover problems. He wants me to act
as liaison between he and his friend. His friend is a
Conch who works on the shrimp boats. I've known him
most of my life, so Aaron naturally feels I should
intervene in this latest breakup."

Quinton felt himself relaxing. "You refused, and he
was angry?" he asked, satisfied. The thought of the
homosexual trying to involve her in his sordid life-style
angered him. She had accused him of being naive;
perhaps he was intolerant too of things he did not
understand. For all he cared, homosexuality could have
remained in the closet. "As for surprising you without
makeup . . ."

"I refused because Aaron's too good for a shrimper," Justine continued. "He's handsome and talented
and sensitive. I told him he was throwing his life away
on a brute. That's what made him angry." She leaned
forward to take a cigarette from the coffee table and the
front of her silk gown opened to reveal her smooth,
tanned legs.

Memories of their night together crowded in on
Quinton's thoughts; he felt a subtle but demanding response in his groin. His mouth became even drier. He

cleared his throat and moistened his lips with his tongue. He watched Justine light her cigarette and exhale a cloud of smoke above her head. She absently drew the material of her robe together over her exposed legs.

"He'll get over his anger when he sees I'm right," she said of Aaron. "He'll meet another man, no doubt a tourist, and that will help him forget his shrimper." Her green eyes fastened on Quinton. "Too many people throw their lives away on bad relationships," she said. "We, women especially, are taught to think love and marriage conquers all. Too many times they're only another trap. But then you know about marriage, don't you, Quinton? Tell me, did you love your wife? When you met her did you think she was your soul mate?"

"I'm afraid soul mates isn't a word I can identify with," he murmured hesitantly. He wanted to cross the room and sit beside Justine on the sofa, even if it was that dreadful Dali creation, and take her in his arms, make love to her, but he restrained himself, thinking she would object.

"Spirits that have lived and loved through many lifetimes," she explained. "When you meet in each lifetime you have this great affinity for one another. You know you were meant to be together, always. All other affairs are only substitutes, diversions until you find that one person." If her expression had not been so serious, he would have thought her teasing him. "Was sex with your wife as good as it was last night between us?" She laughed behind another cloud of cigarette smoke. "My boldness is scandalous to you, isn't it, Quinton? What a suppressed life you must have led."

"Lovemaking with Joanna was . . . was nothing like between you and me," he said quietly. He felt his legs trembling; confession might be good for the soul but it was playing hell with his nervous system. "Justine, I . . ."

"I'm sorry you decided against handling my aunt's auction," she interrupted. She leaned forward and crushed out her cigarette with angry jabs at the side of the crystal ashtray. Eyes averted, she said, "It was good between us, Quinton. I only wish it wasn't so temporary." Leaning back against the upper lip of the Dali sofa, she folded her arms across her stomach in the attitude of a scolded child. "Funny isn't it? When I first saw you in my aunt's study, I thought, 'He could be my soul mate.' Then last night . . . oh, but I should take the advice I gave Aaron. You'll be returning to New York, and I'll . . ."

"I've decided to handle the auction," Quinton blurted.

Excitement sparking behind her green eyes, Justine sprang from the sofa and ran into his arms. "Oh, Quinton, I'm so happy, so very happy! You won't be sorry." She pulled his head down and greedily returned his kisses. Then as suddenly as she had flung herself into his arms, she freed herself. "But we mustn't let her know about us," she said earnestly.

"Your aunt?"

"You don't know her. She can be a real harridan. For all her elegant manners and the concern she expresses over me, she can be as rapacious as a grasping mother. She might dismiss you despite her determination to have you arrange the auction."

"Then we'll see that she doesn't know," Quinton said, ignoring a surge of guilt at the duplicity.

"It won't be easy keeping it from her. Maria is her eyes around the house. If we're seen together too often around the island, her friends will call with gossip."

"She told me she had few friends," Quinton recalled.

"Yes, but those few are the island scandalmongers. Key West is a small community, Quinton. Already she knows we had dinner last night at *Chez Emile*."

"Yes, she told me. She didn't seem to object."

Justine came back into his arms. "She's shrewd, but we'll manage to be private, Quinton." She parted the buttons on his shirt and buried her lips in the triangular patch of hair on his chest. Again, as he started to slip a hand between the folds of her robe, she pulled away from him. "Not now, darling. We have tonight. And many nights to come." She took his hand and gently urged him toward the door. "You'd best get back to her tombs of antiquities before you're missed. I'll expect you tonight."

"Oh, but I promised to have dinner with her tonight."

"Then come after," Justine said. "Anyway, I have to attend a meeting of the Art and Historical Society tonight. I won't be home until around ten o'clock."

"At ten then," Quinton said with anticipation.

He walked across the yard and tried to act nonchalant when he entered the kitchen. Maria, still at the sink, was putting the final touches to a chef salad. "The air's beautiful after a rain," he said, crossing the kitchen.

"Yes, sir," Maria said evenly without turning.

Quinton climbed the stairs and returned to the Bee room. He spent the next few hours examining and appraising the contents of a French vitrine, but even the Sèvres figurines failed to claim his undivided attention. When Justine wasn't foremost on his mind, he found himself struggling with a sharp sense of guilt. Why should he hide his attraction to her niece from Helene

Haymes? He was an unattached—almost unattached—male with a healthy appreciation of the
opposite sex. His intentions, by today's standards,
were honorable. He wasn't sadistic, physically or mentally. He wasn't out to take without giving nor was he
merely preening the ruffled feathers of his male ego
because Joanna was divorcing him. He was attracted to
Justine Haymes in a way he had never been attracted to
another woman. Why should the old woman object to
that—or to him? If Justine had not been so adamant
about her aunt not knowing about them, he would have
expected the old woman to be exceedingly pleased,
especially when he considered her bemoaning Justine's
asexuality and the end of the Haymes' bloodline.
Helene could certainly cast no stones, not with her
notorious past. Still, he did not know Justine. He had
never been one to believe in love at first sight or, in her
words, soul mates. Those were fantasies restricted to
poets and moviemakers and teen-agers smitten for the
first time.

Quinton's thoughts were interrupted as he heard
Maria on the stairs. The housekeeper's heavy steps
passed his door. He heard her enter the room next door
with her employer's lunch and close the door. He
listened for sounds of their voices, but there were none.

Forcing all else from his mind, he concentrated on
his work. The afternoon passed quickly. Having lost
himself to the examination of a collection of French
engravings yielded by one of the armoire drawers, he
worked beyond closing time of the shops. When he
glanced at his wristwatch he found he only had time to
return to *The Pier House,* shower and dress for dinner.
New clothes for the tropical climate would have to
wait.

When he closed the shutters he saw that Justine's

cottage was dark. He supposed she had already left for her meeting of the Art and Historical Society.

He locked the Bee room and handed the keys to Maria as she let him out the front door. Betty was on the front porch holding Lucifer by the collar. Halfway down the walkway, he thought, *Christ! What am I going to do about the Doberman tonight when I sneak back to the cottage?*

Chapter Six

Quinton descended the second floor stairs and paused for a moment at the edge of *The Pier House* beach. The narrow strip of sand had been transformed at sundown; the lounges occupied by day by the sun worshipers had been pulled to the gently lapping edge of the gulf. Chairs and umbrella-ed tables now dotted the sand; gas torches blazed and sputtered in the wind and cast shadows over couples who had come to listen to the calypso band that performed on a thatched-roofed platform. Rock music from one of the nearby bars mingled with the calypso, but no one seemed to notice or care. A couple near Quinton, their newly acquired sunburns evident even in the torch light, held hands and smiled at one another like honeymooners. A middle-aged woman with hennaed hair and wearing the local version of a sarong rose from her table and began dancing provocatively around her embarrassed husband, urged on by cheers from neighboring tables. The overall atmosphere was one of romance and merriment, and Quinton momentarily regretted his commitment to dine with Helene Haymes. It struck him that this was unlike him; he had always been a business-first, fun-later man. Either the island or Justine was working a change in him. Shrugging, he worked his way across the sand and along the wooden walkways to the taxi stand. "The Haymes house," he told the driver as he settled into the back seat.

The driver's eyes confronted him in the rearview mirror. "Sorry, buddy. I'm not a local. Never heard of the Haymes house. Hemingway House, Pigeon House, Pier House, Audubon House, The Oldest the Southernmost House—but not the Haymes House."

Smiling, Quinton gave the address on Simonton Street. "You sound like a New Yorker," he observed.

"Yeah, the Bronx," the driver told him. "My wife wanted to come to Key West to spend the season with her sister. 'We need a vacation, Sammy,' she says and says and says, so here we are."

"But you're working."

"'Cause I was bored," the driver said as he pulled away from *The Pier House*. "Once I rode the Conch train and took a ride on the glass bottom boat I was ready to go back to the Bronx. Don't like the sun, can't stand fishing, beaches are lousy, restaurants crowded with tourists. No, sir, give me the Bronx."

Some people could be bored in paradise, Quinton thought.

"But the wife and the wife's sister, they've begun workin' on me to sell out up north and move down here permanently," the driver continued. " 'What'm I gonna do for a livin'?' I asks her, and she says, 'Why, drive a cab, of course, just like you do at home.' Well, let me tell you, we'd starve to death with me drivin' a cab on a two-by-four sandbar like this. Bicycles, that's all you need here. Bikes everywhere chokin' up the traffic."

Just like the taxis in Manhattan, Quinton refrained from saying.

He was glad when the Haymes house loomed ahead.

He was in too good a mood to have it dampened by a
fellow New Yorker. He climbed out, paid the driver,
and hesitated at the iron gate, his gaze searching the
yard for sight of the Doberman. The dog must have
sensed him, because it rose up from behind the porch
swing and began barking.

Maria appeared immediately. The black woman
shielded her eyes against the glare of the porch light.
"That you, Mr. Armstrong?"

Quinton identified himself.

"Well, come on in then," Maria shouted. "Lucifer's tied to the swing." As he came up the walkway,
she said, "You goin' to be around for a time you better
make friends with that dog."

"How do you make friends with a killer?" Quinton
quipped.

"A killer? Lucifer?" The housekeeper gave one of
her rare laughs. "That dog's a pussycat. 'Less he hates
you. No reason he should hate you." She turned and
pushed open the front door for him to enter. "Betty
Sue, she'll see that you and the dog make friends. She
and that dog sprouted up together. Aside from Miss
Helene, I guess Lucifer's attached to Betty Sue most."

Quinton noted that Maria had changed from her
housedress to the formal black and white attire he
would have expected only of a Park Avenue maid.

Maria caught him looking at her uniform. "This
here's a special occasion, Mr. Armstrong, sir. Miss
Helene, she ain't been down those stairs to dinner in
more years than I can recall. We done everything up
fine, Betty Sue and me. 'Cept there's just the two of
you, tonight's goin' to be like old times."

"I didn't think Miss Haymes ever entertained, not
since her return from Europe," Quinton said. He saw
the excitement waning in Maria's eyes and wished he
had kept the remark unspoken.

"Special times she did," the housekeeper told him. She glanced towards the stairs. "Miss Helene, she's up there dressin' and ain't ready yet. She had me put a velvet case in the study she said would interest you 'till she comes down. I gotta get back to the kitchen, so you entertain yerself. Drinks and all's on the writin' table." The housekeeper turned and shuffled away down the long hallway.

Alone in the study, Quinton mixed himself a scotch and soda and settled on the sofa. The burgundy velvet case Maria had mentioned was on the cocktail table. He opened the lid and caught his breath in awe. Interest him, Helene had said. That was an understatement. He took the case on his lap and stared at the collection of cameos, some of the finest he had ever seen. In Helene Haymes' methodical fashion, a sheet of paper identifying each cameo had been affixed to the lid of the case. The first he examined was a sardonyx of the Greek goddess Aphrodite; it was mounted in gold with miniature fleur-de-lys fastenings. On the base was soldered the royal coat of arms of France surmounted by a crown. An inscription on the crown stated that Charles, King of France, had made a gift of the jewel in the year 1367. Quinton consulted the attached sheet on the case's lid: Helene had written, *French, 1367, authentication inscribed on base*. The next cameo he inspected was of a Roman emperor's head in jasper ware with a green and white enamel setting. Helene's sheet dated it circa 1820; he examined the workmanship and found himself in agreement. The third was of coral, a bird in flight surrounded by a garland of tiny flowers and set in a ring of gold with a dozen or more diamonds. The pin proving the cameo had at one time been a brooch had been snapped off. The sheet described the brooch and listed it as, *Romantic period, about 1845 to 1860*. Quinton was examining a classic example of a brooch

worn as mourning jewelry in the mid-Victorian era
when the study room opened and Maria stepped in.

"Miss Helene says I should get you settled at the
table," the housekeeper told him. "She'll be down
shortly."

So his hostess wanted to make an entrance, he
thought. Well, let her. If company for dinner was a
special occasion, he wouldn't spoil it. He reluctantly
lay aside the case of cameos and followed Maria into
the entryway.

The housekeeper stopped before carved double
doors. "This room ain't been used since before Miss
Helene's brother . . . died," she announced. There
was a note of anticipation in her voice. "You see
somethin' out of place, you say so before Miss Helene
comes down, Mr. Armstrong, sir. I wants everythin' to
be perfect for her."

"Yes, yes, I will," Quinton agreed, touched by the
housekeeper's obvious devotion to her employer.

Quinton, when Maria threw open the doors, was not
prepared for the Haymes formal dining room. The
room was a good thirty feet wide by fifty feet long.
Double French doors stood open onto the side garden
where the thick vegetation appeared to be pressing to
come inside. Carved cherubs supported the ceiling and
gilted draped garlands of carved flowers. The walls
were paneled; here, too, cherubs protruded from the
center of each holding unlighted candle sconces. The
floor was covered by an exquisite fawn-colored Aubus-
son carpet. The fireplace, of the finest Italian marble,
was flanked on either side by life-sized carved and
painted blackamoors wearing gilted togas and holding
candelabra above their turbaned heads, these also unlighted; their teeth and eyes were made of inset ivory
that glimmered in the dim—and only light—coming

from two single candles on the dining table. The table itself would easily accommodate twenty-four. The throne-like side chairs had been pulled away from the table; only the two end chairs remained. Before noting this, Quinton's experienced eye recorded the sterling silver serving pieces on the sideboard, the Steuben crystal and early Worcester dinner service, the plates set on gold liners. Then he realized he had been squinting in his awed examination of the room and noted the dim lighting of the candles and the distance between the two end chairs.

"I think, Maria, we could have been seated closer together considering the length of the table," he said. "And the lighting. Surely you could light a few of the candles in the wall sconces. As it is it will be difficult enough seeing our food. Seeing one another will be near impossible."

Maria looked doubtful. "There's Miss Helene's eyes to consider," she murmured. "If the light's too bright, she says it's like stickin' her with an icepick." She met Quinton's stare and said, "Maybe a couple more candles, Mr. Armstrong. But she told me firmly to seat you as I has."

"But we'll have to shout," Quinton objected.

"Not in this room, Mr. Armstrong. It's done special. You can hear a pin drop clear 'cross it. Miss Helene's brother, he had this room made special for his music. Besides, you gotta consider . . . "

"Consider what, Maria?" Quinton pressed when she let the sentence trail off.

The large black woman fixed her gaze on Quinton, her expression solemn. "You gotta consider Miss Helene," she said with quiet authority. "She was a beautiful woman in her day."

It surprised Quinton hearing Maria speak of her

employer in such a manner. "Yes, she was very beautiful," he said, remembering the photographs Hal Crimmons had showed him.

"She's still got her vanities, Mr. Armstrong," Maria murmured. "Not that she'd admit it. But me, I've seen her lookin' at them old scrapbooks. Then lookin' in her mirror like she can't believe time and age has taken all that beauty 'way from her." Maria shook her head sadly. "You, you're a handsome man, Mr. Armstrong. Miss Helene, she don't have no designs on you, but . . . well, mostly I think she wants t' keep an illusion alive. She's spent all afternoon with her makeup an' stuff, and with you sittin' too close you'd see the truth she worked so hard to hide from you." The large woman looked at him imploringly. "Sometimes you gotta overlook old people's peculiarities," she said. "She's a good woman, Miss Helene is. She don't mean no harm."

"No, of course not," Quinton said, touched by Maria's understanding. "The seating arrangement will be fine."

"You go on an' sit down, Mr. Armstrong," Maria said gratefully. "I'll pour the wine and then get my soup ready. You ever had conch chowder? Well then, you're in for a treat. Folks say I make the best conch chowder in Key West."

Quinton seated himself and quietly watched the heavyset housekeeper busy herself with the wine. Maria's reference to old people's peculiarities had reminded him of his aunt, his mother's older sister. She had continued to set a place for her husband at the table long after he had died, had even, he suspected, carried on polite dinner conversation with the empty chair when no one else had been present. But Aunt Christine had been a bit more than just eccentric. She had eventually, from the confines of a mental ward, gone to join her beloved husband. Despite her obsession for antiques and her shutting out of the outside world in preference of the darkened cocoon of her bedroom, he had not thought of Helene Haymes as a real eccentric. Her illness explained the darkened rooms; the decision to become a recluse a rejection of her past; as for the antique obsession, had he the opportunity and wherewithal he undoubtedly would have been a victim of the same mania.

Quinton was still considering this when he heard the soft footsteps descending the stairs.

A waft of her familiar perfume preceded her into the room.

Helene Haymes hesitated theatrically in the doorway.

She wore a long-sleeved gown of a shimmering grey fabric that caught and reflected pinpoints of light from the candles; form-fitting, the gown had obviously been chosen to prove that she had not lost her famous figure. About her slender throat hung a necklace of emeralds and diamonds; matching emerald and diamond drops sparkled at her ears. Her grey hair had been meticulously coiffured and moved slightly in the breeze coming through the open French windows; the dim light from the entryway behind her giving the illusion of a silvery aura. But the style of her hair, like the design of her gown, was from another era; an era of elegance for which Quinton, looking at her, felt a sudden nostalgic longing. How many nights as a boy had he sat in darkened movie houses fascinated by the glamorous movie queens of his parents' generation? Garbo, Dietrich, Crawford; Helene Haymes was of their era, the glamorous era that had abruptly ended in the fifties and was now almost laughable to the teenagers of today when lack of other late-night programs forced them to watch the old movies.

"Good evening, Quinton," Helene greeted. "No, don't get up. You needn't prove chivalry isn't dead except in rare young men like yourself. I know it is." Her resonant voice had taken on a sultry quality. As she crossed to the table, she explained, "On dull, grey days when the sun is not too much for my eyes I often go to the widow's walk and spy on young people in the streets below. I noted the lack of courtesy and decorum immediately when I returned from Europe. From what I gather it's now as antiquated as my treasures. Ah, Maria has outdone herself." Seated, she surveyed the table setting with a critical eye and found nothing needing correcting. "Except it's a bit too dark. My ailing eyes would, I'm certain, tolerate another candle or two. I wouldn't want to deprive you of seeing the delicious food Maria has prepared for you, Quinton. Would you?" she asked, indicating the candelabra near his end of the table.

She sipped her wine, watching him over the rim of her glass as he obediently rose and set flames to two of the candles. "Much better," she said. "Tell me, Quinton, did you appreciate my cameos?"

Settling back in his chair, Quinton told her they were of the finest quality. He was impatient and unwilling to let the conversation linger on the cameos; she had mentioned talking to him about Justine. At the moment, that was the topic that peaked his interest. Still, he sought patience. There was so much they needed to discuss, including a topic he had determined that afternoon to broach despite the predetermined attitude he knew she would take. Looking at her down the expanse of the table, he decided to wait for an opportune moment. Perhaps the wine would make her mellow. As for the dim lighting and the distance she sat away from

him, if her aim had been, as Maria claimed, to hide the
ravages of age from him, then she had succeeded. The
setting was as complementary to her as was a gauze-
covered camera lens or a photographer's airbrush to an
actress or model. There was a slight tremor in her hands
and her movements were those of someone near
exhaustion, but not necessarily the permanent exhaustion of age. He noted the high-reaching neckline of her
gown and remembered Joanna had once told him that
the neck and hands were the most difficult for plastic
surgeons to correct. But who would look at her neck
with the fire of so many emeralds blazing above her
bosom?

"You are inspecting me, are you not, Quinton?" she
asked suddenly.

Quinton felt the heat of a flush. "I . . . I was
admiring you," he murmured.

"Oh, you're a flatterer," she mused, and smiled. "I
shan't be coy and refuse to admit I didn't dress especially for you. I have not dined with a gentleman in
. . . how many decades? Actually, I believe the last
true gentleman I dined with was Lord Cambray," she
said, and sighed softly.

Quinton recalled the English lord Hal Crimmons has
mentioned as Helene Haymes' last known lover. He
decided to be bold. I remember the name," he told her.
"Didn't he die on his yacht in the Mediterranean?" He
noted the sudden jerk of her head.

"One half hour before reaching Monte Carlo," she
answered evenly. "Tell me, Quinton, why would you
remember Lord Cambray's name? He was noted for
little else beyond his inherited wealth. At the time of his
death I doubt you'd reached puberty." When he did not
answer, she said, "I see. You've been looking up my
old scandals. Would you tell me why?"

All right, out with it, Quinton told himself. No need

now waiting for an opportune moment. "Aside from my interest in you," he began, "it has to do with the auction."

"I fail to see what my past has to do with the auction," she said. Her voice became tinged with sarcasm as she added, "No doubt if I continue to question you, you'll eventually tell me?"

Quinton moved uncomfortably in his chair. "I don't mean to be evasive," he said. Actually, he was remembering how Hal Crimmons had told him she had had him thrown out of her room in Paris when he had tried to interview her. *After throwing everything in sight at him,* Hal had said. Swallowing a gulp of wine, Quinton said, "I did do some research on you before coming to Key West, Helene. Most of what I learned was very sketchy and . . . "

"Much sensationalized and much untrue," she interrupted.

"It appears you were a favorite topic of the press," he agreed. "Jacqueline Onassis's press coverage pales beside yours."

"Is that meant to be flattering? Mrs. Onassis's frequent appearance in the press was and is as boring to me as my own was. I found it intolerable. The familiarity of my face was an albatross that prevented me from moving about freely. As I told you, notoriety kept me from visiting antique shops and museums throughout Europe. Even if I avoided the crowds the shopkeepers recognized me and put premium prices on their merchandise. I had to hire go-betweens to barter with shopkeepers."

"Forgive me, but it did not appear to unduly hamper your collecting. From what I have seen—and I realize I've only touched the surface—you possess one of the most important collections in this country. Perhaps in retrospect you'd consider that your notoriety might have been an asset. People who ordinarily would have disposed of their antiques and art objects through dealers must have heard of your obsessive collecting and come to you instead.'' Quinton paused, waiting for her reaction. When she merely sat staring quietly at him down the expanse of the table, he went on by suggesting, ''Perhaps it was only your private life that suffered. I can see where a woman of your unfortunate notoriety would have difficulty venturing out to public places with . . . may I call them your lovers?''

Helene was silent for a moment more; then she laughed softly. ''Yes, Quinton, lovers will suffice. You are perceptive. Of course my notoriety was a great asset in my collecting. It is difficult to explain Europe at the end of the war to an American who wasn't there. To an American such as yourself who wasn't even born, it might be impossible. There was an exhilaration of the spirit because the war was finally over. People who had buried their hopes through fear and necessity let them burrow to the surface again. There were cities and towns and lives to rebuild. Jewelry and antiques and objects of art that had been hidden away until a better day were brought from their hiding places. Most had to be sold to finance rebirth of families and dreams. The market was bloated with these items, but those I called the ghouls usually got there first. The ownership of so much art was questionable. The ghouls didn't question. They cheated and paid rock-bottom prices and turned over the merchandise for quick profits, never caring about what they were selling, only the money.''

She sighed, as if to gain energy, then went on. ''I cared. I was greedy, but I cared about the preservation of antiquities. Without the preservation of art what would the whole dreadful thing have been for? We'd have been looked back on as another dark ages. I had already attracted some notoriety before and during the war. Newsmen had found that photograph of me on Hitler's arm and it found its way into the press. I've already told you how that came about, how I had to flee Berlin to escape the madman. When I saw that it was inevitable that I was going to be thrown into the public eye again I made sure my obsession with art and antiquities was made known. I developed a reputation for not cheating the honest seller of antiques and they began to seek me out instead of submitting to the ghouls. Then, too, there were men seeking my favors who contributed a good share of what you'll see in this house.

"So, yes, Quinton. To answer your question, my notoriety was definitely an asset in my collecting. As you said, it was my private life that suffered. It was the destruction the press brought down on my private life that eventually caused my resentment. When I met a man I loved and wanted to settle down the press continued to hound me and made his and my life miserable."

Helene stopped speaking. Absently running a finger around the rim of her wine glass, she sat staring at Quinton for several moments before saying, "You still haven't told me what all this had to do with the auction. My past has been buried for almost thirty years. Those who remember Helene Haymes at all probably think she's dead. She soon will be," she murmured as an afterthought. "At least she . . . I will have died in peace." Retracting her hand from the glass and placing it in her lap, she smiled across the vast expanse of table at Quinton. "Perhaps it's a blessing of old age, but sometimes I think of that younger, notorious me as someone else. A character from a play or book, someone I might have known only fleetingly."

Quinton pulled himself up in his chair. His throat was constricted; when he swallowed his wine it hurt. "Then apparently there's no reason for me to go further with my suggestion," he said with difficulty.

"No, please do," Helene urged. "I'm intrigued."

Quinton sat absently drumming his fingers on the tabletop. If his suggestion alienated the old woman, she might dismiss him; if she sought another appraiser and a separate PR firm, then he would be torn away from her niece. That thought gave him hesitation.

"Go on," Helene urged quietly.

"Your auction," he finally said, "would have a greater possibility of attaining your wish to rival the Rothschild's auction if we could ignite interest in the press. I don't just mean nationally, but on a worldwide basis. At our first meeting you said you wanted the buyers worked into a frenzy. Why not push them into that frenzied state even before they arrive in Key West? I have the means of doing just that if you approve the way."

"And that is?"

"Put the notorious Helene Haymes before the public again," Quinton blurted. Before she could react, he went on, "Newspaper, magazine, television coverage. We'd go for the major newspapers and most widely read magazines, perhaps get you a spot on "60 Minutes" with Harry Reasoner or Mike Wallace."

"Oh, my God!" Helene gasped.

"The buyers would come not only to bid for choice antiques but to compete in owning something once belonging to the notorious Helene Haymes, the woman who was seen on Hitler's arm and counted dukes and lords and a king or two as lovers."

Helene's hands went to her breasts as if to quiet her racing heart. "Even to suggest . . . "

"You said since you were forced to dispose of your

treasures you wanted to command top dollar,'' Quinton reminded her. ''Even then success wouldn't be guaranteed, considering the remoteness of this island, but world press coverage would be a decided advantage.''

''But the price,'' Helene murmured so softly he scarcely heard her. ''Do you realize what you're asking of me? To give up the anonymity I fought so hard to obtain? My final months spent hiding from the curious, the religious reformers, the fanatics who once screamed for my head, those unfathomable people who attempt to attach themselves like camp followers to anyone touched by fame or notoriety?''

Quinton said nothing, realizing she was talking more to herself than to him. He sipped his wine and watched her, knowing the struggle going on inside her.

Helene, sitting with her back ramrod straight since the moment of his suggestion, relaxed slightly and let her hands return to her lap. ''Your proposal is so horrifying it makes the mind boggle,'' she told him. ''Still, I bow to its validity. We Americans are peculiar by definition. We like to build bigger than life images of people whether they be heroes or villains. We experience segments of life through them vicariously that would otherwise not touch us, but when we become bored with them or feel they have betrayed that image we like to tear them down off that pedestal we've put them on and grind them into dust as retribution. Yes, I can understand why your proposal would attract American buyers. Helene Haymes betrayed their image of an American. She turned her back on them during the war years and took foreigners as lovers. She socialized with the monster Hitler and, some said, made anti-American radio broadcasts for Goering. She . . . I need to be punished. I escaped their wrath long enough. What better way to punish me than to bid for and carry away my treasures?'' Sighing, she shook her perfectly coiffured head from side to side. ''But what of the other buyers? The Arabs and English? What fascination would stripping an infamous, fallen-from-grace American have for them?''

''The world has become a much smaller place since you hid yourself away in Key West,'' Quinton answered. ''The people of the world are not so very different from Americans any longer, if, indeed, they ever were. Among the wealthy the auction would attract, greed still reigns supreme. Fallen idols and deposed leaders are almost commonplace. Celebrities who were once expected to live exemplary lives now have affairs and babies out of wedlock and talk openly of their sexuality. I don't suggest we make an issue of your past to give the do-gooders a second opportunity for retribution. It won't be retribution that will compel them to come and carry away your treasures.''

''What then?'' Helene inquired.

''You represent a romantic era that no longer exists,'' Quinton answered thoughtfully. ''That era is greatly missed and remembered with more than mere nostalgia. The press has explored and written about it *ad nauseam*. Still, the public can't get enough of it. You're a figure of that era who at your peak fascinated them. I believe the press coverage my firm could secure for you would be phenomenal. In each interview and article we could stress your antique collection and the upcoming auction.''

''I'm beginning to understand,'' said Helene. ''Instead of reliving my life in memory and conversation like any normal old woman, I'm to do it in the press. A retrial of public opinion, so to speak. Of course,'' she said with deliberateness, ''you intend me to be presented as someone who was maligned? No doubt you'll attempt a bit of guilt infliction on the public, so they'll welcome me back into the fold as they welcomed back Miss Bergman after their shoddy treatment of her in the fifties.'' Helene placed her hands on the tabletop as if she would rise, but then, thinking better of it, she sank back into her chair and sat staring pensively through the open French doors.

Quietly, Quinton said, ''There would be an important difference from your past press coverage. You and I would be in control. You needn't dredge up anything you chose to leave buried. I'd act as liaison between you and the press.''

''The friend who recommended you was right, Quinton. You're capable of wearing many hats: appraiser, publicist, press secretary and . . . '' Whatever she was going to add she decided against it and let the statement go unfinished. ''And you think this is important to the success of my auction?''

''I do,'' he answered.

''Then I'll consider it,'' she said in such a way that made further pursuit of the topic impossible.

''Then also consider our time element,'' Quinton insisted.

Helene's mouth formed a sardonic smile. ''The element of time is one I am acutely aware of,'' she muttered. ''Now, where is Maria with our dinner?'' She reached for the crystal bell beside her plate and gave it a demanding jingle.

Maria, as if waiting just beyond the door, pushed into the dining room with a steaming tureen of soup. As she served Quinton her eyes probed his seeking assurance that the dinner was going well for her employer; his answer was to avert his gaze. The housekeeper was forced to content herself with his, ''Delicious,'' when he tasted her conch chowder.

Helene only toyed with the food that followed; she remained distant, thoughtful, speaking only to inquire if Quinton approved of the broiled dolphin. "It isn't the mammal," she said when his fork faltered, "but a seasonal fish to the gulf waters. You must also try our yellowtail. I'll have Maria prepare it for your next dinner. I prefer it to all other fish."

Helene folded her napkin slowly and waved away the caramel dessert, rising. "If you've no objection, Quinton, Maria will serve your coffee in my rooms." She motioned Quinton back into his chair when he made to rise. "You may think me a tedious old woman, but my upstairs rooms have come to represent security for me. Justine even accuses me of suffering from. . . but then Justine likes everything labeled." Her eyes swept about the dining room, like one surveying a favored place for a final time, and then, without another word, she turned and swept from the room, her gown shimmering in the candlelight. Her presence seemed to linger long after her footsteps had died away on the stairs.

Maria, standing with the unwanted bowl of caramel in her hand, pulled her eyes away from the dining room doors through which her employer had vanished, and confronted Quinton. "Miss Helene, she's upset," the housekeeper said accusingly.

"If I upset her, I'm sorry," Quinton apologized, "but our discussion was necessary." His taste for the caramel gone, he pushed the dish away. He was somewhat disturbed also; by broaching the subject of the auction and press coverage he had eliminated Helene's discussion of her niece. He glanced at his wristwatch and saw it was nine-thirty; he was to meet Justine in her cottage in half an hour. If Helene wanted to continue the discussion of the auction over coffee, she might even detain him until midnight. He told himself he should have exercised restraint; still, he had wanted the topic presented. He also felt a consuming need to confess his complicity in agreeing to do the article for Hal Crimmons' magazine. If, after his confession, Helene Haymes still wanted him to arrange her auction, he would dedicate himself to the task with an unfettered conscience.

As he sat pondering, Maria began clearing the table; her attitude toward him was chilled, believing he had upset her employer on the special occasion of a dinner party. Rising, Quinton moved to the French doors and stood looking into the unkept garden, his back to the room. A full and luminous moon hung like a gigantic balloon above the bamboo palms. A trade wind was stirring the branches and causing them to make a rustling sound. Insects with iridescent green backs darted from bush to bush in what appeared to be a frenzied flight of mating. A loud croaking drew his attention to the ground just beyond the French doors. A bloated toad with a horned back sat in the dim shaft of light from the dining room, its tongue flicking in and out as it feasted on the insects. He turned back into the room.

Maria had gone into the kitchen, but her daughter Betty was there, leaning against one side of the fireplace and watching him with her child-like eyes. He forced a friendly, "Hello," despite his dark mood; then, remembering her mother's suggestion, he said, "I understand you and Lucifer are very close friends, Betty."

The girl-woman nodded. "Lucifer's my dog now," she said proudly. "Now he ain't Miss Helene's."

A bell in the kitchen sounded; he heard the housekeeper shuffle into the hallway and climb the stairs.

"Do you suppose you could make Lucifer my friend

also?'' Quinton asked. ''It looks as if I'm going to be around for a while and I'd like Lucifer to take kindly to me.''

Betty cocked her head to one side, considering. Quinton noted that the girl's skin was lightly colored in comparison to her mother's, and he wondered if perhaps she was a mulatto, the offspring of the housekeeper's transgression into the realm of the Southern whites. ''Lucifer takes kindly to some folks,'' Betty said. ''Some he don't. Like Miss Justine.'' Then, as if she felt it necessary to rush to the Doberman's protection, she said quickly, ''But he don't hate Miss Justine. He's just feared of her.''

Quinton recalled the dog's odd behavior when Justine had shouted at him; its retreating, tail between its legs, whining. Well, I'd like him feared of me, he refrained from telling the girl. ''Do you think you could make Lucifer my friend?'' he asked.

''Can't make him,'' Betty answered. ''I can tell him to be your friend, but it's up to him if he wants to be or not.''

''Well, perhaps between the two of us we can convince him I can be a good friend,'' Quinton said. ''I'll bring him a bone or maybe a toy.''

''Gotta lot of bones, and I made him toys,'' the girl said with a tinge of jealousy. ''He don't like toys anyway. Just rocks and sticks. He likes to chase rocks.''

''Yes, I saw you playing with him,'' Quinton said patiently. ''Then I'll bring you a present for helping us become friends,'' he offered as childish blackmail. ''Will you agree to that?''

''What you bring me?'' Her dark eyes sparkled with anticipation.

''What would you like?''

"A new dress."

"All right. A new dress it is," he agreed. He heard Maria descending the stairs. "You can start helping us become friends first thing tomorrow."

Betty glanced toward the entryway doors and the creaking stairs beyond. "A red dress," she said hurriedly, and fled into the kitchen.

Maria shuffled in from the entryway. "Miss Helene, she's got one of her headaches," she told him with scarcely veiled accusation. "She says would you excuse her. She'll talk to you in the mornin'."

Quinton was relieved. Now he could wait for Justine when she returned from her meeting. He nodded simply. "In the morning then," he said. "I'll see myself out."

Maria regarded him with somber gravity and seemed about to speak; instead, she shrugged her heavy shoulders, crossed the dining room and vanished through the swinging door to the kitchen. He heard her say, "All right, Betty Sue, you help with these here dishes now, and I don't want nothin' broke neither."

Quinton let himself out the front door. Lucifer, still tied to the porch swing, rose with a growl and strained at his leash. "Tomorrow we're going to start becoming friends, old boy," Quinton said. "Even if it costs me a new dress for Betty." He made his way around the side of the house, walking softly past the open French doors of the dining room and hoping his feet avoided the bloated toad he had seen earlier.

The cottage was dark, the moonlight reflecting off the darkened windows.

Pressing into the shadows of a nearby tree, Quinton waited for Justine. He desperately craved a cigarette, but did not dare light one for fear the glow would be seen by Maria and Betty or by Helene, whom he suspected had no compunction about spying on Justine, living vicariously through her niece as she had accused the public of having done through her past notoriety.

The wind was cool and welcome after the hot, humid day. He was satiated by Maria's cooking. Despite Helene's abrupt exit at dinner, her reaction to his suggestion of publicity had not been met with the violent objection he had expected. He had a feeling she would agree to his plan and even forgive him when he confessed his devious agreement to write an article on her for Hal Crimmons' magazine. Overall, he had a sense of satisfaction, as if the scales of life's balance had shifted in his favor for the first time since Joanna had announced her intention of divorcing him. Impatience for Justine's return and the anticipation of another night with her were the only strains in his sense of well-being.

Maria finished cleaning the kitchen and turned off the lights. Lights came on in the bedroom the housekeeper shared with her daughter; then in the smaller window of the bathroom. Presently, Quinton heard the shower and the heavyset black woman's singing as she scrubbed away the sweat of the day. He thought the song she sang was a Bessie Smith number, but he could not be certain; since marrying Joanna he had given up his passion for jazz and could no longer distinguish Bessie Smith from Billie Holiday or early Mabel Mercer.

He extended his hand beyond the rim of shadows from the tree under which he stood. The moonlight reflected on the dial of his wristwatch. It was quarter past eleven. His sense of anticipation had waned; his good mood was changing to annoyance. He wondered if Justine had forgotten their rendezvous, if she was one of those women who were perpetually late. He vowed he would wait until exactly eleven-thirty; then he would return to *The Pier House* and console being stood-up by getting morosely drunk.

At eleven-forty-five he heard movement along the side of the main house. He had not heard the noisy front gate open and so expected the Doberman to suddenly appear stalking his scent. Forgetting decorum, he examined the trunk of the tree to determine if he could shimmy to safety away from the animal's fangs. Embarrassing, but Maria would no doubt have to rescue him. What excuse would he give her for being in the back yard? She would probably think him a voyeur, perhaps accuse him of hiding in the darkness to watch her showering. If his situation were not so desperate, he would have appreciated the humor.

But it was Justine, not Lucifer, who emerged into a narrow space of moonlight; she wore white slacks and sweater and carried a white handbag that she swung in rhythm to her step. She was humming, oddly the same number Maria had been singing only moments before. Sight of her caused Quinton's pulse to race; he forgot his annoyance, his anger. Justine's step faltered just before she reached the shadows of the tree. "Who's there?" she asked in a loud whisper.

Quinton stepped away from the shadows.

"Oh, Quint, darling," she murmured. "I'm sorry I'm so late, but the meeting dragged on and on." She came to him, stood on tiptoes and kissed him.

He detected the distinct odor of alcohol on her breath and stopped himself before asking if it was customary for drinks to be served at meetings of the Art and Historical Society. He would have encircled her waist and drawn her to him in a kiss of a more passionate nature, but she pulled back and walked around him toward the cottage door.

"Why are you standing out here, darling? I left the

door unlocked for you.'' She threw the door open and disappeared inside.

As a New Yorker the idea of an unlocked door was remote to Quinton. Feeling somewhat foolish, he followed her into the cottage and closed the door as she switched on the lights. She came to him then, warm and responsive, and let him wrap her in his passionate embrace. She allowed only one lingering kiss; then wedged her hands between them and urged her release. He stood, tasting the alcohol he had smelled earlier on her breath. She crossed to the tray of decanters.

''A drink, darling? I always need one after a performance.''

''Scotch and soda,'' he said. ''What performance is that?''

''Oh my performance at the meeting,'' she said, splashing scotch in a glass. ''Pretending I care what architect is ignoring the building code for Old Town, or what storekeeper isn't keeping his sidewalks clean.''

''If you don't care, why do you attend?''

''Because I'm a Conch and a member and I have to do my duty,'' she answered. ''A Haymes has been on the committee since its formation.''

She handed him the scotch and soda, and he noted the sparkle in her green eyes. He wondered if she was intoxicated; then decided she was on an emotional high. He hoped that emotional high was due to meeting him and not the committee meeting she was protesting.

''Speaking of the Haymeses,'' she said, ''how did your dinner go with the queen of the clan?'' There was a bite of sarcasm in her voice.

''You don't like your aunt much, do you?''

''No, not much,'' she answered. ''Did she lament my neglect to you? Or did she merely suffer her loneli-

ness quietly with only occasional hints of my in-
gratitude?''

"Actually, I don't recall your name coming up."

"Then you must have been a captivating dinner
companion, my darling," she said with a smile. She
lifted her glass, watching him over the rim as she drank.
Her dark hair was pulled straight back from her face and
knotted at the nape of her neck as she had worn it that
morning. Her face had the appearance of being freshly
scrubbed; she wore no makeup aside from a suggestion
of lipstick. Her green eyes, playful now, were unmis-
takably teasing him. He stared at her face intently, at
the high cheekbones that created hollows of her cheeks,
her defiantly tilted chin and perfectly shaped lips, and
he found her beauty startling. The mere sight of her was
enough to awaken the passionate side of his nature that
Joanna had managed to quietly smother in the first
years of their marriage. Her eyes filled with impish
sparks as she asked, "Did the old harridan try to seduce
you?"

"No," he said, smiling despite himself.

"Good. If she had I would truly have hated her."
She drained her glass, set it aside, came and took his
untouched scotch and soda from his hand. "We've
wasted enough time," she murmured. "Let's go to bed
and make love."

Chapter Seven

Quinton awakened suddenly.

In the first moments before his senses adjusted themselves, he suffered from disorientation, and thought the woman snuggled against his side was Joanna; but Joanna had never snuggled, preferring to cling to her side of the bed, as if contact were abhorrent. The sun was already up, bright behind the ethereal Nouveau women woven into the draperies; their lidless eyes confronted him blandly. He blinked, struggling for coherence of senses, and fought to shed the clinging webs of a nightmare that refused to be recalled or remembered but merely clung there in the netherworld of sleep like an unknown threat to be dealt with.

His neck was stiff as he turned it. Then, staring down at Justine's peaceful, sleeping face, he was jolted back to the reality of time and place. The remnants of his nightmare were shattered; he felt curiously alive and rejuvenated. He accredited his sense of revitalization to the woman beside him. He would have kissed her, but that would have awakened her and he wanted to hold on to these moments of well-being, contentment—and yes, love. He had no doubt that what he felt for her was love. He felt as if the delicate emotion needed guarding, protection even from her.

His arm had gone to sleep beneath her head; he flexed his fingers slightly and felt a tingling sensation spread to his shoulder. His feet had become entangled in the sheet. Except for his one free arm, he could have been bound, a prisoner—but a willing one. Sighing, he pressed the crown of his head back into the pillow and lay staring at the patterns of lights and shadows on the ceiling. Various Art Deco vases and bowls were acting as prisms for the morning sun and created rainbow-hued swirls on the plaster. Outside, Lucifer was barking playfully, romping with a laughing Betty.

It was not so much that she stirred, but more of a sense of her that caused him to glance again at Justine. Her green eyes were open, staring at him.

"Why are you smiling?" she asked sleepily, and nestled even closer into the protective curve of his body. The humidity had already touched the day and he could feel the dampness at all points of body contact.

"Because I'm happy," he answered. He moved his arm and felt the throb of blood rushing through his veins.

"No one has a right to be happy first thing in the morning," she murmured against his side. "Especially not a man who moans with nightmares throughout the night."

The elusive sensation of a threat that he had first awakened with returned, but he pushed it away; he did not want to dissipate his springboard feeling—from which he would dive into this new, better day. A day made even better, he thought, because he had realized how he felt about the woman nestled so tightly against his side. Lightly, he said, "It could be worse. I could snore."

"And not sleep with me," she said. "What were you dreaming about?"

"I don't remember, really."

"Well, it must have been dreadful. I wouldn't want to hear even if you did remember."

"Actually," he suddenly recalled, "it had to do with your aunt."

He thought he detected a slight quiver pass through her body. She pushed away from him; before he could reach for her, she was out of bed slipping into a dressing gown. "It's late," she said, her voice strained. "She'll be expecting you. Do you like your coffee strong?" Her last words were thrown back from the adjoining room.

"Yes, strong," he called out, but he doubted she heard him above the rattling of pans and the sudden vibration of the water pipes. Still puzzling over her reaction to the mention of her aunt, he reached for his wristwatch on the bedside table. It was quarter past eight. He was due to meet with Helene at nine o'clock; since she had already expressed her disapproval of tardiness, he dare not be late again. He untangled his feet from the sheet, and rose. The panels of mirrors behind the bed threw back his naked reflections. The male morning syndrome of erection was still with him. No time to coax Justine back into bed; a cold shower would have to suffice.

Her Art Deco-Art Nouveau decorations extended into the bathroom. Plaques of slim-hipped, tiny-breasted ladies cavorted on the walls against brightly colored batik wallpaper. The basin was a gigantic marble shell, the gold spigots adorned with semi-precious stones in the style of the turn of the century. The vanity mirror was framed by gilted rococo floral carvings with a spread-winged dove perched on the top center, a broken garland in its beak. The commode itself was shaped like a clam shell, the silver lamé lid resting on the points. The carpet was a garish mauve color that picked up the least prominent color in the wallpaper. In his epitome of bad taste, Quinton spotted one item that drew his attention, a small painting attached to the back of the door. Closer examination proved it to be an original Beardsley, signed and dated by the artist. Making a note to mention its value to her, he stepped into the shower and turned on the cold spigot. The water trickled out.

He heard Justine back in the bedroom, and called, "There's no water pressure."

She stuck her head through the bathroom door. "One of the flaws in paradise," she said. "Water is a problem at times. Other times it's electricity." She went away before he could comment.

He showered as best he could and redressed in yesterday's clothes. Justine was sitting over a steaming cup of coffee in a nook by the kitchen window when he emerged from the bedroom. Her hair had come away from the bun at the nape of her neck and fell about her shoulders. The silk dressing gown gaped in front and he had a glimpse of naked breast with its ribbon of pale flesh untouched by the tropical sun. Her gaze was directed towards the sheer curtains; as he sat he saw Betty and Lucifer playing in the back yard. His sensitivity to Justine detected a troubled ambiance. He sipped his coffee and said cheerfully, "As a coffee maker, you're also an artist. Speaking of which, when are you taking me to *The Gingerbread Gallery* to see your work?"

Justine pulled her gaze away from the window and fixed him with her green eyes. "Tomorrow or the next day," she said without deep interest. "Today I have other plans."

Quinton refrained from inquiring of those "other

plans." After all, he had no right to question her activities. He would like to have said, "Look here, Justine, I think I'm falling in love with you. No, as sudden as it seems, I *am* in love with you. Loving you, that should give me certain privileges. Like knowing how you spend your days—and with whom." No, definitely the wrong approach. Her spirit was independent; he could not change that by suddenly blundering into her life with his declaration of love. He did say, "Whatever you do today, I hope it puts you in a better mood than you appear to be in now. I hope it wasn't my performance in the bedroom that's caused you to greet the day with such a long face."

Justine managed a weak smile. "No, darling," she assured him. "At the expense of inflating your male ego, you are an exceptional lover, Quinton Armstrong."

"Well, well, that puts me back in high spirits."

"I thought it might," she said with a soft laugh.

"And now what to do about you? Do you want to talk about what's bothering you? I'm a good listener."

Justine looked at him intently, her green eyes calculating whether she should unburden herself.

"It's not as if we're strangers," he encouraged.

"Wasn't it Edna St. Vincent Millay who said pain was easily expressed to strangers on a train, not to friends?"

"If she did, she was wrong," Quinton said. "We are friends, Justine." He put special emphasis on *'friends'* to denote that it encompassed more, much more.

Justine released her grasp of the coffee cup, interlaced her fingers tightly on the tabletop, and stared down at them. "It's her," she said, nodding toward the main house.

"Your aunt?"

"Sometimes just the mention of her name can send me into depression or anger. Like earlier when you said your nightmares were somehow connected to her. She has a way of intruding in my life that's intolerable. She's always tried to replace my mother. She interferes, tries to dictate what I should and shouldn't do, what people I associate with, which ones I should snub because I'm a Conch and a Haymes. Within the normal social order, you see, we Conchs have our own system of class distinction. The lower, the smug middle class, and the wealthy.

"The Haymeses lost their deviously acquired fortune decades ago, but she, in an even more devious manner, managed to restore it. To her, we're part of the island's diminished elite. She expects me to restrict my associations to that inner circle, even, God willing I overcome my imagined asexuality, marry within it. Before my father died she even went so far as to attempt to force an arranged marriage."

The knuckles of Justine's hands had whitened from pressure; she unlaced them and brought them to her lap. "I've always rebelled against any of her suggestions," she said. "If she says something is black, I insist it's white. If she agrees it's white, I insist its black. I hobnob with shrimpers and beach bums and assorted white trash, and make certain her cronies call and report to her. She, in turn, has her own form of retribution. She controls the money, and money, to paraphrase an old saying, makes our island world go around."

Quinton felt discomfort nag him at the knowledge that soon, very soon, everything would pass from the aunt to Justine; the old woman was going to enormous trouble to guarantee her niece full value of her antiques. That did not sound like a woman seeking retribution. Still, he was bound to secrecy.

"The reason I'm telling you all this, Justine went on, "is that this morning when you mentioned her name in regard to your nightmares it occurred to me that she might . . . . she could come between us. There, I've said it," she murmured with a nervous toss of her lovely head. "I've admitted how important you are to me. Now even if she doesn't learn about us and try to interfere, you'll become a typical male. You've conquered, so now you can use me, abuse me, and, when your work with her is over, you can cast me aside." She laughed as if jesting with him, but the jest was belied by the seriousness in her green eyes.

Quinton merely sat staring at her in stricken delight.

"You probably consider me just another foolish woman," she accused. "Only a foolish woman would confess emotional involvement so quickly. There are probably numerous New York females who've reacted to you just as I have."

"How wrong you are," Quinton managed. "You're not a foolish woman and I'm not a typical male, not if a typical male would ever cast someone like you aside. As for other women, you may not believe me, but you're the first since my wife. I'm flattered you think otherwise, but women have never been particularly drawn to me. Either that or my own density has made me unaware of any attractions. I guess the best way to explain myself is to tell you I've always been a one-woman man." He laughed. "Christ, that makes me sound like a cheap country and western lyric."

Joining his laughter, she said, "We'll get Aaron to write the tune."

"Aaron?" His laughter died.

"My gay friend. He writes music."

"Oh," he said. "Is it Aaron you've plans with for today?"

"As a matter of fact, it is. He needs to keep busy to forget about his breakup. We're going water skiing. Oh, poor darling." She reached out and touched his cheek affectionately. "You're not jealous of Aaron? Of a homosexual? Why don't you join us? You're so pale. You could use the sun."

"I have work to do," he said evenly. "I've only a few days to do my appraisal before I have to return to New York and start the procedure for your aunt's auction."

"It doesn't seem fair, me frolicking in the sun while you're locked away in a dusty room of ancient junk."

"It's not junk," Quinton said, almost irritably. "I'm very fond of antiques, and I'm devoted to my job. Your aunt's collection is the most exciting I've seen in private hands."

"I didn't mean to offend you. I guess my reaction to antiques also comes from my opposition to her. I decorated the cottage as I have because I knew she'd find it offensive. I've scoffed at what she calls her treasures for so long I've begun to believe I dislike them. I don't actually. I can share your appreciation of them, if not your excitement." She leaned across the narrow table and kissed him. "I don't want to leave you today," she said. "I'd like to be with you even if I have to sit in a corner and watch while you do your appraisal. I could call Aaron and cancel." It was both a statement and a question.

"No, you go and enjoy yourself," he told her, and meant it.

"What about joining us for an hour later?" she pressed. "You have to take a break. Even she can't object to that. We could pick you up at *The Pier House* beach. Oh, say you will." Her beautiful green eyes sparkled with excitement. "Even an hour with you would make our separation until tonight more tolerable.''

Quinton knew he should devote every hour to the appraisal, but not wanting to disappoint her and still overcome by the flattery of her confessed affection for him, he acquiesced. ''But only for an hour. I'll tell your aunt I have to do some shopping.''

''You needn't tell her anything,'' Justine said with authority. ''She'll never know if you're in that rambling old house or not. Besides, she sleeps most of the afternoons; either that or she pores over her scrapbooks and old love letters.''

Quinton read the disdain in her voice and could not refrain from asking, ''Do you really hate her so much?''

Her answer was a defiant tilt of her chin, a chilled frosting of her eyes.

''Have you considered that perhaps you've misjudged her? That she's only had your best interests at heart?''

''Her interpretation of 'best interests' caused my father's death,'' Justine answered coldly.

''The boating accident?'' he said, remembering Helene mentioning the unfortunate event.

''Oh, is that what she told you?'' Justine said with an angry sneer. ''He didn't die in any boating accident.'' She turned her head away to hide the sudden moisture forming in her eyes. ''It's not the truth,'' she whispered. ''Even if she would like it to be. My father hanged himself from the bell tower of the church. She drove him to it. If nothing else, I'll never forgive her for that.''

As Quinton was about to question her on this startling statement, she said, ''Now, you'd best go to her. If people are late she becomes incensed.'' She wiped at her cheeks impatiently. "You'll have to placate her as well as keep her in the dark about us if we're to enjoy ourselves without her interference." She rose, gathering up their unfinished cups of coffee and carried them to the sink hidden by the Deco screen. From behind the screen, she said, "I'll send Betty on an errand so she won't see you leave the cottage. She might tell her mother, and Maria would most certainly tell my aunt."

How, Quinton wondered, could they continue their affair, separated from the main house by only the unkept yard, and Maria not discover their secret? Discovery was inevitable; then he would have another complicity to explain to Helene Haymes. "Justine, wouldn't it be better to . . ."

The telephone rang and cut him off.

Justine came from behind the screen and answered: "Yes. Yes, it's me. Hello." She glanced at Quinton over her shoulder, and smiled. "Everything's fine. Yes. As expected. Right on schedule. Good-bye." She hung up, explaining, "The gallery wanting to know if a canvas for a New Orleans client is going to be completed on time. Now, darling, we'll pick you up on *The Pier House* beach at two o'clock. Wear a skimpy pair of trunks so I can admire your gorgeous body." She came, stood on tiptoes, and kissed him.

"You're a strange and frustrating creature," Quinton told her. "You flit from mood to mood, topic to topic with such rapidity you make my mind flounder. Promise me tonight we'll sit down and calmly carry one conversation through to a logical conclusion."

"I promise," she said, raising one hand and placing the other on an imaginary Bible. Slipping from his arms, she went to the door to send Betty from the yard.

"Tell her to take the Doberman with her," Quinton said.

Quinton walked around the side of the house, unseen, he thought, and rang the front doorbell. In the short walk from the cottage to the front door, his countenance had changed; his deep-set blue eyes were troubled, his mouth tightly set. From the moment Justine had told him her father had hanged himself from the church bell tower he had been struggling with his nagging indignation. He hated to be lied to; perhaps that explained his own inability to tell even a little white lie without his face undergoing a telltale change. It irritated him that Helene, after entrusting him with her secret of impending death, had then thought so little of him as to lie about her brother's death. Had he not already determined otherwise, he might have forgiven her by thinking her senile, but senile she certainly wasn't; her mind like her tongue could crack like a whip. He tapped his foot impatiently as he waited for Maria to materialize and let him in. When she didn't appear he tried the handle and the door swung inward. As he climbed the stairs his impulse to confront Helene with her lie waned. Confrontation would mean admitting a closeness to her niece, a closeness Justine had warned him to keep hidden.

On the top floor, as he raised his hand to knock, Helene's door opened suddenly and Maria filled the frame with her bulk. Her eyes held an indiscernible expression, both questioning and chilled. "Miss Helene, she ain't dressed yet," the housekeeper told him. "She had a bad night. You do what you gotta do, and she'll send for you when she's ready." The housekeeper spoke with a quiet authority.

"I'll need the keys and her inventory book," Quinton said. He intended to begin marking the most valuable items of her collection, those items he felt should be featured in a brochure with photographs and possibly printed authentication.

Maria, nodding, closed the door; he heard her speaking, her voice muffled by the heavy carved oak, but he did not hear her employer's reply. Presently, the door reopened and the housekeeper shoved the keys and inventory book towards him. "You want coffee, then you help yourself in the kitchen," she said; apparently she had not forgiven Quinton for spoiling last night's dinner party. "Me, I gotta see to Miss Helene. She can't dress without me. She's always worse when she's been upset." Maria tossed him a savage look accusingly, and closed the door in his face.

Quinton flushed darkly. He raised his hand again to knock, thought better of it, and shrugging, turned away from the door. Before beginning the meticulous task of catologuing and appraising, he decided to complete his examination of each and every room. He began on the second floor, but his examination went no further than the first door he opened. What had at one time been a tremendous ballroom was now choked by storage of cloth-covered mounds of furniture. He edged down narrow aisles lifting dust cloth after dust cloth, his excitement growing and being expressed in sighs of bewilderment. At one end of the ballroom he came across Helene's clock collection; he unfurled the dust cloths and let them drop to the floor; table upon table, their tops crowded by antique clocks of every description, a collection that rivaled the one he had viewed at the royal palace in Madrid a few years previous, clocks presented to past kings and queens by the rulers of the world, each trying to outdo the other in their gift to the horology-minded Spanish rulers. Quinton whistled softly, murmuring, "A fortune in clocks alone."

Aware that he was not alone, he turned and found himself confronting Maria. "Miss Helene, she'll see you now," the housekeeper announced. "You want coffee, I'll bring it now," she added, seemingly in a better mood.

"Thank you, Maria," Quinton said graciously. He loosely re-covered the clocks, intending to return to their inspection as soon as he had finished with Helene.

He found Helene's door slightly ajar.

At the sound of his footsteps in the hallway, she called, "Come in, Quinton." She occupied the accustomed Bergère chair. A dim light glowed in an opaque amber globe behind her and fed color into the greyness of her hair and silk dressing gown. The morning sun through the slats of the closed shutters made slashes of light across the outer edges of the carpet. "I trust you had a pleasant evening?"

Quinton sought double meaning in the question, but found none; she had not, he reflected, been aware of his evening spent in the cottage. "Most pleasant," he answered. "I understand you had a bad night. If, as Maria implied, I upset you, I'm . . ."

A pale hand was raised within the darkened periphery of her chair and gestured dismissal of the housekeeper's accusation. "Maria," she said, "is overly protective of me. Sit down, Quinton. I've spent my night weighing our conversation."

Quinton sank into the chair opposite her, prepared to meet her objections to putting herself again in the limelight for the sake of her auction.

"I understand the validity of your suggestion," the old woman said. "You are, of course, correct in stating an auction of the sort I demand requires more than merely top quality antiques. It's easy to forget that the ghouls as well as the true collectors give an auction its impetus. Ironic, I suppose, that the very bastards I hated so much during my days of collecting will be the ones to drive up prices of my treasures at auction. They lost out to me often in the past, but now they'll be carting my treasures away.'' She sighed wearily and appeared to shrink further into the down-filled cushions of her chair. ''The ghouls are the victors in the end,'' she murmured, distantly.

When she remained silent for several moments, Quinton said, ''Am I to assume you're giving permission to extensive press coverage?''

''With limitations,'' she answered. ''I do not wish to be hounded by reporters, nor do I wish to be photographed. You will act as my liaison with the press. I will meet with no one else personally. That must be understood at the outset. As for what past scandals are aired, I leave that entirely to you. I will hold myself at your disposal and, for what good they'll be to you, there are my many scrapbooks, diaries and love letters. Discretion, Quinton, that should be the key word. Remember, it isn't me who'll suffer from this new surge of notoriety, but my . . . Justine.''

''You make it extremely difficult for me,'' Quinton said. ''After the first wave of interest in you every reporter in the industry will no doubt attempt to be granted an interview.''

''I will deny everyone,'' Helene said firmly. ''I repeat, only you, Quinton, will be allowed to interview me personally. Let your public relations firm send out its press releases, or whatever they're called, and we'll judge from there just how effective this scheme of yours will be. As for myself, I think you an extremely enterprising young man. I'm pleased you were recommended to me.''

''Just who did recommend me?'' Quinton asked.

''A friend,'' Helene answered evasively. ''Now, tell me what comes next. What will you do to get my auction in motion?''

Quinton settled back in his chair. "First," he said, "I would like to complete my inspection of the collection. Every room presents new surprises. I just came across your clock collection in the ballroom."

"Ah, yes, the clocks," she said with another sigh. "Those were Lord Cambray's obsession, not mine. He was reputed to own the most extensive collection in private hands, but I can't verify that. I did not meddle in his bailiwick and he left me to mine. I do remember that he once flew halfway around the world when he heard a gallery was touting a find of Viennese bracket clock supposed to have been one of a kind by a master clockmaker. Albert was a man of small stature, not very imposing. I walked into the gallery on his arm that day. He took one look at the clock and drew himself up to his full height, announcing to a gallery filled with noted horologists that the clock was a fraud and the dealer a charlatan. An argument over the clock's authenticity ensued, but Albert clung stubbornly to his appraisal. He was sued for defamation by the gallery owner. After Albert won the case he returned to the gallery, picked up the clock in question and smashed it on the floor. 'So you'll not try to hoodwink another collector,' he said, and turned and stormed out. He was sued again, but the charges were dropped." Her voice had taken on the resonance of one lost in memory. Weeks, months, decades dropped away, and she spoke as if Lord Cambray had lived and been her lover only yesterday. "Albert could be fierce, but he was always gentle with me. And what a sop he was when it came to . . . " She let the sentence trail off suddenly as if catching herself from relating a memory best kept secret.

"You sound as if you loved him very much," Quinton observed.

"I did," Helene said. "He was the only man I ever loved. We could spend hour upon hour together, each of us submerging ourselves in our individual collections, and never become bored. He was born under the astrological sign of Virgo. That gave him a meticulous nature and accounted for his fascination with the mechanisms of clocks. It may interest you to know both Louis XVI and Peter the Great of Russia, both clock fanatics, were also Virgos. Do you believe in astrology, Quinton?"

"No," he answered bluntly.

"Ah, well, then perhaps your beliefs are placed higher," she said. "I always found astrology less mystical than religion. Albert used to chide me about it."

"Then you inherited the clock collection from Lord Cambray?" Quinton asked.

"Yes. That in itself is a story. Everything in our house on the Isle of Wight came to me on Albert's death. Losing him, a man I truly loved, was the most shattering experience of my life, but devastated as I was I rose to the occasion when his family tried to have the will rescinded. It was a long and tiring legal battle and, oddly, one of the few incidents in my life that was kept out of the press. His family was that powerful. It was the threat of notoriety, I think, that in the end made them relinquish their claim. They couldn't continue to battle me and hold the press at bay indefinitely.

"I should like Albert's memory respected in any articles you might release to the press, Quinton," she stated. "It's one of the few restrictions I shall put on you. As for his dead fish of a wife, she's long since been buried and no doubt roasting in that particular nook of hell reserved for English bluenose bitches. Except for one child, his children are of no concern to me." She leaned forward, the amber light spilling full across her face, a face that was captivating in its agelessness. "Which brings us, Quinton, to the topic I wanted to discuss with you, a topic closer to my heart even than my precious treasures. Yes, that is possible—and true. I can see that surprises you."

Quinton said nothing. It amazed him that she could discern his slightest expression in the dimly lit room; her eyes, though sensitive to light, must be extremely keen.

Helene leaned back in her chair and was swallowed again by shadows. "Aside from myself, only one other living person knows what I am about to tell you," she said from within her cocoon of darkness.

Quinton was about to object, to tell her he did not want to be the confidant of more of her secrets, but some instinct told him what she would say concerned Justine, so he held his objection.

Helene began:

"When I first realized I was in love with Albert Cambray, I also realized I had, until then, loved only myself. I, who had been mistress and lover to numerous men and had listened to them confess their love for me with scant regard, had at last become victim to my own ploy. I had been invulnerable to this devastating emotion; now it was awakened in me and I found I had no resources to deal with it. I was as destructible as a schoolgirl experiencing her first infatuation.

"But why Albert Cambray, why this man? I had been mistress to some of the most exciting and dynamic men of the era. Granted, some were beasts, but all had possessed a charisma Albert lacked. As I said, he was a man of small stature, not even handsome. With his walrus moustache, receding Cambray chin and tiny, blazing almond-colored eyes, he often reminded me of a carnival barker or a mad inventor. He had two pas-

sions in life, clocks and boats. I knew that if I succeeded in becoming his third passion, it would also be
in that order of importance. I think he had taken me as
his mistress more because it was fashionable than for
any physical or emotional need. I had agreed to the
arrangement because I needed, in Albert's vernacular,
'a safe harbor in which to scrape the barnacles of the
past years from my soul.' Neither of us anticipated a
poignant attachment becoming a complication. Albert
was safely, if not happily, married; he had his position,
was a man of respectability. Most of his peers kept
mistresses, but these women were interchangeable, and
often were. A friend once remarked that as a mistress
she was no more important to her lover than his favorite
fedora.

"Albert was not that indifferent. He was also generous. He purchased, in my name, a beautiful house on
the Isle of Wight and allowed me to furnish it with the
most expense antiques. He visited frequently, but was
never demanding. The afternoons were generally spent
on his boat; evenings he liked us to sit in the drawing
room, he tinkering with his clocks and me studying the
histories of my treasures. When we retired it was often
merely to fall asleep holding one another. Our
lovemaking was never ardent, but easy and natural,
unlike what I had grown accustomed to; he was gentle,
as concerned for my pleasure as his own. He never
questioned my past, never, like so many of my lovers,
wanted his male ego inflated by being favorably compared to those who had come before him.

"When it came time for his visits to end he would
usually slip away before dawn and not awaken me. No
good-byes or promises of when he would come again. I
was left alone with my housekeeper and the two
Dobermans he had bought me for protection. In the

beginning, I thought I would go mad. I was accustomed to parties and balls and traveling from one chic place to the next with the expensive people. I would, in my loneliness, curse him and swear that when he came again I would break it off and fling myself back into the mainstream of life and living. After all, my madcap life had not been seriously altered by a world war. Why should I make such a drastic change because of an arrangement with Albert Cambray? Had it been an earlier lover, I would merely have called in the movers between his visits and left a hastily scrawled note terminating the affair.

"But when Albert came again I would be there, waiting. The loneliness during his absence would be forgotten. A consuming and uncanny peace would settle over me. I felt all was well with the world, with me, with us. I wanted nothing more than that quiet harbor he had arranged for me. Days on the boat, evenings in the drawing room, nights clinging to one another in the darkness of our bedroom. Nothing more exciting than the acquisition of another treasure, the authentication of a past one. I continued to correspond with dealers of antiquities throughout Europe. I bought and shipped the important pieces to Key West, as if in my subconscious I always knew I'd end here alone with only my treasures for comfort.

"All the while my love for Albert smoldered without my realizing it. I'll never forget the day the revelation struck me. It was summer. I was standing on the cliff behind the house. A summer storm was brewing on the horizon. The water below was laced with whitecaps, Albert's boat straining at its mooring. I had gone out without a sweater and the sudden wind chilled me. Curiously, there was some feeling churning inside me that was, I reflected, as violent as the sea, as contrasting as the sky with its turbulent black horizon and blue, sunlit apex. I both wanted to shout with joy and sob with anguish, and did not know the why or wherefore for either. Ah, at last, I thought, the madness my father predicted for me as the price for the life I chose to lead.

"I had turned and started back towards the house when I saw Albert's Bentley snaking its way up the cliff road. The impact of the revelation struck me. Aloud, increduously, I said, 'I love him'. Those words, once spoken by me without understanding or sincerity, now created an emotion so strong, so profound, so naked and stark that my very strength seemed to be plucked away. I staggered to a bench on the cliff's edge and sat down, weeping.

"Albert's last visit had been only two days prior. It was unusual for him to come again so soon. It occurred to me that maybe fate had dealt him the same staggering realization. Trembling, I rose and went to greet him.

"But it was his precious boat that had brought him back so soon. He had learned of the approaching storm and had wanted to inspect the moorings.

"Love, it appeared, when it came to me was to be one-sided.

"Albert detected some change in me, but he said nothing, avoided any topic that might open itself to a discussion of my newly discovered attitude toward him. Still, I do not think he was without comprehension. Before he departed the following day he made me a gift of one of his prized clocks." Helene lifted a pale hand and indicated the shadowy mantel. "His Peter Rau organ clock," she said with a sigh. "It contains seven melodies by Joseph Haydn. Quite lovely and rare. It plays one melody every hour. I both prized and hated that clock because I looked upon it as a symbol of his appreciation for my not having verbalized my love for him."

Quinton glanced dutifully towards the clock in question, but could make out only its shape in the dim light. Discerning the emotion in the old woman's voice, he now wished he had prevented her from relating her confidence. He wanted to be a collector, a chronicler of her scandalous past, but he was not prepared to be swept up in the emotions those memories might awaken. He chided himself for foolishly having thought a personal life could be related in the same cold, hard, unemotional terms as some historical event. Further proof that he was not, as Hal Crimmons would lead him to believe, a capable reporter for the assignment on Helene Haymes. Then, too, there was his selfish motivation in hoping Helene would reveal something of Justine. Already, he reflected, he had lost his objectivity.

"Life between Albert and me continued much as before," the old woman went on, "except I looked at him through different eyes and with a changed heart. I began to suffer related emotions. Jealousy was the worst; the fact of Albert's wife became unbearable I tortured myself by imagining him making love to her, sharing with her, enjoying her company as much or more than he did mine. She was my enemy, and yet she remained totally unknown to me. Except for a blurred photograph in the social pages, I didn't even know what she looked like. If I questioned Albert about her, he was evasive. I believed he felt it would blemish her if he discussed the mother of his children with *me,* a notorious harlot. What a fool I was. That dear, gentle man. In his mind it was the reverse.

"Once, learning that Lord and Lady Cambray were to attend a social function honoring a foreign diplomat, I traveled to London and, like some character from a 1930s American melodrama, stationed myself in the shadows outside the hall. I saw Albert's wife for the

first time. She was a shrew of a woman, towering
above him, with a hawk-like nose and thin, mean lips.
She smiled for the press, but it did not take a perceptive
person to recognize there was no mirth behind those
hard eyes. She clung to Albert's arm, but with an
attitude of possession; a calculating woman displaying
a prized matrimonial catch; an unspoken statement,
'This man and all his wealth, power and prestige are
mine.' I hated her instantly, but I came away to discover my jealousy had left me. I understood my importance to Albert, understood why if he loved me he had
been unable to bring himself to confess it. He had given
his wife the power of manipulation through the holy
union of matrimony. He feared that I, through the
knowledge of his love, would use that love over him
and become a replica of his wife.

"Years of absorption with myself turned to devoted
absorption with Albert. I found myself longing for
those things my life-style had forced me to surrender.
Most of all I wanted a child, Albert's child."

Here, Helene paused for such a long time that Quinton thought she had decided to end her story. He did not
know what was expected of him, if he should comment
or merely rise and take his leave of her. Indeed, for all
he could see of her in the darkened room, she could
have drifted into a sudden nap.

But then she said, "I was already past the age when a
woman should have children. If I did not think of
myself, I reflected I should at least consider the child of
so unconventional a union. A child born to me then
would, during its most formative years, have an old
woman for a mother. You see, Quinton, I still suffered
from that very American attitude toward age. What
fools we Americans are for thinking the young are to be
envied their youth. We should look on youth as the

caterpillar phase in the life of a butterfly. It isn't until we've gone through the awkward, crawling stage of the caterpillar that we can spread our wings and truly soar.

"Ah, but I mustn't get on the topic of youth versus age," Helene muttered. "I came to my conclusions too late for my own benefit."

"My decision, like most of those I'd made, was selfish. I wanted a child, Albert's child. My want won over my sensibilities. I didn't tell Albert because I knew he would object, didn't tell him I had deliberately gotten myself pregnant until my body made confession necessary. At first he was furious. His face swelled with rage. He screamed at me for the first time since I'd known him. He had been working on a delicate ormolu clock when I delivered my news. He shoved the clock aside, and rising, strode to the fireplace and stood with his back to me, staring down at the freshly scrubbed hearth. 'You'll naturally have an abortion,' he said darkly. 'No,' I told him. 'I will have this child.' 'You would bring a bastard into this world?' he demanded. 'I cannot give our child my name, and you, forgive me, Helene, will inflict the legacy of your past upon the child regardless of how carefully you might conceal your identity to prevent doing so.'

"It was the first time Albert had ever made any reference to my past. I felt as if he had struck me a physical blow. It was made all the more painful because I knew what he said was the truth. It was one of the considerations I had ignored when I had decided to become pregnant. I had laughed at my notoriety, but the laughter had now taken on the sting of gallows humor. It would be the child who suffered my infamy. Albert was twenty years older than I. He would not be capable of maintaining a 'safe harbor' for many years more. At the same time this struck me, I realized that because I would have to lose Albert eventually, I wanted the child even more. 'I'll have this child with or without you!' I shouted at him. 'I'll not be left with only memories.' And I stormed from the room, firm in my decision.

"Later that night he came to me. He crept into bed and pressed his face against my stiff, unyielding back, and whispered, 'All right, Helene. You win, my darling. I'll make what arrangements possible to protect our child.'"

Helene now rose from her chair. She moved through the darkened room to the sideboard, a shimmering vision of pale silk. Quinton heard the stopper of the decanter removed, heard liquor being splashed into a glass. He even heard, or imagined he heard the liquor being gulped down her constricted throat. Turning, she leaned against the sideboard and confronted him with eyes he felt could uncannily pierce the room's heavy shadows.

"Three weeks before the following spring turned into the summer of Albert's death a daughter was born to me," the old woman said quietly. "A precious new life created of our bodies out of love, the only love I've ever known. Albert named our daughter Justine."

Chapter Eight

"Justine!" Quinton rose from his chair as he cried the name. "Are you telling me that . . . that Justine isn't your niece? That she's . . . "

"My daughter," Helene Haymes confirmed.

The old woman moved back to her chair and sat down.

"But how could you not have told her? Why wouldn't you have told her?" Quinton demanded. "I find it incredible."

"Do sit down, Quinton," Helene said evenly. She waited until he had reseated himself before saying, "After Albert died and the legalities were settled over my inheritance I decided to return to America. As I told you, Albert's sudden death devastated me. If it had not been for our daughter, I think I would have joined him. I loved him that much. But there was our daughter to be considered. As for myself, I suppose I could have remained in Europe even though I no longer had any friends there. I had severed all relationships when I'd become Albert's mistress. I needed to be consoled, but there was no one to turn to. Here in Key West, I had a brother I scarcely knew and a sister-in-law I'd never met. Be what it may, it was home, and in times of deep trouble the home is always thought of as a safe haven.

Besides, I wanted my daughter raised as American.
Despite my own desertion, I retrained a strong sense of
country. The problem was that here those that didn't
think of me as a traitor because of those stories linking
me with Hitler considered me an unredeemable slut.
Albert's words came back to haunt me. I was a marked
woman, and my past would mark our daughter. I
couldn't have that, wouldn't have it.

"It was my original intention to return to this old
house and hide away until I could make plans. Key
West being my hometown and the small town it is, I
knew I'd have to go elsewhere, assume a new identity
to protect my daughter and myself. I flew into Miami
and hired a private plane to fly me to Key West in the
middle of the night, a fitting homecoming, the inter-
national whore returning home under the cover of darkness with her bastard."

Quinton winced at the bitterness in the old woman's
voice. He could sense her anguish as the emotion of that
time in her life was brought back into focus.

"My father had died the month before," she went
on, "and word had not reached me. There was only a
young black woman and her half-caste lover here to
greet me when I arrived with my baby. My brother's
wife had always refused to live in the house. Since
before the war the locals had taken to calling it the
Whore's Mausoleum. They watched the arrivals of
shipments of my antiquities and called them my sinful
bounties. Rumor had it that when I was old and men no
longer wanted me I intended to return here to wallow
among my treasures. Little boys used to throw stones at
the house and scribble obscenities on the walls. My
sister-in-law, I later learned, was from the Bible Belt,
the daughter of a Baptist preacher; she'd have no part of
the house, and considered me Satan's brand on her
husband's soul.

"Maria made up my old room for me and Justine. I swore her to secrecy about my return, and sent her to fetch my brother. His wife wouldn't allow him to come. He hadn't even been allowed to visit our father in his last, dying days. He was a born-again Christian and the objects I had filled the house with belonged to the Devil.

"Outraged, I left Justine in Maria's care and walked to my brother's house. It had been the whore's money that had supported him for years. I needed his help in establishing a new life for my daughter and myself, and by God, I intended to have that help.

"His wife was a pale, chinless creature with dung-colored hair who kept calling out to her Jesus to protect her soul and the soul of the baby she carried from the contamination of me, the harlot. My brother had changed. He had once been a robust man with an eye for pretty women and an unquenchable thirst for rum. He now had the pouch of a beer drinker. His jowls sagged. The color had drained from his green eyes and with it the zest for life and living. He flushed scarlet when I told his wife to shut up and leave us in private. He stammered some weak defense, and ordered me out of his house. A house, I reminded him, bought with my money, my whore's money, making it no less corrupt than the family home his wife refused to allow him to enter to either visit a dying father or assist a sister in need. I also reminded him that the many loans I had made him had enabled him to open his real estate business. 'It's time,' I said, 'to pay the piper.' His heavyset body appeared to cave in on itself. 'You wouldn't call those loans in?' he cried, and I assured him I would, that I had every intention of doing so even if it destroyed him. 'You'll be stealing from the poor box of your wife's church just to feed your family, and I'll have no mercy, none.' He collapsed onto the sofa, that fat stomach of his snapping the buttons on his shirt. 'Damn you,' he wept. 'Damn you to Hell.' I waited until he had calmed down. Then I told him I had no need for money, that I would sign off all his loans if he would help me establish a new identity and a new life for myself and my daughter. I would even, I told him, pay him a sizable bonus for his assistance. Something sparked behind his eyes then, and it was greed.

"With a promise that he would help me, I returned to the house and locked myself inside. Black curtains were placed on the windows to hide any unusal lights that would attract the neighbors' attention. Maria shopped at two separate stores so the purchase of additional food wouldn't raise suspicions. The windows had to be kept closed in the event Justine would cry and be overheard. We made diapers of towels and when we did the wash it was hung to dry in the passageways. Only when Justine became ill was Dr. Webb, my brother's classmate and friend, brought in on our secret.

"Still, even as a hidden prisoner in my own home, there was a growing satisfaction in being back. I could wander for hours upon hour from room to room and admire the treasures I had shipped from Europe. I had Maria's half-caste lover open cartons and reassemble furniture. I began my inventory book and organized papers of authentication.

"Meantime, my brother began arranging new identities for myself and Justine, a task that in the end proved unnecessary. Fate stepped in with what I thought a preferable solution.

"My sister-in-law was old-fashioned as she was religious. She had a terror of hospitals matched only by her hatred of me and what she called my sinful life. She chose to give birth to her baby at home in her own bed with only Dr. Webb in attendance.

"The baby, I was told, was a breach birth. Had my sister-in-law consented to give birth in a hospital, Dr. Webb might have been able to handle the complications. As it happened, he could not save the mother or the unfortunate child. Maria had gone to offer what assistance she could; she returned with the news and I sent her back immediately to bring my brother to me. I should have considered his loss, his grief, but the scheme that had occurred to me when Maria had told me about the death of his wife and baby had seized me as a perfect solution and time was of the utmost importance. I had to gain my brother's approval before the doctor could register or report the deaths."

Helene paused, and Quinton, caught up, unconsciously leaned forward in his chair in an encouraging gesture for her to go on.

"What better identity for my daughter," Helene said, "than that of my brother's child? She would not only be a Haymes, she would legally carry the name. Dr. Webb could be bribed through money and friendship. He could register Justine and quietly dispose of the body of my brother's dead son. Who would question him? For what reason? He, like us, was a Conch; he was respected and trusted. If he was hesitant, he could be reminded that the land on which his contractors had erroneously extended one end of his Olympic-sized swimming pool was still owned by me. Then, too, with Justine accepted as my brother's daughter my right to be with her would not be questioned. I could remain in Key West in the home of my birth and with my treasures around me. Perhaps the locals would never forgive me my past, but they could not inflict my shame on a child they thought to be my niece, not the daughter of the righteous widower Haymes.

"All this I poured out to my brother, and the bodies of his wife and son not yet cold. It was heartless, I know, and I make no excuses. My brother sat where you're sitting now, and he glared at me with such hatred I can feel it still. He said nothing, but his silence and glaring hatred told me more than mere words could have. When he rose and left me I knew he would do as I demanded, but I also understood he would be my enemy for life.

"What I did not know was that his revenge would be so overwhelming. I did not think him capable of nurturing a vendetta that required years of patience and careful planning. Ah, but I should have understood. He was a Haymes, and we've always been known for our scheming.

"Dr. Webb announced my brother's wife had died giving birth to a daughter, that the child had to be flown to a hospital in Miami for specialized care. My brother moved back into this house. He received sympathetic neighbors downstairs while I hid up here. His wife's church members shook the rafters with their gospel singing and shrieking prayers. Dr. Webb was given a deed to cover the infringement made by his contractors. He later told me he had arranged for my brother's son's body to be buried with his mother, the secret of his existence hidden at her feet all through the funeral services and into the grave.

"I exited Key West as I had arrived, in the dead of night, and returned the following day at high noon to make my homecoming public. Locals streamed past the house for days, some shouting obscenities, others just gawking at the windows. I had to have the telephones removed. Maria's lover had to stand guard on the front porch with a shotgun. It wasn't loaded, but no one knew that. The newspaper had a field day; all the old scandals were reopened and flourished upon. The photograph with me on Hitler's arm was reprinted with a story claiming I was his favorite even over the stupid Eva. There was talk of opening a federal investigation. I was a Communist, a Socialist, an atheist, a Satanist, and various other sundry beings. Newspaper photos from the past were dug up from foreign news agencies and reprinted. There was even one of me with Lord Cambray—a photo I wasn't even aware was in existence, of us in a sidewalk cafe in Paris just after the liberation. It had been taken the day we had met. He was in uniform. The other man with him, the man who had introduced us, was an American general; the press, not wishing to taint the memory of that hero, had snipped him from the photo when it was printed.

"Through all of this I remained indoors. I spent my days with Justine and continued the inventory of my collection. In the evenings when my brother returned home, the commotion outside would cease out of respect for him. The Widower Haymes was a respected pillar of the community; he mustn't suffer because fate had given him such a sister. It was suggested that I was adopted, the bad seed of a maid who had died in childbirth, that my mother had been raped and impregnated by a Navy man—that was a favorite since the Navy was resented. They had overstayed their welcome in Key West; the war was over and they were no longer needed.

"I pride myself on retaining a sense of humor, Quinton, but it is difficult even now to look back on those days with anything near amusement."

"And I want to start all that over," Quinton said darkly.

"Ah, but for a different reason," the old woman said, "and these are different times. No doubt the curiosity seekers will come to peer at my house. I might be put in the local guide book and included on the

Conch Train Tours, but the hostility, I think not. The
moral standards of this country have changed drastically. We are not quite so quick to throw stones, not with
drug-addicted, sexually perverse children in almost
every family and crooked politicians being exposed in
the highest offices. The Victorian wind has been
knocked out of the Americans. This time the publicity
will, I think, do just what you intend of it. It will bring
the wealthy collectors to my auction.

"But during that time I feared most for Justine.
There was always the possibility some neighbor might
suspect her real parentage and start a vicious rumor;
Justine looked nothing like anyone but me. I refrained
from going near a window for fear of being seen and
compared to the child. I became the recluse I am today.

"And I was happy, as happy as I deserved until . . ."

The old woman turned in her chair so that the pale
light from the slats of the closed shutters outlined her
profile; yes, Quinton reflected, there was a definite
resemblance to Justine.

" . . . until I realized my brother had maliciously,
subtly turned my daughter against me. How cleverly he
had played the role of her loving father, poisoning her
against me to such an extent that the harder I tried to
express my love for her the deeper her resentment
became. How obsessive his hatred of me must have
been. He made it impossible for me to ever confess the
truth to Justine. How he gloated the night he admitted
his revenge. I cursed him to Hell, not knowing that was
exactly where he'd be the following day.

"But it did not end there," Helene said passionately.
"No, not even there! My brother was so demented he
even used his own death to drive a final wedge between
Justine and me. He left her a letter telling her he could

no longer live with the shame I had brought on them, especially on her, his beloved daughter.'' The old woman clenched her pale hands and pounded repeatedly on the chair arms. "Actually, he suffered the same malady that now attacks me. Rather than fight for the last months of life he chose the coward's way.''

Quinton rose as the old woman moaned in torment. His first instinct was to go to her, to still her hands and calm her, but he merely stood staring down at her pale, silk-draped shape in the dark cocoon of her chair and he felt curiously incapable of approaching her. He knew himself inept in expressing an understanding of malice so vicious as her brother's or of anguish so deeply felt as hers. Finally, he heard himself saying, "You told me your brother died in a boating accident. Why did you lie?''

Her hands became stilled. "I had not yet decided how much of the truth to tell you,'' she whispered, her voice still racked by emotion. "We Southern families guard our skeletons, Quinton. It is part of our tradition. Of course, his death is a matter of record. You would have learned of it sooner or later from some gossiping neighbor. When your purpose on the island is known you will undoubtedly be questioned about the salacious Helene Haymes. The locals' curiosity will again be sparked. You will be told stories, legends, fabrications and perhaps a spattering of the truth. You might as well hear the entire truth from me.'' She hesitated, sighing. "Besides, I have an ulterior motive for trusting you.''

Quinton sank slowly back into his chair. "And what is that motive?'' he asked, scarcely above a whisper.'' Beneath the window, he heard the Doberman barking; heard Betty laughing, and Maria call out to her to keep the noise down.

"I want you to know certain things so you will avoid

using them in any way that might hurt Justine," Helene answered. "Then, too, I wish to ask a favor of you. Are you a loving man, Quinton?"

Quinton instantly thought of Justine, and felt the color rise to his face. "I . . . I consider myself capable of loving," he answered simply.

"It's the most dangerous of the virtues," Helene said with authority. "Love of God, wars have been fought over that. Women, love of women has driven men to murder, has caused empires to fall. More personal, something I witnessed was the German people's love for Hitler. Their love for that madman allowed them to be turned into sadistic swine. I'm mentioning all this because I want you to form a opinion while you are here. I love my daughter, Quinton. Her animosity toward me had not dulled that love. Before I die I would like her to know who she is. I would like her to know her father was a gentle Englishman and her mother not so horrible a creature as she was made out to be. She should know she came from loving stock. But this may be selfishness on my part. Justine has always been a strange young woman. I blame this on my brother. In breeding her hatred of me he also bred discontentment and a perverse outlook on life. I'm afraid the fortune she will inherit from me will impel her to live the life of a superficial woman who flits from country to country, one party and good time to another as I did before I met Albert Cambray. She would have no need to live the life of a courtesan, not with the fortune she will have. Those days are finished anyway. But there is still the emptiness and anyone who doesn't take command of her own life will be its victim. I've given it much thought, and I believe Justine may be saved by the truth."

"I still don't understand what you are asking of me," Quinton told her.

"I want you to get to know my daughter, Quinton. I want you to pave the way for my confession. I want your opinion before the auction is over as to whether you agree that the truth would benefit her or if my determination to tell her is only an old woman's selfish need to end the charade before her death."

"You . . . no! You can't ask that of me!" Quinton cried. He was shaken to his depths by her request. He had already become entangled in their lives through his attachment to Justine; the old woman apparently intended to hopelessly ensnare him. He didn't understand why, but he already, just by listening to Helene, felt a conspirator against Justine. "You employed me to appraise *objets d'art*," he stated. "I'm not an appraiser of human beings, of their motivations or their life-styles. I'm not a psychiatrist, nor can I allow myself to play God. I couldn't presume to give an opinion on how such a confession might affect Jus . . . your daughter."

"Calm yourself," Helene told him. "Mix yourself a drink. You seem to need it."

Obediently, Quinton rose and moved to the sideboard. He poured himself a healthy serving of what, in the darkness, turned out to be bourbon. The liquor burned his throat, but he instantly felt his nerves relaxing. His breath became normal; the muscles in his abdomen grew less cramped. He experienced a sudden desire to flee the old woman's room, her house, the island, and return to the sanity of his familiar world. He had spent his life surrounded by antiquities; he had, by the very nature of his existence, shielded himself from extreme emotions. People like Helene Haymes and, yes, even Justine—they belonged to the vivid, imaginary world of movies and plays and novels. The most demonstrative events in his life before coming to Key West had been his marriage and divorce from Joanna;

otherwise his life had been tranquil. He had been left to his complacent absorption in his antiquities, the slightly more bothersome PR business and, to a lesser degree, in himself. Joanna had called him dull. It struck him now that she had been correct. There were people actually living the lives of which movies and plays and novels were made. He loved such a person—he loved Justine; the thought made his heart suddenly pound with a mingling of ecstasy and confusion. He had never felt more aware of Joanna's accused dullness. He gulped the remainder of the bourbon and set the glass aside. His legs felt weak as he returned to his chair and sat down. His eyes narrowed to mere slits as he attempted to pierce the darkness dividing him from the old woman, but she remained a pale blur of shimmering silk and gray hair.

Evenly, he said, "I'm a good appraiser. Perhaps the best in the business. If you want to employ me for that service and to arrange your auction, then I'm at your disposal, but as much as I may sympathize with your situation I can't involve myself in your personal problem with your daughter. I couldn't assume the responsiblity of the effect your confession might have on her."

Several moments past, the silence broken only by the ticking of the organ clock and the occasional barking of the Doberman.

Then, her voice completely composed, Helene said, "Thank you for your honesty, Quinton. I naturally want to retain you professionally. As for what I've told you today, think of it as an old woman's tale of no importance."

The nuance of her voice was an obvious dismissal.

As Quinton rose and bid her good day, he also thought her voice contained the nuance of victory.

* * *

Quinton followed Betty onto the front porch and sat down on the steps beside her.

The girl used one hand to tightly grasp the chain collar around the Doberman's neck; in the other she held what she had told Quinton were Lucifer's favorite treats, dried strips of smoked beef. "He'll be your friend for sure after you give him these," she said, and thrust out the first of the bribes she meant Quinton to offer the dog. Lucifer cocked his head questioningly to one side; then, realizing, as Betty did, that Quinton was not going to feed him, he made a lunge for the tasty morsels. Betty snapped him back to a sitting position beside her. "You goin' to make friends or not?" she demanded.

"What? Oh, not now," Quinton murmured. "I'm sorry. I'm not in the mood."

Betty looked at him quizzically. He had a strange, thoughtful expression. His deep-set eyes were troubled, fixed faraway, like her mother's sometimes became when she talked about times before Betty's Papa had gone up north. "You don't make friends, I still get a new red dress," she challenged. Her lower lip protruded stubbornly in the pouting defiance of a much younger child.

"Yes, yes, I promise," Quinton told her. "You run along now and play with Lucifer. I just want to sit here a few minutes and . . . rest."

"No rest for the wicked," Betty quoted her mother mockingly, "and the righteous don't need it. You wanna play a game?"

"Not now," Quinton persisted.

"Miss Justine, she plays games with me," the girl told him.

"Does she? Do you like Miss Justine, Betty?" He had no idea why he asked such a question; perhaps because he had been considering his own feelings towards Justine.

The girl took a moment to contemplate her answer. "Lucifer, he don't like her much," she concluded. "I can't make him like her either. Me, Mama says I gotta like her." Going into the voice that mocked her mother's again, she said, " 'Little nigger girls gotta like them that feeds 'em.' "

"Do you like Miss Helene?" he queried.

A definite, "Yeah. Miss Helene, she gave me a doll. You wanna see it?"

"Not now. Later, maybe."

"Can't show it to you anyway. Mama keeps it put up. Says it's a rich white girl's doll ain't meant to be played with. Why'd someone wanna doll can't be played with?" She thoughtfully peeled away a single strip of beef and tossed it into the yard, releasing Lucifer's collar so he could dash after it. "Miss Justine, she says I'm too old for dolls anyway, so stop complainin'."

The dog dashed back to the foot of the steps; salivating, barking for another offering. Quinton heard the screen door open behind them and Maria shuffle onto the porch.

"You teasin' that dog, Betty Sue? Suppose to be makin' him and Mr. Armstrong friends. She talkin' your ears off, Mr. Armstrong? Always talks too much, that girl."

Quinton raised his head and looked up at the heavy-set housekeeper. Although he didn't recall noting the humidity having an affect on her before, there was perspiration on her brow, yet he had seen her climb the stairs without so much as a labored breath. Her dark eyes were piercing, probing, searching both his and her daughter's faces.

"Don't neither talk too much," Betty mumbled defiantly.

"No, she doesn't," Quinton defended. "We're friends, Betty and me. We were having a friendly chat."

The girl beamed. "Mr. Quinton's goin' to buy me a red dress," she told her mother. Bored with Lucifer, she tossed him the remaining strips of beef.

"Hmm, so you told me," Maria said. "Your lunch's in the kitchen. Run along now and eat. You want some lunch, Mr. Armstrong?"

Quinton rose from the steps and absently dusted off the seat of his trousers. "No, thank you, Maria. I thought I'd take a break and see some of the town." He had half an hour before meeting Justine at the beach.

"You want Betty Sue to go with you?" The question was asked too quickly, as if she feared for him to wander about by himself.

Disappointed when he said no, Betty, Lucifer at her heels, ran around the side of the house and to the lunch waiting in the kitchen.

Reading the housekeeper's expression, Quinton said, "She told me people would talk and ask questions." He indicated the upper floors and the woman living there with a toss of his head. "You needn't worry, Maria. I'm still a stranger on the island. Besides, I'm a very discreet man. I don't talk about my employers or listen to gossip."

Maria shrugged away inference to her concern. Absently, she lifted the hem of her apron and wiped her hands. "When do I tell her you'll be back if she asks?"

"In a couple of hours. It's a beautiful day. As long as I'm in paradise, I might as well see some of it."

Maria nodded, and turned to go back inside.

Quinton stopped her. "Maria?"

"Yes, sir?"

"You've been with Helene Haymes since she returned to Key West?"

"That I have, and her father before," the black woman answered proudly. "I had my baby right back there in that room off the kitchen. When my time comes to go, the Lord willin', I'll die there, too."

"You must know everything that's gone on in this house," Quinton said. "Between Helene and her brother—and Justine. You're an intimate part of their lives. Does the old woman ever demand your opinion on . . ."

"Listen here, Mr. Armstrong," the housekeeper interrupted. "Me, I know everything and nothin'. What I do know, I don't say. I'm a housekeeper, always have been and always will be a housekeeper. A housekeeper knows things, but she ain't what you call intimate. I've loved Miss Helene since she came home with her . . . since she came home. Sure, she tells me things, but it's like she's talkin' to herself."

"But surely after all these years you're on intimate . . ."

"You gotta understand, Mr. Armstrong," Maria said matter-of-factly, her voice lowered as if she feared it would travel over the wall, "this island may be paradise to you, but to a nigger housekeeper like me it's just another small town in the South of these United States. I've got my place, and I know what it is. I ain't no Northern nigger. So don't go askin' me things about Miss Helene and what's gone on here, 'cause I can't give you no answers." Her dark eyes narrowed; she wiped the perspiration from her brow with an impatient gesture. "I'd no more tell you things about Miss Helene than I'd tell her about you spendin' the night in Miss Justine's cottage," she said.

Quinton flinched, swallowed. "I understand," he said. "Thank you, Maria."

He went hurriedly through the gate as the blunt housekeeper went back inside.

Chapter Nine

Quinton sat in the back of the boat; the sun was hot, but the spray of water refreshed him. He divided his time between watching Justine, who was operating the boat, and Aaron, who zigzagged behind on water skis. Justine wore a scant bikini, and he noted again with appreciation the beauty of her body. Her dark hair was pulled back from her face and tied at the nape of her slender neck with a fuchsia scarf that fluttered in the wind. When she glanced periodically over her shoulder to check Aaron's progress she flashed a smile at Quinton. Strange, he reflected, that a smile was enough; when Aaron had gone into the water all sense of jealousy had left him. Not so when he had first boarded the small boat—he had envied the younger man's body, his handsomeness, and his closeness to Justine.

Aaron was motioning for Justine to turn the boat toward the island; she had apparently gone too close to the ship lane and the swells were making skiing more chore than pleasure. Laughing, she turned the boat and increased its speed. "Watch him go down now!" she shouted at Quinton.

Just as Quinton turned, Aaron's body rose over a swell. The skis fell from his feet and he released the towing bar. Christ, Quinton thought irritably, he isn't even awkward when he falls. Instead, Aaron was propelled over the water with the grace of a flying fish, and then splashed out of sight with scarcely a ripple of the surface.

"He'll be furious," Justine laughed. She cut the speed of the boat and turned it in a wide arch to retrieve her friend. She killed the motor several yards before reaching Aaron, and coming to the rear of the boat, sat down beside Quinton. "Aaron's very competitive," she told him. "When it's my turn to ski he'll give me one hell of a turn." Her green eyes sparkled. "Of course, I'll go down. If I out-skied him, he'd go into one of his black moods and spoil the rest of our day."

"I'm afraid my part of your day is only another half an hour," Quinton said. "I've work to do and . . . "

"And you suffer the Protestant guilt when you goof off," she finished. "Tell me, Quinton, have you always been so conscientious?"

"Always," he said lightly. He found he could not stare at her breasts, exposed except for the narrow ribbon of her halter, without being threatened by arousal of his desires. He averted his gaze and found himself staring at her thighs; there was a dark mole on her right thigh that he had not noticed before. What else about her was waiting his discovery?

Justine let her head fall back, exposing her tanned face fully to the sun. "You'll be infected by the Key West ambience soon," she said. "This isn't New York. The pace is much slower, much. Nothing is completed on schedule, nor do the locals expect it to be. It's frustrating for the tourists and part-time residents, but they adjust."

"I doubt I would," Quinton said seriously. "Not with the horrendous task ahead of me."

"The auction?"

"Hmm."

Without opening her eyes, Justine said, "She's waited all these years. Another few days, even a few weeks can't matter. If you want, I'll talk to her, convince her not to treat you like a family retainer." As always, animosity had crept into her voice when she spoke of Helene.

Quinton had started to comment, but Aaron's arrival beside the boat stopped. Again, that nagging jealousy tugged at his chest. Why couldn't she have arranged for them to be alone? He had so little time before he had to return to New York; her queer friend could occupy her time after he had gone.

"You tried to throw me into a whip on purpose," Aaron accused from the water.

Laughing, Justine sprang to her feet and moved to the side of the boat to offer him a hand. "Don't blame me because you loused it up," she laughed. "Now I'm going to beat you, Aaron Clarke."

"Don't count on it," he challenged.

Quinton watched their exchange with interest. They were obviously very much at ease with one another; he wondered how long they had been friends. What common denominator allowed a homosexual male and a heterosexual female to establish a friendship? Was he jealous of their relationship, or was he refusing to admit that the presence of a homosexual was making him question his own masculinity? He studied Aaron intently as the man climbed into the boat. If he compared himself to Aaron, he, Quinton, would be the loser. Justine's friend was perhaps the most handsome man Quinton had ever seen; tall, with broad shoulders, narrow waist and slim buttocks. Obviously a body freak, Quinton reflected; no man had a body that beautiful without daily workouts. Dark brown hair streaked by the sun; large almond-colored eyes, chiseled features, possibly of Italian or Greek origin. As he gained his footing in the boat, he ran his hands down over his body to shed the excess water and the sun glistened off rippling muscles. He laughed, his teeth flashing white against the deeply tanned flesh. He did not glance once at Quinton, but Quinton knew he was aware of his scrutiny, perhaps even of the intense, masculine comparison.

Justine leaned toward Aaron and said something Quinton could not hear. The young man nodded, and moving to the front of the boat, started the engine. Justine returned to the seat beside Quinton. She took Quinton's arm and moved it behind her neck, leaning into him. "We've decided to give you a tour around the island," she told him. "We can continue our skiing contest after you've returned to the dreary world of antiquities." She brought his hand down over her breasts and pressed it there. She must have sensed his discomfort, because she lifted her head and stared up at him. "Does Aaron's being here inhibit you, darling?"

Of course, it did. He was not a man who easily expressed affection in front of people, but if he told her that she would accuse him of being Victorian, so he pretended her question had been drowned by the roar of the engine. To disavow his inhibitions, he spread the fingers of his hand and dug them gently into the flesh of her breasts. She responded by kissing the underside of his chin. Even the salt water had not destroyed the familiar fragrance of her perfume. With her snuggled against him, it assaulted his nostrils, and he searched again for its name, trying to recall Joanna having mentioned it, but the name evaded him. He would buy her a bottle on his trip to New York.

"Why were you staring at Aaron so attentively?"

she asked. She pulled back so she could look into his face.

"I . . . I wasn't," he lied, and he felt the lie registering on his face.

"You were," she said. "I saw you. Don't tell me that beneath that conservative exterior lurks a slightly bent, capricious male? You're not a closet homosexual, are you, darling?" She was teasing him, but he discerned a hidden note of apprehension.

"Definitely not," he answered with an equal blending of teasing and seriousness. "Actually, I find him curious. You say he's a homosexual, and yet there's isn't the slightest hint of feminity about him." He glanced toward Aaron's back as if he might overhear the conversation. "When he climbed into the boat he looked like some Greek god rising from the sea. It occurred to me that women, when they find out his preference, must consider it a great waste. No doubt they're constantly throwing themselves at him in a resort like Key West." He hesitated; then decided he would match her boldness: "Is that how you met him? Making a play for him?"

Justine threw her head back in a loud laugh that caused Aaron to glance around. "No, darling. When I met him he was sitting on the beach holding hands with his shrimper-lover. Watch where you're going, Aaron," she called. "We're only saying nice things about you." To Quinton, she said, "Now, that's out of the way. Your male ego doesn't have to do battle with Aaron's, and I don't have to concern myself with your possibly divided sexual preferences. I'll only have to guard against other females trying to steal you away from me."

"No one could steal me away even if they wanted to," he said, and despite Aaron's presence in the boat, he tilted her head back and kissed her full on the mouth. The open display of affection, entirely unique to him, gave him a curious sense of power and freedom. He would have repeated the act had Justine not suddenly turned away from him.

Pointing towards the shoreline, she said, "This is the gulf side of the island, darling. The channel we're in was deepened by the navy. The smaller island on our right is the result of the dredging."

Quinton followed her pointing finger and noted the man-made island was covered by trees; Australian pines, he judged. At one end of the island two house-boats bobbed in the wake of a passing fishing boat; one with its aft sunken beneath the water, the other appearing ready to join it.

"Abandoned," Justine said, reading his thoughts, and turned her attention back to the main island. "There's *The Pier House* where you're staying, and there, that's where the locals and tourists mingle each night to worship the sunset."

"To do what?" Quinton noted an expanse of brick wall eroded by many high tides and behind it what appeared to be a parking lot.

"We simply call it 'Sunset,' " Justine explained. "I don't know when or why it started, but people gather there every late afternoon to watch the sunset. It becomes a sort of spontaneous sideshow. There are musicians and singers and dancers, all performing. Then there's the local color. The Iguana Man with his pet iguanas crawling all over his body, Mad Mary who wears a different hat each week and embellishes stories about Key Westers and its history for the price of a drink, Old Jonsy who sells drawings he says he does but that are actually drawn by his invalid wife. There's drinking and singing. People meet and leave together."

Her voice took on a somber tone. "Sometimes it's strange," she whispered, her voice almost lost to the engine and the wind battering at their head.

"Strange how?" he encouraged.

"I don't know, just strange. Sometimes the singing is happy, sometimes it reminds me of a canticle to a sun that's going down never to rise again. Oh, that's morose." She laughed, and turned her attention to pointing out what she told him was a mooring platform for navy submarines. "As you can see, the navy still controls our best beach and the choicest waterfront property, but there are negotiations for its return. Quinton, when you're alone with my aunt does she tell you personal things about the family? Does she tell you things about me?"

"There you go again," he said. "From one subject to another without a pause between."

"Well, does she?"

"Yes. Today she did," he answered truthfully.

For a few moments she stared at him with something like fright in her green eyes; this changed to hate and bitterness. "Quinton, don't let her come between us," she said fervently. The wind had torn her dark hair from the fuchsia scarf and it lashed about her beautiful, intense face. "She's always spoiled everything that's been important to me, always! You're important to me, Quinton. If she's made aware of that importance, she'll stop at nothing to shatter me, us."

"I won't let anyone come between us, Justine," Quinton assured her. "But isn't it just possible you've misjudged her? That all these years she's had only your welfare at heart?"

"First of all, there's a vacuum where he heart should be," Justine said caustically. "Secondly, you don't misjudge my aunt, and survive to tell about it. She's like a cobra mesmerizing its victim. If the prey doesn't flee immediately . . . '' She stopped speaking and stared at him. Her eyebrows arched questioningly above eyes that did not blink even against the hair whipping about her lovely face. ''You like her, don't you?'' she asked increduously.

''The truth is I do,'' Quinton answered evenly. ''I . . . I have compassion for her.''

''Don't waste compassion on someone who doesn't understand its meaning,'' Justine snapped. ''She had no compassion for my mother or father. The night he hanged himself she opened a rare bottle of champagne and celebrated. She's a monster! The only human feelings I've ever seen her express are over her damnable treasures. I don't know why she's decided suddenly to auction them, but if it's painful for her when they're carted away I'll be jubilant.'' She glanced towards Aaron, aware that he had slowed the boat, and motioned him to return to shore. ''The tour to be continued another time,'' she said with waning anger.

''Justine, I . . . '' Quinton began to placate.

But she stopped him by saying, ''Will we be able to have dinner together tonight, or do you have another command performance with her?'' Before he could answer, she leaned back into him. ''I'm sorry,'' she said. ''I didn't mean to spoil our time together by discussing her. If you're forced to dine with her, I'll understand.''

''I'll be dining with the woman I love,'' Quinton said with a smile.

Justine's returning smile was belied by the seriousness remaining in her green eyes. ''And who might that be?''

''As if you didn't know.'' He pulled her head down into the curve of his neck, and he held her closely. The

expression in his own eyes was serious as he realized
the hatred Justine felt for Helene was so intense it must
be purged or she would never truly know peace of mind
or spirit. Earlier, he had fought Helene's suggestion
that he involve himself in their emotional conflicts, but
now he knew he must reverse his decision. If he could
somehow bring mother and daughter together, he must
try—for Justine's sake, but he doubted that Justine's
hatred, even when she learned the truth of her birth,
would be completely dispelled in Helene's short remaining lifetime.

Dark storm clouds were gathering over the gulf waters. Aaron, noting the darker cylinder of a rain funnel,
turned to point it out to Justine and Quinton. When he
saw the couple huddled in the back of the boat, their
arms about one another in a loving embrace, his
almond-colored eyes narrowed and his handsome face
was etched with an ugliness that truly would have
baffled Quinton, if he had seen it.

A fishing boat crowded with tourists on their way to
fish over the reef sounded its horn in greeting. Happy,
carefree tourists waved and shouted at the ardent couple
in the back of the speedboat. In response, Aaron extended his middle finger in a universal gesture.

When Quinton returned to the house on Simonton
Street it was difficult to channel his interest in antiquities. He was told by Maria that Helene was taking
her afternoon nap; she promised to call him as soon as
the old woman had awakened. He went into the
antique-cluttered ballroom and spent an hour rearrang-
ing furniture to create space for a working area for
himself and the assistant it would be necessary to
employ. Even after his efforts, the space he created was
inadequate. He would, he reflected, require an entire

room to house himself and the necessary equipment of his trade. Telephones would have to be installed, and desks for secretaries to answer them. As the designated time for the auction drew nearer, the old house would hum with activity. He wondered if Helene had taken this into consideration. Then, too, since she had refused to see reporters personally, some burly man would have to be employed to stand guard at the gate.

He located a pad and pencil and made a list of people and items he would require. He then made a detailed schedule of the things he must attend to on his return to New York. Once the mechanism of the auction was in operation he would like to commute from New York to Key West as seldom as possible. Time spent in New York would be time away from Justine and separation at this stage in their relationship would be painful.

Once the image of Justine filled his mind, he could not shake it. He lay his pencil aside and leaned lazily back in his chair, his gaze fixed with half-sight outside the windows as daylight began to wane. The air in the ballroom was sultry; he was tired from the little sleep he had had since arriving and he was in the disposition for daydreaming, a luxury foreign to his nature. He closed his eyes and tried to imagine a future with Justine, but instead of the happiness he intended to envision his thoughts swirled with confusion. The future, even an imagined future, evaded him. He experienced a sense of quiet desperation; love and happiness of the sort Justine evoked seemed now, in his thoughtful state, more fantasy than reality. When he was with her he felt secure; away from her the security crumbled. When he was with her it was possible to look into her green eyes and believe the love she felt for him, but alone some inner voice disputed the validity of that love.

With considerable effort, he forced Justine from his

thoughts. Beyond the dirty windows, he saw that traffic was growing heavier on the street: cars and bicycles and two Conch tour trains following one closely behind the other. The tour guide's voice came over the loud-speaker:

". . . the Civil War, Key West, although its sympathies were Southern, was a stronghold of the North. On your left you'll see one of the island's oldest mansions. Built by Samuel Haymes in the first quarter of the 1800s, the house is still maintained by his ancestors. Some of the locals claim it's haunted by . . ."

The first train passed on and the second train's tour guide's voice prevailed: " . . . example of the period's architecture. Notice the widow's walk and the gingerbread carvings along the eaves. Samuel Haymes made his original fortune in salvage. Subsequent ancestors added to that fortune through the sponge and tobacco industries. The house is said to now be only in partial use. The present ancestor of Samuel Haymes is a recluse and refuses to have the house included on our annual tours of historic houses. On your right is a beautiful example of the poinciana trees that make the island burst with color during their blooming season, and behind the poinciana you'll see a strain of the monkey tree Ernest Hemingway had brought from Africa and planted in the yard of his . . ."

Quinton's attention was claimed by Justine as she pedaled her bicycle between the two tour trains and stopped at the gate. Even from his distance, with his view hampered by the dirty panes of the windows, her beauty was strikingly evident. It occurred to him that when Helene's notoriety was again made public Justine would be pointed out for more than her beauty; she would be labeled as the ancestor of Samuel Haymes and the scandalous twentieth-century harlot. As he watched her move up the walkway and disappear below, it occurred to him also that the price of a successful auction might be too great to pay for the woman he loved, especially if she chose to remain in Key West.

He was still contemplating this when the ballroom door opened and Maria announced that Helene would now see him.

Helene was not in her usual bergère chair, but instead was propped up against the carved rococo headboard. One of the shutters on the opposite wall had been opened to let in the twilight, the soft, diffused light illuminating the room more adequately than during his other visits. The old woman wore a bed jacket of grey satin, a lace collar turned up about her throat and neck. Her slender fingers were encased in fingerless gloves, more, he imagined, to conceal the ravaged veins than for warmth. She was staring through the distant shutters as he entered and did not pull her gaze away as she said, "A beautiful sunset tonight, Quinton."

He glanced through the shutters and saw a darkening sky streaked by vivid colors. "Yes, beautiful," he agreed. He crossed to the bed where a chair had obviously been arranged for his visit, and sat down.

"You're staring at me," Helene said. "Why? You expected me to be more beautiful, is that why? I shouldn't have allowed Maria to open the shutters."

"No, that's not why," Quinton hastened to assure her. "Quite the contrary. Actually, I was taken by your strong resemblance to your daughter." This was the truth; in this better light he could distinguish the high cheekbones, the perfectly defined nose and defiantly tilted chin, and nestled within the puffy flesh about her eyes the green irises so like Justine's. "The resemblance is uncanny," he said. "I'm surprised that Justine hasn't suspected the truth of her birth merely by comparison."

"It's the Haymes look," the old woman said. "If

you go through our family albums, you'll see it often. She's had no reason to suspect.'' She turned back to him, the twilight already fading and shielding her age. ''Maria said you wished to speak with me.''

''I've made a list of items I'll require,'' he told her. ''Including the necessary staff.''

''This staff is absolutely necessary?'' she challenged.

''It is,'' Quinton assured her.

''Understand, Quinton, I'm not objecting to the salaries, only the presence of outsiders in my house. I'm unaccustomed to people tramping about, making noise and gawking at my treatures.'' She sighed wearily and drew the lace collar of her bed jacket closer about her neck. ''Ah, well, it shouldn't matter, confining myself as I have to this room. You will, of course, warn your staff not to intrude on my privacy. No one is to consult me personally on anything related to the auction. They're to come to you or to Justine. Give the list of your requirements to Justine. She will see to them. My only other request is that no locals are to be hired, but I've already informed Justine of that. I can't abide the idea of other Conchs rummaging through my house and carrying away tales.''

''That's going to make hiring a staff difficult,'' Quinton pointed out.

''Justine will know who to hire and who not to,'' Helene said. ''She knows I don't want Conchs or Fresh Water Conchs.''

''Fresh Water Conchs?''

''Key Westers of two or three generations,'' Helene explained. ''I told you we had our peculiar system of snobbery, Quinton,'' she said with amusement. ''Justine will also give you whatever advance you require.''

''You've already discussed this with her?''

"I have," the old woman answered. "She does consent to visit me on rare occasions. Generally when I send for her."

"Didn't she demand to know why you had suddenly decided to auction off you antiquities?"

"Not demand," Helene said. "Naturally, she asked. Naturally, I evaded the question. She may hate me, but she respects the purse strings I hold. My daughter has no money of her own, Quinton. My brother squandered what little he had before he hanged himself, so he left her nothing except debts. I paid those and arranged an allowance for her."

"But not too much of an allowance?" Quinton dared.

Helene stared at him for several moments before saying, "Control was necessary. I didn't want her running off to New York to pursue a career in the theater again. She doesn't want for anything except cash. She can charge her clothes to my accounts. She eats from my kitchen. She doesn't pay rent. I've established trust funds for her. Her only out-of-pocket expense is for her leisure. For that she has the revenue from her paintings. Do you consider me an ogre, Quinton?"

"No," he answered thoughtfully. "I was just considering that your fear of her running off to New York couldn't have any foundation. If that was her desire, she need only take an object, or objects from your collection and sell them for enough to live well even in expensive Manhattan."

"Members of my family may have been many things, but we never bread thieves," Helene said with a measure of pride. "Now, Quinton, is there anything else? If not, I'm very weary. I had a bad last evening and an even worse day. I've taken a medicine that puts me mercifully into a painless state bordering on coma. If there's more, tell me before the medicine takes effect.''

Quinton rose to take his leave.

"When do you plan on returning to New York to make your arrangements for a photographer and printer?'' the old woman asked.

From the door, he answered, "Within a couple of days.''

"Then you'll also want information for your magazine article,'' she reminded him. "I'll have Maria leave my scrapbooks and diaries for you in the morning. I won't ask you for final approval of your article, Quinton. I trust you. Should you have questions, I'll meet with you tomorrow at this time. Good night, Quinton.''

"Good night,'' he answered quietly, and let himself out of her room just as Maria arrived with a covered silver tray.

As he descended the staircase, he wondered if, through her illness, Helene Haymes had become addicted to drugs. This visit had been the first time he had had an unhampered look at her, and in her face he had detected something that continued to trouble him.

They had driven twenty minutes to half-an-hour up the keys. The restaurant Justine instructed him to turn into was on Sugar Loaf Key and was rather remote, with a lodge or motel in the rear. The restaurant was crowded with tourists, but the maitre d' seated them immediately when he recognized Justine. Locals, Quinton reflected, apparently received preference over tourists.

Now, after Justine had deserted him for the women's room, he avoided the angry glances of the tourists waiting to be seated, and stared off through the plate glass window. Beyond was a narrow balcony, below that a lighted lagoon where a dolphin swam about pushing an innertube with its snout. At first he couldn't imagine why the dolphin reminded him of Joanna; then he remembered the committee she had headed to save the dolphin from the tuna fishermen who were killing them in their nets. As with all her causes, she had been fervent in her "Save the Dolphins" efforts.

He remembered the night she had come home from a day at the supermarket, a day spent trying to convince shoppers to boycott tuna and to sign a petititon against the tuna industry. There had been a nasty bruise on her cheek, and when he had questioned her she had admitted being attacked by a man who had turned out to be a retired tuna fisherman objecting to the pressure being put on the industry that paid his retirement benefits. "Good God!" he had cried. "You'll get yourself killed on one of these crusades! I want you to stop, Joanna. If you must devote yourself to a cause, find a nice peaceful one." Joanna had glared at him, absently stroking her injured cheek. Finally, she had retorted, "By peaceful, you mean dull, don't you, Quinton? Dullness, that's your nature. Well, I won't let you make such a person of me!" Later that night as he was drifting into a troubled sleep, she had said, "You're staid, Quinton!" Then she had spelled out the word, "S-T-A-I-D," as if it had been an accusation of his responsibility for her bruised cheek and pride.

"A penny." Justine broke into his thoughts.

"What? Oh, my thoughts aren't worth it," Quinton said. He rose and pulled out her chair, aware of the continued hostile glances of the tourists who had been waiting ahead of them for tables. As he reseated himself, he asked, "Why did you insist on this restaurant, Justine?"

"You don't like it, darling? The food's excellent. As

for the crowds, you'll find them everywhere this time
of year."

"Could it be that it's a place your Key West friends
don't frequent?" he asked. "I'm getting the impression
you're trying to tell me ours is a back street affair."

"I do feel it would be wise not to be seen together too
often, not yet," she said. She smiled at him teasingly.
"I've my reputation to consider."

"But you'd pick me up on a crowded Key West
beach and neck with me in an open boat," Quinton
said. "You're a woman of contradictions."

She dismissed all pretense of a smile. "I told you
why, darling. If someone should tell her about a little
flirtation in the afternoon, she won't consider it serious, but too many dinners together and she'd get suspicious. I love you, Quinton. If she even imagined that,
she'd go to any lengths to destroy . . . " She glanced
up at the approaching waitress. "I'd like a key lime
daiquiri. Would you like to try one, darling?"

Quinton disliked exotic drinks, but rather than inter-
rupt their conversation he nodded so as to dismiss the
waitress. "Justine, why, if you hate her so much, have
you stayed with her?"

"I ran away once, and failed, remember?"

"But you could have tried again," he suggested.
"There are probably more struggling artists in New
York than Key West. I guess what I want to know is—is
it the money?"

"Money? Her money?"

"You will inherit it one day."

"It would be like her to leave it to charity," Justine
told him. "No, darling, it's not the money."

"The place, then? Key West? You love it, and I
don't blame you. It's unlike any place I've seen in the
United States, a tropical paradise."

Justine's green eyes fixed on him probingly. To-night, she was wearing an emerald-colored silk blouse that emphasized her eyes; her hair was worn loose and cascaded about her tanned shoulders. The only jewelry she wore was the Faberge pendant; it was on the pendant that Quinton fixed his gaze. "You ask if I stay because I love Key West, and then you make an effort to answer affirmatively for me," Justine said. "Is that because you're afraid the answer could be something else, something dark and foreboding? Could it be you think my hatred of Aunt Helene is obsessive, so fanatical I can't walk away from her, or it?"

That was exactly what Quinton had been considering, but now that she had voiced it it rang false. Rather than lie, he said nothing.

"If I didn't think I know you better, I'd say you read too many novels by Southern writers," she said, again assuming a teasing attitude. "We're not all Tennessee Williams heroines with tortured souls and pasts of harlots, or Faulkner women with . . . ah, here's our drinks."

"Helene also mentioned Mr. Williams's heroines," Quinton said as he lifted the glass of pale green crushed ice and liquor.

"Did she?" Justine said without interest. "Well, maybe her eyes are better than she claims and she spends all that time alone comparing herself to fictional heroines. God knows she'd be a perfect character for Williams." She sipped her drink and set it aside. "Now, let's forbid my aunt entry into further conversation. I proclaim this my evening, and I want to know about you, Quinton Armstrong, my lover."

"You know all that's important," he said uneasily. "I'm an about-to-be-divorced man in his mid-thirties. An appraiser. And I'm in love with you."

"What sort of child were you?" she persisted.

"Ordinary."

"I'll bet you were an honor student."

"I was."

"Artistic?"

Quinton felt color come to his face. "I thought I was when I was in my late teens," he admitted. "Like hundreds of other young men, I planned to be the next Hemingway."

"Are those aspirations dead?"

He said nothing.

"You discovered the world of antiquities and turned away from the world of words," Justine supplied. "I'll bet your wife didn't encourage you to write. When did you put aside your aspiration to become a writer? No doubt after you were married."

"I had to make a living," Quinton said; oddly, he felt defensive about Joanna. She had not encouraged or discouraged the completion of his novel; neither had she expressed any interest in reading what he had written. Once when they were first married she had said at a party that he would one day be a famous novelist. She had said it with conviction, but then everything Joanna said was with conviction; few people understood the kinks of uncertainty in her nature. He sipped the key lime daiquiri, and found the taste pleasant. "I always thought of daiquiris as a woman's drink," he said in an effort to turn the conversation.

But Justine was persistent: "Why are you so fond of antiquities, Quinton?"

"I guess because they're proven," he answered. "They've withstood the test of time. That, and the fact that the workmanship and care of past eras can't be duplicated in today's society. Today it's fast, cheap manufacturing, prefabrication and inferior materials.

When a piece of furniture goes home with a family it's destined to be discarded and replaced within their lifetime. No need to worry about what chair or table is willed to which child. Just moving it is often to snap the legs. Then, too, antiques are investments. You can live with and enjoy an antique and when you're ready to sell it or leave it to . . . '' Quinton, noting Justine's smile, stopped talking abruptly. ''I tend to get carried away on the subject,'' he apologized. He drained his glass and set it aside.

''Like Helene,'' Justine said, and then added, ''I'm sorry. Would you like another drink, or should we order?''

''It's up to you.''

''You may drink as much as you like,'' she said. She nodded her head to indicate the lodgings beyond the lagoon. ''I've made arrangements. We won't be driving back immediately.'' She smiled at him seductively. ''We're registered as Mr. and Mrs. Jones from Dubuque.''

Quinton laughed.

''What's so amusing?'' Justine demanded. ''The choice of name or the city?''

''Neither. It's just that this will be another first for me. I've never checked into a motel with a woman other than my wife.''

''This will be different,'' Justine said with promise.

They had several drinks; Quinton lost count. He was pleasantly high when their dinners arrived: broiled yellowtail, the delicate local fish Helene had recommended for one of their future meals together. By the time they had finished, the crowd in the restaurant had begun to thin out. The dolphin in the lagoon had grown weary of pushing around the tube and the surface of the water was still, reflecting a silvery, full moon. Beyond

the doors to the cocktail lounge, a combo had begun to
play a tune Quinton tried but failed to recognize; halfway into the number, a female vocalist joined in, her
voice gravelly with age and too much bourbon. Justine
ordered two cognacs and coffees.

"I shouldn't," Quinton said. "If you ply me with
drink, you can't expect me to be an adequate lover."

"I'll take my chances, darling. I'm not expecting
you to be perfect every . . . " She stopped speaking,
and when Quinton glanced at her he saw her face had
paled.

He turned to follow her gaze and saw a woman
approaching their table. She was about fifty, with hair
bleached the color of cornsilk and swept up in a French
twist. She had the appearance of someone who had
recently lost considerable weight, loose flesh not yet
contoured to her jaw, and hanging in swaying folds
beneath her upper arms. She wore heavy makeup with
eyebrows penciled in by an unsteady hand. Her dress
was of a brightly printed fabric that, beneath the chandelier, gave her flesh an unhealthy yellowish tint. As
she stopped at their table, her small dark eyes considered Quinton with interest. She scarcely pulled her
gaze away from him as she addressed Justine: "Justine,
darling. Imagine running into you here. How are you,
darling? Hello, young man. I'm Ernesta Calder."

"Ernesta, may I introduce Quinton Armstrong.
Quinton, Ernesta Calder."

Quinton rose politely. "Mrs. Calder, a pleasure."

"Miss Calder," the woman corrected. "Justine,
wherever did you find such a handsome man? Are you a
tourist, Quinton?" Her badly etched eyebrows lifted
with the question and were thrown even more out of
line, giving her dark eyes the illusion of being badly
crossed.

"Actually, I'm here to appraise . . . " Quinton began.

"Quinton is visiting from New York," Justine interrupted.

"Oh, a long visit, I hope," the woman said, casting her dark eyes up and down him in a blatant sexual appraisal. "Do tell me you won't be leaving before the weekend. I'm having a little get-together. I'd adore for Justine to bring you."

"I'm afraid Quinton is leaving in a couple of days," Justine answered for him.

"Oh, such a shame," the woman cooed and, considering him removed from seduction because of his early departure, turned her attention to Justine. "Where have you been keeping yourself, my dear? The Art and Historical Society meetings are so dull without you. I haven't seen you since your aunt . . ."

"I've been busy with my painting," Justine again interrupted. "I'd forgotten you lived on Sugar Loaf, Ernesta." The comment carried the undertone of an insult.

"We haven't finished the house here yet, my dear." The insult had not been lost on the woman; her backbone straightened noticeably and fire sparked behind her dark eyes. "Frankly, I'll be delighted to move outside Key West. In sympathy with you Conchs, the island is becoming a nest for homosexuals and drug addicts. Have you noticed, Quinton?"

"I've only been struck by the island's beauty," Quinton responded.

"Oh. Generally outsiders are more observant than those who live with a problem from day to day. How is your aunt, my dear? Dr. Webb says she's fine, but to him everyone who isn't dead is fine."

"Helene is the same," Justine answered.

"Well, give her my regards. Good night, my dear. A pleasure meeting you, Mr. Armstrong. Perhaps on your next visit . . . " she let the sentence trail off suggestively. She walked away, tossing a final glare of hostility over her shoulder at Justine as she exited the dining room.

"Ernesta Calder is an ex-showgirl turned respectable," Justine said as Quinton reseated himself. "That is, she married into respectability. Her husband is a retired attorney from an old Conch family. He met her on a trip to Atlanta and shocked the locals by bringing her back and introducing her as his wife. His first wife had only been dead six months. Ernesta is as lecherous as they come. She's also one of the island's biggest gossips. My plan to drag you out of Key West boomeranged. Tomorrow it'll be all over the island that we were seen dining on Sugar Loaf."

Quinton was only half-listening. "She said the Art and Historical Society meetings were dull without you," he said.

Justine read the implication immediately. "Ernesta frequently misses meetings," she told him. "She was absent the other night. Ah, here're our cognacs. Drink up, darling. Mrs. Jones wants to retire."

Chapter Ten

Quinton carried the hefty stack of scrapbooks to his desk before the window, and sat down. The books, over a dozen in number, were yellowed by age. Many of the bindings were broken; pages were carelessly stuffed inside out of sequence, as if the owner and subject had long since lost interest in the life she was documenting.

He opened the first book at random and read:

Last night at the Royal Opera House the Prince made an entrance with a mysterious woman clinging to his arm. Most men would be flattered by escorting such a woman, but, dear readers, this woman succeeded in eclipsing even the heir to the throne. Royalty gave homage to beauty. As she paused at the top of the Grand Staircase to sweep back the folds of her cape, every eye turned in her direction. There was a decided hush, and then a swelling wave of whispers as Viennese Soeiety questioned her identity. Looking neither to the left nor right, she descended the Grand Staircase with such regality no wonder rumor started that she was the Grand Duchess Marta returned from exile. No Grand Duchess this. Sources close to the Prince tell me the woman is an American named Helene Haymes. The Prince, I'm told, is thoroughly bewitched by this dazzling American beauty.

Another page carried a photograph of a young Helene. Beneath it, the caption read: *Great Britain had Wallis Simpson. This American could become her Austrian counterpart.*

Smiling, Quinton turned the page.

American Fortune Hunter Attacked by Irate Citizens

Helene Haymes, the American whose name has been frequently linked to a royal personage, was attacked yesterday outside her hotel. Women, shouting accusations, threw stones and demanded the American be expelled from the country. Miss Haymes, who was treated privately by hotel doctors, declined comment. A spokesman for the hotel later reported that Miss Haymes had departed after the unfortunate incident. No forwarding address was left with the hotel.

Quinton flipped through the pages reading incident after incident of Helene's earlier encounters in Europe. A prince, a duke, a famous French actor; the press always attacking her for her liaisons, many articles comparing her to the still-remembered Isadora Duncan, others to Marlene Dietrich and Greta Garbo, whose films were the present rage.

"So here you are," Justine said. After their return drive from Sugar Loaf Key, she had changed into white slacks and a loose-fitting blouse. She wore no makeup and had applied a slightly greasy coat of oil to her face, apparently in preparation for an excursion to the beach. She threaded her way around the antiques to his desk, bent and kissed his cheek. "What have you here?" She glanced over his shoulder and the smile left her lips when she saw the scrapbooks. "Oh, her bibles," she murmured scarcely above a whisper; still, that whisper stung with sarcasm. Her face turned tense. She withdrew her hand from his shoulder, but not before he felt its trembling.

"Have you seen these?" Quinton asked.

"I have, many times."

"I'm surprised she allowed it," he remarked.

Turning away from him, Justine stared through the grimy windowpanes at the street below. "She didn't. My father showed them to me," she said. "He wanted me to understand how she had contaminated our family name."

"I don't think that's quite fair," Quinton said, "or honorable. I'm sorry, Justine, but I have to say what I feel. I can't help but think of Helene as a victim of a self-righteous era. The contamination should be blamed on a press that pandered to a phony moralism of the time."

Justine's green eyes turned on him. "You're defending what she was?" she demanded increduously.

"I'm neither defending nor attacking what Helene was," Quinton told her. "It was the life she chose to lead. No one has the right to judge her. Certainly not me. Or her brother. Or you."

"How pompous you sound, Quinton." It was the first time her bitterness had been aimed directly at him, and she appeared to regret it as soon as the words left her lips. Instead of apologizing, however, she turned again to stare out the window.

Quinton watched her in silence. He could detect the outline of her scant bikini through her white slacks, the contours of her slim, boyish buttocks, and the passion he felt for her rose up inside him. He did not want to discuss Helene with her; when he was with her he found concentration on anything but her presence difficult. He started to reach for her, but his hand fell back to his lap. Quietly, he said, "You realize, of course, that your own outlook on life is in conflict with what you think of Helene's? Isn't it true that you consider yourself a modern woman?"

She mumbled affirmatively without turning.

"If Helene lived today as she did in her own era it wouldn't even create a ripple of moral indignation," he said. "Why can't you think of her as a woman who existed before her time?"

"Because I can only feel my father's shame," Justine answered. "She drove him to that belltower and put the rope about his neck! He was all I had, and she took him away from me! You don't know her, Quinton. It's not just her past. It's what she is, what she's always been. A clawing, manipulative female. A shrike. She thinks of no one or nothing except herself and her precious antiquities."

"Have you honestly tried to look at her objectively?"

"I've known her all my life," Justine said sharply, turning to face him. "You've known her only a few days. And don't tell me a stranger can be more objective. Of course I've tried to consider her differently. Do you think I want to hate my only living relative? That I like to think of myself bound to her by something other than love?" Her shoulders suddenly stooped with the burden of emotion. "The truth is I'm bound to her by hatred."

"Justine, have you read these books in their entirety? Or did your father only show you certain unflattering articles?"

"What are you implying?" she demanded.

Quinton flipped the pages of the book he had been reading to an article. Tapping the page with his fingers, he said, "Could a woman such as you described Helene write an article like this?" he said. "Even before Hitler came to full power she wrote this, denouncing him as a madman. She had the strength and foresight to attack Winston Churchill and George Bernard Shaw because they made public statements praising Hitler and Musso-

lini. If she cared only for herself, would she have
bothered? Such outspokenness must have made it very
difficult for her in the circles in which she traveled. If
she hadn't cared for others, she would have kept her
insights to herself.''

Justine moved from the window and once again
glanced over his shoulder. It was evident from her
expression that she had never read the article.

''And here,'' Quinton said hurriedly, flipping more
pages. He stopped at a faded photograph of Helene
dressed in soldier's fatigues. The photograph had been
printed in a French newspaper after the armistice. Quinton translated from the French: ''The *Legion of Honor*
was awarded to Helene Haymes, an American, in a
ceremony on Friday for her outstanding contributions
to the war effort. Miss Haymes, in addition to her
weekly radio broadcasts, gave of herself untiringly,
often entertaining troops near the front lines, under fire
and in danger of losing her life.'' Quinton pushed the
scrapbook towards Justine. ''Do you know how few
Americans were awarded the *Legion of Honor?*''

Justine stared unbelievingly at the photograph. ''I
. . . I never knew about this,'' she stammered. She
sank into the chair beside Quinton's, and began thumb-
ing through the worn book. Then, as suddenly as her
interest had been sparked, it waned. She snapped the
cover closed. ''It still doesn't change things,'' she said
evenly.

But there was the ring of doubt in her voice, and that
had been all Quinton had meant to plant.

''Why are you going through these?'' she asked with
suspicion. ''And don't tell me you happened to come
across them. She had them taken to her room when she
suspected my father of showing them to me.'' Her
green eyes met his unblinkingly. ''Did she ask you to
show me the flattering articles?''

"She did not." Quinton explained that he would be writing several pieces on Helene for the auction and that she had offered her scrapbooks as a source of information. He did not mention the diaries now resting in the desk drawer.

Justine pulled her gaze from him and stared thoughtfully down at the scrapbooks. The sunlight streaming through the window highlighted her dark hair and created the illusion of a red aura.

Quinton said nothing, leaving her to her thoughts.

She stood and walked around the desk distractedly. When she spoke her words surprised him: "I'll have Maria clean these windows. If you must stay inside you should be able to see out." She looked at him and saw his expression. "You realize we've done it again don't you?" she said. "She's intruded in our conversation and managed to come between us. She's manipulating you. I suppose to get to me. For what purpose, I don't know."

"Justine . . ."

"Oh, all right! She has a *Legion of Honor* medal and she attacked Hitler as a madman long before it was fashionable, but I don't trust her, Quinton. I somehow feel she's going to drive a wedge between us." She moved behind him, put her arms around his neck and rested her chin on top of his head. "You're so kind, so gentle, and so unsuspecting, my darling. Don't let her captivate you with her stories. Believe me, she has an ulterior motive. She has an ulterior motive for everything. Father convinced me of that."

Quinton wanted to say, "Your father was an English lord." But, of course, he refrained himself. If the edge of her hatred could ever be dulled, it would have to be Helene who told her the truth. Despite her words, he heard the nuance of doubt in her voice. He had done all he could for the moment, all Helene could expect of him.

"Are you going to be able to get away any time today?" she asked, nibbling at his ear. "I could continue the tour of the island."

Regrettably, Quinton told her he would have to stay and work. "There's a lot I have to do before going back to New York tomorrow," he said.

"Then I'll leave you to it," Justine said. She kissed his cheek and pulled away before his hands could clutch at her. "I won't be away long, darling. I'm going for a swim, and then I have to drop by the gallery. Another of my paintings sold."

"Congratulations." He turned in his chair to watch her as she moved towards the door. "When you come back I'd like to discuss the staff Helene said you'd be responsible for hiring."

"Oh, I've already done that, darling. When Helene commands, I obey immediately. I've hired two young women. Neither is madly attractive, so I'll feel secure about leaving them alone with you in these dank rooms." She stopped in the open doorway, and turned. "I've also hired Aaron. He needs the money, and since he's not a Conch, salt or fresh water, he fits her requirements." She blew him a kiss and disappeared before he could object to Aaron as one of his employees.

He felt a vague hostility not only toward but from Aaron. If, however, he confessed his feelings to Justine she would think it pure jealousy on his part. He would, he reflected, simply have to make the best of working with the homosexual. He only hoped the handsome beach bum would not create any difficulties; the scope of the auction required everyone to work in unison.

Rising, Quinton stepped to the window and watched

Justine go down the walkway and let herself out
through the front gate. On the street, as she was about to
get on her bicycle, she glanced up at the window.
Feeling as if he had been spying on her, Quinton
stepped quickly out of sight.

By the time Maria delivered his lunch tray, he had
already read Helene's scrapbooks and had made an
outline for the article he had been commissioned to
write for Hal Crimmons' magazine. If, as Hal had
suggested, the story received cover treatment, he hoped
interest would be stimulated in Helene—that would
make the agency's task easier; magazines, like book
publishers, tended to imitate each other's successes.

"You liked the conch chowder so much the other
evenin', I fixed it again," the housekeeper said as she
removed the silver cover from his tray. "You got
special likes, you gotta tell me."

Quinton perceived Maria's coolness. He had too
much on his mind already without searching for a
reason he might have offended her. "Whatever you
prepare will be fine, Maria," he said amicably. Actually, last night's excessive drinking had left him with a
queasy feeling in the pit of his stomach and he had no
desire for food. "Is Helene up and about?" he asked.

The housekeeper regarded him even more coolly.
"Miss Helene, she had an awful night. I had to send for
Dr. Webb. Sent for Miss Justine, too, but she wasn't
home." Her eyebrows lifted accusingly. Then, with a
shrug of her heavy shoulders, she said, "When Miss
Helene sends for me, I'll tell her you want to see her."
She turned to leave.

"Dr. Webb is still practicing then?" Quinton said.
"He must be a very old man." Helene's story remained
vividly in his mind.

"He's only carin' for special patients," Maria

answered without interrupting her shuffle towards the door. ''Miss Helene, she's his special patient.''

Conspiratorial partners, Quinton thought, and wondered if doctor and patient ever discussed their secret of the tiny body hidden away in its mother's coffin; if the doctor's guilt made Helene a special patient.

By midafternoon, Justine had not returned, nor had Maria summoned him to Helene's room. Quinton had written up a proposal to present to his partner at the agency, outlining the publicity campaign he envisioned for Helene and the auction. A few credit card lunches and promises of returned favors and his partner Horace would have the campaign launched. He then made a list of photographers he thought capable of handling the collections, and said a silent prayer that one of them would be between assignments and willing to travel to Key West. Next he listed potential publishers for the auction's brochure; he had worked with Leeman & Farris on his own book, *The History of Porcelains*, and decided to approach them first.

Beyond the window, the outside drew him like a magnet. It was a warm, sunny day, not as humid as the past few days had been; floral fragrances blew through the open window to entice him out. He dropped his pen and pushed the pad aside. If Justine had returned, she easily could have convinced him to join her in frivolous play. He stood and moved to the window. A postman was stopping at the gate. As he reached through to the metal mailbox, Lucifer charged threateningly. Instead of being alarmed, the postman stooped, reached through the grating and patted the Doberman's head. Amazing, Quinton thought. As the postman toyed with the dog, Quinton noticed light reflecting off something shiny in his left ear. He pulled back the curtain for a clearer view and smiled when he realized the man was wearing a gold earring. A standard government regulation uniform and a gold earring—only in Key West, he thought. The postman lifted his gaze to the house, and Quinton let the curtain fall back into place; no need starting rumors about the occupants of the Haymes House peering from behind curtains.

Leaving the ballroom, Quinton wandered into the hallway. He could hear Maria singing below as she went about her duties; instead of disturbing her, he decided to climb the stairs and knock gently on Helene's door. If there was no answer, he would slip quietly away. If she invited him in and he saw she was in a bad state, he would make polite inquiries about her health and take up his questions about the auction at a more opportune time.

As he approached the top floor, Betty was sitting on the steps. The girl had a drawing pad spread out on the edge of the landing and was so involved with her activity she didn't hear him until he had almost reached her. Startled, she sprang to her feet, dropping her pencil. As it bounced down the steps, Quinton stooped and retrieved it. Noting it was an expensive sketching pencil, probably Justine's he handed it back to the girl.

"It's an awfully nice day for you to be inside," he told her.

Betty sat back down, stretching her long legs across the top step as if to block his path. "Don't wanna be inside," she said. She flexed the pencil between both hands as if she might suddenly snap it. "Wanna go out an' play with Lucifer."

"But your mother has you listening for Miss Helene should she call, huh? Too bad. I can sympathize because I'd like to be outside myself." He sat down on the step below hers and reached for her sketch pad. "What have we here?"

"Pictures," she said, still pouting.

"Yours?" The question came out with doubt, because as he flipped through the pages he found the drawings far too sophisticated and well-executed to believe them Betty's. Most likely she had taken Justine's sketch pad when she had taken the pencil. The first drawing was of Justine's cottage, with the poinciana tree in full bloom and Lucifer sitting on the steps. The second was of the front wall and iron gate, again with Lucifer sitting quietly in the walkway. "Are these yours?" he asked again.

Betty nodded, her dark eyes expecting criticism. "Miss Justine, she taught me to draw," she confessed. She leaned over him and examined the next sheet of the pad. The drawing was of the back yard as seen from an upper window. "That's from Miss Helene's window," she said. "I did that one a lot when I used to have to sit with Miss Helene."

Quinton flipped through the next few pages, all scenes of the back yard. The major difference in each was that Lucifer sat or stood in various areas, always looking up mournfully in the artist's direction. "These are quite wonderful," Quinton said. He stopped at the next drawing, a cemetery with the stones and obelisks tilted at odd angles, as if about to topple to the vine-choked ground. Lucifer sat on one of the slabs, his legs crossed as if in prayer, his head raised as if baying at the moon, one charcoal tear falling from his one visible eye. The mood of the drawing struck Quinton despite the fact that it was the least well executed. Probably done hurriedly, he thought. "Where's this, Betty?" he asked, hoping for insight into why the girl had made the drawing.

"Cemetery 'course," she responded. "Them's graves. Old graves." She leaned back against the banister as if the drawings were of no further interest.

"Why's Lucifer so sad?" Quinton pressed. "That's a tear in his eye, isn't it?"

"Hmm. Dogs cry just like people," she said. "They gets mad an' happy an' sometimes they cry. Only people don't notice." She closed her eyes, brought up her legs and wrapped her arms about her knees. "Dogs are smart. They feels things that people don't."

"I daresay you're right there," Quinton told her. He continued to flip through the sketch pad; all the drawings except for that of the cemetery were made in or around the Haymes house. The girl's world, he thought, and was reminded of Wyeth's painting titled *Christine's World,* one that evoked an unexplored melancholy in him. "Have you ever been to school with other children, Betty?" he asked.

The girl's eyes opened and she contemplated him thoughtfully before saying, "Don't have to go to school. Mama teaches me to cook and clean."

"Mama also teaches ya not to scatter yer stuff on the stairs," Maria suddenly said from the middle of the stairs. "She talkin' your ears off again, Mr. Armstrong?" The heavyset housekeeper continued climbing the stairs with her remarkable agility. Her eyes were kept on her daughter, questioning, scolding.

"Actually, I was asking her about these drawings," Quinton explained. "I'm very impressed. They show talent. Undeveloped, but talent that should be nurtured."

Maria transferred her gaze from her daughter to Quinton. She looked at him intently, seemed about to say something, and then turned back to Betty. "You run along now and play with Lucifer," she told the girl. She waited until Betty had retrieved her sketch pad and had gone running joyfully down the stairs. Then she said, "Don't go puttin' fancy ideas in her head, Mr. Armstrong. She's a dreamer enough."

"But your daughter does have talent," Quinton insisted. "She should be enrolled with an art teacher, someone who can bring that talent out."

"How old you think my Betty Sue is?" Maria said. "She ain't no little girl 'cept in her head. She don't think right 'cause the Lord saw fit t' punish me for my sins. Betty Sue, she's too old t' learn now, t' learn more than I teach her, and that's how t' survive. How's drawin' fancy pictures goin' t' help her? Even if she could be taught?"

Quinton felt his anger rising. "It could open an entirely new world for her. I don't care how old she is, or even if she is retarded. She should have the opportunity to explore and expand her talent. A real sin would be to deny her her potential." Even as he spoke he tried to get his anger in check. Why was he, a man who had always, as Joanna had frequently reminded him, been so complaisant, suddenly stepping in where before he would have walked away.

Maria smiled benignly at his anger.

"I don't understand why Helene or Justine didn't assume the responsibility of seeing to the girl's education," Quinton said. "There are special classes, special teachers for exceptional children. Surely this island is not so frivolous as to not have such programs."

"You're gettin' yourself all worked up over somethin' you don't understand," Maria said calmly. "I dress my Betty Sue young 'cause that helps me to think of her that way, but she's done past her time of learnin'. She an' Miss Justine, they been drawin' them pictures since they was girls together. Betty Sue, she don't get no better at it. That's right, Mr. Armstrong. My Betty Sue's not much younger than Miss Justine. I had my punishment in Betty Sue, and Miss Helene, well, she had hers not much different than mine. It's often through the children that the Lord chooses to make us pay for His wrath. When I think of who's payin' the most, Miss Helene or me, I think I'm luckier. My Betty Sue's always goin' t' be my little girl. She ain't smart and she ain't goin' t' learn more than she knows right now, but she loves me. She's goin' to go on lovin' me, too, unless someone who don't understand tries to put fancy ideas in her head and make her feel like her Mama's not done right by her.'' Here, the heavyset housekeeper pulled herself up to her full height. ''So you listen t' me, Mr. Armstrong. I may get fired for sayin' my mind, but I'm sayin' it anyway. You wanna be my little girl's friend, that's okay by me. But you don't put no notions in her head 'bout bein' better than she is. Miss Helene, she may want you to change things for her, but me, I don't want things changed with me and Betty Sue. Any changes to be made with me and mine, I change 'em myself.''

Quinton had never heard the housekeeper make such a long speech. He had the distinct impression she had carefully thought out what she said to him, perhaps having anticipated his unwelcomed intrusion in her life from the moment he arrived. ''Very well,'' he said, averting his eyes from her steady gaze. ''I won't interfere. However, I would like you to consider that if you honestly believe your Lord caused Betty's condition as a punishment for you, He also gave her the gift of her talent. Not to nurture that seed would be against Him.'' He glanced back at the housekeeper's impassive face. ''I won't bring it up again,'' he promised, and sighed his defeat.

Maria nodded in affirmation. ''I think you're a good man, Mr. Armstrong,'' she said. ''I don't hold you no malice. I just want things straight between us, understand? Before all else, I got to protect my little girl. What else you do here, that's no concern of mine.''

Quinton's eyebrows shot up. "Exactly what do you mean by that, Maria?"

"Enough said already," she dismissed the question. Moving by him to the top landing, she turned and her eyes were on a level with his. "Don't look like Miss Helene's goin' to be up to seein' you 'till evenin'," she said. "When the doctor gives her a needle she sometimes sleeps right through the day. That's merciful, I guess."

"Is she in that much pain?"

"Can't one person measure another's pain," Maria answered profoundly. "You run along, Mr. Armstrong," she said in the same tone of voice she had used minutes before with her daughter. "You go an' have some fun an' relax. You look like a man could use some relaxin'. You can talk business with Miss Helene later."

"Yes, I suppose I can," Quinton agreed, feeling again the pull to escape the gloomy house for the outdoors.

Maria moved down the hallway to her employer's door.

Quinton noted she inserted a key in the lock and turned it before entering. Odd, he thought. Had she been locking visitors—him—out, or the old woman inside?

Quinton walked to Duval Street and purchased a cotton shirt and denim trousers at a department store with the unlikely name of *Fast Buck Freddie's*. The clerk was a young woman with frizzed blonde hair and unintelligent blue eyes; to his question of where to find *The Gingerbread Gallery,* she merely motioned the direction with a toss of her head, not interrupting the rhythm of her gum-chewing jaw.

The gallery was filled with customers or browsing

tourists. Quinton could not distinguish which. The clerk—or owner—was a tall man with two distinctive grey streaks in his black beard. When Quinton managed to get his attention and ask if Justine Haymes had been in yet, the man shook his head in a negative response.

"When do you expect her?" Quinton pressed.

"With Justine, you expect her when she walks through the door," the man answered, and was pulled away before Quinton could question him further.

As long as he was there, Quinton decided to look around. Two of Justine's paintings occupied spaces near the door. One, a view of the man-made island he had seen during their boat trip, was striking in its use of vivid colors. As in all Justine's paintings, the sky consisted of dark storm clouds with a mere wisp of blue visible at the horizon; the two abandoned houseboats bobbed on turbulent gulf waters and a gull swooped downward in a plunge for a fish swimming too near the surface. The second painting was of a lush terrace garden with the azure blue of the water visible between giant palms; parrots, their legs chained to bamboo perches, confronted one another with spread wings; here, too, the sky was darkened by storm clouds. Quinton leaned towards the attached cards and saw the prices were slightly over seven hundred dollars for each; a short biography listed the artist, Justine Haymes, as a local whose work had been exhibited in New York, Los Angeles and Atlanta. He stepped back and viewed the paintings from a distance. Objectively, he saw talent in the canvases, but not of the quality to demand the asking prices. Next to Justine's work hung a painting by Tennessee Williams. Quinton considered the local celebrity fortunate to have established himself as a playwright; one of the greatest, he reflected, the country had ever produced.

Quinton spent the next half-hour roaming about the gallery hoping Justine would suddenly materialize. When she didn't, he left the gallery and wandered down Duval Street. The street was crowded by bicyclists and motorists, many of the automobile-driving tourists driven to frustrated horn-honking by the uncourteous road manners of the cyclists. The crowd was mostly young, late teens to mid-twenties, and in gay, holiday spirits. A few of the bicycles had their frames decorated with garlands of plastic flowers, adding to the festive air.

When he reached the end of the street and entered *The Pier House* his clothes were soaked with perspiration; he wished he had changed into the lightweight trousers and shirt at the department store. Although the humidity was not as high as previous days, he was unaccustomed to it. His legs felt weak and his thirst was demanding. Instead of going to his room, he went to the upstairs bar and ordered a tall Tom Collins. He dropped into a rattan chair and swilled half the drink in one gulp. The cold drink and the air conditioner revived him. He looked around at the other customers and suddenly became aware of his age; in his mid-thirties, he must be considered an old man. Most of the afternoon drinkers didn't look old enough to purchase liquor, yet he heard them calling for expensive Russian vodkas to be defiled by orange, guava or mango juices. A girl young enough to be his daughter tugged straight blonde hair away from her eyes and winked at him invitingly. The young man with her caught the exchange, turned to look at Quinton, and then laughed aloud.

Embarrassed, Quinton rose and moved onto the deck. The humidity again assaulted him, but at least here there was a slight breeze off the gulf. He walked to

the railing and stood staring down at the narrow beach
area. The sand and the water were as crowded as Jones
Beach could be on a hot weekend afternoon. He
scanned the bodies on the lounges looking for Justine,
but if she was among the mass of oiled bodies he could
not detect her. He turned his attention to the channel.
There were several boats, but none of the type Justine
and Aaron had taken him out in. A fishing boat was
returning from the reef, the decks crowded with waving
tourists.

Quinton finished his drink and was about to go to his
room to shower and change into his new clothes when
he heard:

"Mr. Armstrong?"

He turned to see the woman who had approached his
and Justine's table last night at the Sugar Loaf Key
restaurant.

"It is Mr. Armstrong, isn't it?" the woman said. She
came directly up to him, standing too close for polite-
ness, and stared up into his face with blatant inquisi-
tiveness.

"Yes, Quinton Armstrong," Quinton responded as
he searched his memory for her name. All that came to
mind was Justine having told him the woman was an
ex-show-girl whose marriage to a respected attorney
shocked local society. He smiled and asked, "How are
you? It's nice to run into you again so soon."

"Yes, well, it's a small island." The woman's penciled eyebrows arched in a decidedly appraising
glance. "Come. Sit over here, Quinton. May I call you
Quinton? We don't stand on formalities for long in Key
West. That is, most of us don't." Before he could
refuse her invitation, she took his arm and led him to
where she had been sitting. "Would you like another
drink? Waiter!" She sat as she spoke and motioned him

into the chair beside her. "Move your chair closer, Quinton. We don't want to shout."

Quinton moved the chair scarcely an inch closer. He noted the woman wore a long, brightly colored dress similar to the one she had worn the previous evening, and he wondered if it was to hide a body gone to flab by overindulgence. She also leaned forward in her chair so that to look directly at her Quinton was forced to squint into the sunlight.

"So unfortunate you'll be leaving before my party, Quinton," she said. "Everyone talks about Ernesta Calder parties from one season to the next."

"I'm sorry I won't be able to attend," he said. He had only spent moments with the woman and already felt trapped; he cursed himself for not going directly to his room. He wanted to get back to Helene's; Justine was undoubtedly there by now, waiting for him.

"Ah, well, we have now," Ernesta said suggestively. "And—exactly when do you leave Key West, Quinton?"

"Tomorrow," he answered.

"Back to New York and the cold, hmm?" She laughed. "Well, that gives you tonight."

"Yes, tonight," Quinton repeated. *Just tonight with Justine before they would be separated for several days*. He stared down at the ice melting in his glass, feeling a sudden wave of depression.

"So sad you look," Ernesta observed. "I hate to see handsome young men look sad." She reached and lay her hand on his knee.

Quinton felt the heat from her hand penetrate to his flesh. He shifted his gaze away from his glass. The diamond on her ring finger sparkled in the sunlight. The back of her hand was heavily veined, freckled, a telltale scar revealing surgery had been performed to stretch the skin tightly over skeletal bones and tendons. Still, her hand looked old, almost like a talon.

"Perhaps I might cheer you up," she suggested. "Tonight, perhaps."

Good God, Quinton thought. Is she trying to pick me up right here in public? She must have sensed his revulsion, because she withdrew her hand abruptly. He felt he had put himself in an awkward position and said with forced easiness, "I'm afraid my last evening is engaged. But thank you. You're most considerate."

"Considerate," she repeated stiffly. "I've never been accused of being considerate. With Justine, I suppose? Your last evening?"

"Actually, with her aunt," he said.

Ernesta Calder sat forward in her chair. "Helene Haymes?" Her irritation at being rejected was replaced by obvious interest.

Quinton nodded. He had saved himself from facing her ire, but he had opened himself to her curiosity.

"This is fascinating," Ernesta said. "You've actually seen Helene Haymes? You've done something none of us locals have managed. Tell me, Quinton, in what capacity have you come to Key West to visit the infamous Miss Helene?"

"I'm an appraiser," Quinton offered, and said no more.

"Appraiser of what?" the woman pressed. "Land?"

"Antiquities."

"Antiquities. Ah, the fascination increases. You know there are rumors about the antiques and *objets d'art* hidden away in that mausoleum on Simonton Street. But no one gets beyond the front door. That black Amazon guards the house as if it was her own. People stopped trying to pay their respects years ago, even before I came to the island."

"I assumed you'd met Helene Haymes," Quinton said, "since you inquired after her last night."

"Met her? My dear young man, you could count the number of locals who've met Helene Haymes on one hand, and those who have are curiously closed-mouthed. I tried to meet her," she said with an edge of bitterness. "I thought as a newcomer it would be a *coup d'etat* as a hostess if I could achieve what the other l-a-d-i-e-s had failed to accomplish. When I went to the house I was practically devoured by a killer dog and then rudely informed by that rotund maid that Miss Helene didn't accept invitations from anyone. The scene was apparently witnessed by a passerby and I became a laughing stock for months."

Quinton lowered his head to conceal his smile as he visualized Ernesta Calder confronted by Maria and the Doberman. Her next comment almost made him burst into laughter.

"It's disconcerting the number of eccentrics who people this island, Quinton. Helene Haymes the worst of them."

Apparently eccentrics, like Ernesta Calder, saw themselves as conventional. Here she sat, a woman evidently older than the fifty years he had judged her to be last night, in a garishly colored print dress, her bleached hair perfectly coiffured in the style of a much younger woman, diamonds sparkling on hands surgery had been unable to make youthful, trying to seduce him, and still referring to Helene Haymes as an eccentric.

"Why does she continue to hide herself away?" the woman asked, more of herself than of him. "Her shame is long past forgotten."

"Is it?" Quinton said pointedly.

"Oh, of course there are those who would be cruel given the opportunity," Ernesta conceded. "Cruelty

rivals eccentricities. On the surface they can be so very
charming, so very Southern. One always thinks of
Southerners as being charming and gracious. Well,
they haven't been gracious to me. I don't mind telling
you they've made my life hell. But I haven't locked
myself away as she has. Can you imagine what it's like
to be accepted only as your husband's wife, never for
yourself? Oh, I'm invited to parties and people come to
mine. I'm allowed to be on committees. But all out of
respect to my husband. They snub me in subtle ways.
My husband, too, for marrying me, but he's too dense
to see it. They whisper about Helene Haymes, but they
respect her. She could emerge from that tomb and
become the toast of Key West.''

Quinton refrained from saying, ''Perhaps she
doesn't want to be the toast of Key West or any other
city. She's been that, had that.'' Instead, he merely sat
and stared at the woman who was working herself into a
state of excitement and wished he could escape grace-
fully.

''Well, I'll tell you *I* don't respect her,'' Ernesta said
vehemently. ''I hate people who don't fight for what
they want out of life. What are these society matrons
anyway? Ancestors of pirates and cutthroats and
scavengers of the sea, that's what most of the Conchs
are. And the others, I have a theory about them, too.
They're runners. They can't run any further than here,
to Key West, these losers, so they ban together in a tight
little circle. They create a hierarchy and help each other
pretend they'd be just as important in any other city,
that they're not losers.''

Quinton noted that people at nearby tables had turned
to stare at them. He cleared his throat in a gesture meant
to call Ernesta Calder's attention to her raised voice, to
the notice she was attracting. For the first time since he

had sat down, he realized the woman was intoxicated. His need to escape her became intensified; he shifted uncomfortably in his chair.

"Well, I'd like to bring down their social pyramid of cards," Ernesta went on bitterly. "There's no Golden Gate Bridge for them to jump from, but it'd be just as rewarding hearing that some of them had walked into the sea." She laughed hollowly. "Like Virginia Woolf, with their hats on and every hair in place."

"Excuse me," Quinton began, "but I must . . ."

"I don't have that power and never will" Ernesta refused to be interrupted. "Instead, I find compensation in other ways. But Helene Haymes, she could have given me that power by simply accepting my invitation."

Quinton rose. "I'm sorry, Mrs. Calder, but I'm late for an appointment."

Ernesta Calder's hostile concentration was broken. She became aware of the attention she had attracted. Her makeup seemed to become even more harsh as the color drained from her face. Her frightened eyes scanned the nearby tables determining if anyone of importance had overheard and might spread her bitter words. She set down the drink she had been holding with enough force to make the metal tabletop reverberate. Extending a hand toward Quinton, she rose with his gentlemanly assistance. "For God's sake, walk me out of her," she whispered. "Please! Just off the deck. I'll make it on my own from there."

Quinton took her arm and felt her trembling. He opened the sliding glass doors and walked her into the expansive bar.

"Dear, dear," she murmured. "I do tend to get dramatic. A holdover from the old days. I was on the stage, you know?" She glanced over her shoulder

through the glass doors, her eyes still searching the
faces of those who had been sitting within earshot of
their conversation. "Only tourists," she finally said
with a sigh of relief. The expression of concern left her
eyes as she turned them back on Quinton. "I'd be
curious to know if Helene Haymes has retained even a
remnant of her former beauty. She's only a few years
older than . . . she was supposed to have been quite a
beauty. My husband speaks of her as if she were a
goddess."

Quinton shrugged and said nothing.

Ernesta continued to walk slowly toward the exit,
still clinging to his arm. "I have two questions for you,
Quinton," she said, assuming the attitude of an old
friend. "Why did she do it? Why did she lock herself
away like that all these years? She had everything:
wealth, beauty, social standing. The scandal would
have been forgotten and forgiven."

Quinton gently removed her hand from his arm.
"I'm afraid I can't answer that question," he said.

"Well, you can certainly answer my second," Ernesta said. "Why are you appraising her antiques? "
When she saw he was not going to answer, she cried,
"Why are handsome men always so exasperating?"
She moved to the stairwell, stopped and turned, clinging to the banister. "I should like you to meet my
husband, Quinton. There's something about you that
reminds me of him, something in your eyes. They're
the mirrors of the soul, you know, the eyes."

"Good-bye, Mrs. Calder." Quinton planned to take
another exit and retreat to his room.

"My husband was madly in love with Helene
Haymes," Ernesta said, stopping his departure. "He
married his first wife on the rebound when Helene ran
off to set Europe on its heels. I think he still loves her,

or at least the memory of her. Strange, isn't it, how some women have the power to possess a man?" She cocked her head thoughtfully to one side. "Or is it that some men have a natural debility that demands they be possessed by a woman? Good-bye, Quinton." Despite her intoxication, she maneuvered the steep staircase with ease, saying over her shoulder, "I could have cheered you up tonight, Quinton. Too bad you have to spend the night with . . . " Her voice was cut off by the bend in the stairs.

Quinton went to his room, showered and changed into the clothes he had purchased earlier. It was almost twilight when he came out of his room; people had begun to wander away from the beach and the ritual Justine had called *Sunset*. Instead of wasting time waiting for a taxi, he walked the few blocks to Simonton Street.

Lucifer rose up on the porch as Quinton let himself through the front gate. The dog growled, and then came forward wagging its tail.

"Good boy," Quinton said. "Good boy." He bent and cautiously patted the Doberman's head. Lucifer nuzzled him with his cold nose, hoping, it appeared, to be given an offering. "Next time, old boy. We may not be friends yet, but we have an agreement, don't we? Good boy." Not wishing to press his luck, Quinton moved slowly up the walkway, the dog trotting along beside him.

The front door was unlocked. He let himself in and would have gone up the stairs had he not heard Justine's voice coming from the direction of the kitchen. He threaded his way along the maze of paneled passageways, using Justine's and Maria's voices as a guide.

". . . no call to shout at me, Miss Justine," Maria said angrily. "I ain't no jailer, I'm a housekeeper!"

"You are what I say you are!" Justine retorted; Quinton had never heard her voice so angry.

"You listen t' me, Miss Justine," Maria cried fretfully. "I've been with Miss Helene since she came home t' Key West and I've seen and heard things made me go down on my knees to the Lord, but I ain't goin' to stand by and get myself and Betty Sue in so deep we can't . . ."

The floorboards creaked beneath Quinton's weight and the voices instantly stopped. Forcing a smile, he pushed through the swinging door into the kitchen.

Justine and Maria were standing in the middle of the room. Both were facing the door, both had surprised and questioning expressions on their faces.

"Oh, there you are," Justine cried. She smiled, but there was still anger blazing in her green eyes. "Aunt Helene has been asking for you, but I think she's gone back into a drug-induced sleep. Maria, see if Aunt Helene still wants to see Quinton tonight."

"Yes, ma'am," the housekeeper muttered. She pushed passed Quinton without glancing at him, perspiration beaded on her forehead and her dark eyes holding an expression not unlike the anger in Justine's.

When the swinging door had slapped closed behind the housekeeper and Quinton heard her footsteps fading in the labyrinth of the passageways, he asked Justine, "What was that all about?"

Justine came to him, stood on tiptoes and kissed him. "Only a domestic problem," she answered. "Even Maria gets out of line once in a while." She wrapped her arms about his waist and leaned the side of her face against his chest. "Where have you been, darling?"

Quinton refrained from asking her with the same question; oddly, he felt defensive. "Having a cocktail with Ernesta Calder," he said, and he felt her body stiffen against him. "You didn't tell me her husband was one of Helene's old beaus."

She pulled back and looked up into his face. "I didn't know," she answered with amusement. "No wonder she hates me so."

"I don't think that has anything to do with her liking or not liking you," Quinton told her. "She considers herself a social outcast, a woman forced to live on the fringes of the island's social set."

"I wouldn't have believed Ernesta was that perceptive," Justine said. "I always thought she considered herself firmly 'in.' God knows, she acts it." She stepped close against Quinton again, wrapping her arms about him. "If the old harridan doesn't feel up to demanding your time tonight, shall we have a quiet dinner in the cottage? It'll be our last night together until you return from New York. Beside, I have to prove to you I can cook, that I'm not just another spoiled Southern belle." She undid two buttons of his shirt and kissed his chest.

"Justine, I love you," he whispered. *God knows how it happened so quickly, but I love you.*

"I love you too, darling." She stepped away from him when she heard Maria's returning footsteps.

Maria pushed through the door without looking at either of them. On her way to the sink, she said, "Miss Helene, she's still sleepin'." She turned on the tap and began scrubbing a skillet, her back to them.

Justine winked at Quinton. She nodded toward the cottage. "In an hour," she whispered. She brought a hand to her lips, blew him a kiss, and then turned and left through the back door.

Maria looked around, seemed about to speak, then turned back to the sink, scrubbing the skillet with even greater fury.

Quinton went up to his makeshift office to waste an hour.

Quinton rose from bed in the middle of the night. He lit a cigarette and stood smoking in the darkness. Behind him, Justine was sleeping, naked, the sheets kicked away into a shimmering pile of pale silk on the floor. Her body was a dark silhouette, legs and arms thrown helter-skelter like one would expect of a child. He stood looking down at her, the glow from the tip of his cigarette occasionally piercing the darkness, and he tried to sort out and understand the portent that kept him from sleeping beside her. But whatever had brought on his insomnia would not leave him or surface. To keep from waking her, he went into the living room of the cottage, drew open the draperies and stood staring out toward the main house as he finished his cigarette.

He didn't know how long he had stared at the lighted upper window before comprehending what he saw. A bright light behind Helene's partially closed shutters! As he watched, a shadow moved across the shutters. A man!

"What is it, darling?"

He turned to see Justine standing in the bedroom doorway. Silhouetted in the moonlight, she resembled one of the Art Nouveau women used in her decor. "I woke and you weren't there and . . . "

"There's a light in Helene's room," he told her, "and I distinctly saw the shadow of a man cross behind the shutters."

"Oh." She crossed the darkened room and, standing beside him, looked up at the lighted window. The shadow again moved behind the shutters. "Maria," she said knowingly.

"No, a man," Quinton said firmly. "And the bright light of her eyes . . . "

"Dr. Webb, then," Justine said with a hint of irritation. "Perhaps she's taken ill and Maria's called him in. It's not uncommon. Helene's a bit of a hypochondriac."

"But the bright light," he repeated. "Her eyes are so sensitive . . . "

"She wears an eye mask when he examines her," Justine said flatly. "After all, he can't examine her in the dark." Reaching for the cord, she pulled the draperies closed. "Come back to bed, darling."

"But shouldn't we check with Maria? It might be serious."

"If it's serious, Maria will call me," she answered, irritation still evident in her voice. But her body was soft and yielding as she pressed against him, repeating suggestively, "Come back to bed, darling."

Obediently, he followed her across the darkened room, the light in Helene's room and the evasive portent that had given him insomnia forgotten.

Chapter Eleven

"Don't despair, Quinton," Helene said from the shadows of her bed. "It's only a temporary setback. I'm not going to die on you before the auction."

"I hadn't thought that," Quinton said, embarrassed because the thought had occurred to him only moments before as he had entered her room.

"In any event," the old woman continued, "I had documents drawn up guaranteeing you payment should the unexpected happen. But it won't," she added with conviction. "Sit down, please," she said with impatience. "We needn't stand on formalities, you and I."

Obediently, he slipped into the chair beside her bed.

"How long do you expect to be in New York?"

"Three, four days," he answered. "Possibly a week. It depends on the cooperation I get from my partner. I've already telephoned and instructed him to add to our staff." As if to justify the additional expenses, he added, "We'll need someone working with the galleries and auction houses here and in Europe. We'll need their mailing lists of top collectors and dealers. Then there're those who'll work directly with the press and . . ."

"You needn't explain," Helene interrupted. "Have you seen Justine this morning?"

"Yes. In the kitchen." And before that, in her cottage, in the shower together where they had made love with the trickling spray playing over their bodies. Just the memory was enough to excite him.

"She was supposed to join us," the old woman said irritably. "I wanted to impress on her the responsibility she will be taking on by assisting you. Ring the bell cord and have Maria send her up."

"I'm afraid she's left the house," Quinton said. "She said something about errands."

"Hmm, errands," Helene murmured doubtfully. "I've given the documents I mentioned to her. Watch her, Quinton. Promise me. If she doesn't serve you well, I want to know. I'm afraid she still won't take me seriously. She thinks I'll back down at the last moment and refuse to auction my treasures."

That thought also had occurred to Quinton, that he would perform all the preliminary tasks only to have the old woman cancel the auction until after her death: people, after all, even those who had been given a set date for death, tended to believe in their immortality. Should Helene suddenly want to keep her collection around her until after her death, he would understand. Aloud, he said, "I believe Justine will serve you well even though she might not understand your reasons for the auction."

"Oh, you've spent time with her?"

"Well, no, I've . . . I've chatted with her. She seems quite intelligent and not lazy."

"Do you find her beautiful, Quinton?"

"Yes," he admitted without hesitation. He decided the old woman was fishing for a compliment. "She's very beautiful. She resembles you."

Helene laughed softly. "You needn't appeal to my vanity, Quinton. I know I was beautiful. *Was*. But I

worked at my beauty. Justine doesn't. Her beauty is
natural. Perhaps that's why it's so unimportant to her.''
She sighed and slightly changed her position on the
bed. ''In the days I've spent locked in this house, in this
room, I've often wondered in retrospect how different
my life would have been if I had been homely. I don't,
however, think I would have wanted anything different
than it was. Except for my relationship with my daughter. In your *chats* with Justine, have you given any
thought to our discussion? Have you determined if
telling her the truth would be of any advantage to her?''

"Naturally I've given it thought," Quinton said,
almost angrily. "You knew it would be impossible not
to. As for a determination, I haven't made one.''

"Haven't, or have and refused to commit yourself?"
the old woman challenged. "Well, no matter. In the
end the decision is mine. I didn't mean to burden you
with more than the auction. As you told me, you're an
appraiser of antiquities, not of people. Were my scrapbooks and diaries of use to you?''

Quinton was thankful for the change in conversation.
He told her he had finished thhe article he had been
commissioned to write. "If you would allow it, I'd like
to take your scrapbooks and diaries to New York with
me. Since you refuse to meet reporters personally, I'll
have to commit most of the information to memory.
Then, too, they may be of use to the publicity staff.''

Helene was silent for several moments, moments in
which he expected her to be formulating a gentle refusal. His eyes were becoming accustomed to the dim
lighting and he could make out the outline of her head
against the white linen, tiny beads of light reflected in
her eyes—eyes that were fixed on him.

Finally, she said, "So long as you remove all entries
referring to the conception and birth of my daughter. I

may decide to tell her the truth of her birth, but what she tells the world is for her to determine.''

"Agreed," he said.

"Then take them," she said wearily. "Why I kept them I don't know. A silly woman's egotism, I suppose." He heard the sudden intake of her breath, as if she had been stabbed by sudden pain.

"Is there something I can do?" he asked with concern.

"No, nothing," she told him. "It will pass." Her pale hand came away from the linen, reaching for him.

Quinton took her hand, held it. A great pity for her began to well up inside him and he struggled to keep it at bay; already she had drawn too many emotions out of him. He was, he reflected, as enmeshed with Helene Haymes as he was with Justine. She pulled her hand from his, as if aware of his discomfort. "Are you sure you wouldn't like me to call Maria?" he asked, and realized there was a quaver to his voice.

"No. She'll only give me more medicine," Helene answered. "I'm kept drugged enough as it is. I'd rather face the pain than be constantly in a netherworld of semiconsciousness."

"But surely . . . ''

"There," the old woman said with cheerfulness he knew was faked, "it's gone. A moment or two of pain is preferable to hours of drug-induced sleep. But I am weary, Quinton. If there's nothing more, I'll say good-bye until youu return from New York."

"Yes, certainly." Quinton rose to leave.

"You're a good man, Quinton Armstrong," Helene said. "Should Justine ever conquer her asexuality, you're the sort of man I hope she finds."

Quinton's immediate thought was that she was probing, had heard something from Maria or Betty Sue and

was leading up to questioning him about his relationship with her daughter. He felt his mouth go dry; when
he swallowed his throat was constricted. He recalled
Justine's warning: *if she knows about us she'll do
anything to destroy what we have*. Still, as he stood
looking down at her silhouette on the bed he had to fight
his compulsion to admit his love for Justine regardless
of the consequences. He was certain Justine was wrong
about how Helene would take the news. Wouldn't she,
after all, welcome information that dispelled her erro-
neous belief in her daughter's asexuality? He opened
his mouth to speak, but a lingering doubt kept the words
from coming out. "Now you're appealing to *my* vanity," he said with forced lightheartedness. "I know I'm
a good catch. Was, and still am." Joanna would certainly have challenged that statement even if it was
made in jest.

He was relieved when the old woman laughed softly.
"A safe journey, Quinton," she said. "I've grown
accustomed to you in the past few days. I shall miss our
times together."

"I only hope I return with good news for you," he
told her.

"Oh, you shall," she said with assurance. "We're a
good combination, the two of us. With my collection
and your expertise, our auction has to be successful."

Outside her room, Quinton moved slowly, thoughtfully to the landing. He gripped the banister and stood
staring down at the funnel effect of the entryway far
below. It had struck him like a revelation when he had
been about to confess his love for Justine to Helene that
it had not only been the doubt of the old woman's
reception of the news that had kept him mute. He had
also not wanted to shatter the romance's aura of the
forbidden. That, he had realized, had somehow, mys-

teriously, made it all the more beguiling and exciting.

"Quinton," he whispered, "you're discovering things about yourself you never suspected existed."

His vision focused on Maria who had appeared in the entryway and was staring up at him.

"Somethin' wrong, Mr. Armstrong?" the house-keeper called, her voice filled with anxiety.

"No, nothing wrong, Maria," he called down to her, adding quietly to himself, "At least, I don't think there is . . ."

As previously arranged with Justine, Quinton took a taxi to the ocean side of the island; a pass to enter the navy base had been left with him at the guard house. The sailor, a young man with close-cropped blond hair and a Cary Grant dimple in the middle of his chin, directed him to the navy beach.

Justine was already there—alone. She was stretched out on the narrow strip of sand on a multi-colored beach towel; she was on her stomach, head face down in the crooks of her arms. She did not stir as he approached and he assumed she was sleeping. He sat down beside her and removed his shoes and shirt, rising to step out of his trousers. He hadn't thought to bring his own towel and had to settle himself on the sand. The sun was hot; he immediately felt it on his skin, rekindling the pain from the sunburn he had received the day they had gone boating. He looked to her beach bag, wondering if she had brought suntan lotion; her unoiled back told him she had not. She was so darkly tanned she had no need for oils and lotions. Waiting for her to awaken, he let his gaze travel along the beach. It was man-made, but was, he determined, the best stretch of beach on the island; leave it to the navy to supply adequate beaches for the officers and their families. Resting on his elbows, he let his head fall back and closed his eyes. The sun and the humidity caused the perspiration to bead over his body; he felt it run into his eyes and wiped it away, and in so doing transferred the sand from his hands to his face. "Damn," he swore. He had never been a beach lover. He rose, moved to the water's edge and waded in, scooping water onto his face to wash away the sand. The water felt refreshing; he glanced back at Justine, saw she had not moved, and then he dove beneath the surface.

Justine was sitting up when when next he glanced in her direction. She waved and blew him a kiss.

"Come in," he called. "The water's beautiful."

She rose and came to the line of the surf. The straps of her halter were unfastened, dangling; just above the strip of green fabric he could see the upper crescents of her nipples. Instead of stepping into the water, she sat down cross-legged, watching him. Even from his distance he could discern the troubled expression on her face.

Quinton came out of the water and sat down beside her. "What is it, Justine?" he asked. "To use a cliché, you look as if you'd lost your best friend."

Justine fixed him with her green eyes. "I'm losing you," she said so softly he almost missed her words. She gave him a perplexed smile. "Silly, isn't it? You're only going to be gone a few days and I feel as if I'm losing you forever."

Quinton reached for her, held her, feeling her body respond to the sudden coldness of the water still clinging to him. "Only a few days," he repeated. But he felt it, too, that sense of losing her if he went away, of her not waiting until he returned, of things somehow being different between them; it had happened so quickly that their relationship had a sense of unreality. "I'll call you every day,'' he promised. ''Every night, too.''

Justine nestled against him. ''I'm a possessive lover,'' she said. ''I always knew I would be when I found a man I loved.'' Leaning her head against his right shoulder, she brought up her hand and gently brushed her fingertips over the flesh of his chest, tracing the outlines of his nipples, then moving lower over the muscles of his abdomen.

Quinton's response was waves of electric-like current surging to his chest and groin. God, how easily she aroused him! He felt himself straining against the elastic of his swim trunks, felt her fingers slipping beneath the waistband. She pushed him to his back, leaning over him on her elbow, her faced pressed so close to his he could feel her breath on his cheek.

''Possessive and demanding,'' she murmured, and her fingers found what they sought.

''Not here, Justine!'' he said in a smothered cry. He opened his eyes and stared up at her, at her sullen expression. ''I'm sorry,'' he said, ''but someone might come along.'' Lightly, he added, ''Good God, you might change me from the staid individual I was, but you're not going to make an exhibitionist of me.'' He managed a laugh.

Justine smiled sardonically. ''But you do want me, don't you, Quinton? Even here? If you had a capricious nature, you'd take me whether someone saw or not?''

''Words are unnecessary. My body's answering your question.'' He tugged at the constricting fabric of his swim trunks, gently pushing her hand away, and sat up.

''Will you always want me as much as you do now?''

''I've no doubt about it,'' he answered. ''But apparently you do.''

''Perhaps I'm insecure. It happened so quickly between us. Sometimes I still can't believe it. I tell myself it's just one of those resort affairs, for you. When you get back to New York you'll think the whole thing foolish, or you'll blame it on the exotic setting and tropical climate.'' She brought her halter straps behind her neck and tied them as she spoke. "You'll get involved in your preparations for the auction and forget about me.''

His voice was firm: "No chance of that. Ever. Nothing like you has ever happened to me, Justine. I admit it baffles me that . . . that I've found you and you feel the same. I never expected to live a storybook romance, but that's exactly what it is with you. How could I forget that or you for a single moment?''

Something sparked behind her green eyes; she appeared satisfied, reassured. Still, she asked, "Then you're as much under my spell as I am under yours?''

"Totally under your spell,'' Quinton answered, and the truth of it struck him with an impact that caused him to avert his gaze from her probing stare; an uneasiness nagged at him ever so gently.

Justine placed her fingers beneath his chin and raised his head so that their eyes met once again. "I've always heard it said that in every relationship one person loved more than the other. Perhaps that won't be so for us, Quinton. Perhaps we'll be unique.''

Quinton then had the impression she was teasing him; his uneasiness increased; he wanted to cry that their relationship was no teasing matter, nothing to be discussed lightly. But it suddenly occurred to him that she had assumed the resonance of teasing to keep their last hour alone less serious. He shed his concern and assumed a parallel attitude. His gaze was caught by something in her dark hair. "Here, what's this?'' He plucked away a blond strand, turning it between his fingers as he showed it to her. "No, it's grey. Well, well, you're cheating on me already, and with an older man."

A grave expression flickered across her face, and then quickly vanished. Smiling, she said, "I see you're the suspicious type. I'll have to watch myself. My appraiser is also an amateur detective." She laughed, leaped to her feet and dashed into the water until it reached her knees. "But this time you haven't caught me," she laughed over her shoulder. "I used Aunt Helene's hairbrush this morning. The grey hair is hers."

"A likely story," Quinton teased, rising to follow her into the water.

"Likely, and true. I have to do something while she's lecturing me." She scooped the cool water onto her arms and thighs. "I use her brush because it irritates her. When she's particularly cranky I even count the strokes aloud." She splashed water in his direction. "Am I found guilty or innocent?"

"The detective finds you innocent," Quinton said. "The appraiser finds you lovely." He reached for her, but before his hands made contact she dove beneath the surface and swam away from him.

"I won't go with you to the airport," Justine told Quinton. "I loathe good-byes. Saying good-bye to you, even temporarily, is already painful enough." She tilted her head to receive his kiss, clinging to him long after their lips parted. She pulled away, turning to snatch her beach bag and towel from the sand. "Hurry back, Quinton," she said. "My days and nights are going to be agony without you."

"You'll be too busy to even miss me," Quinton told her. "That is, if you see to all the instructions I've left you." He took her towel from her, shook out the sand, and folded it to fit into her beach bag. "I've made sure you'll be occupied."

A spark of defiance flashed behind Justine's eyes. "I'll do all I'm expected to do, but not for her. For you." She took the towel from him and stuffed it into her bag. "Hire a staff, see to the installation of telephones, have the ballroom rearranged into office cubicles, establish myself as liaison with the Chamber of Commerce, so on and so on. She's told me a hundred times what's expected of me, Quinton. If it wasn't for you, I'd tell her what she could do with her auction." Her expression softened. "But there is you, darling. I'll do whatever I can to help it run smoothly for you."

Quinton's brow furrowed. "I wish you didn't hate her so," he said quietly.

Justine gave him a look that bordered on being savage.

"All right," he placated. "We won't discuss it now. But promise me, Justine, that while I'm away you'll attempt to consider Helene objectively and not with the hatred instilled in you by her . . . by your father."

"I promise nothing other than to miss you, darling," she said.

"And I you," Quinton assured her. He would have pursued the topic of Helene, but Justine came back against him for a parting kiss. He held her, wishing he could cancel his flight for a later one, knowing he couldn't because the airline had been heavily booked when he had made his original reservations.

"You must go now," Justine said, "or you'll miss your plane. Good-bye, darling." She kissed him again, lightly on the cheek. Then, she turned and went without hurry towards the building where she had left her bicycle. She waved without turning as she pedaled away, disappearing between abandoned navy buildings.

Quinton, depressed, returned to *The Pier House* packed his suitcase and took a taxi to the airport.

An hour later his plane was climbing through billowing white clouds. When the plane broke out of the clouds into the sunlight, the keys below were mere dots of green strung together like a necklace by bridges and framed by white surf against a blue, blue sea.

Ahead, New York waited, days of hard work, a confrontation, a final one, with Joanna—and then, gratefully, his return to Justine. He missed her already, missed her desperately, evidence of how completely he was, in her words, under her spell.

PART II

Chapter Twelve

Quinton bolted upright in bed.

A dim light glowed behind the slats of the Venetian blinds; the radiator was hissing—despite its clamoring, the room was cold. Outside in the street a car horn honked, sounding curiously deadened. An alarm clock buzzed in the apartment next door. It was six a.m. by his clock, his own alarm had been set for quarter to eight.

Quinton continued to sit, unmoving, trying to recall the dream that had awakened him so abruptly. Dreams, he thought, are warnings from the subconscious; yet, this dream, this warning evaded recollection. He slipped his feet over the side of the bed and onto the cold floor, remembering the warmth of Key West he had left behind the day before. He moved to the window, parted the blinds, and looked out. Four floors below exclusive Gramercy Park was blanketed by freshly fallen snow, the naked tree limbs bending beneath their burden. The benches and pathways, available only to those park residents with keys, were mere mounds and valleys of whiteness; the surrounding sidewalks had not yet been marred by footprints. A picture postcard wonderland, he thought, and shuddered from the cold. By eight o'clock, the cars and pedestrians would have turned the fresh snow to slush;

the beauty would be gone and the snow would only be an inconvenience.

He came away from the window, slipped into his terry cloth robe and bedroom slippers, and went to the kitchen to plug in the coffeepot. Then he shaved and showered. Drying himself, he confronted his image in the vanity mirror. His face was deeply tanned, emphasizing the blueness of his eyes. He leaned closer to the mirror, examining himself, feeling he had changed but unable to detect that change visibly.

When he came out of the bathroom the aroma of coffee permeated the apartment. He added powdered milk and a teaspoon of sugar in his one and only coffee mug and carried the coffee into the living room. Very little mail had accumulated during his absence, evidence of the singular life he had lived since moving away from Joanna: utility bills, a bank statement with a pathetically low balance, an announcement of an upcoming auction at Parke Bernet—and lastly, a notice from his attorney reminding him of a meeting with Joanna at her attorney's offices on Park Avenue at noon on the twentieth. The twentieth—that was today; fitting, he thought, *High Noon,* a battle to the death, only on fashionable Park Avenue instead of some western town; the weapons—divorce legalities instead of trusty six-shooters. He put the reminder of the meeting aside and lit his first cigarette of the day. As he sat smoking, the quietness of the apartment seemed to close in on him; in Key West he had always awakened to the chirping of birds and had not really noticed the silence of his New York existence until now. He thought of Justine and felt remarkably lonely. Rising, he switched on the radio and went into the kitchen for more coffee.

'' . . . *on this snowy morning. Subway crime has doubled in the last quarter of the year. A committee of concerned citizens presented a petition to the mayor yesterday demanding more police protection. An apartment house fire in the Bronx left sixty homeless. Arson is suspected. A seventy-year-old woman was found frozen to death last night in her East Village apartment. Authorities are investigating the building's failure to supply adequate heat to its . . ."*

Quinton snapped off the radio on his return to the living room. Better to feel lonely than depressed by the news. He paced back into the bedroom, set his coffee on the bureau and began unpacking, which he had been too tired to do last night. He cautiously unwrapped the Holbein miniature of Anne of Cleves that Helene Haymes had given him to show her generosity. He carried the miniature back into the living room, adding it to the collection in his curio cabinet. His gaze fell on the *biscuit de Sèvres* figurine he had purchased from Parke Bernet. "You started the whole thing, you little devil," he said aloud. Now, in examining the figurine, he found it paled in comparison to those he had viewed in Helene's collection. He wondered why he had wanted to own it so badly, badly enough to have risked his integrity by accepting the assignment from Hal Crimmons' magazine, and then it occurred to him that the *biscuit de Sèvre* had been a mere part of a fatalistic plan to bring him and Justine together. While he considered this, the telephone began to ring. He carefully closed the curio cabinet and returned to the bedroom to answer.

"Quinton, this is Joanna. Where the hell have you been? I've been calling for days."

"Good morning, Joanna."

"That partner of yours acted as if your whereabouts were a state secret. All he'd tell me is that you were away. Away where, Quinton?"

"Good morning, Joanna," he repeated pointedly.

"Oh, good morning, Quinton," she conceded with irritation.

"How are you?"

"Do you really care?"

"If I didn't, I wouldn't ask," he answered.

"If you cared you wouldn't have vanished without a word to me."

"I didn't think my whereabouts would be of interest to you. We're separated, you remember that, don't you? That should be even more firmly established this afternoon in your attorney's office."

"Then you are aware of the meeting," she said, sighing. "I wasn't certain. You can be so vague."

"Yes, so you've told me. Often. Vague and staid and boring. Old before my time. Sensitive to antiquities and art, but not to people. Do I have the routine right?"

"Don't mock me, please, Quinton." There was an unusual tone of pleading in her voice. "This isn't easy for me either, you know."

"I'm sorry," he said, and meant it. He could imagine her sitting at her Louis XVI *bona du jour*, the desk he had bought for her during one of his appraisals, a fragile, feminine, hard-carved piece of furniture with ormolu that he had felt so fitted her, as it had once fitted a lady of the French court.

"I keep asking myself if I'm doing the right thing by divorcing you."

After a long moment, Quinton said, "I think you are, Joanna. For both of us." He could sense her shocked reaction as clearly as if she had verbalized it.

"Are you going to explain that statement?" she demanded coolly.

"No, I think not," he told her. "There's no point to explaining."

"Then, I guess there's nothing else to say," she said awkwardly. "I'll meet you at my attorney's at noon."

"Yes, high noon," he said. "Good-bye, Joanna."

After he hung up, he felt curiously empty. Even when he forced his thoughts back to Justine he could not shed the disturbing mood that had descended on him with Joanna's phone call.

He dressed hurriedly and, to escape the loneliness of his apartment, left early for the office. Taxis were naturally unavailable because of the snowstorm; he trudged around Gramercy Park and headed up Park Avenue, his body bent into the chill wind; cursing, he wished himself back in Key West, with Justine, on the deserted navy beach. He forgot the cold as he fantasized making love to her, as she had wanted, on the warm sand, the hot tropical sun beating down on their entwined bodies.

Joanna Armstrong, née Freytag, as it stated on the document handed to Quinton, was a woman of grace and dignity. The daughter of a Connecticicut industrialist who traced his ancestry back to the *Mayflower* and a mother whose father and grandfather had served honorably in the United States Senate, Joanna dressed and conducted herself with breeding. At thirty-seven, two years older than Quinton, her face showed promise of aging with equal refinement. Her forehead was too high, emphasized by the severe style of her auburn hair, and her hazel eyes set too far apart. Her upper lip was too thin for her liking and the high points of her cheekbones were not quite balanced, a hereditary curse that caused her to keep her head slightly tilted to one side because she felt it made the imbalance less noticeable. Viewed as a whole her face was attractive, even beautiful, but she saw only its faults. She did grant herself the shapeliness of her body—her dimensions had not changed since she had been nineteen and won a college beauty contest. She attributed retention of her shape to a sensible diet, exercise, and her refusal to bear children. Quinton had often thought it her fear of pregnancy that had made her so sexually paranoid.

Joanna now sat iin the straight-backed chair beside her attorney's desk, her shapely legs crossed, the toe of her Gucci shoe soundlessly tapping the air. She had dressed somberly in a two-piece navy woolen suit. She wore no jewelry, but the indentation of her ring finger gave evidence of recent removal of her wedding band. Her sable coat, a gift from her parents on her thirtieth birthday, lay flung over the arm of a nearby leather sofa. The Gucci handbag matching her shoes was oversized and stuffed to capacity; she had set it beside her chair and unknowingly it had tipped, spilling a clutter of papers onto the brown and black tweed carpet. Quinton could read the bold print on one paper—SAVE THE WHALES—and he smiled sadly to himself; Joanna and her causes, her good intentions, her involvements, her substitutes for facing herself. It occurred to him that perhaps the most important decision she had made with regard to herself personally was to divorce him, he looked at her more closely, trying to view her as an outsider, as one who did not know why she had dressed so severely. However, he could not step outside himself and consider her as a stranger. To him, she had dressed severely to appear impregnable, only she had failed and looked even more vulnerable than she was. He had to fight down a sense of guilt, as if they were here because of him, not her. But it is me, he thought, and the guilt flooded over him. Justine awakened in me what Joanna could not. He averted his gaze when Joanna lifted her hazel eyes to meet his.

"Now there's the question of the car," Matt Foreman broke in. Matt, her attorney, ran a stubby index finger down a list of their assets. "Ah, a Mercedes, 280D. 1979 model. My client will, of course, demand clear title to the Mercedes." The attorney glanced not at Quinton whom he knew socially, but at Quinton's attorney, Tom Korman. His wrinkled brow furrowed as he prepared himself for a challenge.

"My friend at Chase Manhattan holds the title," Quinton said quietly. "An outstanding balance, if memory serves me correctly, of seven thousand two hundred dollars." He hadn't wanted the expensive car, Joanna had; driving to Connecticut to visit her parents and friends in an ancient Buick had been embarrassing to her.

"The Mercedes should be sold and the proceeds divided equally," Tom Korman countered.

"Nonsense! My client needs transportation!"

"My client is presently resorting to taxis, buses and walking," Quinton's attorney announced hotly. "If the Mercedes isn't to be sold, he should retain possession. It's necessary to his business."

Matt Foreman, a friend of Joanna's family since they were children together, glanced at his client for instructions; she had apparently not made her wishes concerning the Mercedes known to him.

Joanna stared thoughtfully into space, and said nothing; only Quinton was aware of her discomfort, of the indignities she was feeling.

"Mr. Armstrong," Matt Foreman began, taking a stand on his own, "does his appraising almost exclusively in Manhattan. He, therefore, for all legal purposes, lives and works within, the same borough of New York; within, as you put it, taxi, bus and walking distances. My client on the other hand lives in Scarsdale where public transportation is . . ."

"Your information about my client is incorrect," Korman interrupted. "Mr. Armstrong is one of the most respected appraisers of antiquities in the country and in Europe. He travels extensively and requires the Mercedes. He's now involved in an important appraisal in Key West, Florida, and is considering driving the Mercedes to . . . ''

"Let Joanna have the Mercedes," Quinton said with quiet authority. "I won't be needing it. A bicycle will suffice."

Korman's face paled. "Mr. Armstrong, I warned you. If you want to make concessions . . . ''

"Yes, I remember the warning," Quinton said. "Call a conference in an outer room. Don't show any weakness in the face of opposition. No emotional displays. Keep everything cool, calculating and businesslike." He turned to Joanna. "I suppose you were given the same advice?"

She nodded, the hint of a smile playing about her mouth.

"It's all nonsense," Quinton said, speaking to her and ignoring both attorneys. "We could settle this between us, quietly. No arguments, or at least no serious ones. After all, it isn't as if there are children to involve us in a custody battle—" Joanna flinched at that—"and what we own, aside from my personal collections, could be divided by us to our mutual satisfaction. We could finish the entire matter over lunch and that would be the end of it."

"I'm afraid it isn't done that way," Matt Foreman said stiffly.

"Definitely not," Korman agreed.

"But it could be," Quinton said, not taking his eyes from Joanna. "It isn't as if we're parting enemies. We're simply two people who found our marriage incompatible. It's the marriage we want to destroy, not each other."

"Mr. Armstrong, I must insist . . . ''

Joanna silenced Matt Foreman with a gesture of her hand. She sat, the three of them staring at her, for several silent moments, her eyes boring into Quinton as indiscernible thoughts flashed through her mind. Her Gucci-shoed toe ceased movement, her back straightened. Then, gradually, a smile spread across her face. She bent, scooped the spilled papers back into her purse, rose and retrieved her sable coat, flinging it around her shoulders. "Where would you like to lunch?" she asked, and swept across the office and out the door.

"We'll contact you later, gentlemen," Quinton said, and followed. When he closed the door he heard Joanna laugh for the first time in a very long while.

"That's the first time I've known you to create a ripple, to make a stand against convention," she said as they waited for the elevator. "You might have given poor Matt a coronary." She stared at him through thought-slitted eyes. "There's something else about you, too," she mused. "Something different. I don't know quite what. Tell me, Quinton, what are you up to?" When he didn't answer, she sighed and said, "An exciting new collection to appraise, I suppose. That's the only thing I've ever known to stimulate you."

"Actually, an exciting new collection is only part of it," Quinton said. He took her arm and they stepped into the crowded elevator, Quinton feeling self-satisfaction in knowing he had aroused her interest and curiosity to the point where she was having difficulty containing her questions. He thought: *After all, my dear Joanna, you're not the only one embarking on a new life.* He pretended to be unaware of her sideways glances. *Wouldn't the new Quinton Armstrong astound her! It certainly did him!* "How about a steak?" he asked casually.

"But you never liked steak for lunch."

"I do now. I'm ravenous."

"Whatever," she said, trying to sound bored. "It's the settlement that interests me, not your sudden appetite." She pulled her arms into her sable coat as the elevator opened onto the chilled lobby. "It's going to be a cold winter," she said, shuddering.

"Not for me." He said nothing more.

"And what does that mean?" she demanded. "Why are you suddenly trying to be so mysterious?"

"I'll explain over lunch."

"Damn you," she whispered. "I think this was a mistake." She glanced at him curiously. "You were always so predictable, before. Now I don't know what you're thinking, what you're feeling."

"I believe," Quinton said, "that was one of your chief complaints, that I was too predictable, that there were no longer any surprises between us." He pushed open the doors to the street and stood back for her to exit.

"Damn you," she said again.

The downtown restaurant was crowded, but the maitre d' managed to get them a corner table in the front. "Two dry martinis," Joanna told the waiter.

"No, wait. A lime daiquiri," Quinton stopped the waiter. "I've developed a taste for them," he told Joanna. "Now, about the Mercedes and . . ."

"Forget the settlement for a moment," Joanna said peevishly. "Quinton, what's going on with you? And don't say nothing. I know you. Or at least I thought I did. But there's something . . . something different. You even look different. I can't say how, but you do. Younger, I think. More purposeful. You're also acting younger. Almost, God forbid, like a young man who'd been smitten.'' She glanced through the plate glass window at the snow swirling in the street. ''And it isn't even spring,'' she said, and laughed because she had used the familiar lyrics of the song in a musical delivery.

Quinton glanced up from the table. ''You're different, too, Joanna,'' he said quietly. ''I haven't heard you laugh in a long while.''

Her smile faded. ''I haven't been happy for a long while, Quinton.''

''I'm sorry.''

''No, I didn't say that to make you feel guilty. My unhappiness wasn't your fault, not entirely. I've come to see that since you moved out.'' She smiled again, but without humor in her hazel eyes. ''As the old cliché goes, I couldn't live with you, but I'm having difficulty adjusting to living without you.''

''I'm sorry,'' Quinton said again.

''Will you stop saying that?'' she said irritably. ''The house seems empty without . . . '' She broke off as the waiter returned with their drinks. When he had set down their drinks and departed, she absently fingered the stem of her martini glass, waiting, it seemed, for Quinton to speak. When he did not but just sat staring at her, she said, ''You do understand that because I'm divorcing you doesn't mean I've stopped loving you? It's just . . . well, just that our entire relationship had become so hopeless. I'd felt the futility of it for a long while.''

''I didn't realize that until later,'' he confessed. ''I guess, Joanna, we never really communicated with one another.''

''You were too busy with your precious antiquities.''

''And you with your committees and causes.''

"They didn't mean anything to me, Quinton. They were a substitute."

Surprised, Quinton asked, "For what?"

"For the life that was passing me by. I was doing nothing except growing older as I went from one meaningless day to the next."

"I admit now to having been a lousy husband if that's any consolation."

"No more than I was a lousy wife," Joanna told him. "The problem, Quinton, is that we never really shared anything. Not even in the bed . . . well, I don't want to go into that."

Quinton sipped his lime daiquiri and curiously found the taste not to his liking; so unlike when he had had the drink with Justine. Still, the taste did bring memories to mind that he forced away for another time. It seemed unjust to think of Justine when he was supposed to be listening to Joanna. "Perhaps," he said, "we should go into our physical relationship."

"No!" Realizing she had raised her voice, Joanna glanced nervously at the surrounding tables, relaxing when she saw none of the lunch crowd was paying the slightest attention to them.

"We're both starting new lives," Quinton said. "I only thought it would help us by understanding where we had failed one another."

"Where I failed you," Joanna snapped. "That's what you really mean." Slightly above a whisper, she said, "Do you think I'm unaware of the frustration I must have caused you? The frustrations I suffered?"

"I never complained."

"Not verbally," she retorted. "I'm certain you told yourself you were above complaining, above pleading with your own wife for sexual fulfillment. If you had only been more forceful."

"Am I to understand you wanted me to rape you?"

"Don't be ridiculous!" she cried; still, he could see by the expression in her eyes the thought had occurred to her as a possible solution to their—her—problem. "Those clumsy routines of yours when you wanted sex. Your leg suddenly touching mine with *accidental* purpose, your hand creeping slowly towards me under the sheets, your sighs, the way you'd act—like the thought of sex had just occurred to you upon contact with my body. You never could just come straight out and say, 'Let's fuck!'"

"Joanna!" Now it was Quinton's turn to glance at the neighboring tables, his tanned face coloring with embarrassment. Then he burst into laughter. He turned back to Joanna. "Well, that was a shocker." He'd never known her to use words stronger than *damn*.

His laughter was contagious; Joanna smiled despite herself.

"What are we doing?" she said. "It really doesn't matter, the past. It's senseless to go over it now."

"Yes, senseless," he agreed. He pushed the unfinished daiquiri away.

"Would you like that martini now?" she asked pointedly.

"I don't need it, not if we're going to stop taking bites out of one another."

"A truce, then," she said. "Seriously, I hope we can become friends, Quinton. I do appreciate your fine qualities. Yes, I grant you many fine qualities. You're loyal, dependable and . . ."

"A regular boy scout," he finished without sarcasm.

Joanna's eyebrows lifted as she determined whether he intended to continue the battle.

"Friends," he said, and extended his hand across the expanse of the table.

Uncertain, she touched his hand gently, pulling it away before he could clasp it. She motioned to the waiter for a second martini, something she customarily never did. "All right," she said, fixing Quinton with a steady gaze, "tell me what you've been doing. Where did you get the tan?"

"Key West."

"Oh, vacationing? I didn't think your finances allowed for . . ."

"Working," he interrupted.

"You've obviously been combining work with pleasure," she said. "That's what's different about you, you're relaxed." She smiled. "That's amusing."

"What?"

"In all the years we were married I don't remember seeing you so relaxed. Or so self-assured. Not since you stopped writing that novel of yours."

"I thought you'd forgotten about the novel."

"No."

"You never mentioned it," he said. "Only once, in the beginning."

"I guess I was jealous," she admitted. "You had a way of expressing yourself. I didn't."

"You wrote poetry."

"Dreadful romantic stuff that would have embarrassed a school girl in love. But we're getting back to the past again. What possible work could you be doing in Key West?"

"You make it sound like Key West is a depressed area," he observed.

"I wouldn't think anyone on the island possessed an antique collection of the stature you appraise," she said as the waiter set her second martini in front of her.

"I didn't know you'd ever been there."

"When I was a young girl my father used to take my

mother and me there during the winters. My father's a reverse snob. All our friends went to Miami, so he refused to go there. I hated Key West.''

"Why?" Quinton asked, genuinely interested.

"I could never make friends there. I remember being so lonely, so anxious to get back to Connecticut. Besides, I hate tropical climates. I don't know why, reading all those Somerset Maugham short stories, I suppose, but I always equate tropical climates with decadence. Absurd, isn't it? There must be another reason, some impression I had as a young girl, but I don't remember it.'' She sipped her martini, staring at him over the rim of the glass. "Now suppose you tell me why you like Key West?"

"I simply find the island fascinating," he answered.

"The island, or someone you met on the island?"

"Have you ever heard of Helene Haymes?" he asked.

"Wasn't she an actress or . . . oh, no, I remember her. Well, not really remember her. Most of what I know about her I researched at the local library.''

"Researched Helene Haymes?" he asked incredulously. "Why?"

"Because of something I overheard once between my father and a professor friend of his,'' Joanna explained. "It was one of the first adult parties of my parents' that I was allowed to attend. It was when all the furor over Tokyo Rose surfaced long after the war. My father's friend said Toyko Rose should be shot, living in America before and after the war and making all those broadcasts to injure our boys' morale. Then he said Helene Haymes should be shot also for consorting with Adolf Hitler. "A traitor and a common whore,' he said. It impressed me, all that talk about women being traitors and whores—it was the first time I'd ever heard that word used in my company. I remember my father laughed and told the professor there was certainly nothing common about the Haymes woman, that she was indisputably one of the most beautiful women in the world. The next day I went to the library and read every periodical I could find on both Tokyo Rose and Helene Haymes. Don't tell me that's who your client is, Helene Haymes? I remember she was supposed to be a fanatical collector of antiquities."

Quinton nodded. "One and the same," he said.

Joanna considered him thoughtfully for a moment before saying, "That's interesting, Quinton, but there's more, isn't there? It took more than an old woman with a past to make a noticeable difference in you."

Quinton considered how much he should confess.

Joanna suddenly set her martini down with such force the liquor splashed onto the tablecloth. "You're having an affair, aren't you? With some woman you met in Key West?" The tremor in her voice displayed both incredulity and undertones of jealousy.

Quinton knew that lying to her would be pointless. He merely nodded in affirmation.

Joanna paled. "Good God, I don't believe it," she gasped. "You! An affair! So soon!" She lifted her glass and drained the contents. "You bastard!"

"I don't understand why you're reacting this way," he said. "We're separated, divorcing. You said we both had new lives ahead of us. Really, Joanna. There's no call for you to act the betrayed wife."

Joanna's breath was coming in gasps, her well-rounded breasts heaving beneath her jacket. Her hazel eyes were blazing. One hand rose to her neck, her habit being to toy absently with her necklace whenever she was upset. Her hand fell into her lap when she realized she had worn no jewelry. "Bastard," she repeated in a near-whisper.

Quinton, despite himself, felt a rush of guilt. He saw her eyes filling and knew how openly she gave into her emotions once her tears came. "I suggest you get a hold on yourself," he told her. "I'm sorry. If I'd known how you'd have taken this, I wouldn't . . . "

"I won't make a scene," she said with conviction, and visibly shook herself, straightening her back and putting her other hand in her lap. She lowered her head and stared down at the tabletop as if drawing strength from the checkered blue and white design. "You're right, of course," she said. "I shouldn't feel like a betrayed wife. But the sad truth is I do. Stupid isn't it? Tell me about her, this woman who's replaced me already."

"I don't think we should discuss her," Quinton said. "You were right. This lunch was a mistake. We should have concluded the settlement as our attorneys wanted. Would you prefer to leave?"

"No. I'll be fine in a moment. Is this new woman in your life related to Helene Haymes?"

"Joanna, I don't think . . . All right, yes, she's her dau . . . her niece. Now, let's not pursue it any further."

"Is she as beautiful as the legendary Haymes woman?"

"I'm not answering any more questions," Quinton said firmly. "I think we should leave. I have an appointment with Hal Crimmons at three and . . . "

"Give me a few minutes," Joanna demanded angrily. "I'd like enough time to digest this so I can stand up and walk out of here with my dignity."

Anger shot through Quinton like a sudden charge of electric current. "For God's sake, Joanna! *You* threw me out! *You're* the one who wanted the divorce, remember? Now, because I've met someone else, someone who's important to me, you're suddenly a betrayed, injured wife and accusing me of robbing you of your dignity! This is incredible, simply incredible!" He raised his hands and dropped them back into his lap in a gesture of disbelief.

"You could have at least waited until . . ." She let the sentence trail off.

"Until what?" Quinton finished.

"Nothing," Joanna said sharply. "And lower your voice. People are beginning to stare."

"I'll damn well shout if I want to! Until what, Joanna? I could have at least waited until what?"

Joanna fumbled to pull her sable coat over her shoulders. She moved to get up, but Quinton reached a restraining hand across the table and grabbed her wrist.

"Until you had established your new life, that's the crux of what you were going to say, isn't it, Joanna?"

Joanna, glaring at him, tried to pull her wrist free. "Let me go, damn you!"

But Quinton's grasp remained firm. "You thought I'd retreat entirely into my world of antiquities, didn't you? You find it inconceivable that I could have a life without you. Christ! I haven't robbed you of your dignity, Joanna. You don't even feel betrayed or jealous because I'm having an affair. No, that's not it at all. It's that I'm functioning without you, and you thought that impossible. You looked on me as a puppet and yourself the puppeteer."

"You're out of your mind," Joanna accused bitterly.

"Why didn't I see it this clearly before?" Quinton went on. "It's the image of yourself I've managed to offend. All these years I've let you manipulate me, and so you thought of me as powerless to lead my own life without you. You've thought of yourself as almost omnipotent in comparison.'' He released her wrist, slumped back in his chair, and fixed Joanna with an odd, distant stare. ''You always had the power to make me feel guilty,'' he said. ''You could put me on the defensive with only a hurt look, and that was your greatest source of power over me. A moment ago my misdirected guilt cast a shadow over my feelings toward Justine Haymes.'' He sighed. ''That'll never happen again,'' he vowed.

Joanna had risen and stood staring down at him, her face frozen in a mask of emotions she could not express.

''Justine has brought out a better side of me,'' Quinton told her. ''She doesn't manipulate me. She makes me feel like a man instead of a puppet.''

Joanna stiffened. ''I only hope you haven't merely changed puppeteers,'' she said tersely, and walked out of the restaurant without a backward glance.

Quinton reached for her unfinished martini and drained the contents. The liquor burned his throat. Outside, the snow was getting heavier, pedestrians bending into the wind. A sudden longing to return to Key West and Justine swept over Quinton. He signaled the waiter for the check.

Chapter Thirteen

Hal Crimmons ran a hand absently through his grey, unruly hair, brushing it back from his eyes, eyes that he did not take from the pages on the table before him. Since beginning Quinton's article on Helene Haymes, the magazine writer had ignored his Scotch and water; the ice had melted and turned the drink to colored water. Unlike Hal, Quinton thought. Nothing stood between the writer and his liquor. Was that a good sign? Perhaps Hal's intense attention to the article could be attributed to his horror at the writing; perhaps he was formulating some polite words to disguise its poor merit. They were, after all, friends, drinking buddies—you didn't tell a friend his literary efforts were crap.

Quinton leaned back in his chair, struggling with his nervousness. It wasn't until he had given Hal the article that his doubts had surfaced. Why was it he was so self-assured when it came to appraising antiquities, but when it came to his writing . . . It had been the same with his novel. He had written every night; then, in the morning when he had reread his work, he had doubted its value. That inability to appraise his writing objectively—that and Joanna's lack of encouragement —were why his unfinished novel now gathered dust, the pages yellowing, in some forgotten cardboard carton.

Moriarty's was quiet; it was the mid-point between lunch and dinner. Their waiter lounged against a near wall, giving them glances between staring through the window at the heavy snowfall. Quinton caught his attention and signaled for fresh drinks.

Hal turned a page, not looking up, and Quinton watched him, his expression. He could discern nothing except the writer's intensity.

"Of course it needs editing," Quinton ventured. "I'm not a professional . . ."

Hal silenced him with a gesture of his hand.

What the hell did it matter anyway? Quinton asked himself. The agency employed free-lance writers and editors; it would be their task to turn out acceptable articles on Helene for the publicity and promotional campaign he planned.

To occupy himself while Hal finished the article, Quinton took his briefcase from the floor and removed one of Helene's scrapbooks. He scanned the pages with scant attention. *American Antique Collector Purchases Items Belonging To Marie Antoinette. At the Paris Auction House last night, Helene Haymes, an American, purchased several items authenticated as once belonging to Marie Antoinette. The French government is attempting to curtail auction of historic . . .* Quinton's eyes roamed to the facing page. The article was from *Yank* magazine and was titled *Heavenly Helene. Take your Betty Grable, keep your Rita Hayworth and your Lana Turner. If a pinup hangs on this soldier's locker, it's going to be of Helene Haymes. Her legs are better than Grable's. She looks more provocative in a negligee than Hayworth and fills out a sweater better than Turner. And she is American, too. Maybe not as American as Mom's apple pie,*

*but she's from H-O-M-E, as only the South can grow
them. She hails from Key West, Florida, and you can't
get any further south than that; just in the event you
G.I.s don't know your geography, Key West is the
southernmost city in the good old U.S. of A. Georgia
may be known for its peaches, but Key West will hereaf-
ter be known for its sophisticated beauties—all because
of Helene Haymes. And here's an astounding fact for
you—the most beautiful woman I've laid eyes on spent
the war years right here in Europe waiting for us, her
fellow Americans, to come and put an end to . . .*

"Damn good," Hal finally said. "I knew you had it
in you, old man." Hal collected the pages and pushed
them to one side of the table. His faded blue eyes fixed
on Quinton. "It's got flair," he said. "My publisher
got a bargain."

"You're not just being polite?" Quinton pressed,
sitting forward. "I mean, I can take criticism, Hal. You
don't have to flatter me for friendship's sake."

"Flattery's not my style," Hal assured him. "Hell,
Quinton. I'm leveling with you. It's damn good character piece. Granted, it needs a copy editor's attention,
you're a damn poor typist, but nothing major needs
changing in the guts of the piece. Damn good."

"It's important to me," Quinton said. "Not just
because I contracted to do it and like to do the best I can.
It's more than that." He pushed his empty glass away
to make room for the refill the waiter was setting before
him. "I'm considering getting back into my writing,
making another attempt."

The older man's bushy eyebrows rose expressively.
"Back to writing the great American novel, huh?" he
said, his voice tinged with sarcasm. "Well, I wish you
more luck than I had. As you know, I resigned from a
D.C. newspaper to write the great American novel
—which died on the reviewers' desks along with my

self-confidence and belief in the American dream.
After my novel bombed they didn't want me back on
the paper. No major newspaper wanted me. They
didn't want a loser. The American Way," he said with
a sigh. "But what the hell, old man, it might work out
differently for you. You don't have to put your career
on the line. If the novel bombs you can go on appraising
antiques and . . ."

"That's the point," Quinton interrupted, "I won't
be able to. Hal, I'm considering getting out of the
appraising business after Helene Haymes' auction."
He lowered his gaze, stared at the ice bobbing in his
drink. Quietly, he said, "There won't be much of a call
for antique appraisers in Key West." His eyes lifted to
judge Hal's reaction.

"Oh, oh! Don't tell me you've been bitten by the
tropical bug? Not the no-nonsense Quinton Armstrong of my acquaintance? Who'd have thought you
could be tempted by the beach bum—starving artist
life-style? You're joking, of course?" Hal sipped his
drink, his eyes studying the silent Quinton. "No, I see
you're not jokin," he said seriously. "Well, old man, I
guess we had best do some talking. Soul-searching has
never been my forte, but either me or some high-priced
analyst is going to have to talk you out of insanity."

"It's not a decision I made lightly," Quinton said.

"If I didn't know you better I'd say you're taking an
early step into the male-menopause-at-forty syndrome," Hal said, laughing to give the statement a less
serious edge. "Mid-life crisis and all that. You are
going through a divorce, old man, and that can be
rough. Then, hell—" he nodded towards the window
—"coming from sunshine, swaying palm trees and
pretty little numbers in bikinis into this can give anyone
Florida fever."

"I made the decision the night before I left Key

West," Quinton told him. "I don't know how to explain this, Hal, but . . . well, I feel as if I've undergone an important change. It's almost as if I'm a totally different man. As a different man, I'm forced to look at my life as I'd been living it."

"And you don't like what you see? Definitely a mid-life crisis, old man." He reached across the table and shoved Quinton's drink closer to his hand. "Get drunk, find yourself a professional woman, and keep busy until it passes, that's my advice. You're not the sort of man to drop out, Quinton."

Quinton scowled. "That's what I'd expect Joanna to say," he murmured. "'Staid, boring Quinton isn't the sort of man to drop out. He's as antiquated as the antiques he appraises.'" Without intending to, he had affected Joanna's manner of speaking; the mockery instantly made him feel guilty, disloyal. He gulped a swallow of Scotch and soda. "Sorry. I shouldn't have brought Joanna into it. It doesn't concern her, not really. I don't blame her. It's a just chance, fate. You believe in fate, Hal?"

"If I'm controlling mine," Hal mumbled. "You've met a woman, haven't you, old man?"

"Why do you say that?"

"Classic symptoms," Hal answered. "A beauty, no doubt? Younger than you? Makes you feel alive for the first time? Understands you unlike your wife ever did? Awakens your lagging sexuality?"

"Good God!" Quinton cried. "What are you? Psychic?"

"Just an observer of life, old man," Hal said faintly, pretending to transfer his interest to the snowy scene beyond the window. "We'll never get a taxi in this," he said, "so we might as well go on drinking. Waiter, another round."

"I've too much to do to let myself get drunk,"

Quinton said. "All right, Hal, give. Why did you peg it as a woman in my life?"

"Percentages," Hal said. "Let's leave it at that. Tell me more about Helene Haymes. I want details, more than you've put in your article. Has time and age been kind to her?"

"I can't really answer," Quinton said. "She exists in a world of semidarkness, so it's impossible to see her clearly. Her room, even the dining room when we had dinner together, is carefully lighted to . . . "

"Ah, vanity," Hal interrupted.

"No, I think not," Quinton said. "An illness has made her eyes extremely sensitive to light." He decided not to tell Hal about the old woman's terminal illness; Hal was a reporter, and even statements made off the record had a way of finding their way into print. "But even in the dim lighting, the woman's charisma is evident," he went on. "She must have been devastating when young."

Quinton's glance fell to the tabletop and open scrapbook. His voice faltered as for the first time he noticed the byline on the *Yank* magazine article. *Heavenly Helene by Sgt. Harold Crimmons.*

Hal's glance followed his. "What have you there?" He turned the scrapbook around. "Ah, the printed word always outlasts the author."

"I thought you'd never met Helene Haymes," Quinton challenged. "You told me she had you thrown out of her hotel room in Paris and you never "

"That's true. I never interviewed the lady. But the editor of *Yank* didn't know that. The quoted lines in the middle of the article were my own invention. Don't look so shocked, Quinton. I was a young reporter trying to impress the editor. What would she care? With all the bad press she was receiving, I was kind to her I thought she'd be grateful. I even had a copy of the issue delivered to her hotel with a note, but she never responded. Now, years later, I find out she kept the article. I'd be flattered if it didn't now seem like such childish reporting.'' He closed the scrapbook, thumping his fingers on the faded leather cover. ''I'll give you some advice. Never read your own work once it's been printed.'' He grinned ruefully.

''Are her expectations of an auction comparable to Rothschild's only an old woman's madness as you once thought?'' Hal then asked.

''There's nothing mad about her or her expectations,'' Quinton answered. ''I agreed to handle the auction for her. Perhaps there's a touch of madness in me. The assignment will be the most demanding of my career.'' He glanced at his wristwatch as the waiter returned with additional drinks. ''I'm going to have to decline another,'' he told Hal. ''I have to get back to the office before my partner leaves for the day.''

''Then drink it quickly,'' Hal said. ''I can't stand to see a man waste liquor.'' He lifted his glass in the gesture of a toast. ''Are you doubting your ability to pull off her auction? If so, don't. You're the best in the business. Or so I've heard.''

''And where would you hear that? From me?'' Quinton laughed. Hal Crimmons, like most of Quinton's friends, wouldn't know one antique period from another, an original from an early copy or a fake. ''I have a tendency to brag under the influence,'' he said. He took a sip of the Scotch and soda and decided he wanted no more; discreetly, he pushed the glass to one side. Getting his briefcase from the floor by his chair, he glanced at Hal and caught the reporter staring at him with a totally serious expression. ''What is it?'' he asked. ''Did I say something?''

"What? Oh, no. It's nothing."

"Well, in that case, I'd better hurry." He started to rise.

"You don't doubt your ability to carry the auction off, do you, Quinton?" Hal's faded blue eyes held an intense expression; his bushy eyebrows were drawn together thoughtfully. "I mean, it would be a shame to fail, this being your swan song, so to speak."

He's really concerned about me as a friend, as a person, Quinton reflected; he had never really thought of Hal Crimmons as more than a casual friend, a drinking and lunch companion when time and appointments allowed. He put the reporter's mind at ease by saying, "All I know, Hal, is if anyone can pull off an auction of this stature in a remote place like Key West, then no one has a better chance than yours truly." He smiled. "As you said, I'm the best in the business."

"Well, the best of luck to you, old man. I admire you. Really, I do. This auction is going to put you in an enviable position. You do realize that? If you pull it off, you're going to be in demand throughout this country and Europe. You'll be able to name your price." He sighed and shook his head slowly from side to side as if it was incomprehensible. "And you're going to bow out for the love of a woman, retire to an island, and make an attempt at writing the great American novel at a time when publishers only want commercial garbage. What about the woman in question? Does she know what you're planning?"

Quinton, staring down at the reporter, wished suddenly he had kept his plans to himself.

"No, I see she doesn't," Hal went on. "Well, Quinton, she just might think you're a romantic fool. I'd discuss it with her before I made any serious plans. But, then, I don't have to tell you that, do I? Women can be strange creatures by definition. They like a man to be romantic until it gets to the bottom line. Then . . . ''

"Hal, I've got to go," Quinton said. If he had not recognized the slur in the reporter's voice caused by his fast drinking, he might have been angered by his well-intended advice; but, he reasoned, it was the liquor talking. "I'll call you for lunch before I return to Key West, Hal. Take it easy.''

As he exited across the deserted dining room, Quinton heard the reporter mumble, "My lifetime ambition, to take it easy, but who can afford to?"

Quinton dialed the phone number in Justine's cottage. He counted the rings—twenty-four—before hanging up the receiver. The digital clock beside his bed read five minutes to midnight. Where could she be? Perhaps at a late meeting of the Art and Historical Society, perhaps with Helene, the old woman could have taken a turn for the worse. He wished to hell there was a telephone in the main house; then, remembering that Justine was to have had telephones installed, he dialed Key West information and requested new listings for the address on Simonton Street.

"Nothing listed,''the operator told him in her southern accent.

He switched off the light and pulled the electric blanket up to his chin. Outside, it was still snowing, cold; something was wrong with the radiator in the bedroom and the chill penetrated the windowpanes. He turned the electric blanket to "High" and settled down to wait for sleep to claim him. Half an hour later he got up and dialed Justine's cottage again; still no answer. "Damn!" he grumbled, and decided she was probably with her fag friend Aaron. That awakened his jealousy, and he told himself again how insane it was to be

jealous of a homosexual. He supposed a woman like
Justine would feel safe with a homosexual friend; they
could communicate without the question of sex rearing
its head. But then, why was he still jealous? His own
insecurities? Perhaps because it was difficult to accept a
man as handsome as Aaron being a homosexual?
Perhaps the handsome beach bum had heterosexual
inclinations even Justine didn't realize.

To keep his mind off Justine, he mentally went over
the arrangements he had completed that day. It had
been a real coup getting a promise of articles on the
Haymes Collection from the major financial publications. More and more investors were putting their
capital in antiques, increasing their scarcity and driving
up prices. The curator of a local museum had told him
that afternoon that an antique sideboard the museum
had considered last year for six thousand dollars had
been purchased eleven months later for sixteen
thousand, and they considered themselves fortunate to
get it at that price. The same curator had assured him
that if the merchandise was of the quality he had described they would certainly have representatives at the
Haymes auction regardless of where it was held, Key
West or Timbuktu.

He had also called Hal Crimmons at the magazine
offices around six o'clock and had been surprised the
reporter was there and not still at Moriarty's. "Yes, the
publisher's read you article," Hal had told him, "and
he loved it." Quinton had requested a meeting with the
publisher for the following morning. "I'll arrange it,"
Hal had said without questioning his reasons, and had
hung up.

Joanna crept into Quinton's thoughts; he felt a rush
of guilt as disturbing as the jealousy he had felt moments before. He had, he thought in retrospect, been

too hard on her. They were both victims of their up-
bringings, she of her New England Puritanical heri-
tage, and he the unfortunate product of an overly protective mother and an indifferent father, a condition
that had lasted until only months before he had met
Joanna. And then rebelled further by marrying her
despite his mother's objections. He was breaking free
now, finding himself; he wished Joanna the same success. Tomorrow, he vowed, he'd call her and try to
smooth over the hostilities they had awakened in one
another today.

The telephone rang, jarring him. He fumbled for the
receiver, knocking the ashtray to the floor. "Hello."

"Darling?"

"Justine!" He sat up and switched on the lamp. The
cigarette ashes were all over the corner of the Chinese
carpet, something that ordinarily would have sent him
rushing for the vacuum cleaner. "I've been trying to
call you all evening."

"I imagined you were," she said regretfully. "I
miss you, darling. Desperately."

"I miss you, too." He bit his lower lip; then said,
"Where have you been? A meeting?"

"Yes, a meeting. The Society is fighting a building
on Duval Street that doesn't conform to restrictions. I
thought I'd go mad when it dragged on and on, because
I knew you'd be calling. I rushed home to call you as
soon as the meeting ended. How are you, darling?"

"Freezing," he said. "We're in the middle of a
snowstorm."

"It was eighty degrees here today. I went swimming
before the meeting."

"Don't be sadistic," he said, and laughed.

"When are you coming home?"

"*Home*?" he echoed. "Darling, I'm a New Yorker,

as unappealing as that now seems.'' He lit a cigarette. ''Justine, I love you.''

''And I love you, Quinton. That's why I want you back as quickly as possible. When?''

''If all goes well tomorrow, then the day after,'' he said, knowing he should remain for a full week instead of leaving additional responsibilities with his partner.

''Then the arrangements are going well?''

''Yes.'' He told her his article on Helene had been well-received; then he briefly mentioned some of the other arrangements, and ended by asking after Helene.

''The harridan is the same,'' she answered, the familiar sarcasm coming into her voice as it always did when she spoke of Helene.

Quinton wondered just how much he should ask Justine on the telephone. Cautiously, he said, ''Has she . . . talked to you?''

''Talked *at* me,'' Justine answered. ''She talks. I listen. But I must admit you certainly impressed her. She thinks you're a handsome young genius. I could hardly keep from telling her I agreed. I think, Quinton, if you were a Conch with a good background and an enviable position, she'd find you a suitable husband for me, even though she still thinks of me as asexual. As it is, darling, I'm afraid our affair will have to remain illicit.''

''Justine, don't jest about . . . about us,'' he said. ''There are some things too sacred for gallows humor.''

''Yes, that's true. I'm sorry, darling. I love you, and that's nothing to jest about. Perhaps when the auction is over . . . '' Something crashed in the background and she let the sentence go unfinished.

''Did you drop something?'' The crash had sounded distant, across the room. It struck him that perhaps she was not alone—that perhaps Aaron had come home with her from the meeting for a nightcap. Jealousy rose up in him again like bile. "Justine, are you alone?"

"Alone? Of course, darling. It's one o'clock in the morning. I just bumped a table and knocked a vase to the floor. It's shattered, but then you won't mind. It's that dreadful Art Deco piece you hated."

Quinton detected, or thought he detected, a nervousness in her voice. It occurred to him that she might be lying; perhaps she was aware of his jealousy, was having an innocent drink with Aaron, and wanted to spare him the anguish she suspected it would arouse in him. "Tell me you love me again," he said.

"I love you," she said without hesitation.

There, he thought. At least if Aaron was there, he had heard her confess her feelings. But what satisfaction was that? Foolish, Quinton, he reflected. A part of this new you is a monster that has to learn trust. Something Hal Crimmons had said that afternoon flashed through his thoughts. "Justine, how would you feel if I was a struggling writer? If we had to live frugally on what we both made from our art?" He certainly didn't intend for her to support him, even if she would soon be a very wealthy young woman. "Would that change how you feel about me?"

"If you're being serious, then I should be insulted," Justine answered. There was a silence on the line, as if she was waiting for him to apologize. When he remained mute, she said, "Quinton, I love you. I'd be proud of you whatever you did for a living. As for living frugally, the parsimonious Aunt Helene has accustomed me to that. I wouldn't know how to live otherwise. Is this a form of proposal?"

Quinton laughed, relieved. "I guess it is," he said. "At least the preliminary to one."

"Then when you ask me—after the auction—the answer will be yes, darling. With that, I shall hang up, go to bed, and dream about becoming Mrs. Quinton Armstrong. Good night, darling."

"Good night, Justine." Reluctant to break the connection, he said, "I'll dream about you too."

"Until day after tomorrow," she said. There was a click and then the sound of the dial tone.

Quinton continued to hold the receiver, the dial tone buzzing in his ear, hoping he had been mistaken, that he had not heard a man's voice in the instant before the click of the disconnection.

Troubled, he switched off the lamp and settled back in to wait for sleep. It came fitfully. His last memorable nightmare repeated itself. He was on a large yacht somewhere on the calm, blue waters of the Gulf of Mexico, bound to the mast; his clothes had been stripped away and he was naked. Justine, Joanna and a shadowy Helene Haymes stood contemplating his nakedness; behind them, Aaron stood, arms crossed over his muscular chest, smiling humorlessly, the front of his scant bikini bulging from an erection the fabric could scarcely contain. Over the side of the yacht, Quinton could see the grey shadows darting beneath the blue surface of the calm water; waiting to be fed, the sharks had gathered for their sacrificial offering. "He'd make a good husband," Justine said, "even though he'd make me live frugally." "He isn't a Conch," Helene countered. "And he's a lousy husband," Joanna contributed knowledgeably. "He was a Mama's boy, you know. If it hadn't been for me, he'd have ended up like your friend here." She indicated the still-smiling Aaron, and then confronted Quinton with an unpleasant smirk. "You'd probably have been better off being a sexual deviate instead of an emotional

defective, Quinton." Turning to Aaron, she put her
hand firmly on the bulge in his bikini. Aaron displayed
no reaction; he merely continued to smile at Quinton,
an accusing, demented smile that evoked unexplain-
able terror. "But I love him!" Justine cried in his defense. "He isn't a Conch," Helene repeated. Still
encased in shadows, the old woman turned and signaled to the cabin. "A frenzy!" she cried. "You must
create a frenzy for the auction to succeed!"

The same old man as in the past dream emerged from
the cabin, his green eyes cold and determined. But
instead of a carcass, this time he carried various pieces
from Helene's antique collection—a Doré bronze, *biscuit de Sèvres* figurines, an oil painting; these he flung
over the side of the yacht and the sharks attacked them
as if they were living, bleeding beings.

As Quinton watched the frenzy of the sharks, he
became aware of the heat on his naked body—the sun
was burning him—but what difference did sunburn
make when soon all sensation would be denied him? He
looked to Justine; unable to speak, he pleaded with his
eyes. She stood, hands on hips, gently swaying with the
motion of the yacht. Her dark hair had been tied back
from her face, her green eyes, emerald-colored and
glowing in the bright sunlight, were filled with tears,
but beneath the tears was a glimmer of emotion he
could not discern. "I can't help you," she said. "You
didn't trust me, and now she's going to destroy you."
"He's only a romantic fool," the old man said in Hal
Crimmons's voice. "The sharks are ready for him."
Joanna, stepping forward, threw back her head, forgetting to keep it tilted to hide the imbalance of her cheekbones, and laughed: "So much for your new life,
Quinton!" "I love him." "He isn't a Conch." "A
romantic fool." "A lousy husband." "An emotional

defective." "The best in the business." Burning,
burning—the sun was going to burn him to death before
he could be fed to the sharks! His body was on fire, his
chest, his groin—

Quinton was jolted awake.

The blanket! The goddamned electric blanket! He
threw the blanket off him, sat up and turned down the
controls. His head was throbbing. Rising, he stumbled
into the bathroom and took the last two aspirins in the
bottle. The aspirins lodged in his throat. He leaned over
the basin, clutching the sides, until the aspirins went
down his throat and the threat of retching had passed.
His face only inches from the medicine cabinet mirror,
and confronted his reflection. There was exhaustion
mirrored in his eyes and the yellow shower curtain cast
an unhealthy glow over his tanned flesh. Without turning from the mirror, he reached out and yanked the
shower curtain to one side; the sickly pallor immediately left him.

Christ, what do these nightmares mean? Some sort of
unconscious flagellation? Mid-life crisis, Hal Crimmons had said. Bunk, pure bunk. Anxieties, no doubt,
caused by the demands of Helene's auction, by the
divorce from Joanna, by the tearing away of old values
and patterns and the establishment of a new life-style.
Hell, the phoenix had to burn before it could rise from
the ashes and begin a new cycle. If nightmares were the
only price he had to pay . . .

He came away from the mirror and returned to bed.
The electric blanket had cooled. He wrapped himself in
it and turned his face into the pillow. His senses were
acutely alert. He could hear the numbers of the digital
clock turning over, the faucet dripping in the distant
kitchen, someone snoring in the apartment next door;
outside, a dog barked and someone's footsteps
crunched in the snow. Tomorrow, he vowed, he'd call

the doctor and get a prescription for sleeping tablets.
With all the work ahead of him he couldn't afford to
lose sleep to nightmares or insomnia.

It was almost dawn before he fell into an untroubled
sleep.

"Hal convinced me you were the man to write this
article," the magazine publisher said, "and you've
proven him right."

His name was Thomas Riggs, and he looked to
Quinton's surprise, not a day over thirty. He had sandy
hair, worn over his collar, and eyebrows that had an
annoying habit of contracting as he spoke. His eyes
were pale blue and were in constant movement, never
settling for longer than an instant on anything; their
expression was not sharp or keen and did not mirror the
intelligence Quinton expected in the publisher of an
important magazine. He wore a beard despite the fact
that his hair was thin. His suit was expensive, unmis-
takably English tailoring, and his necktie a subdued
burgundy and grey stripe. He sat behind a massive
mahogany desk cluttered with manuscripts and proof
sheets. A porcelain pencil cup carried Harry Truman's
favorite slogan: The Buck Stops Here. Only beneath
the slogan was the caricature of a male deer poised over
a sprawled doe.

Quinton sat in an overstuffed leather chair facing the
desk. "I'm glad you like the piece, Mr. Riggs," he
said.

"Like it?" Riggs said, eyebrows contracting. "It's
damn good. A great character piece. Your writing
shows a real flair."

Hal's words almost exactly, Quinton thought. Was
this a conspiracy to make him think of himself as a
writer?

Riggs lay the article aside and leaned back in his

swivel chair. "Now what can I do for you, Mr.
Armstrong? If it's another assignment you're after,
you've got it."

"Perhaps at a later date," Quinton said. "Right now
I'm interested in the treatment you're going to give the
article on Helene Haymes. In the beginning, Hal mentioned something about a possible cover."

Riggs' eyes darted to his intercom. "Oh, he did, did
he? Well, Mr. Armstrong, your article's great, just
great, but I can't guarantee cover treatment."

"I'm also interested in the timing of publication,"
Quinton went on. "I don't know if Hal told you, but
I'm arranging an important auction of Helene Haymes'
antique collection. If my article's publication is prop-
erly timed it can spark interest with other publications.
That can help the auction. You see, the entire concept
of an auction of this caliber is unprecedented in the
United States and . . ."

Riggs' swivel chair snapped into an upright position
so quickly it threatened to throw him across his desk.
"Let me understand this, Mr. Armstrong. You sell me
an article and now you're trying to tell me not only how
but when to publish it? I must say, you're not lacking
in . . ."

There was a timely knock on the door, and Hal
Crimmons entered without waiting to be invited. "I
thought I heard a familiar voice in here," the reporter
said. "Good morning, Quinton. Riggs." He closed the
door behind him and crossed to the only other vacant
chair. "Mind if I join this discussion?"

"Perhaps you'd better," Riggs said. "Your discovery seems to be thinking of himself as an award win-
ner." The publisher's nervous eyes darted from Hal to
Quinton and back again. "He was telling me how and
when to publish his article."

"Hold on," Quinton said. "I haven't presumed to tell you anything of the sort. I merely came to explain the circumstances surrounding the Haymes auction and to convince you, if possible, to print the article as quickly as possible."

"I'm not in the business to give promotion to commercial ventures, Mr. Armstrong," Riggs said hotly. "I realize you own a promotional agency as a sideline, but my magazine's policy is . . ."

"Tom!" Hal said with authority.

Surprisingly, the publisher fell silent, looking to Hal Crimmons like a young man called down by a father figure.

"I think I can explain this better than Quinton here. He doesn't understand the jargon or the sensitivities of us publishing people." A twisted smile played about the corners of the reporter's mouth. "Quinton, why don't you wait outside while I plead your case? I think I understand both sides and I don't mind offering myself as liaison. Providing you buy me a liquid lunch before you fly off to your island paradise." He winked and nodded toward the door, his expression saying, I can handle this, old man. Leave it to me.

Quinton glanced at Riggs, noted his acquiescence to Hal's suggestion, rose and let himself out of the office. In the reception room, he paced, chiding himself for getting off on the wrong foot with the publisher. If he had had more sleep . . .

"Riggs is sensitive about his authority," Hal explained later when he joined Quinton. "The magazine's a toy, a present from Pop, who made his fortune in Texas oil. Only Riggs doesn't want it to be a toy. He takes himself seriously, wants to be a genuine publisher who browbeats his staff the way Papa browbeat him. If some writer or art director doesn't murder him first, he might make it, too.''

"I wouldn't gamble on his chances," Quinton said sourly.

"Anyway, you've got your timing," Hal told him. "I convinced him we'd be scooping the other magazines if we brought the article out quickly. Now about the cover. Can you get a recent photograph of Helene Haymes? I thought perhaps a divided cover. Then and now.''

"No recent photographs," Quinton said. "She forbids them.''

"No recent photographs and no personal interviews with anyone except you," Hal said. "She's not making it easy for you, is she, old man?"

Quinton said nothing.

"You've taken on one hell of a challenge." Hal slipped his arm about Quinton's shoulder and walked with him to the door. "I'll do what I can, which is considerable," he said. "I'll call you this afternoon."

"Thanks, Hal. About that liquid lunch, I'll have to owe you. I'm returning to Key West tomorrow."

"I see," Hal said abstractly. "Well, good luck, old man. In both endeavors." He winked mischievously as he closed the door behind Quinton.

Quinton went from the magazine to the first printer on his list. Within an hour he had settled a deal for the publication of the auction's elaborate brochure. How elaborate, would depend on the photographer and the firm that was contracted to do the color separations. He returned to his office and started making phone calls. Keith Johnston, his second choice as photographer, was available and willing to travel to Key West, providing the client would agree to per diem and the additional expense of employing his assistant, a young woman named Ruthie who was also currently sharing his bed.

Quinton agreed on his client's behalf. He dialed Justine's number to instruct her to wire the photographer a retainer, but there was no answer.

An hour later, she called him. "The telephones are in the ballroom," she told him, and he jotted down the numbers. "I've also employed two people in addition to Aaron so, darling, you'd better come back to me tomorrow or they're just going to be sitting around collecting salaries. The harridan won't like that."

"I wish you'd stop referring to her as that," Quinton said.

"It's more polite than what I'd prefer to call her," Justine told him.

No sense in battling that now, Quinton decided. Apparently, Helene had decided against telling Justine the truth of her parentage, at least temporarily.

"I love you," Justine whispered, and he could imagine Maria standing nearby.

"So much so that you had a man in the cottage last night?" he said. He hadn't meant to bring that up! Damn, if he had slept, he'd have had better control.

There was a heavy silence before Justine said, "What man?"

"Just before the connection was broken I heard a man's voice. I thought perhaps it was Aaron."

"Aaron?" she laughed. "Aaron's gone back to his shrimper, darling. What you heard was the television."

"I don't remember a television in the cottage."

"That's because I keep it under the skirt of a table unless it's in use," she said. "Blank TV screens remind me of Orwell's *1984*."

"Justine, I'm sorry. I've never been a jealous or suspicious person. I don't know why I've suddenly . . ."

"Maybe it proves you love me," she said. "Only

you have no reason to be jealous or suspicious, Quinton. You're the only man in my life. The only man I want in my life, now and forever. Oh, I'm being summoned by the harridan. I'll call you tonight, darling. Good-bye.'' She hung up before Quinton could tell her about wiring a retainer to the photographer.

Oh, well, he reasoned, he could do that tonight. The photographer wouldn't be needed for another week or two.

The only man I want in my life, now and forever, Justine had said. Christ, what a fool he'd been to be jealous of her! What a fool!

Hal Crimmons called shortly after Justine and informed Quinton the boy wonder publisher had agreed to publish the Helene Haymes article in their next issue; also, that the magazine would carry a follow-up piece on the auction itself if Quinton agreed to write it. The pay was the same as for the first assignment. Quinton readily agreed. News of the pending auction had already begun to spread throughout the antique trade of New York; several calls came into the office from dealers seeking dates and further information about the merchandise. It would be only a matter of weeks until word of mouth spread from dealers to collectors and investors, from New York to California and the Texas oil barons between, from the capitals of Europe to the fanatical Arabian collectors of the Middle East. The frenzy had begun.

Quinton returned to his apartment in high spirits. He had picked up food at a Third Avenue deli and ate corned beef on rye and German potato salad while listening to Beethoven blaring on the stereo; he wondered if Justine liked classical music—a thought that made him realize how very little he knew about her. Odd, he reflected, to love a woman who was still a comparative stranger.

He packed his suitcase, including lightweight summer clothes, showered, and because of last night's lack of sleep, went to bed early.

When the telephone awakened him, he answered expecting it to be Justine: "Hello, darling."

"This is Joanna." Her voice was cold, offended.

"Oh, Joanna!" He sat up, forcing his mind alert. "I meant to call you this morning, but my schedule has been so hectic."

"I know. I've tried to reach you."

"I want to apologize for yesterday," he told her. "There's no sense ending this on a note of hostility."

"*This* being our marriage?" she said caustically.

"I'm sorry," was all he could say.

"I never really thought it would come to this," she said, her voice breaking. "I . . . I don't really know what I thought, only that I had to jar you out of your . . . Quinton, how serious is it with . . . with this woman?"

"Joanna, I don't want to discuss that," he said decisively. He switched on the lamp and was irritated to find he had left his cigarettes in the living room. "Could you hold on a moment?" He lay the receiver down, stumbled into the living room in the darkness and came back with his cigarettes. He sat on the bed, staring at the receiver lying on the pillow.

"Quinton! Quinton!" Her voice sounded distant and hostile and slightly muffled by the receiver's bed of goose down.

He snatched up the receiver. "Yes, Joanna. I'm here. Sorry. I left my cigarettes in the other room."

"Are you alone?" she asked accusingly.

"Yes, and trying to sleep."

"Sleep," she said. "I can't sleep without pills. I can't adjust to being alone, Quinton. Every noise in the house awakens me. I spend the nights pacing."

"Why don't you spend some time with your parents?" he suggested. "Give yourself time to adjust."

Joanna laughed without humor. "My parents," she said critically, "are horrified that their daughter is divorcing. There hasn't been a divorce in our family, ever. By their reaction, you'd think I'd committed all of the seven deadly sins. My father said he'd . . . Quinton," her voice broke again, "I . . . I don't know if I'm going to make it through this adjustment . . . I'm not as strong as I thought . . . I'm so . . . so lonely . . . I miss you so . . ." She began to cry.

Quinton's felt the perspiration on his hand gripping the receiver. He was filled with mixed emotions, sympathy and annoyance. He wanted to console her and at the same time remind her that the divorce had been her decision. Aloud, he said, "Joanna, stop crying. Take a sedative and go to bed."

"Quinton, I need to see you. I need . . . I need to talk to you."

"That's impossible, Joanna. I leave for Key West in the morning."

"Back to her!" she yelled.

"Yes," he said quietly. "Back to her."

Her voice sobered. "Then it is serious between you?"

Quinton refused to answer.

"It must be," she said. "Your wife calls you in desperation and you can't see her because you're going back to some . . ."

"Don't say anything you'll regret later, Joanna," he warned. "And may I remind you that you are in the process of becoming an ex-wife. My allegiance ended the day you filed for a separation."

"You can be so goddamned cruel, Quinton! After all these years you found the strength to speak your mind only to hurt me, probably the only person who ever truly cared about you.''

"Joanna, it won't work this time," he said patiently. "I'm not going to feel guilty because you're feeling desperate and alone."

"You never really loved me," she accused.

Quinton flinched. If what he felt for Justine was love, then Joanna was right, he had never really loved her. He crushed out his cigarette with vehemence, cursing beneath his breath that she had destroyed his sense of well-being, angry that she had awakened him from a sleep without nightmares. "Joanna, I'm going to say good night and hang up now," he said evenly.

"You think this woman's changed you, don't you, Quinton?" Joanna shouted. "You think she's made you strong, given you something I didn't? You haven't changed! You've just added cruelty to your other faults! You're still a weak man, Quinton. You're still naive! You're no doubt still easily manipulat . . .''

"Good night!" Quinton repeated, and dropped the receiver back into its cradle. Cursing, he rose from the edge of the bed, lit another cigarette and paced through the apartment, smoking. He stopped at the liquor cabinet and poured himself a neat Scotch, downing it in one greedy gulp. The telephone rang again, but he refused to answer. When the ringing eventually stopped he went into the bedroom and dialed Justine's number in case it had been her calling and not Joanna. There was no answer. Finishing his cigarette, he curled up back in bed, expecting sleep not to come, or to come with nightmares if it did.

Instead, his next awareness was sunlight bright against the Venetian blinds and the digital clock alarming at precisely seven forty-five. The radiator was hissing, and he could hear the sounds of traffic. He rose and peered through the slats of the blinds. The snow had turned to slush. The sky was clear, a chilled blue. A good day for flying, he reflected. He made his bed, ignoring his nagging sense of depression, readied the apartment for desertion, and then showered and shaved. After dressing, he called the office and went over last-minute details with his partner for arrangements on the Haymes auction. When he hung up he dialed Justine's number again, wondering why she hadn't called last night as promised: again, there was no answer.

By the time he disembarked in Miami to change planes to Key West, his depression had lifted. Joanna was pushed to the recesses of his mind. Breathing the hot, humid Florida air, he felt as if he had come home; his anticipation at seeing Justine increased. The work he had brought to go over on the smaller plane to Key West lay untouched on his lap. He stared through the plane's double windows, a dreamer, his gaze fixed on the billowy white clouds, his thoughts on a future with Justine that would be, that *had* to be as close to perfection as a man could hope for. The only imperfection was the guilt he felt because of Joanna, a guilt he had no cause to feel, and yet could not entirely shed.

The plane to Key West was filled to capacity, tourists in brightly colored sports shirts and linen jackets, women in summer cottons and sweaters thrown over their shoulders, everyone friendly and talkative. Quinton retreated from conversation, not wanting to dull his sense of expectation at being with Justine again. When Key West came into view, a green jewel in a blue and turquoise sea, he returned the untouched work to his briefcase.

He took a taxi from the airport, impatiently urging the driver beyond speed limits.

Lucifer ran to the gate of the old mansion on Simon-ton Street, barking, not threateningly but in greeting. Quinton patted the Doberman's head: "Good boy, Lucifer, good boy!"

The front door opened and Maria stepped onto the porch. "So, you're back, Mr. Armstrong," she said, her voice oddly pitched.

Quinton saw Betty standing in the hallway behind her mother. "And with a red dress for you, Betty," he said. He took the package from beneath his arm and extended it to the wide-eyed girl. While she excitedly tore off the wrappings, he turned his attention back to the housekeeper. "I've some good news for Helene," he said. "Is she awake? And Justine, is she home?"

Maria looked at him gravely. "Miss Helene, she took worse during the night," she said. "Miss Justine, she flew with her to the clinic in North Carolina."

Quinton could only stare, his elation at returning suddenly gone.

"Miss Justine, she'll be back this afternoon," Maria told him. "You come on in, Mr. Armstrong. She had me make a room up for you on the second floor."

Solemnly, Quinton followed the massive house-keeper into the house and up the staircase, not even hearing Betty who was thanking him gratefully for the grown-up woman's dress she was holding up to her body as she danced happily around the barking Dober-man.

Chapter Fourteen

Feigning sleep, Quinton watched through lowered lashes as Justine sat up, stretched languidly, and then pulled herself up against the elaborate headboard. She drew the sheet about her breasts, tucking it beneath her arms to hold it in place, and lit a cigarette. She inhaled deeply and allowed the smoke to lazily escape her parted lips. Staring thoughtfully into the room now bathed in morning sunlight, there was a suggestion of a smile hovering about the corners of her mouth.

It had struck him that she was experiencing some perverse pleasure in having made love in Helene's bed and that almost provoked a continuation of his last night's objections. Instead, he refrained from intruding on her thoughts and continued to stare at her, thinking how fortunate he was to be loved by a woman so beautiful and exciting. He fought the impulse to reach out and caress her, draw her to him and make love to her again. Sometimes when he looked at her—like now—he felt emotion swell within him. You're a man possessed, he thought with amusement, and he vowed he must never allow anything to come between them, not the nagging guilt over Joanna that he had brought away from New York, not Helene and her secret, not even the importance of the auction.

Without looking at him, Justine said quietly, ''A woman always knows when she's being admired, Quinton. It's a characteristic of the gender. So you might as well stop faking sleep.'' She turned to him then and smiled.

''Shall I ring Maria for coffee, darling? It would . . .''

''No!''

''It would be amusing to see the expression on her face when she saw us naked in Aunt Helene's bed,'' she finished. ''Despite having a bastard daughter, Maria's devoutly moralistic. Shall I ring?'' She started to rise from the bed, laughing.

But Quinton was quick to restrain her, drawing her into his arms. ''You're a devil,'' he told her. Then, as he kissed her, he wondered what her reaction would be when and if Helene ever confessed that Justine was also a bastard. Perhaps it would be more shattering than either he or Helene had anticipated.

Justine, sensing a change in him, pulled back and met his gaze. ''What is it?'' she asked, her green eyes narrowing.

To cover his thoughts, he said, ''This room. This bed, her bed. Sleeping together here was . . . well . . .''

''Was what?'' Justine pressed. ''Sacrilegious? Sometimes I believe you think of the harridan as some sort of goddess.''

''No, it was merely childish,'' he said, instantly regretful that he had been critical.

Justine pulled herself entirely away from him and returned to her position with her back against the headboard. Her face became a mask behind which she hid her emotions. ''Perhaps it was childish,'' she admitted, ''but she'll never know, so what's the harm?''

Quinton said nothing.

"I suppose it was wicked to want to make love to you in her bed for poetic revenge against a harpy who thinks of me as asexual." Her voice softened, became introspective. "I guess I've always sought satisfaction in childish ways because of the things she's done."

"I'm sorry if I took that satisfaction away, but you must . . ."

"No, I can't blame you for that," she interrupted. "The satisfaction last night was sexual and perfect and just what I wanted."

Quinton detected an expression of puzzlement in her eyes. In an attempt to draw her out of the seriousness into which she was sinking, he said, "Thank you, madame. A man likes to be told when he gives sexual satisfaction. It's a characteristic of the gender."

Her mood altered with chameleon swiftness. She lifted his hand to her lips and kissed it. "Darling, I love you," she said. "You know how to keep me in a good disposition."

He started to move closer when she suddenly pushed his hand away and sprang from the bed.

"Your staff is due in half an hour," she said, "so no more lovemaking until tonight. In the cottage." She snatched Helene's grey silk dressing gown from a chair's back and disappeared into the bathroom.

"Wench," he called after her.

He heard her turn on the shower, then heard the water springing off her body onto the plastic curtain. He pulled himself up in bed and lit a cigarette. As he smoked, he let his gaze travel about the room. He had never seen it in full light, and he found himself instinctively appraising. The mantel clock, a bisque figurine of three muses, a gilt Louis Philippe mirror. The chest where the crystal liquor decanters were kept was undoubtedly a Robert Adam design with *scagliola* panels, dating from the last quarter of the eighteenth century. The old woman's writing desk was Spanish with the rich marquetry decoration popular during the reign of Charles IV; the chair facing it was also Spanish, with the carved ornament typical of that country's work of the late eighteenth century. There was a japanned cabinet that was most likely German and made by Martin Schnell in Dresden in the mid-1700s; he had seen only one other like it, that in the Victoria and Albert Museum. Fine pieces, all of them—but not what he would have expected a collector of Helene Haymes' distinction to select to live with day in and day out. He wondered if the pieces she had chosen for her room were, like the mantel clock, of sentimental value. His attention was caught by an oil painting on the side wall—he recognized the work as that of the French painter Andre Derain, one of his personal favorites. The subject was a young woman with a blue drape falling across her right breast, her left breast exposed. Rising, Quinton crossed the room and opened the shutter nearest the painting. He didn't need the brightness of the sunlight to recognize the artist's model as Helene herself.

"Good God," he murmured aloud, "she was even painted by Derain."

"What was that, darling?" Justine had emerged from the bathroom wearing Helene's silk dressing gown, a towel wrapped about her wet hair.

"I said she was even painted by Andre Derain," he repeated. He changed his position to view the painting from a different angle.

"And by Picasso and Dali," Justine said dully. "There's even a very cryptic sketch done of her by Gertrude Stein when she visited her during the war. In time I'm certain she'll inform you of how sought after she was as a model. And how willingly she posed, egotist that she was.''

Quinton, ignoring Justine's barb, continued to consider the Derain painting. Something about it bothered him, but he could not determine what.

"Is it valuable?" Justine asked.

"Hmm,'' he murmured, unable to pull his gaze from the painting.

"The Picasso's on loan to a museum in New Orleans,'' Justine said. "She loaned the Dali for exhibition in Europe. Of course you'll want them returned for the auction since . . . ''

"I've got it!'' Quinton said. "Her eyes!'' He pointed to the canvas. "Why would Derain paint her eyes blue?''

Justine laughed. "Because she insisted,'' she said. She walked back into the bathroom, toweling dry her hair.

"Insisted?'' Quinton followed her to the bathroom door. "Why?''

Justine had tossed the towel onto the edge of the tub and was leaning into the mirror for a morning inspection of her flawless face. "Aunt Helene,'' she said without turning from the mirror, "might have been considered feminine perfection by her admirers, but like many women she had her own conception of what she thought she should look like.''

Quinton shrugged his naked shoulders. "I don't understand.''

"Well, darling, some women dislike their noses or their chins and they simply go to plastic surgeons and have them changed. Aunt Helene's vanity was different. According to my father, she always wanted blue eyes. She somehow was convinced green eyes were a sign of bad breeding. Shanty Irish, something like that. She apparently only agreed to pose for Derain if he would paint her with blue eyes.''

"I can't imagine Derain agreeing," Quinton said thoughtfully. "He was such a perfectionist. Picasso and Dali, did they both agree to the alteration of eye coloring to flatter her idiosyncracy?''

Justine ran a comb through her wet hair. "Dali, I don't recall," she said, bored. "With Picasso, who could tell? Now, darling, unless you want Maria to catch you here, I suggest you slip quietly down to your own room.''

Quinton stepped out of his room as if he were leaving it for the first time that morning. He was wearing the summer clothes he had brought back from New York, dull, perhaps, in color, a beige cotton shirt and khaki trousers, but then he had always been a conservative dresser: he hadn't a flair for color like the Key Westers.

Maria, who had knocked on his door, looked at him appraisingly, then said: "Two people who says they're new employees has arrived. I put them in the ball-room.''

"Thank you, Maria.''

The housekeeper hesitated.

"Is there something else, Maria?''

"About the dress you brought Betty Sue," Maria said uncomfortably. "I want to thank you, Mr. Armstrong. I ain't seen her so happy, ever.'' The heavyset housekeeper lowered her eyes to conceal the emotion mirrored there. "That dress makes her look like a grown-up woman," she mused. "Can't say that I like that, but it makes her happy. Thank you for that, Mr. Armstrong.''

"I'm glad Betty likes the dress," Quinton told her.

As she began to move away, Quinton said, "Maria, tell me about Helene, please. Justine dismissed her setback as a mental whim, maybe just a wish not to witness strangers in her house, but I'd like your opinion. Did Helene really take a turn for the worse?"

Maria's dark eyes probed his for several moments; she appeared to be calculating her answer. "Miss Justine, she knows best," she said, her voice unemotional, almost a mimicry of herself. With a nod, she turned and descended the staircase, leaving Quinton just as puzzled as before.

Upon entering the ballroom, Quinton found a young man and woman standing at a desk that had been placed near the window, their backs to him. Neither had heard him enter. The man was tall, at least six feet, and the woman short, the top of her blonde head scarcely reaching his shoulder. Both wore faded denim trousers, the man's worn low on his hips in the style of the fifties, the woman's tied around the waist with a brightly colored scarf. Their shirts were also matching, the thin white cotton fabric and loose design popular in imports from India, with fancy needlework about the collars and the cuffs, so thin the flesh could be seen clearly; there were no bra straps visible beneath the woman's. Her hair was in need of combing. They were examining a map they had unfolded from the spine of a postal zip code book Quinton had had Justine pick up at the local post office.

The woman giggled softly. "You ever notice how Florida resembles a limp prick?" Her Bostonian accent was evident.

"Hmm," the man mused. "That makes the rest of the South the country's groin." He laughed at his own humor and reached to place his arm around her waist.

Quinton walked toward them with deliberate noise.

"Good morning," he said, pretending not to notice how quickly they moved apart. "I'm Quinton Armstrong."

"Then you're the man we'll be working for," the young man said, stepping forward, hand extended. "I'm Alex Reed." His handshake was firm, his palm dry despite the humidity. "This is Lucenda Racina."

The young woman bobbed her head in a nod. She looked no more than nineteen, Quinton judged. Her eyebrows were too bushy for the delicate lines of her face and the fingernails of the hand she had brought nervously to brush away some hair had been bitten to the quicks.

Alex could have been in his early or late twenties; it was difficult to determine his age. He wore his auburn hair long, slightly curled below the ears, but it was clean and brushed to a fine sheen; obviously he was proud of the full head of hair. His eyes were blue, startlingly pale, but the pupils were slightly dilated and gave his eyes an intensity that was belied by the easy carriage of his body. His shirt was open at the throat and there was a long scar running horizontally just below his neck.

Lucenda's eyes were a pale hazel; her pupils, too, were dilated.

Neither sported the customary suntans of Key Westers or tourists.

Quinton recalled reading a statement by James Kirkwood that Key West would undoubtedly be the last stronghold for hippies. Disturbed, he moved to his desk and sat down. "Are either of you accustomed to handling valuable antiques?" he asked pointedly. "Rare porcelains, crystal, paper thin glass?"

Lucenda lowered her thin lashes and fixed her gaze on the parquet floor. "My mother collected paperweights,'' she said barely above a whisper, ''but she'd never let me touch them.'' She lifted her eyes and met Quinton's gaze. ''She called me a klutz, but I'm not. That's what you want to know, isn't it? If we drop things?''

Quinton nodded.

''I worked in a gift shop in San Francisco,'' Alex said. ''No accidents. If you broke something, they took it out of your pay.''

''How long did you work there?'' Quinton asked.

''Two months. Look, Mr. Armstrong, we need the work. Lucenda and me, we don't have any bread. There are plenty of places to crash in Key West, but we need money to buy co . . . food and essentials. We'd both be good workers not be late and not just flake off. 'We'd be careful, too, and not break anything. We're not thieves, that counts for something when you're working with valuable stuff like you mentioned. I may not like antiques, but I respect them because of their value.''

Quinton smiled despite himself. ''Value rather than esthetics is unfortunately why most people respect antiques,'' he said. ''How long have you been in Key West?''

''Since the day before Miss Haymes approached us about working,'' Alex answered. ''Do we have the jobs, Mr. Armstrong?''

''It's going to be dusty, hard work,'' Quinton told them discouragingly.

''We need the bread,'' Alex repeated tonelessly.

''All right, we'll try you out,'' Quinton said despite his reservations.

Later in the morning when Justine came to the ballroom, Quinton told her, ''I know Helene's restrictions about locals being in her house, but we have to hire some responsible people. Did you notice how nervous that girl was? She's like an alcoholic with d.t.'s. I can't in all conscience allow her to handle collectibles worth thousands of dollars. It would be insanity, sheer insanity.'' His brow furrowed. ''Damn,'' he said. ''Why does it matter if the employees are locals or strangers?''

''Just another of the harridan's idiosyncrasies,'' Justine said. She moved behind his chair and began massaging his tense neck muscles. ''She's called eccentric because she's wealthy,'' she said. ''Poor, she'd just be a crazy old lady. But don't despair, darling. You have me and you have Aaron. We can both handle her precious treasures without breaking them. I've spent my life in this museum. My first memories are of being warned not to touch, not to run, not to play indoors because there might be an accident. I lived in fear of shattering something and causing her fury.''

''Was she really so terrible?'' Quinton asked. ''Or were those fears instilled in you by . . . by someone else?''

Justine's hands stilled on his neck. ''My father and Maria were only repeating her orders,'' she said. ''She was the queen and we her subjects, afraid we'd break something and be punished.''

''Now you're being dramatic,'' he accused. ''I doubt that any one or all of her possessions were as valuable to her as you. She loves you, Justine.''

''Oh, does she? And how do you know? Because she told you?'' Her hands continued massaging, only this time without gentleness. ''She might have convinced you of that, darling, but I know her too well to be convinced by her performances. Aunt Helene loves only herself and her horde of antiquities. Perhaps that's a blessing. She certainly isn't lovable.''

"What if her expressions of love aren't performances?" Quinton suggested. "What if she genuinely
loved you, only certain circumstances prevented her
from exhibiting that love? What if she could not break
through a barrier to make her love believable?"

Justine moved away from him to seat herself in a side
chair. She turned to stare throughtfully through the
window, the sunlight through the sheer white curtains
outlining her profile and giving her a Madonna-like
appearance.

Finally, she turned to him and said, "She was
strange during the flight to the clinic, not really like
herself. She told me about a man in her life who had
died. A man I'd never heard her mention. An English
lord. Lord Cambray. When she spoke of him I was
aware of a change in her. All her hardness, her bitterness and self-involvement left her and beneath her cold
exterior I had a glimpse of a stranger." Justine sighed,
rose and perched on the edge of Quinton's desk. "I felt
myself responding to her, to the only person in my life I
have really hated, but it was only fleeting. I suddenly
realized she was lecturing me, using me in some perverse way to gain approval of an affair with a man she
was remembering with perfection. I don't know why
she suddenly felt she needed my approval, but all the
same, she did, and I resented her for it. I realized that
while she had been talking she had taken my hand. That
. . . . that disturbed me more than I can tell you. It was
all I could do to choke down my revulsion. I sat staring
at that wrinkled hand holding mine and I told myself
this was the woman who had driven my father to
suicide, the woman who thought of herself as a family
matriarch who controlled my father and now me with
promises of future rewards, and I hated myself as much
as I hated her. I snatched my hand away and had to fight

an impulse to physically attack her.'' Justine's voice had risen with emotion; her body had tensed. "She stopped talking and scarcely said another dozen words for the remainder of the trip."

Quinton felt sympathy for both women, for Helene who wanted to be united with her daughter before her death, and for Justine, unknowingly that daughter, whose emotionally crippling hatred had been so solidly instilled by a man with a vendetta. Rising, he put his arms about Justine and held her. With her head nestled against his neck, he wondered if indeed it would be better if the truth Helene was so determined to confess came from him. A knock on the door ended his consideration, and he moved away from her.

Maria opened the door. "Mr. Armstrong, I've got your lunch ready," she said, "and, Miss Justine, there's a Mr. Clarke askin' for you.''

"Is your friend always so late?" Quinton asked Justine, unable to keep the anger from his voice.

"I told him to come at noon," she said, "so he's actually five minutes early." To Maria, "Tell him to go to the cottage. I'll meet him there in a few minutes."

Nodding, Maria left them.

"Why the cottage?" Quinton demanded.

Laughing, Justine kissed his cheek. "Because, darling, I'm having all the Art Deco and Art Nouveau you hate so much removed. I'm turning the cottage into your offices."

Quinton was astounded. "You're giving up your privacy? Why?"

"It seems the logical thing to do," she told him. "I'll move back into the main house, not to please the harridan but I'm sure she'll be elated. Don't worry, darling, I'll take a room far removed from hers, and we'll keep a sofa bed in your offices in the event

passion intrudes on your work habits.'' She kissed him
again and then pulled back. ''Now down to business.
Later, darling.'' She walked away from him; stopping
at the door and smiling back at him, she said teasingly,
''And don't fret about Aaron and I being alone, darling.
His lover didn't go out on the shrimp boat this week.
He's helping with the macho work.''

Quinton heard her amused laughter through the
closed door.

Quinton elected to have his lunch in the kitchen.

It was a comfortable room, large and immaculate and
permeated by the aromas of Maria's cooking. The
housekeeper had set out his lunch—shrimp in beer
batter and an avocado, tomato and lettuce salad—on
the table where she had her meals with her daughter.
The oilcloth covering the table had been scrubbed for so
many years the pattern was almost indiscernible. The
kitchen door stood open, and Quinton could hear noises
from the cottage, occasionally laughter, Justine's and
Aaron's, and he lost his appetite.

Maria peered through the window, checking on
Betty who was playing in the yard with Lucifer. ''Don't
you bother them in the cottage,'' she called, and Betty's weak, ''No, Mama,'' came floating back. ''You
want coffee, Mr. Armstrong?'' Maria asked. ''You
don't like shrimp, I won't fix them no more.''

''I'm very fond of shrimp,'' Quinton told her. ''I'm
just not too hungry today.'' He pushed his plate away
and turned to the door as Justine's laughter reached out
to him like a magnet. Only minutes ago she had been
perched on the edge of his desk with tears in her eyes.
Her moods, he decided, were mercurial, and he wished
he was now a part of her lighter, happier tenor, a
disposition Aaron had apparently brought out in her.

Maria brought him coffee although he had not asked for it. She eyed the untouched shrimp on his plate critically as she carried it back to the sink. Her back was to him, but he saw her carefully picking off the shrimp, possibly for her own and Betty's dinner.

"What were Betty's and Justine's childhoods like in this house?" he asked.

Maria glanced at him before she turned to scrape the lettuce from his plate into a pail. "You interested in Betty Sue's or Miss Justine's childhood?" she said pointedly.

"Would you say they had happy childhoods?" he said, pressing the issue.

"Compared to?" Maria asked. She turned, leaning against the sink, and met his gaze.

"Well, to other children," he answered.

"I can't compare 'em to other children," Maria said, "but I can't see either one has room to complain. Miss Justine, she had everythin' money could buy, and Betty Sue, she got her castoffs and hand-me-downs. That's better than I could have done fer her on my own."

"Was it a happy house?"

"Sometimes it were, sometimes it weren't," the housekeeper said. "Like all houses, I suppose. You gotta take the good and bad of life, that's what my mama taught me." She had apparently warmed to him, Quinton thought, since he had brought the red dress for her daughter.

"What was Mr. Haymes like? Miss Helene's brother?"

Maria turned back to the sink. "You'll have to ask Miss Justine that," she said.

"Did you like him?"

"Don't matter whether I did or didn't. He's dead anyway. It ain't good to talk about the dead. Brings 'em

back, keeps 'em from goin' on to where they're supposed to be.''

"That's spiritualism,'' Quinton told her. "Do you
believe in spiritualism, Maria?''

"Maybe,'' she said evasively. "Why'd you want to
know?''

"Because I've read that it helps troubled spirits to
pass on to different planes if the living discuss them and
help them to understand the transgressions that keep
them earthbound.''

Maria, her hands sudsy from the dishwater, faced
him again. There was a hint of a smile playing behind
her dark eyes. "You wouldn't be tryin' to dupe me,
would you, Mr. Armstrong? To get me to answer
questions so your curiosity can be put to rest?''

Quinton laughed good-naturedly. "I confess,'' he
said. "Guilty as charged.''

Maria, wiping her hands on her apron, crossed the
room and sank into the chair opposite him. "I told you I
wasn't goin' to answer no questions,'' she said, "but
I'll tell you this about Mr. Haymes. Maybe he's the
one who caused most of the trouble. He wasn't the
man people thought him to be. He was always smilin'
in public, talkin' nice to people and actin' like he cared
'bout 'em. Acted that way with Miss Helene and Miss
Justine, too. He was always caterin' to Miss Helene and
spendin' time with Miss Justine, spoilin' her even
though Miss Helene was always tellin' him not to.

"But Mr. Haymes, he was a hypocrite, always was,
even before he buried his wife. It was her dyin' that put
the deep hate behind his eyes, hate no one seemed to see
except me, and that because he didn't care if I saw him
fer what he was, a man with the Devil's sickness in
him. It was the sickness that made him do what he did,
and in a house of God too!'' She shook her head

gravely. "No, no talkin' about Mr. Haymes' transgressions is goin' to help his spirit. The Devil had his spirit before that rope snapped his neck and took it from his earthly body, and the Devil, he don't waste no time in takin' his own t' Hell. Mr. Haymes' spirit ain't floatin' around. It's been burnin' in brimstone several years now. You can call that spiritualism or Baptist preachin' or nigger superstition, but it's what I believe."

"Did you try to warn Miss Helene of his influence on Justine?" Quinton asked.

Maria's face, more expressive than Quinton had ever seen it, suddenly reverted back to its impenetrable mask. "I ain't sayin' no more," she told him stubbornly. She started to rise, then settled back in her chair as if the effort was too much for her. "Except this," she said, " 'cause you made my Betty Sue happy and 'cause I think you're a good, God-fearin' man despite . . ." She let the sentence trail off. "People ain't always what they seem to be on the surface, Mr. Armstrong. I've lived long enough to know that. When the Devil gets in 'em he can make dark patches in the soul like rot in an apple. The surface is all shiny and you don't know the rot's there until you bite into . . ."

"Well, what have we here?" Justine asked from the open doorway. "Kitchen gossip?" She was smiling, but the expression in her green eyes, as she looked disapprovingly from Quinton to Maria, was without humor.

"I was just asking Maria how she prepared the batter for her shrimp," Quinton lied.

Justine came into the kitchen. She was wearing a scarf about her head; there was a smudge on her forehead. She had on a man's shirt, the sleeves rolled up to her elbows. "I didn't know you were interested in recipes, Quinton." She slipped into Maria's chair as the housekeeper abandoned it and returned to the sink. "You are apparently a man of many talents," she said, winking at him. "I can't wait until you reveal them all." She reached for his cup and sipped his coffee, her eyes probing his above the rim.

Quinton wondered just how much of Maria's conversation she had heard. "How's the renovation coming? You certainly seem to be enjoying yourselves." I'm putting her on the defensive, he thought, to prevent her from being angry at Maria; the tactic had been used often enough on him by Joanna to understand its workings.

"Aaron and his friend are very amusing," she said openly. "Maria take some lemonade to the cottage. My friends are thirsty."

"Yes, Miss Justine."

Justine's gaze swept from the housekeeper to the open door, drawn by Lucifer's barking. "And have Betty keep that damn dog quiet," she ordered.

"Yes, Miss Justine," Maria repeated.

Quinton was acutely aware of the anger in Justine's voice, and he wondered why, if finding him questioning Maria in the kitchen irritated her, she did not vent it towards him instead of the housekeeper? From tears to laughter to anger, all within minutes; definitely mercurial, he thought.

"Would you like to meet Aaron's shrimper?" she asked him.

"No, not now," Quinton told her. "I think I'll take a walk before getting back to work."

"Oh, but I can't go with you," Justine objected. "I have to show them where to store the contents of the cottage. Aaron's practically helpless and his lover's ninety percent muscle. If you'd care to wait for an hour or so, I'll . . ."

"I'm only going around the block," Quinton told her. "I've too much to do to take more time." Quietly, so Maria wouldn't hear, he added, "I'll knock off early and we'll go for a lover's stroll."

"All right," Justine agreed. "I just hope on your walk around the block you don't run into the seductive Ernesta Calder again," she said with a hollow laugh.

"Heaven forbid," he said.

It pleased him that Justine's attitude was one of jealousy—although he knew it was only pretense.

Chapter Fifteen

In the following weeks Quinton became deeply involved in the preparations for the auction. He rose every morning at six a.m., had breakfast with Justine, and then retired to his cottage office, often working until well past eight o'clock at night. There were problems, but none he couldn't deal with. Lucenda, after receiving her first week's salary, disappeared. An upset and mournful Alex received a letter from her the following week telling him she had decided to return home to Boston and had been too weak to tell him good-bye in person. "I was going to marry her," the youth told Quinton, his pale blue eyes rimmed by dark circles of worry. "I'll never get involved with an addict again!"

Justine hired another transient girl of about Lucenda's age and within the week Alex had forgotten Lucenda. Janet Darcy was more efficient than her predecessor. From New Orleans, she had come to Key West to get over her first disastrous affair; she was shy, well-mannered, and proved to Quinton during her interview that she was knowledgeable about antiques by giving him the proper names and even partial period placement of every item in the ballroom where he met with her. "My mother was a fanatical collector," she told him. "She had more books about antiques than she

had antiques, and I'm a chronic reader. I also have
eighty-three percent retention.'' Quinton was impressed. Janet was pleasant looking, if not beautiful,
with large almond-colored eyes and straw-colored hair.
She moved about the house so silently that she seemed
to suddenly materialize in a room instead of entering it.
Alex did not seem the sort of man she would be attracted to, but the old adage of opposites attracting
apparently applied. Justine, for no reason she could
explain, disliked the girl and deliberately avoided her.

The New York photographer arrived, photographed
the collection in four days, spent the fifth day on the
beach, and returned to Manhattan to develop his work.
An ad in the local paper had produced a retired editor
now living in Key West; she was hired to edit—and to
flourish—Quinton's blurbs. Aaron, always late,
proved to be a competent worker if he could be kept
from socializing with Justine; he took on the task of
assigning lot numbers and of keeping records of where
each item was stored. He avoided Quinton with almost
as much abviousness as Justine avoided Janet Darcy.

Quinton's New York partner had obtained the choicest mailing lists from famous worldwide auction houses
and antique dealers; an elaborate brochure was printed
and mailed. An article on Helene Haymes appeared in
the *New York Post;* it was, as expected, sensationalized, with particular emphasis given to the
accusations of a romantic interlude with Adolf
Hitler and the infamous American. The photograph of
Helene clinging to the madman's arm was so blurred
she was scarcely recognizable. The article gave
Helene's current residence as Key West, Florida, *''that
frivolous island, the Capital of Camp, which was becoming known as Fire Island South because of the
influx of homosexuals.''* The pending auction was not

mentioned. Interest was sparked with numerous magazines; telephone calls and telegrams came in from *Life*, *Newsweek*, *Time*, *Cosmopolitan* and *New Yorker*. Offers were received from book publishers for an autobiography. An independent television production company wanted to do a documentary. Hollywood was interested in a film. The Miami division of the women's liberation movement wanted Helene to write an article on how she had been exploited. A scandal sheet wanted to know what Hitler was *really* like in bed. In response to the auction brochures, several museums requested public showings of the Haymes collection before it was sold.

Yet, in Key West itself, the comings-and-goings at the Haymes house elicited surprisingly mild interest. A few locals came by, Ernesta Calder one of them, but Maria told them Miss Helene was away on a trip and barred their entrance; no, Miss Justine was busy and couldn't receive them.

As for Justine, Quinton seldom saw her during the day. At her insistence, he had given her specific assignments and when he checked they had been completed, but he had the uneasy feeling that she often slipped away from the house without telling him.

Maria, since the day when Justine had caught them huddled together at the kitchen table, had retreated back into impenetrability and seldom spoke except to acknowledge instructions or inform them meals were ready. Betty, however, took to sitting quietly in rooms where Quinton was working, or following in his shadow as he moved about the old mansion. "You're my friend," she once told him when he questioned her, "so I likes to be around you." Since she bothered nothing and seldom disturbed his thoughts by chatting, Quinton, flattered, allowed her to do as she pleased. But should Justine ever enter a room, Betty quickly left, not returning until she was certain Justine had made an exit. Sometimes she would huddle in a chair, sketch pad propped against her knees, and draw him. One likeness was quite good; when Quinton commented on it, she beamed with pleasure, tore it from the pad and gave it to him.

During the weeks of her confinement to the clinic in North Carolina, Quinton never heard from Helene directly. Once she called when he had gone to the post office and another time when he was out for a walk. She had left word that she was feeling "much improved" and might be returning in the near future, but she had hinted at no specific date. Quinton was upset, but not greatly. There were details relating to the auction that he had to speak to her about, but he reasoned she would return in adequate time. Meantime, he was enjoying the freedom of the old mansion, just himself and Justine wandering freely from room to room, because once Maria and Betty retired they never emerged again until morning. Justine never again suggested they make love in Helene's bedroom, but they had met on occasion, accidentally, during working hours in the storage rooms, and once they had made love on a dusty empire sofa surrounded by a barrier of armoires that had prevented them from being seen when Aaron had entered and called Justine's name, leaving when she had not responded.

"He dislikes me," Quinton had told her after Aaron had gone. "He avoids me whenever possible."

Justine, slipping back into her clothes, had said thoughtfully, "Maybe he avoids you because he knows he makes you uncomfortable. Aaron's very sensitive. He's aware you suspect he'll make a sexual advance toward you if ever the two of you find yourselves alone. He's simply sparing you the discomfort until you adjust to his homosexuality and understand that homosexuals are as discriminating about their sexual partners as straights.''

"Go tell that to Anita Bryant," Quinton had retorted, miffed by her haughty understanding. "But, he had conceded, ''he's an excellent worker, as conscientious as I've ever seen. I can't understand why he's a beach bum when he devotes himself so completely to his work. It's almost as if he had greater stakes in it than a mere salary. The job, after all, is only temporary.''

"Perhaps that's why he can devote himself to it," Justine had said perceptively. "Because it *is* only temporary. He doesn't feel trapped by it.''

That explains Aaron, he had refrained from saying. Now tell me why you avoid Janet Darcy, a shy, intelligent girl you dislike for no apparent reason.

Hal Crimmons called from New York and informed Quinton that the proofs for his article on Helene had been received by the magazine. "We've decided to go with a still photograph from one of her two movies for the cover," the reporter told him. "Very glamorous and not too dated. Inside, we're using more stills and a reduction of the Picasso painting.''

Surprised, Quinton asked, "How did you know about the Picasso?''

"I have friends in art circles. I lied to the museum in New Orleans, told them I was representing Helene Haymes. They're airmailing me a color transparency. Is there a chance of getting photographs of the Dali and the Derain?''

Quinton, uncertain if Helene meant the Derain to go up at auction, had had the photographer take slides of it in any event. He gave Hal the photographer's studio telephone number and then called to approve the release of the slide to the magazine's delivery service. He made a note to question Justine about the European museum exhibiting the Dali.

Justine was working closely with the Chamber of Commerce. Apartments and condominiums and houses where part-time residents were not going to be in occupancy were arranged with the owners as rentals. Letters went out to all collectors and dealers anticipated to attend the auction advising them to make their reservations early; a list of hotels, motels and guest houses was included, along with ratings where available. Those who could not obtain lodgings in Key West itself were advised to try other keys, Sugar Loaf, Marathon and even the distant Key Largo. Quinton suspected that many of the wealthy patrons would prefer the more elegant hotels of Miami and Miami Beach and would fly down the mornings of the auction and back at nights to take advantage of the city's nightlife. The Palm Beach crowd would undoubtedly come and go in private yachts and planes.

Each day the mails became heavier until the earringed mailman began to complain. The telephones rang incessantly. An additional employee, an elderly retired school teacher from Santa Something, California, was hired to take messages and correlate mail requests for further information.

The frenzy Helene had requested had begun early.

And still she did not return.

Quinton ignored a sense of panic that had begun to plague him.

It was nearing noon on Friday.

A storm over the gulf had driven the humidity higher than customary for the season. The sun was high, blazing and hot, and the cooling storm clouds on the horizon were threatening to pass the island and relieve only the mainland.

Quinton had opened every window in the cottage, but the old mansion in front, the wall behind and the

surrounding palms blocked any possible breeze that
might reach him. The ceiling fans seemed only to
intensify the heat. He changed into walking shorts,
sandals and a cotton tank top, gifts from Justine, but
perspiration continued to seep from his pores To add to
his discomfort, the cottage had filled with flies that
buzzed and dove at him like kamikaze pilots. Between
wiping perspiration from his eyes and palms and swat-
ting at flies, he brooded over the conversation he had
had that morning at breakfast with Justine.

He had stared at the eggs, toast and fruit Maria had
set before them with no appetite. The beginning of
congestion in his chest and a familiar ache in his
stomach told him he was coming down with a cold. He
seldom got colds, the damnable things, but when he did
it always took weeks to shake them. "I'd better call Dr.
Webb and get a shot," he had said. "I don't have the
time now to pamper a cold."

Justine without looking up from her plate, had said,
"Dr. Webb doesn't practice any longer." She, too, had
been quietly moody since getting up.

"Well, he comes running when Helene needs him,"
he had said irritably, "so I think you could prevail on
him for a simple shot."

Justine had looked at him blandly. "I'll call, but I
think he's away. There are other doctors. Any one of
them could, as you put it, give a simple shot. I'll find
someone." She had turned her attention back to peeling
a guava.

"I'd also like Helene's phone number at the clinic,"
he had told her. "Since she won't call to let us know
when she's returning, I intend to call her. There are
papers she must sign, decisions only she can make. I
don't mind accepting my responsibilities, she pays me
well enough for it, but as my employer she also has
obligations."

Maria, busy at the sink, had suddenly become stilled, the dishes no longer passing through her sudsy hands. She had turned: "Miss Helene, she hates telephones."

Justine had silenced the housekeeper with a glance. "What papers? What decisions?" she had asked Quinton. "I have power of attorney to act on her behalf."

Odd, Quinton had thought. I would have imagined she would be elated at the prospect of disturbing Helene on the hated telephone. He had pressed, "Are you refusing to give me the clinic's number?"

"No, of course not. Not if it's essential. Is it essential?"

Suddenly it had all seemed so unwarranted, his irritability and his insistence on being given the clinic's number. The papers requiring her signature were simple releases that Justine was authorized to sign; the decisions could wait until shortly before the auction. He had sat staring at Justine silently, feeling childish and guilty for having given in to the effects of the heat and the beginnings of a cold. He was not a man who customarily inflicted his ill moods on others. It was, he had reasoned, the pressures of the auction and his long working hours. The person he least wanted to argue with was Justine. He needed, in Hal Crimmons's vernacular, R & R, rest and recreation. He had wanted to apologize—always, he had been good at apologies, even when he hadn't felt blamable—but his well-controlled stubbornness had surfaced and he had continued to sit silently, broodingly.

Justine's green eyes had suddenly softened. Despite Maria's presence, she had said, "Darling, there's something else bothering you. What is it?"

There had been—there was—but it was buried so deep that he was unable to discern it. It, whatever it was, was tenaciously gnawing at him and would, he assumed, like the symptoms of the cold, eventually make itself known.

"It's only the cold," he had told her. "Colds always make me irascible. I'm sorry." He had attempted to alter his mood, saying "It's a cruel god who allows common colds to exist in paradise," but even that had come out like a complaint, and Maria had voiced her objection to censuring God by clucking her tongue against the roof of her mouth.

"Maria, bring Mr. Armstrong aspirins and orange juice," Justine had instructed. "I'll locate a doctor to give you a shot, darling."

As she had risen from the table, he had said, "Am I forgiven for being such an ill-tempered bastard?"

"You are forgiven," she had said, and had bent and kissed his cheek, whispering, "I love you."

But when she had left the kitchen to telephone a doctor, he had noted her verbal forgiveness had not yet reached her piercing green eyes. Her expression had haunted him all morning.

Quinton swatted at another fly and succeeded only in striking his own neck and spattering beads of perspiration onto the personal letter he was in the process of penning to the curator of San Francisco's de Young Museum. The moisture immediately caused the ink to spread. He crumbled the sheet and flung it into the wastebasket. Rising, he stood directly under the ceiling fan and let the movement of air play over his upper body. His right buttock was sore where the doctor had given him an injection. He massaged the sore cheek and some satisfaction must have showed on his face, because he became aware of Betty's muffled laughter; he had forgotten she was there, sitting in the corner with her sketch pad, the Doberman curled up on the floor beside her.

"I do that when I gets spanked," she told him. "It makes the hurt go 'way."

"Well, it doesn't help too much with shots," Quinton said. "That doctor must have been a quack."

"What's a quack?" she asked.

"A bad doctor," he answered.

"Dr. Webb, he's a bad doctor," Betty said seriously. "I hide when he comes."

"You're a smart girl," he mumbled beneath his breath.

He left Betty in the cottage and crossed the yard to the back door. The kitchen was empty. He helped himself to lemonade and carried the glass into the heart of the house. Here, since the ceiling fans were not used, the heat was more intense. He pitied Justine, Alex, Janet and Aaron, who were working somewhere on the upper floors; the retired school teacher had already asked permission to leave for the day—new to the area, she was not accustomed to the heat and humidity and had appeared on the verge of collapse. Quinton had told her to stay home tomorrow if the weather did not make a change, the others could share the answering of telephones.

The house was now quiet. He stood in the entryway and stared up the stairwell past the chandelier. There was no sound of ringing phones, no footsteps, no conversation muffled in the labyrinth of the upper floors, no Maria humming hymns as she cleaned. What, he asked himself, if they had all passed out up there from the heat? No, a silly thought. Justine, Maria and Aaron were used to the tropical heat; Alex and Janet were young and resistant. Still, he should give them the balance of the day off, perhaps change their work schedule to nights when the trade winds made the old mansion bearable.

He climbed the stairs to the second floor landing, aware of his dizziness and the acceleration of his heartbeat. Either the cold or the injection or both were intensifying the effects of the heat. He clutched the banister and held the surface of the lemonade glass against his forehead to cool himself. His legs felt as if they were turning to sponge. He staggered to a side chair, sat down and drank the lemonade. Removing the ice cube, he held it against one wrist and then the other. His dizziness passed and his heartbeat became normal. Only an uneasiness remained. He had never been seriously ill a day of his life, but he remembered vividly the lingering illness that had eventually claimed his maternal grandmother, her cries and whimpering and drugged ramblings, and consequently, his fear of personal illness bordered on a phobia. That's why he had related with such heartfelt compassion to Helene's condition. Leaning his head back against the wall, he remained in the chair, eyes closed, the remains of the ice cube melting in his hand and dripping onto his naked leg. He felt extremely weak.

The windows at either end of the hallway were open. A sudden hot breeze stirred the sheer curtains. A door creaked. Quinton opened his eyes and saw the ballroom door moving slowly inward from the breeze. "Christ," he muttered outloud, "I hope the storm is going to hit." Then he sat upright, aware of a voice, Justine's voice, coming from the ballroom. He stood unsteadily and moved to the door.

When the cottage had been converted into offices much of thhe furnishings, plus furnishings from the room Justine now occupied, had been moved into the ballroom. Rows of chests and armoires and dressing tables, ornate cabinets and sofas standing on end blocked the windows and the two crowded desks where Alex and Janet performed their duties. The ballroom was somewhat cooler than the hallway; he heard the whirring sounds of electric fans. Justine's voice was louder and he used it as a guide to make his way through the maze of passageways.

"Yes. Even ahead of schedule."

The dizziness struck Quinton again like a blow. He staggered, supported himself against a Louis XV aromoire, and leaned his forehead against the cooler surface of its beveled mirror.

" . . . demon for work."

He opened his mouth to call out, then decided he did not want to alarm Justine. She was apparently on the telephone judging from the lapses at her end of the conversation. He wondered vaguely if she was alone.

" . . . but do we really need him any longer?"

Quinton pushed away from the armoire.

"It's becoming more difficult to sustain my . . . "

His foot struck the leg of an Italian vitrine and the panels of glass reverberated.

"Who's there?" Justine called.

He managed to proceed to the end of the row of furniture.

She was alone, standing behind one of the desks, the telephone receiver held to her ear. The fan on the window ledge was lifting her hair from about her shoulders and whipping it about her face as the large blade rotated. Her face went pale when she saw him. "Quinton, what are you . . . ?" She suddenly said into the receiver, "I'll call you back later," and hung up. "Quinton?"

"I feel so . . . who were you talking to?" He moved unsurely to the desk chair and sank into it.

"Helene," Justine said. "I called the clinic this morning and left a message for her to return my call. You look awful, darling."

"I feel awful. Where are the others?"

"I sent them to the beach for a break. This heat is unbearable." She came to him, bent and placed a hand on his forehead. "You're burning up," she said with concern.

"I'll be all right. It must be the heat and this cold." He reached for her hand and held it. "I'm sorry about being so cranky this morning. I don't want you to think your lover is so . . . "

"Forget it," she said. She stooped beside his chair, her green eyes probing his. "Darling, I think I should call the doctor back."

"No, it'll pass. How is Helene?"

Justine bit her lower lip. "She's better. She said she'd be coming home in another week."

"Good." There were tiny tiny explosions of light before his eyes. Good God, he thought, I'm going to pass out. "Justine, I don't want to alarm you, but I think I'm . . . "

"Quinton!"

His head fell down to his chest. The explosions of light vanished and darkness pressed in.

He seemed to be existing in a netherworld halfway between reality and unconsciousness. He heard Justine call out, and then almost immediately—or had time elapsed?—Aaron was there beside his chair.

"He's fainted," Justine said, as if from a great distance.

"Fainted? From what?" Aaron's voice sounded slightly amused.

"How the hell should I know? Get him to his room. I'm going to call the doctor." There was a loud clicking sound, as if the dialing of the telephone had been magnified.

"I don't know if I can lift him," Aaron complained.

Quinton felt himself being handled roughly. He tried

to speak, to tell Aaron to leave him be, that he would be all right, but he could not find his voice.

"Then drag . . . "

Sounds, awareness came and went like images on a screen when the film was breaking. He felt himself being lifted, carried. He opened his eyes and saw the shadowy shapes of finials and ornate carvings on the bonnets of tall cabinets. He recalled his nightmare of being thrown to sharks. In his confusion, the furniture became masts, the roaring in his ears the sound of the ocean lapping against the sides of a yacht, Aaron's heels against the naked floor the snapping of jaws, jaws waiting for a sacrifical offering. "Justine! Save me!" he cried, and then the blackness claimed him completely.

He became aware first of the coolness.

He opened his eyes and found himself in his bed. The shutters had been drawn, but there was still shafts of bright light behind them. He felt disoriented, thought he had overslept, and then he remembered passing out in the ballroom. He tried to sit up, groaned against the sudden pain in his head, and let himself fall back against the down-filled pillows. A noise caused him to turn to his right.

Maria was struggling out of a chair. "You just lay still now, Mr. Armstrong," she said, her voice making it evident that she had been sleeping and he had awakened her. She took a washcloth from a pan, ice clanking against the sides, and dabbed it on his forehead; the coldness drove the remaining cobwebs away.

"What's wrong with me?" he demanded.

"Nothing serious," the housekeeer answered. "Just a touch of the heat. Too much work, too, I'd say.

Doctor said you'd be fine by mornin'.''

"Probably a reaction to his damn shot," he complained. "Why is it suddenly so much cooler?"

Maria returned the cloth to the pan. " 'Cause it rained," she said. "Cooled things down for a time. But now it'll get even hotter than before. You don't have to worry. Miss Justine, she had a cooler brought in fer you.'' She nodded toward the far side of the room where a large air-cooler was shirring quietly.

"What time is it?" he asked.

"'Round five o'clock. But don't you go worryin' 'bout the time. You just rest. Go back to sleep maybe. Betty and me, we'll take turns sittin' with you for a spell. You want anythin' you just tell us.'' She maneuvered her bulk back to the chair and sat down.

"What I want," he said, "is to get up." He started to throw the covers away and that brought Maria back out of her chair with surprising agility.

"You oughtn't do that, Mr. Armstrong," she warned, and gently pushed him back against the mattress. "Doctor said you was to stay in bed 'til morning'. Miss Justine, she'll get mad at me if I let you get up.''

"Where is she?" Quinton asked. The throbbing at his temples was becoming less painful; his thought were clearing. "Damn, I've never passed out in my life.''

"Miss Justine's dressin' for the party," Maria told him. "She said she'd stop by before she goes.''

"Party?" Well, he couldn't be seriously ill if Justine was leaving him to attend a party. Still, it seemed rather callous of her to go with him confined to his bed.

The door opened and Justine entered. She was wearing a long white dress that clung suggestively to her body and highlighted her deep suntan. Her dark hair was pulled back from her face and worn in a French twist. The only jewelry she wore was the Faberge pendant of the astrological sign of Gemini; it reminded him of the first time they had met when he had tried to impress her by identifying the workmanship. She had applied makeup to her eyes; the green irises taking on the depth and color of emeralds. "Darling, you're awake," she said, and came to the edge of the bed, bending down to plant a kiss on his forehead. "Your fever's broken, too. You certainly gave me a fright," she said as she straightened. "If Aaron hadn't decided not to go to the beach with the others . . . " She let the sentence go unfinished.

Maria had walked to the opposite side of the room, and with her back to them, was absently dusting the top of the bureau with the hem of her apron.

"You look especially beautiful," Quinton said. "What's the occasion?" He had tried to keep the childish sense of abandonment from his voice, but despite his efforts the nuance of it was there; he saw it register on her lovely face.

"Oh, darling, would you rather I stay with you?" She sank to the edge of the mattress. "It's only a silly party for some visiting novelist, nothing important. I just thought that since you would probably sleep until morning . . . " She, too, was unsuccessful in burying her true feelings; he could tell she wanted to attend the party. "Actually, I only wanted to see the new compound where the party's being held. I've been told the residents have turned it into a veritable paradise of tropical plants and fountains." She sighed almost undetectably. "I'll call Maggie and simply tell her I can't make it," she said, and started to rise.

"No. You go," Quinton insisted. "I understand I've been ordered to bed until morning anyway."

"Are you sure you don't mind?"

"Not at all," he lied. "I'll read, perhaps start that second magazine article I'm supposed to write." He reached for her hand and pressed it affectionately.

"You're supposed to be resting," she said with mock scolding. "Are you sure you wouldn't rather I stayed? We could play backgammon or cribbage. Or I could read to you."

Quinton laughed. "I haven't been read to since I was six," he said. "Go and enjoy yourself." He pulled himself up against the headboard and the movement made him aware of the soreness in his right arm and along his side; he vaguely remembered the pain as Aaron had hoisted him from the ballroom chair. He grimaced and said, "Your gay friend must also be a sadist. He almost dislocated my shoulder."

"I don't know what I would have done without him," Justine said. "I was so frightened I could scarcely dial the telephone."

'How the hell should I know? Get him to his room,' Quinton remembered her shouting as if in a dream. *'I'll call the doctor!'* He recalled thinking at the time how composed and in charge she had been, and he had felt relieved. "Poor darling," he said. "I'm sorry I frightened you. It happened so suddenly I . . ."

The doorbell cut him off.

"Oh, that must be Aaron," Justine said, rising.

"Aaron?"

"He's acting as my escort to the party in your absence," Justine explained. She stooped and kissed his cheek. "Promise to rest and not work," she said. "Maria, make sure he drinks plenty of liquids. Goodbye, darling. I'll look in on you when I return." She crossed the room and let herself out without glancing back at him; Quinton heard her footsteps moving quickly down the hallway.

Maria, eyes averted, moved back toward her chair to

resume her vigil. Before she had reseated herself, Quinton said, "Maria, would you get me a glass of cold milk, please?"

"Y'sir, Mr. Armstrong," she said, obviously glad to escape the confines of the sickroom.

After she had gone, Quinton rose and walked, without dizziness, to the windows. He opened the shutters and looked out onto the front yard. He witnessed Justine and Aaron going down the walkway, Justine clinging to the handsome homosexual's arm. Jealousy swept over him like a torment that could not be dismissed. There was something in the manner in which she clung to Aaron's arm, something in the tilt of her head when she looked up at him—no, damn! It was his own interminable jealousy! What the hell was wrong with him? Justine loved him, Aaron was only her friend and a goddamn pervert at that. When the couple reached the gate, Quinton stepped back from the window so he could not been seen, placing himself so he could scarcely see their heads over the window ledge. His heart skipped a beat. As Aaron leaned forward to open the latch, Justine laughingly placed a quick kiss on his cheek. Then they passed through, the gate closed, and they were gone.

Quinton was still standing at the window when Maria returned with his milk.

"Mr. Armstrong," she reproached, "you ain't suppose to be outta bed."

Quinton moved silently back to the bed, lay down, and closed his eyes. "Leave the milk on the nightstand, Maria," he instructed dully. He heard the glass being set down on the marble top. "And, Maria, it isn't necessary for you to remain with me. I'd like to be left alone. Even as a child I couldn't sleep with someone watching over me."

"Yes, Mr. Armstrong, if that's what you want,"

Maria answered. "I've my chores to do."

He heard her shuffling footsteps cross to the door. "Maria, where is this compound where the party's being given?" he asked without opening his eyes.

"Over on Catherine Street," she answered.

"Good night, Maria."

Hesitantly, she echoed, "Good night," and then crept quietly from the room.

When he came out onto the porch Quinton saw the last colored streaks of the sunset fading on the horizon. The trade winds had begun to blow gently over the island, but they carried little promise of cooling the temperature. The storm had apparently passed on to the mainland while he had been unconscious, leaving only enough rain to raise the humidity.

Quinton glanced back at the front door. Maria had not heard him descending the stairs, and Betty, whom he had found stationed outside his door, thinking his exit was a game, had promised not to tattle on him.

He moved down the walkway and quietly let himself out of the metal gate. He walked to Duval Street and at the taxi stand asked the dispatcher if he was familiar with a new compound on Catherine Street. "Written up in yesterday's newspaper," the burly man told him. Quinton ordered a taxi and ten minutes later climbed out; he paid the driver and stood waiting on the sidewalk until the taxi had driven away.

The street was crowded with parked cars, every make from Mercedes to Volkswagen and American compacts jammed onto the edges of the tarmac and leaving only space for a single car to pass. Overhead, the thick branches of poinciana trees stirred in a breeze. The wooden gate before which Quinton stood was closed; the gate, like the surrounding wall, was slightly above eye-level. He stood on tiptoes, but only managed to see the tops of flaming torches scattered among palms and hibiscus bushes. There was the sound of soft music almost lost beneath voices. He heard footsteps approaching on the opposite side of the gate and stepped quickly between parked cars so the guests who were leaving would not find him standing directly in front of the gate. A matronly looking woman in a flowing print gown emerged with a young man. The woman's laughter denoted alcohol-lost control. The young man clung supportively to her arm. They moved down the sidewalk, the woman weaving, and climbed into a vintage black Cadillac. They had left the gate ajar.

Inside the compound, a brick pathway wound itself between shrubs and palms. Near the center, he could see the corner of a swimming pool, its shimmering light reflected on a crowd of people. He looked for a long white dress, but when he spotted one it was worn by a heavyset woman, the flame from a torch feeding color into her white hair.

He stepped to the open gate, then stopped. Christ, he thought, what made me think I could crash a party? I can't, I just can't! He had meant to slip in, cling to the fringes of the crowd and watch Justine and Aaron. Seeing them together, unsuspecting, he had thought he could put an end, once and for all, to his nagging suspicions and jealousy. Ridiculous, he now decided. I've become demented. The kiss he had seen Justine give Aaron could have meant nothing more than friendship. Why did he have such difficulty accepting their friendship? Accepting Aaron as a man whose sexual preference encompassed only other males? Go back, he told himself. Get your ass back into bed, and if you try very hard, you can rid yourself of this ludicrous jealousy.

"Mr. Armstrong, isn't it? Quinton Armstrong?"

Quinton had heard no one approaching. He spun about, startled, and found himself facing Ernesta Calder and an elderly white-headed man with a heavily wrinkled, bloated face. Composing himself, he took the ex-show girl's extended hand.

"Mr. Calder, my husband," she introduced, making the gulf between their ages sound even greater by her formality.

Quinton took the man's hand and found his handshake firm and youthful.

"Mr. Armstrong is the young man I was telling you about," Ernesta told her husband. "He's appraising Helene Haymes's antique collection."

"Ah, yes," Mr. Calder said with obvious interest. "That sparked my curiosity."

"Everything about that woman sparks your curiosity," Ernesta stated.

Ignoring his wife, the man said, "You see, I'm Miss Haymes's attorney. I was wondering why she would require an appraisal. I called at the house, but her maid told me she was in a clinic in North Carolina." His colorless eyebrows lifted questioningly. "Curious, most curious."

"She'll be returning in a week," Quinton offered. Wasn't that what Justine had told him just before he had passed out?

"I was wondering if perhaps the museum had reconsidered . . ."

"Enough about that woman," Ernesta cut in. "Why are you standing out here, Mr. Armstrong? You needn't be shy about being alone."

"I'm afraid I wasn't invited," Quinton told her. "I was just passing and heard the sound of a party and . . ."

"Well, come along in then," she said, taking his arm.

"I'd rather not. I was just out for a walk and . . ."

"Nonsense, my boy," Mr. Calder said. "Ernesta's right. Come along in and meet some of the locals. If they're a bore—and they can be believe me—at least you'll get a free buzz on and hopefully something to eat. Who's giving this party anyway, Ernesta, dear?" He nudged Quinton good-naturedly. "So hard to know who your host and hostess are at these compound parties."

"He once thanked another guest for inviting him," Ernesta said dryly. "The Dawes, Fred and Dorothy, are the hosts tonight and novelist Jack Mayfield is the guest of honor." She pulled Quinton through the gate.

"Never heard of him," Mr. Calder said from behind.

"Well, pretend you've read every word he's written," Ernesta shot over her shoulder. She squeezed Quinton's arm. "Don't let him start talking about Helene Haymes or he'll monopolize you all evening," she warned in a near-whisper. "Boring, boring, boring. Perhaps you and I can . . . Oh, Dorothy. How are you, darling? May I present Mr. Quinton Armstrong from New York City?"

Quinton spotted Justine almost immediately.

She was standing across the pool talking to a woman in a blue pantsuit. The ripples across the surface of the pool were causing the light to shimmer over her white gown, giving her an eerie quality of unreality. She was easily the most beautiful woman present.

Aaron was standing next to her conversing with a man in a too bright, plaid sportscoat. Aaron was, Quinton hated to admit, the handsomest man present.

Both were visible to him in profile. They appeared conscious of one another's presence, but not intimately so. Justine turned to Aaron, said something, and he took a cigarette from his pocket, lit it, and then turned back to his conversation. He used his hands expressively; perhaps that could be taken for a feminine trait—he certainly had no others. Dressed in tight-fitting white slacks and a blue silk shirt open at the neck, Aaron looked like a paperback cover artist's conception of a superstud.

Justine, looking for an ashtray, turned in Quinton's direction.

He stepped quickly back away from the lighted edge of the pool. He realized how extremely foolish he would feel if she saw him. It was devious enough to spy on her, unworthy of him not to trust her; it would certainly be unwise to be caught. He decided he must leave as inconspicuously as possible. More guests were arriving and Ernesta, who had been watching him from where she had been cornered by three other women, had turned away to greet a newcomer. He set his drink down on a table and stepped into the crowd surrounding the buffet, intending to skirt the group and make for the exit.

Instead, he found himself confronted by Ernesta's husband. The attorney held a plate heaped high with food. "Been trying to have a word with you," he said. "Oh," he turned to the man at his elbow, "this is Jack Mayfield, the guest of honor. Good writer. Jack, meet Quinton Armstrong."

The two shook hands.

"Quinton's down here from New York doing an appraisal for a client of mine. Most . . . hmm . . ." he took time to pluck a shrimp from his plate and pop it into his mouth . . . "most curious, young man. But then Helene has always been unpredictable and changeable. Didn't think she'd change her mind about her collection though. She was always inflexible about what she wanted to happen to it. But having it appraised, well, I guess . . . hmm, delicious shrimp, you should try them . . . what was I saying? Oh, yes, Helene's collection. A remarkable woman. We grew up together. Our families go back to the days when salvage was Key West's biggest business. Actually, hers goes back even further, back to when the island was a haven for pirates, but don't tell her I told you that. That's probably where she got most of her spunk. Remarkable woman, remarkable.''

The novelist winked at Quinton over the old man's shoulder.

"You were going to tell us something about her collection,'' Quinton reminded the attorney.

"Oh, yes, indeed I was,'' Mr. Calder said. "I'm probably the only person outside of Justine and her maid who's seen her collection. Now you, of course, Mr. Armstrong. She was always terrified of people viewing the collection. Afraid they'd recognize its value and rob her.'' He laughed. "If she hadn't kept guests out of the house, I'm sure she'd follow them to the door and search them before they left. She has pirate's blood and thinks everyone's a filcher. When we were drawing up her will and making arrangements for her museum, she made me stress that all items that could find their way into tourists' pockets had to be kept under glass and lock and key. I put the most stringent regulations any attorney's ever . . . ''

"Excuse me,'' Quinton interrupted. "Are you telling me Miss Haymes's original intention was to set up a museum for her collection?''

"It certainly was. In that old mansion of hers,'' the attorney answered. "Although it would never hold all of it. It's crammed already and she has two storage sheds filled to the ceilings on Stock Island. But she's apparently changed her mind. Wisely, too, I'd say. The

tourists who come to Key West don't come to look at
antiques. They come for sun and fishing, for sun and
swimming, for sun and fun. By fun, you know what I
mean?'' he winked. ''The tourists are getting younger
and younger. I have to believe that because I can't
accept that I'm getting older and older, that's what my
wife tells me.'' He laughed with amusement. ''But kids
nowadays, they don't have any interest in antiques.''
He leaned closer to Quinton and the novelist and said
quietly, ''If you can't screw it, smoke it or sniff it,
they're not interested.'' He popped another shrimp into
his mouth. ''I guess I'd better get some of these to my
wife before she comes looking for me.'' He turned and
walked away through the crowd.

''Quite a character,'' the novelist said.

Quinton nodded. He was still considering the news
the attorney had related about Helene's intention of
establishing a local museum to house her collection. He
became aware of the novelist staring at him and pulled
himself away from his thoughts. ''Sorry,'' he said. ''I
didn't mean to be rude to the guest of honor.''

The novelist laughed. ''The party's really to show
off the compound,'' he said. ''I'm just an excuse so it
won't appear too pretentious.''

''Is it your first visit?''

''No. I come down often to unwind from New York
and try to get my perspective back. My agent owns the
house at the end. Usually I keep a low profile, but this
time I agreed to playing the role of guest of honor.
They've done such a damn good job with the compound
I wanted to help them show it off. This was practically a
slum when they started.''

The novelist went on talking about the changes that
had been necessary to create the compound, but Quinton's thoughts wandered. Finally, the novelist, recog-

nizing his preoccupation, excused himself and moved away.

Quinton glanced suddenly to where he had seen Justine last standing. She wasn't there; neither was Aaron. His gaze swept the crowd seeking a glimpse of Justine's white gown. She was nowhere in sight, but the compound was now so crowded she could be near him and he'd miss her in the sea of bodies.

Voices all around him were blending in a confused den of sounds: " . . . when I was the social editor on the newspaper . . . " " . . . oh, Tenn, yes, he's a darling, always saying those outrageous things to shock people and . . . " " . . . turned their boat into one of the small keys and stumbled right onto a drug drop. She was shot in the arm and . . . " " . . . and there they were, the three of them on the float doing obscene things and everyone lunching at *The Pier House* watching. It was the most . . . " " . . . I think he's actually begun to believe he was Hemingway's buddy, but let me tell you . . . " " . . . darling, my husband's only homosexual when he's drunk!" " . . . because of the Russians in Cuba, that's why they're there. I tell you, the Cuban resurgence is more of a threat than they're . . . " " . . . at *Shoe Fly*, my dear. They have the most adorable python boots and . . . " " . . . won't be back for the season . . . " " . . . say his adopted son is more of a legally snared lover who isn't . . . "

Quinton stepped as far back into the shadows as the vegetation would allow. Still watching for Justine, he worked his way around the crowd and found the brick pathway. Ernesta was near the fringe of a group huddled around a bar. Waiting until she was engaged in conversation and couldn't see him, he walked quickly away.

On the sidewalk, he pulled the gate closed behind

him and breathed a sigh of relief. Now which way did he walk to get back to the house and into bed before Justine returned home? He shoved his hands into his pockets and started walking towards a distant intersection where he could see a flashing red light.

"You're going the wrong way, darling!"

He practically leaped off the sidewalk, crying out in shock. Turning, he saw Justine step away from the shadows about the trunk of a poinciana tree.

"Did you enjoy yourself?" she asked.

Her white gown shimmered in the moonlight as she walked towards him. The whites of her eyes caught a glint from the distant streetlight. She held something in her hand—a drink, the ice clanking against the sides of the glass with a curiously hollow sound.

Quinton felt himself choking on guilt. Was it any wonder he had never had affairs while he had been married to Joanna? The slightest infraction, and he was destined to be caught.

"Justine," he said, "forgive me! I'll never doubt you again. I'll smother my jealousy if it kills me!"

Justine hesitated; then stopped approaching him altogether, just stood quietly staring at him as if she was making an important decision.

Finally, she said, "Let's go home, darling. These parties bore me. I'd rather be alone with you."

Chapter Sixteen

Quinton made his second trip to New York.

He collected the transparencies from the photographer and delivered them personally to the publishing house, recommending the firm he thought outstanding in color separation; he spent four hours with the art director and his assistant, another hour with the woman who would edit *The Haymes Collection* catalogue. He returned to his office too late to meet his partner who had left a memorandum outlining the progress of the Haymes account; the London, New York and Los Angeles *Times* would be carrying a feature story on Helene with an emphasis on the auction. *You owe me one for that,* had been penciled in the margin. *Antiques* magazine would carry a lead feature on the collection with a publication date three weeks prior to the auction. Quinton skimmed the remainder of the memo until he came to the final paragraph:

The *Post* article had an interesting response from groups outraged to discover our client was still alive and had not been dealt with for what they referred to as 'War Crimes.' Some accused her of being a spy, others of collaboration with the enemy, still others of specific crimes against individuals known to have been executed by the Nazis. Most were cranks—others misguided American patriots ever on the lookout for a possi-

ble witch hunt. One woman, however, who was
referred to me by the *Post*, was of interest; she
claims to have been an acquaintance of our client's
while they were living in Berlin during the war.
Thinking it might mean a possible article, I returned her call. When she learned you were in
charge of the account and the Haymes auction, she
insisted on speaking to you personally. I think the
lady wants to sell 'her story.' Your decision.
Telephone number in the file under Charlotte Engels.

When Quinton dialed Charlotte Engels's number the
telephone was answered by a gravel-voiced woman
with a heavy German accent.

"I talk only in person," she told him. "You come.
I'll tell you about Helene Haymes." She gave him an
address on Hudson Street in Greenwich Village, and
hung up.

Quinton glanced at his wristwatch. He had three
hours before his flight to Miami. If he missed the flight,
he wouldn't make the last flight of the day from Miami
to Key West. There was nothing urgent demanding he
return to Key West until tomorrow, nothing except his
wish not to be separated from Justine. Still, the woman
had sounded mysterious and his curiosity had been
stimulated. He decided to give Charlotte Engels an
hour of his time; calls to his attorney, Joanna and Hal
Crimmons could wait until the next trip.

Charlotte Engels's apartment was in a building slated
for demolition. A sign posted over the mailboxes gave
the tenants three weeks to vacate the premises. When
the buzzer sounded and he opened the lobby door,
Quinton's nostrils were assaulted by a pungent odor
from a pile of garbage left to rot under the stairwell;
something scurried out of sight at the sound of his

footsteps. Somewhere in the labyrinth of the building, a baby cried, a dog barked. The walls, unpainted for at least a decade, showed signs of water damage from the morning rainstorm. Mud had been tracked across the lobby and up the staircase. Covering his nose with a handkerchief, he moved to the elevator and pressed the button.

"Elevator don't work any more," a voice called down the stairwell. The accent told him it was Charlotte Engels.

Quinton went to the base of the stairs and looked up. Several floors above a woman's straggly grey head protruded over the banister. The naked lightbulb behind her made it impossible to see her features.

"You're young, liebling. The climb won't hurt you. Fourth floor in the rear," she called and retreated. "Don't let the rats bite you," was almost lost as she moved away.

Quinton stopped on the fourth floor landing to catch his breath. Charlotte Engels's door stood partially open. From behind another door, two women were arguing in Spanish, their voices baiting their neighbor's dog to barking.

Charlotte Engels appeared in her doorway. "Come, come," she told him impatiently, and motioned him into her apartment.

Charlotte Engels was, he judged, about Helene's age, but unlike Helene, every year of her age was on her face. Her colorless eyes were sunken into her head, her cheekbones hollow, her grey hair unkempt and so thin areas of pink scalp showed through. She wore a green dress that belonged to another era, its hem reaching the mid-point of her bony legs. As she tugged at the dress, it struck him that it had at one time been elegant and she had donned it to receive a guest. About her stooped shoulders she wore a yellowed white shawl. "Sit," she said, pointing to an overstuffed chair with collapsed springs. "You want tea, I have one bag."

"No, no tea," Quinton said, and she looked relieved.

"I used it this morning anyway," she admitted. "How much you pay to know about Helene Haymes?"

"You're certainly direct."

"Not direct. Hungry," she said. She moved to the sofa, which was in no better condition than the chair, and sat down. "Soon I have no place to live. I become one of those women, those bag women. Me, Charlotte Engels! I who once wore jewels and beautiful dresses! Men once fought over me, wealthy men. Now they won't give me a quarter for a cup of coffee. I'm dried up, ugly. But it happened long ago. Before the years did it naturally. It was her fault, Helene's. She did it to me, the American whore!" Her voice had risen with vehemence; suddenly exhausted, she slumped against the sofa back, her concave chest heaving, eyes partially closed as she fought for breath.

Concerned, Quinton started to rise.

"No, sit!" she ordered. "It will pass." She pointed a skeletal finger to the cluttered table at his elbow. "See, liebling, how pretty I was," indicating a photograph in a metal frame.

Quinton, to please her, picked up the photograph. She had been about twenty when it had been taken, and indeed beautiful, her short hair worn in the black patent-leather bob that actress Louise Brooks had made a coiffure trend. Her eyes were large and pale and heavily made-up, and hinted at intelligence and wit. Her skin was smooth, flawless. The woman who now sat on the sofa across from him was not even a shadow of the beauty in the photograph. "Very beautiful," he said. His compassionate nature caused him to be shaken by emotion. He returned the photograph to the table. "If there's something in your relationship with Helene Haymes that we can use in an article," he said, "I'm prepared to pay you two hundred dollars." He had three hundred in his wallet; he would have given her the entire three hundred if he hadn't needed traveling money.

Charlotte Engels laughed without humor. When her laughter died, she said, "It's her I want to pay. Pay big. Pay so I don't tell my story. She always wanted fame. It was almost as important to her as the antiques she collected. But she won't want to see my story in print." The old woman was talking so rapidly spittle ran from the corners of her mouth onto her chin. She wiped it away with a trembling hand. "You work for her, you tell her she pays me big to be *stumm,* mute."

Quinton tried to conceal his bewilderment, but before he could stop himself, he cried, "Blackmail?"

The old woman looked at him calmly, nodding.

"You can't be serious," he said incredulously.

"Most serious, liebling," she assured him. Her eyes blazed within the hollows of their sockets with an intensity that convinced him. "All these years I thought her dead," she said. "In Hell with her lover, the Führer."

"Their relationship was only rumor," Quinton said. "She had to flee Berlin to keep from being murdered by the madman."

"Rumor?" the old woman cried. "You tell me rumor? I was there! I know! There was me and Greta and Helene. Helene wanted to be number one with him, but she could never replace Eva in his affections. Eva was smart. Look what it got her. But Greta and me, she got rid of us. Greta, she drove off. Me she had arrested.''

"I don't believe any of this!" Quinton said, and rose. She was obviously mad; she had seen the *Post* article on Helene and had focused her madness on a past that her demented mind now believed included Helene. As the old woman struggled to get to her feet, he fumbled in his wallet and drew out a twenty dollar bill.

"I don't want your money," she snapped. "I won't be bought off cheap." Still, her gaze focused on the crisp bill and she seemed to be calculating whether she should or shouldn't accept it. "She must pay big or I tell my story to the papers."

"No respectable newspaper would believe you," Quinton told her. "Helene Haymes is a citizen and . . .''

"I'm a citizen too!" the old woman cried. "They listen! I make them listen!" Her accent became heavier as she became more agitated. "She make Gestapo believe I was a Jew!" Fumbling with the frayed sleeve of her dress, she exposed her wrist, as thin as a chicken bone, and shoved it towards him so he could see the numbers tattooed there. "I'm no Jew! She knew, the Führer knew! He let the Gestapo take me to please the American whore!"

Quinton realized she was on the verge of hysteria. "Please , Miss . . . Mrs. Engels . . . Charlotte, please calm yourself." He reached for her arm to help her back to the sofa, but she pulled away defiantly, forbidding him to touch her.

"She had a way with her," Charlotte Engels said bitterly. "She could make men do what she wanted, buy her things, always antiques. What they couldn't buy, they *stehlen* . . . steal! From the Jews they took away." The old woman turned her back to him; she walked to the curtainless window and stood staring into the space between the buildings.

Quinton was undecided; he was convinced she was mad, age and the horrors of her past had driven her to a point where she peopled her memories with celebrities she read about in newspapers and magazines. He wanted to turn and walk out of her apartment, forget he had been here, but compassion held him in place.

When Charlotte Engels spoke again, it was without a trace of hysteria. "At first they used me for the officers," she said. "There were little rooms with beds. The officers, they make jokes about sleeping with one of the Führer's whores. They say they'll have the American next. When we not being used we sleep, over a hundred, in a big room with no heat and no . . ."

"Miss Engels, please," Quinton pleaded. "I don't think you should torment yourself by remembering . . ."

"Mrs. Engels," she corrected without turning. "I marry a Jew from the camp after the Americans free us. We come to America. He was jeweler before the war, but he . . . When they tire of us the officers give us to enlisted soldiers. They only keep the pretty ones. There are so many. If you get sick . . . my husband died after ten years in America. He was thrity-six, but he looked old. Like me. They put me in experiment group when I am no longer pretty. A doctor removed my breasts without giving me . . ."

"Mrs. Engels, I'm sorry," Quinton interrupted. "I'm so sorry. Please believe me, but . . ." he decided not to ignite her hysteria again by telling her Helene Haymes could not have been responsible for her horrors . . . "I must be going. I have a plane to catch and . . ."

"You tell her you saw me. Charlotte Immendorfer,"

the old woman said, turning from the window. "You tell her what they did to me. You tell her I want money or I tell the newspapers about her. They listen to me. The officers tell me things when I slept with them. Things I can prove. Money's not much to pay for what she did to me. I don't want to be woman with shopping bags and no place to go. You tell her she has three weeks. That's when they throw me in street. You tell her."

"Yes," Quinton placated. "Yes, I'll tell her."

"When you tell her you see I speak the truth," the old woman said. "You don't believe me, liebling. But you look in her eyes and you see the truth." She turned again and stood staring through the grimy window at the grey, desolate building beyond the courtyard. "If my husband had not died, he would kill her for what she did to me. You tell her. You tell her I wait for her in *Holle*. She be number one there. *Holle,* that's Hell, liebling. You tell her."

"Yes, I'll tell her," Quinton repeated dully. He dropped the twenty dollar bill in the clutter of the table and let himself quickly out of her apartment.

A Puerto Rican woman with curlers in her hair was standing in her open door looking down towards Charlotte Engels's apartment, apparently drawn by the old woman's earlier hysteria. "She okay?" she asked suspiciously.

Quinton stopped, aware the woman thought he had attacked her neighbor or perhaps brought more distressing news from the contractor who was to demolish the building. Embarrassed, he said, "She was upset about the past. I couldn't control . . . she'll be fine now."

"Ah, si," the woman said. "Sometimes I walk her to her synagogue and she tells me things that upset her."

Quinton, who had moved on to the stairs, stopped. "Then she is Jewish?" he asked.

"Si. And devout," the woman answered. With a final suspicious glance at him, she closed her door and he heard a series of locks being clicked into place.

The rain had begun again, a thin mist that to Quinton, who had become acclimatized to Key West, chilled him to the bone. He checked his wristwatch and was surprised to discover he had been with Charlotte Engels, née Immendorfer, for less than half an hour. He still had time before going to the airport. Taxis were plentiful on Hudson Street because one of the company's many stations was located a block away. He hailed a cab and gave the driver the address of the bar where he knew Hal Crimmons would undoubtedly be preparing himself for the night ahead. He sat moodily in the backseat and contemplated Charlotte Engels's accusations agaiinst Helene. Even if there was no truth in them and he was convinced there was not there were unscrupulous reporters who might give newspaper space, if not credence, to her story. Such publicity could only hurt the auction, Helene—and Justine.

When Hal Crimmons saw Quinton he immediately ordered another drink for himself and one for Quinton. "You look as if you could use this," he said as he pushed the martini towards Quinton. "Auction problems? Or are they romantic?"

"No surprise that I'm in New York?" Quinton said. "Just have a drink and unburden yourself?"

"Well, I've never seen a gloomier countenance, so it appears you need the drink and a good listenener," the older man said. He picked up both their drinks. "Let's move to a table so we can keep it private."

They settled in at the table and Quinton, after a steadying gulp of his martini, said, "This is strictly off the record, Hal. No calls to reporter friends to sell a scoop. Understood?"

Hal gave him a look of mock indignation. "I'm

strictly old school,'' he said. ''If you say off the record, it's off the record. Besides, old man, we're friends. What's the problem?''

Quinton told him about his visit with Charlotte Engels. ''We want publicity for the auction,'' he concluded, ''but not this sort. It could be damaging in a very serious way. Do you realize how many of the antique dealers, museum curators and collectors I deal with are Jewish? If Charlotte Engels's story was written convincingly . . .'' He sipped his martini thoughtfully. ''Even if it was proven to be fantasy, the product of a sick old woman's mind, there might still be doubts that would keep some of the most important bidders away from the auction.''

''Then the woman simply has to be dealt with,'' Hal said flatly.

''What do you mean by dealt with?''

''Appeased, held off until after the auction,'' Hal told him. ''Find her an apartment, pay the rent, give her some walking around money and the promise of more to come.''

''That would be dishonest!'' Quinton was appalled.

''Helene Haymes can obviously afford the expense,'' Hal said. ''Look on it as insurance money. A few dollars given to the old dame will buy her silence and not threaten a boycott of the auction by your important bidders. It makes sense and it's no more dishonest than any other kind of insurance.''

''But it would give foundation to Charlotte Engels' story if she attempted to sell it later,'' Quinton pointed out.

''Then deal with her through a third party,'' Hal said. ''Someone who won't be connected to Helene Haymes should the occasion arise. Deal only in cash. No checks.''

"You read too many detective stories," Quinton said, but his expression revealed that he was considering the reporter's suggestion. "I'll tell Helene," he said. "It'll have to be her decision. The Engels woman gave her three weeks."

"Now that I've settled that problem, how's the romance going? Are you still planning to pull a writer's version of Gauguin?"

Quinton nodded.

"She must really be something, this woman you've fallen for," Hal said.

"She is, as you put it, something," Quinton told him. "She's become everything to me. It still astonishes me that I can feel such . . . such passion. I admit I was never a passionate man with Joanna. I thought it was a quirk of my nature that . . ." Quinton laughed. "Why is it you always manage to get me talking? I'm supposed to be the strong, silent type. One more drink, a quick one, and I have to get to the airport. If I miss this flight, I'll be stuck in Miami for the night."

"I could give you a long list of men who'd love to be stuck in Miami for the night," Hal laughed.

"But those men don't have someone like Justine waiting for them," Quinton said, signaling the waiter for refills.

"By the way, should you need that third party to deal with the Engels woman," Hal said, "I'd be available for a nominal fee."

Quinton, who had slipped into a better mood with the talk of Justine, was drawn back into the problem reluctantly. "As I said, it'll be Helene's decision. Should there be a need, I'll recommend you."

Now Helene, as she had promised Justine, had better come home from the clinic, Quinton reflected. There

were some decisions she could not leave to others. As
for Justine, he had already determined not to tell her
about Charlotte Engels. Should Helene elect not to
return home, he would travel to North Carolina to visit
her.

Quinton glanced up from his desk when he heard the
back door of the old mansion slam.

Justine had emerged and stood on the back stoop.
Hands on hips, she turned her face up to the morning
sun, eyes closed, and took several deep breaths. She
wore a pale blue shirt, unbuttoned, the tails tied together at her midriff. Her hair was loose, cascading
about her shoulders. In the past two weeks she had had
little time for the beach and her suntan had begun to
fade. She had complained weakly, accusing him of
being a slave driver. The work schedule had been
grueling, sometimes extending into twelve and four-
teen hours a day; they worked, ate, slept, with little
time for lovemaking. No weekend excursions to the
other keys, no afternoon boating trips. But, Quinton
told her proudly, they were on schedule.

An auctioneer had been hired. The brochure, printed
and offered for sale, had already gone back to press a
third time. The local hotels, motels and guest houses
were already boasting a 100 percent booking for the
week of the auction. Letters and telegrams had been
received from wealthy collectors demanding preferen-
tial treatment, reserved seating and special lucky bidding numbers, others made offers to purchase items
directly from the brochure "to prevent the owner from
losing profits to what would surely be low bidding." A
Texas oil baron requested Helene to be his guest on his
yacht while it was moored in the harbor, and an Arabian
sheik requested that she invite him as her guest. To all,

Quinton wrote polite but firm letters of refusal. A gardener had been hired to beautify the old mansion's backyard, and carpenters to build a platform at one end for the auctioneer. Key Westers, drawn by curiosity, came daily to stand across the street and watch the comings and goings of workmen. The local newspaper sent a reporter for an interview with Helene and did not believe Maria when she told them her employer was still away on an extended trip. Reporters kept calling daily, demanding interviews, and Maria kept sending them away.

Quinton lay his pencil down, rose and moved to the open door of the cottage.

There were three carpenters constructing the auctioneer's platform. Because of the morning heat, they had stripped away their shirts and worked only in cut-off dungarees, their hard, tanned bodies glistening with sweat. Quinton saw Justine watching them and he felt the Old Demon Jealousy struggle to rise up within him and claim his reasoning. Since the night he had followed Justine to the party he had managed to control his jealousy; she, in turn, had appeared more cautious not to provoke it. Quinton leaned against the door frame, thinking: What's wrong with her admiring a handsome man? Before he could contemplate the answer, he walked back to his desk and sat down.

Janet, at the desk across from his, averted her gaze when he glanced in her direction, but not before he saw her disturbed expression. He had developed a friendship with the young woman. She was an extremely conscientious worker and had proved to be knowledgeable about antiques; what she had not learned from her mother's books, she had quickly picked up. Privately, she had told Quinton that Alex had asked her to marry him once the auction was over. ''But, he's really just a child. I would like someone more mature and settled.''

Quinton had smiled. ''You're only nineteen, Janet. I wouldn't recommend marriage, but then I also think you have time before you commit yourself to a mature, settled man.'' He had been especially kind to her, aware of her interest in him.

Justine's dislike of the girl had taken the form of completely ignoring her. So now, when Justine appeared inn the cottage door, Janet rose from her desk, gathering up papers Quinton knew were to be filed in the cabinets behind her. ''I'll just take these over to Alex,'' she said, and slipped passed Justine into the yard.

''The Mouse is in love with you, darling,'' Justine told him. She came into the room and perched on the edge of his desk.

''I wish you wouldn't call her that,'' Quinton said. ''She's a very sensitve and thoughtful girl, and my best worker.''

''Better than me?'' Her eyebrows arched.

''Yes, even you,'' he laughed.

''But then she gets wages,'' Justine said dryly. ''I work only for the harridan's gratitude.''

''You handle the checkbooks,'' Quinton reminded her. ''Pay yourself a salary.''

''And put her in a tirade? No, thank you.'' She moved from the desk and wandered aimlessly about the office, perhaps remembering when it had been her private retreat from the main house. ''She's already complaining. About the carpenters' hammering, the snipping of the gardener's shears, the   ''

Quinton pushed his chair away from his desk. ''You mean she's back?'' he cried incredulously. ''When? Why wasn't I told?''

Justine turned and smiled at him teasingly. ''The great Helene returned last night,'' she told him, ''in the hours before dawn, like a vampire returning to its coffin.'' Her smile faded. ''She's displeased with you, Quinton. She's not accustomed to being given ultimatums. She returned in a cantankerous mood.''

''I can't help that,'' Quinton said. ''I told you to tell her she either returns home or I go to the clinic. There are things I have to discuss with her.''

''Whatever they are, she'll tell you you should have trusted my judgment,'' Justine said.

''Perhaps.''

''Not perhaps. She will,'' Justine assured him. ''I know her.''

Do you really? Quinton refrained from asking.

''She'll say, 'Quinton, I told you Justine would handle everything in my absence. I am not accustomed to being dictated to by a man, especially not an employee.'''

''You imitate her very well,'' Quinton said, ''but I doubt she'll be as hard on me as you suggest.'' Secretly, he hoped not. ''You've given me her mental condition, but how is she physically?''

''Her eyes, you mean? No change, I guess. She immediately ordered all the shutters closed.'' Moving to the window, Justine stared up at the top floor of the old mansion. ''I don't think there's anything wrong with her eyes,'' she murmured. ''I think she prefers the darkness for psychological reasons.''

''That's a strange thing to say.''

''Maybe her personal demons are less taunting in the darkness.''

Quinton looked at Justine's profile trying to discern a subtle change in her voice. Was she weakening? Feeling sympathetic towards the woman she claimed to hate to vehemently? Her next statement answered the questions.

''If I thought that were true, I'd barge in and fling her

shutters open to the sunlight," she said bitterly. "Her
demons should be allowed to devour her. I wish you
hadn't called her back. Now she'll spoil everything.
We'll have to slip around again to be together. I wish
. . . I wish she had died in that clinic!''

"Justine! You don't mean that!''

Justine spun around from the window. "Don't I? Is it
so wrong to hate someone who's manipulated you all
your life? Someone who drove your father to suicide?''
Her eyes were moist, the expression angry. "Why
can't you see her for what she is? An evil old woman,
not a glamorous, fading legend?'' A single tear broke
from her eye and ran down her cheek.

Quinton went to her and held her in his arms. He
kissed her forehead, her temples, her eyes, tasting the
salt of her tears, and he made reassuring sounds, wishing he were less inept at comforting her. He wished he
could be less objective, too, that he could hate Helene
as much as she, and therefore side with her. But he
could not. He loved Justine, but he had feelings for both
women. He was the man between, a man snared in the
web of their love-hate relationship, and if he was not
careful he might lose Justine.

Justine's trembling subsided. She turned from him,
wiping her eyes. "I'm sorry," she murmured. Then,
suddenly flinging herself back into his arms, she said,
"Quinton, when this auction is over, can we go away?
Just the two of us, for a trip to Bermuda, Africa,
Morocco, Monte Carlo—anywhere? I'd like to get
away from Key West for a while. Away from her.''

"Yes," he told her. "We'll go away. Anywhere you
like. For two, three weeks, a month. I owe myself a
vacation before I launch my new career.'' He caught
his breath, summoned up courage. "Justine, can we
. . . can we make it a honeymoon?''

At first she blinked at him, not comprehending; then

a sparkle came to her green eyes, and she cried, "Oh, yes, my darling! Yes, yes! I didn't think you were ever going to ask!"

"It'll have to be Mexico," he said logically. "My divorce isn't final. We'll marry again when . . ."

"Oh, yes!" She clung to him, laughing. Then, quickly she pulled away and stared up into his face. "Don't tell her, darling," she said. "Not until we're ready to leave. I don't know how, but she'd find some way to stop us."

"Justine, I've just proposed to you and you've accepted. We're both adults. There's no way anyone could stop us. Not even Helene, not even if she should want to."

"You don't know her."

Quinton said, "Would you change your opinion of her if she wished us well and sent us on our honeymoon with her blessing?"

"She wouldn't!"

"But if she did?" he pressed. "Then would you consider that in some ways you might have misjudged her all these years?"

"Perhaps," Justine conceded stubbornly. She lifted his wrist and glanced at his watch. "It's time for my audience," she said sourly. "I was to tell you yours is in an hour." She kissed him hurriedly. "You've made me very happy, darling." She rushed through the cottage door, calling over her shoulder, "I love you!"

Almost immediately, the screen door opened again, and Janet, who had apparently been standing outside waiting for Justine to leave, entered. Her expression was clouded, morose. She dropped the file papers back on her desk and sat in her chair, pretending to be occupied by a brochure she had mailed out weeks ago to potential customers.

"You heard?" Quinton said.

The young woman nodded without looking up. "You're always reminding me how young I am," she said. "But, Quinton . . . " She rose and crossing the door, added . . . "I'm not as naive as you." With no further explanation, she pushed through the screen door and fled across the yard to the main house.

Chapter Seventeen

"Well, Quinton," Helene greeted him from the shadows of her favorite bergère chair, "you insisted on my coming back, so here, at your command, I am. Come in, sit down, tell me what's so important that Justine couldn't make the decisions on my behalf".

Quinton, now familiar with the room despite the semidarkness, crossed to the chair opposite her and sat down. "I could have come to you," he said. "Indeed, I expected to."

"Well, no matter. I'm here now," she said with a tone of dismissal. "Will that hammering go on indefinitely?"

"The carpenters will be finished this afternoon." He crossed his legs and realized relaxing was a struggle; the muscles at the back of his neck had tightened on the climb up the staircase. Or had the tension begun the moment he had learned she had returned? "Do you agree with my decision to hold the auction outdoors?"

Helene was silent a moment before saying, "Surely this isn't the indecision I must settle?"

"Of course not." She was, as Justine had warned him, in a cantankerous mood. "It was only an incidental question." He tried to make his voice sound firm, challenging.

"Well, then, an incidental question in return," she

said. "What if there is a tropical storm for which we are famous? It would be a shame to draw bidders from across the world and then expect them to be doused."

"The ballroom will be ready in the event of a storm," Quinton answered.

"Then that's settled," she said with a weary sigh. "What else?"

"Charlotte Immendorfer."

Her right elbow was resting on the chair arm, her hand, the slender fingers extended, resting against her chin. Her head did not jerk, her hand did not move. She waited clamly for him to continue. When he did not, she said, "Is this a puzzle, Quinton? Are we to play games? Who, or what, is Charlotte Immendorfer?"

"A woman who claims to have known you in Berlin," he told her.

"In Berlin?"

"During the war."

"Ah, I see. And this woman made accusations?" Her voice sounded amused.

"Startling accusations."

"About myself and the madman, no doubt?"

"About that, yes. And more." He then told her about Charlotte Engels contacting his New York office, about his visit to the pathetic woman and the accusations she had made.

When he had finished, Helene leaned forward in her chair, a pale shaft of shaded light from between the slats of the shutters illuminating her grey hair and planting pinpoints of light in both her eyes. "What do you want of me, Quinton? To deny her accusations? I do. They are lies." Her chin was defiantly tilted, as Justine tilted hers when she was angry or upset. "Lies," she repeated, and slumped back into the contours of the chair. "So, it has begun again. But we knew it would. Why did the woman come as such a surprise to you?"

"I didn't believe her," Quinton said hastily, "but she was so . . . so convincing."

"Many of them have been," Helene said wearily. "There have been many who have tried to bilk me. No doubt the rest of the woman's story was the truth. Only she read the article on me and saw one last desperate attempt to save herself from a future that can only mean her death. To have survived those horrors in Germany only to end . . . " She shook her head helplessly, and fell silent.

"She knew about your antiques," Quinton said.

"Easily researched in the public library," she responded.

"I went through your diaries. There were none for the period the woman placed your involvement with Hitler."

"I was too occupied with survival to keep diaries then. Is this a cross-examination? Do you still doubt me?"

"No. I'm merely trying to stress a point."

"Then make it and don't stretch it out beyond endurance."

Quinton told her of the danger of Charlotte Engels selling her story to a newspaper, of the harm it could cause the auction, and then of Hal Crimmons's recommendation. "You can see," he concluded, "the decision had to rest with you. I would not, could not bring it to Justine."

Helene's voice softened. "You were proper to bring it only to me. I agree with your friend. The woman must be appeased until after the auction. Perhaps by then we can find some some agency to help her. I'm not altruistic, but I can sympathize with her situation. I authorize you to contact your friend and have him act on our behalf. Have Justine wire whatever monies he thinks necessary within reason. Say it's a promotional ex-

pense, whatever you feel she won't question. Tell me,
Quinton, did Justine speak of me often during my
absence?''

"No, not often," Quinton lied.

"I will still talk to her, but when the time is right. Is
there anything else? Travel exhausts me. But, I must
confess, it is good to be home. At the clinic the doctors
are inexhaustible. They run tests and then tests of
tests, but I never surrendered to optimism. There was
no disappointment when I learned there was no change
of prognosis. I have a guarantee past spring, so do not
fear for the auction, but, well, I'll not plan on seeing the
poincianas bloom again. You must arrange to be in Key
West for that occasion, Quinton. It's a sight worth
seeing. The island blazes with color.'' There was no
self-pity in her voice; she spoke matter-of-factly, moving from her death to the beauty of the poincianas in
bloom without the slightest alteration of emotion.

But Quinton felt pity. It required considerable effort
to keep his emotion from his voice when he said, ''I
believe the auction will be the success you demand of
it.'' He told her of his progress, of the many acceptance
letters. Then he ended by telling her how admirably
Justine had labored.

Helene was silent a moment, then said, ''You like
her, don't you, Quinton?''

He wanted to blurt, *I love her!* Instead, he simply
said, ''Yes, I like her.''

"I'm pleased," she told him. "Now, Quinton, if
there is nothing further . . . ''

Quinton rose, hesitated. "There is something I'm
curious about.''

"And that is?''

"I met your attorney, a Mr. Calder.''

"Oh!'' The exclamation expressed surprise.

"He was surprised to learn you had hired an appraiser. He seemed to be under the impression appraisals were made before he drew up your will to . . . ''

"The old fool!" Helene snapped angrily. "I haven't spoken to him since he married that show girl. He meant to shock Key West society and only succeeded in damaging his own social esteem." She rose and moved towards the bed. "I suppose he told you my original will made arrangements for a museum."

"Yes. He mentioned it."

"I made that will when Justine ran away to New York to become an actress," the old woman said, stooping to turn down her bed. "I was hurt and angry and meant to disinherit her. When she came home I always meant to change it, but I never did."

"Mr. Calder also mentioned something about storage sheds filled with antiques on Stock Island. If there are items I haven't catalogued . . . "

"No. Those antiques were brought to the house," she interrupted. "I didn't trust leaving them in the sheds. Will you ring for Maria as you leave, Quinton?"

The request was also a definite dismissal. He bid her good day and let himself out.

From the ballroom, he called Hal Crimmons, told him Helene had accepted his recommendation concerning "the Greenwich Village Problem," and asked how much he estimated would be required for appeasement. Hal had apparently given the matter consideration because he answered without hesitation: "Four thousand and a thousand for me, old man." Quinton told him the money would be wired that afternoon. The entire affair bothered him, but he told himself not to let himself get further involved than he was; he had turned the matter over to Helene and the solution had been her decision. He was shouldering enough responsibili-

ties—and guilts. Still, memory of Charlotte Engels
haunted him; he would for the next twenty-four hours
find thoughts of her popping into his head and disrupt-
ing his concentration. In twenty-four hours, Charlotte
Engels would no longer be a problem.

Alex was working at the second desk in the ballroom. Since Janet had joined the staff, the youth had
had his hair cut and trimmed his beard. In place of the
loose-fitting suits and sloppy trousers that had become
his trademark, he wore dungarees and plaid shirts,
thinking they gave him an older, more rugged image.
When Quinton dropped the receiver back into the cradle, Alex glanced up from the newspaper clippings he
had been reading on Helene Haymes. "Quite a woman," he said. "I understand she's back. Will we get
to meet her?"

"That," Quinton said, "is a question I couldn't
answer."

"Janet says she's eccentric. Like Mrs. Winchester in
California." Mrs. Winchester, the heir to the Winchester rifle fortune, was rumored to have been seen very
little by her employees and servants, but was always
spying on them. Among other things, she felt the spirits
of those killed by Winchester rifles were seeking revenge against her. The servants, she felt, were out to
poison her and earn rewards from the spirits, and she
had had various architectural changes made in her old
mansion to enable her to watch them unseen. "You've
seen her," Alex pressed. "Is she anything like Mrs.
Winchester?"

Quinton had toured the Winchester House to
examine the fine examples of Tiffany glass doors and
windows the old woman had used in her ceaseless
additions to the old mansion. "No, she's nothing like
Mrs. Winchester," he told Alex, and refrained from

adding, "Helene Haymes's eccentricities are different."

"What'd you say to Janet anyway?" the youth asked. "When she came in from the cottage she was almost in tears." His voice was suspicious, protective.

"I didn't say anything to Janet," Quinton said evasively.

"She was cussing you," Alex told him. "I never heard Janet use obscenities before. Said you were a clown, that any woman could hoodwink you."

"Probably just tension. We've all been pushing ourselves. Have you seen Justine?" he asked, wanting to change the subject.

"Not since she went up to see her aunt," Alex said, and went back to the newspaper clippings on Helene Haymes that had arrived from the New York office. The blues—the editing copies for magazines—had also arrived from Hal Crimmons, but Quinton had not had time to read his article; he had assigned the editing to Janet and could see various pencil marks on the sheets at Alex's elbow. He told Alex to bring them to the cottage, and then went to look for Justine.

She was not in her room, or in any of the storage rooms he checked. He hoped her meeting with Helene had not upset her. She had been in such a good mood, so happy, after he had asked her to marry him. Regardless of the outcome of the auction, they were going to be happy.

Aaron was descending the stairs from an upper floor when Quinton emerged a second time from the ballroom. The handsome young man was supposed to have been working in the downstairs study. When his present task of assigning lot numbers to the less important items was completed he would no longer be needed on the staff. Justine had already told him and had

reported to Quinton that he had been relieved, wanting
she had said, to escape the gloomy old mansion an
return to his beach life anyway.

Since the night of the party, Aaron had become eve
more distant and unfriendly, avoiding Quinto
whenever possible. Justine had apparently said some
thing to him, perhaps told him about Quinton'
jealousy, and they had temporarily cooled their friend
ship, something for which Quinton felt pangs of guil
whenever he was in Aaron's company. He felt he mus
make amends to Aaron—and Justine—for his foolis
jealousy, but he had been unable to break through th
barrier the young man had thrown up. Sometimes whe
Aaron looked at him he felt not only his discomfort, bu
hatred.

"Good morning, Aaron," he now greeted. "How
are you?"

Aaron nodded, mumbled, "Okay," and continue
down the stairs. "Have you seen Justine?"

Aaron stopped his descent, turned and looked up a
Quinton, his almond-colored eyes cold and challeng
ing. He appeared on the verge of unleashing a torrent o
anger, but then, shrugging his broad shoulders, he
merely said, "No, I haven't seen her," and continue
down the stairs, disappearing into the study and slam
ming the door.

Quinton was in the *Fleur-de-Lys* room, the first roor
of Helene's collection he had previewed the day of hi
arrival. Janet had reported that one of the Dresder
figurines had been broken, and he had come to check or
it.

Indeed, the figurine had been shattered—and not b
accident. There were smudges of porcelain dust stil
clinging to the wall where the valuable object had beer

thrown. The many small fragments scattered about the floor told him repair was impossible. He wondered whose anger—and at what—had caused such wanton destruction. Fortunately, the figurine was not one of the complete Dresden set of the monkey band which, if complete, would bring bids in the six figures. He collected the pieces and dropped them into a small box should the insurance investigator require them to make a settlement. If the figurine was the only casualty of the auction, they would indeed be fortunate.

He was about to leave the room when his eye fell on a cigarette butt ground into the dark-stained wood floor. He had forbidden any of the staff to smoke anywhere except at their desks. The old mansion, with its invaluable collection of antiques, would go up like a tinderbox. He crossed to where the light from the shutters' slats was falling across the ground-out butt, and picked it up. To his knowledge, aside from himself, only Alex and Justine smoked. It was not the typical white paper-wrapped cigarette; the paper was dark brown and the tobacco still had a sweet, exotic aroma. Someone had been in here recently. The aroma awakened an awareness that someone he knew or had met briefly smoked such cigarettes, but for the moment he could not recall who.

He determined then and there that a security guard would be stationed at the front gate at all times. Since there were so many workmen coming and going, Lucifer had had to be tied to a metal stake in the backyard and could not keep intruders out. The staff was too busy to patrol the large house. If a reporter managed to gain admittance and confront Helene—he shuddered—the old woman would never forgive him for calling her back from the clinic where she had been safe from those who would invade her privacy.

Quinton shoved the cigarette butt into his shirt pocket and left. He stopped in the ballroom and instructed Alex to call and arrange for around-the-clock security guards. Then he went down to the kitchen to see what Maria had prepared for lunch.

Just as he pushed through the swinging door, Justine had exited through the back screen. He started to call out to her, but then noted that instead of turning towards the cottage she was going to the end of the yard where the carpenters were finishing up the auctioneer's platform. As she crossed the yard, she had to pass by Lucifer who, angry at being staked and excited by the unaccustomed workmen, barked at her. Justine stopped and shouted for the Doberman to be silent. When he persisted in barking, she turned to Betty who was sitting nearby with her sketch pads.

Maria, drawn away from the stove by the sound of Justine's anger, moved to the window and peered out.

"Keep that damn dog quiet!" Justine shouted at Betty.

Lucifer's excited barking turned to angry snarls when Justine shouted at Betty. Shackles raised, he lunged for Justine. The chain, stretched to its limits from the stake, flipped the enraged dog to the ground only inches from Justine. He was instantly on his feet and straining at his chain to reach Justine, who was standing as if frozen by fear, staring at the dog's exposed, threatening teeth.

"Good Lord!" Maria mumbled. "Now there'll be hell to pay!" She pushed out of the screen door ahead of Quinton.

"I'll have that goddamned dog put to sleep!" Justine cried, finding her voice.

Betty had leaped to her feet, flung her sketch pad aside, and rushed to grab Lucifer's collar. Her eyes widened at Justine's threat. She pulled Lucifer back against her legs, crying, ''You won't hurt my dog! You won't put him to sleep!''

''Your dog!'' Justine shouted, her voice near hysteria. ''He's not your dog! He was . . . '' She turned as she became aware of Quinton approaching with Maria. Her face was contorted with anger, her green eyes as cold as agates. ''That awful beast has always hated me,'' she cried. ''I should have had him put to sleep months ago. He's dangerous!''.

''No!'' Betty wailed. ''Mama, don't let her hurt Lucifer!''

Maria had pulled herself up to her full height, which was formidable. Her dark eyes were as angry as Justine's. ''She ain't hurtin' yer dog,'' the housekeeper promised, her gaze never leaving Justine's face.

Justine cried, ''Maria, don't you dictate to me! It's not your little . . . ''

''Justine, please!'' Quinton interceded. ''There's no call for this hysteria. Come inside,'' he suggested, and reached for her arm.

She pulled stubbornly away.

''We'll settle this calmly,'' he said. ''Over coffee.''

''No. We'll settle it now,'' she snapped, still meeting Maria's unfaltering gaze. ''You work for me! You'll do as I say! I want that dog destroyed!''

''Ain't no dog bein' destroyed,'' Maria told her with authority. ''Miss Justine, you're forgettin' yerself. You listen to Mr. Armstrong, and go calm yerself down.''

''Don't tell me what to do! Do I have to remind you of your position? You're nothing more than . . . ''

''Justine, please!'' Quinton repeated pleadingly. ''For Christ's sake, what's gotten into you? You're making a spectacle of yourself.'' He nodded towards the carpenters who had stopped their hammering and were watching with interest.

"You don't understand, Quinton," she cried. To Maria, she said with the last of her vehemence, "You call and have that dog taken away, you understand? That's an order."

Betty's whimpering grew louder and that caused Lucifer to break into a renewed bout of snarling and barking.

Maria firmly stood her ground. "I ain't goin' to do that, Miss Justine," she said. Turning, she pointed a heavy hand towards the upstairs windows where, it occurred suddenly to Quinton, Helene might be concealed behind the shutters watching the entire scene. " 'Cause if you insist in killin' this here dog, my Betty's dog since Miss Helene gave him to her, then I'm goin' to have to take a stand against you. That's somethin' I ain't never done, but nobody's goin' to break my baby's heart by killin' her dog. I'll have somethin' to say even if I am just a housekeeper an' close to a slave. I knows where to say it too and it won't make no matter to me." The heavyset woman's breasts heaved with emotion. "Now, you tell that girl you ain't goin' to hurt her dog and you get yerself in the house and calm yerself down, or by all that's holy, I'll thrash you myself for the first time in yer life!"

Justine had gone extremely pale. The anger in her face had changed to what Quinton interpreted as fear. Her arms fell to her sides, her shoulders slumped in defeat. She avoided Quinton's gaze. "You're right, Maria," she said weakly. "Betty, I'm not going to hurt your dog."

The frightened girl had unfastened Lucifer's leash from the stake and walked away with him in tow, saying over her shoulder, "I ain't goin' to play your game no more."

"Get inside," Maria warned her. "Lock that dog in yer room an' keep it quiet, ya hear?" Turning back to Justine, the housekeeper seemed about to speak, to say more, perhaps apologize, but suddenly words were lost to her. Sighing, she followed her daughter back into the house.

Quinton took Justine's arm and led her towards the cottage, indicating to the carpenters with a nod that the show was over and they should get back to their work. In the cottage, he poured a stiff Scotch from the bottle he kept in his desk drawer and handed it to Justine. "Drink this."

"No, I don't need it." She met Quinton's gaze with moist eyes, a trembling smile playing about her lips. "I feel like such a fool," she said. "I don't know what came over me. What must you think of me?"

"What I think is that you're exhausted," he told her. "I've been pushing you, the staff, myself, all to keep a schedule. What we all need is some time off. How about an afternoon swim and a few drinks at *The Pier House?* Maybe we could catch one of those sunset ceremonies you were telling me about."

"What I need is sleep," she told him. "I *am* exhausted and you *are* a slave driver." She leaned into his chest and wrapped her arms about his waist. "But I love you anyway," She said, and turned her face up to receive his kiss. "I'm going to take a nap, darling. Since Maria probably isn't speaking to me, would you tell her to say I've gone out if Aunt Helene sends for me? I'm too worn out to go through the strain of listening to her again today."

Quinton nodded.

He watched from the cottage door as Justine walked across the yard and entered the main house. As he was about to turn away, he caught a glimpse of Aaron standing at an upstairs window; he, too, had been watching, his handsome countenance stamped with concern.

Later, when Quinton knocked off working, he looked into Justine's room and saw her still in bed, covered form head to toe by a sheet. Rather than awaken her, he tiptoed out and retired to his own room. He, too, was exhausted. He showered, cursing the trickle of water caused by poor pressure, toweled himself roughly dry, and climbed into bed. He reread the articles on Helene from the New York, London and Los Angeles *Times*, and then the proofs of his own article. It read well, and he was pleased. There was also a test run copy of the cover to be used. Somewhere the staff had come up with a color photograph, a still from one of the movies Helene had made in Europe; it had been taken in the early fifties, before Helene had met Lord Cambray, and showed her in a low cut evening gown with sequined sleeve straps. Her blonde hair had been swept back from her lovely face on one side and cascaded over her shoulder on the other, a style actresses of the fifties had found glamorous. About her slender neck she wore the emerald and diamond necklace reputed to have belonged to the ill-fated Marie Antoinette, the necklace that in a few short weeks would go up at auction and undoubtedly adorn the neck of another beautiful woman. How like Marlene Dietrich Helene had looked, Quinton reflected, and wondered if that was the reason her film career had been so short-lived.

Something about the cover photograph bothered him. He examined it, but exhaustion took over before he could determine exactly what. He lay the cover, article and newspaper clippings aside, and shut his eyes.

It was as sleep claimed him that he realized Helene's eyes in the cover photograph had been blue, not green. He smiled as he drifted off into a dreamless sleep, amused at how far a woman's vanity would go, even to convincing studio photographers to alter the coloring of their eyes.

He did not hear the footsteps retreating cautiously down the staircase outside his room, nor the front door open and close with careful stillness.

The following morning Justine was in high spirits when she came down to breakfast. She gave Quinton a kiss on the cheek and greeted Maria with a cheerful good morning, giving her a sketch pad and several artist's pencils "For Betty."

"A good sleep did wonders for you," Quinton told her as she joined him at the table. He felt refreshed, too, more vitalized than he had been in days.

Maria gave both of them a glance from the stove, saying nothing.

"Is Helene awake yet?" Quinton asked.

Justine stirred her coffee, saying, "I didn't stop by her room. Is she up, Maria?"

"No, she ain't up," the housekeeper answered. "You want eggs or fruit for breakfast, Miss Justine?"

"Both, I think," Justine said laughingly. She reached across the table and covered Quinton's hand with her own. "I've got my man," she said quietly, "so I can afford to gain a few pounds."

After breakfast, Quinton retired to the cottage to answer yesterday's correspondence. Janet was already there, filing; she mumbled a toneless, "Good morning," and went on with her work.

It was nearing noon when Hal Crimmons called.

"I went to see your Greenwich Village Problem," he said. "You can tell your employer I'm returning four thousand of her dollars."

Quinton was immediately disturbed. "Charlotte Engels refused to be bought off temporarily," he said.

"I was afraid of that. Well, we'll just have to take our chances no reporter will take her seriously. If they do, we'll have to hope the important Jewish collectors won't let her story effect them."

"Hold it, old man," Hal said. "I'm certain she would have gladly accepted the money if she'd been offered it."

"Well, then, I don't . . . ''

"Charlotte Engels fell down the stairs of her apartment building," Hal explained. "Her neck was broken in the fall. She's dead."

"Oh!"

"One of her neighbors said the old woman died instantly, so that's that."

"You sound almost happy," Quinton observed.

"I'm not grief-stricken, old man," Hal said, hesitated, and then added, "But of course you would be. You've got to harden up to life, Quinton. Otherwise you'll get a nervous stomach, ulcers and die at a young age. Your depth of sensitivity belongs to the very young and very old. Well, my publisher is screaming for me. See you on your next trip to New York." He hung up before Quinton could say good-bye.

Quinton returned the buzzing receiver to its cradle and sat staring thoughtfully through the cottage window. Hal's news about Charlotte Engels had somehow awakened his nagging sense of something not being quite right. Not about the old woman; Christ, the stairwells in her building had been littered with enough garbage to trip a much younger, healthier person.

"Quinton?"

Janet was standing at his elbow, had apparently been standing there for several moments waiting to get his attention. She placed what looked like an invoice on the desk in front of him. She had been arranging the bills,

separating them from correspondence and the large
number of advertisements Helene's publicity had
brought in the mail, and segregating those bills related
to the auction from those for regular household expense.

Quinton glanced at the bill with half-interest.

"I don't know which this belongs with," Janet told
him, "auction or household. Did you rent storage sheds
on Stock Island to store additional antiques?"

Quinton snatched up the bill. Forty-five dollars for
two sheds. The invoice had been written in ink by a
shaky hand. *Monthly rental* had been printed, and
below that, *Thank you. Lester Santos*.

Helene had told him the antiques stored on Stock
Island had been incorporated with those in the house a
long while ago. Yet she continued to receive monthly
bills. Why had she lied to him?

"I'll take care of this, Janet," he said. He folded the
invoice and put it in his shirt pocket.

Later when Maria called him to lunch, he told her he
had some errands to run and would skip eating. He
walked to the taxi stand on Duval Street and gave the
driver the address on Stock Island.

Lester Santos was a retired fisherman. A bent little
man with a head of unruly grey hair and skin tanned to
the consistency of leather, he met Quinton in the drive-
way. Obviously eager for conversation, he cast aside
any suspicions he might have about Quinton representing the legendary Helene Haymes and led him around
the side of the house, pointing to two good sized sheds.
"I used them for tools and boat parts before I retired,"
he said. "That was nineteen years ago next September.
Sold everything then and ran an ad in the paper to rent
the sheds for storage. Miss Haymes, she answered the
ad and has had them ever since. That's why she gets

them so cheap. Twenty-two-fifty each. I've only raised the rent once. She pays promptly, never late like most folks would be.''

"Did you meet her personally?'' Quinton asked the old man.

"Nope, not when she rented from me, not since. But I'd seen her around when we were kids. She was a wild one. The most beautiful woman I've ever seen. I knew who she was. People talk. She made me promise not to tell anyone she'd rented the sheds.'' The old man motioned Quinton to a wooden bench, and perched on the opposite end. "Fact is,'' he said, "I never saw no one come or go after the sheds were filled until about eight months ago. Then Miss Justine started coming and taking things away.''

"Miss Justine?''

"Her and that pretty boyfriend of hers,'' the old man went on. "I figured she had the right, her being Miss Helene's niece. There's no problem, is there?''

"No, no problem,'' Quinton assured him. "Mr. Santos, could you show me inside the sheds?''

"Not much left now,'' the old man said. "Miss Justine took most everything away a piece at a time. Besides, I don't have keys. Didn't want the responsibility. But you can see through the transom window.'' He pointed a stubby wrinkled finger toward the small windows above each of the sheds. "Really no need for her to rent both sheds now,'' he said. "What's left would fit in one. I didn't say anything. Didn't want the bother of running ads again.''

"What sort of antiques did Miss Helene keep in the sheds?'' Quinton asked. He saw the old man's eyebrows arch, and said, "I mean were the pieces large, small, strictly furniture?''

"Small,'' Lester Santos said. "Old, but small, things Miss Justine could put in a car. I figured that's why she left what she did. Just large pieces that would require a truck. She took the statues and boxes, that sort of thing. Figured she was selling off things for Miss Helene. People are seldom as rich as rumor has them being and it's expensive living nowadays. I figured Miss Helene had come up against hard times.''

"Someone obviously did," Quinton murmured to himself. He rose, thanked the old man, and left.

When he returned to the house Maria told him Justine and Aaron had decided to have lunch at *The Pier House*. "Said fer you to join them," the housekeeper told him, "if you got back 'fore they did.''

"Is Helene up and about?"

Maria shook her head negatively. "She took some of her pills and went back to sleep," she said. "Told me not to disturb her 'til dinner time.''

Quinton walked to *The Pier House*.

Justine and Aaron were seated at a table on the narrow strip of sand between two buildings. They were having tall, colorful drinks. "Piña coladas," Justine said. "Want one?"

"I'm not much in the mood for drinking," Quinton told her.

The sparkle went out of Justine's green eyes. "Something's wrong." "What? Is it Aunt Helene? She's not . . .''

"It's not Helene," Quinton said. He glanced at Aaron, made a decision not to ask him to excuse them, and said, "Justine, why have you and Aaron been periodically removing antiques from Helene's storage sheds on Stock Island?"

Aaron, slumped in his chair, bolted upright. His hand struck his glass and the drink spilled onto the tabletop.

Justine remained calm, not even glancing at Aaron,

holding Quinton's gaze. After several moments, she said evenly, "I had to have money to live, and she wouldn't give me any. I had Aaron take a few items at a time to Miami and sell them for me. I didn't think she'd miss them." She reached across the table and took Quinton's hand; her own was cold from holding her glass and it sent a shiver through him. "I know it was stealing," she said, "and as much as I hate her, I felt guilty because of it."

"Is that why you've worked so diligently on the auction?"

"That, and because I wanted you to be a success, darling."

Quinton stared gloomily at Aaron's drink oozing over the edge of the tabletop onto the sand.

"How did you find out, Quinton?" she asked.

He told her about the invoice and his conversation with Lester Santos.

"I know I've disappointed and shocked you, darling. Can you forgive me?"

Quinton looked at her for several moments before saying, "I'm going to shock you, too, Justine. Helene knew. All the time you were selling the antiques from the sheds, she knew. She even lied to me to cover up for you. She told me the antiques from the sheds had been incorporated with those in the house. And this," he concluded, "is the woman you claim has always treated you unjustly."

"Yes, I knew she was selling the items from the sheds," Helene said. She rose from the bergère chair and moved slowly about the room, her silk dressing gown giving her a ghostly appearance.

"Why didn't you tell her?" Quinton asked. "Why didn't you simply give her money?"

"Because I was afraid to confront her," Helene told him. "We had argued so often. She visited me seldom as it was. I was afraid if I accused her of being a thief I'd drive her away again. Besides, what did it matter that I'd found out? I'd already learned about my illness, already determined to arrange an auction for her benefit. The items stored in the sheds were mostly second-rate." She continued to pace, nervously nervously wringing her pale hands. "Now *you've* confronted her," she said. "If she runs away again, I'll have your meddling to thank, and just when I had determined to tell her the truth about myself and her father."

"I don't want you to do that," Quinton said firmly. "Not just yet."

"What did you say?" Her pacing stopped abruptly. "You don't want me to tell her? *You?* Forgive me, Quinton, but what do you have to do with it?"

Quinton drew a long breath deep into his lungs, exhaled. "Perhaps you'd best sit down," he suggested, determined.

"Yes, perhaps I had," she said pointedly, and returned to her chair.

"I don't believe Justine is strong enough at this point to handle the truth," he told her. "The auction has put all of us under considerable tension. Mentally, I think you confession might have dangerous repercussions."

"I wasn't aware you were a doctor as well as an appraiser," Helene said caustically.

"What I am," Quinton said firmly, "is in love with your daughter."

Helene said nothing, just sat there staring at him in the semidarkness.

"Justine returns my love," Quinton went on. "We're going to be married after the auction. I'll take her away on a honeymoon. She'll rest, become herself.

If you must tell her about her parentage, it would be best when we return.''

Still, Helene did not speak.

"Helene?" He thought she might have fainted, and started to rise to go to her.

"Forgive me," she whispered, holding out a pale hand to gesture him back into his chair, "but you've just dazed an old woman. Give me a moment to absorb this remarkable announcement.'' She sounded neither distressed nor vexed, only stunned.

"I've given it considerable thought," Quinton said quietly. "I have, in fact, had to turn my ability to appraise antiquities to appraising myself, my future, and what I can offer Justine. I am convinced I can make her happy.''

"And you, Quinton?" the old woman asked. "Did your appraisal conclude that she would make you happy?''

"My time with Justine has been the happiest of my life," he said. His gaze fell on the shadowy tabletop between them. He saw the cigarette butt in the ashtray, and it held his attention. It had the same dark brown paper wrapping as the butt he had found in the *Fleur-de-Lys* room.

"The Justine you know now makes you happy, Quinton," Helene said. "Have you considered that she may change? She'll soon be a very wealthy young woman. Wealth has a way of altering personalities.''

As he reached for the cigarette butt, Quinton said, "I've considered that also. I think Justine will be the same wonderful and loving woman she is, with or without her inheritance.'' He turned the cigarette butt beneath his nose; the aroma was the same.

"You are very sure of yourself," Helene said. "And of Justine. Why does that cigarette butt fascinate you so?''

"I found one like it in one of the rooms. It isn't Justine's or mine. Whose is it?"

"I'm sure I don't know," Helene answered impatiently. "You tell me you're in love with my daughter, that you're going to marry her, and then you want to discuss disgusting cigarette butts. For all your charm, Quinton, you can be exasperating."

"I'm sorry." He shoved the butt into his pocket. "Justine pleaded with me not to tell you about us, but I felt I must."

"Undoubtedly, she thought I'd try to interfere," Helene said. "I promise you I won't. When I've managed to digest this, I may even give you my blessing. I must say I never thought I'd live to see my daughter married. She was playing with me then, all the time, deceiving me into believing she was asexual, uninterested in men." The old woman sighed wearily. "I can thank my brother for her deception," she said. "Justine isn't to blame."

"Another thing I'd like to tell you," Quinton said. "When I first came to speak to you about the auction I was unsure of myself, unsure if I could pull it off when I saw the extent of your fabulous collection. I was going to decline the charge and suggest you seek advice from a European or New York auction house, but I was intrigued by you and fascinated by Justine. I believe I fell in love with her the moment I saw her. Even then, I considered resigning from the responsibllity of the auction, but I became enmeshed in your lives. I determined that no one, even if they met my standards as an appraiser, could do for both of you what you wanted better than I."

"Why are you telling me this, Quinton?"

"It's something I wanted you to know," he said. "Regardless of how the auction turns out, I want you to know I did my best, for both of you."

"You still have doubts about the auction's success?"

"No, none," he answered truthfully. "If all indications are correct, it'll be the auction of the century."

"Thank you for that, Quinton," Helen said. "I never doubted you."

When he left Helene, Quinton felt considerably better, relieved. Even if she hadn't yet given her blessing to his forthcoming marriage to Justine, he felt less a conspirator, less deceitful.

Still, and it continued to nag him, he intuitively felt something was wrong.

He wasn't to discover that horror until the day of the auction.

PART III

Chapter Eighteen

To Quinton, Key West became like New Orleans during Mardi Gras.

The channel was filled with yachts, one larger and more expensive than the next; rumor had it that Jacqueline Onassis was aboard one, several movie stars aboard others, and crowds gathered along the beach to watch the passengers being boated ashore.

The wealthy collectors, curators and investors gathered from the four corners of the globe. The airlines were forced to put on additional flights and the air terminal had to divert private planes to Marathan because of lack of space. Highway 1 was jammed by the curious as well as those attending the auction from Miami. Every available living space had been rented and special arrangements had been made for tents to be pitched along the beaches to accommodate the overflow. The regulation against parking along the highway was abandoned, an unbroken line of vans and cars lined the beach from the Stock Island Bridge to the Casa Marina. The police force, even with additional men, was taxed to keep order. Drug dealers, always active because of the accessibility to Mexico and Cuba, tried to take advantage of the carnival atmosphere to land a ten-ton shipment of marijuana and cocaine, but the authorities had been tipped off and were waiting for them. Grocery stores and restaurants ran out of food, and emergency calls had to be placed to neighboring keys and Miami.

Crowds began collecting on the sidewalks outside the Haymes' mansion as early as sunrise; barricades had to be used to keep the streets open to traffic. Quinton, gazing from the ballroom window, remarked to Justine that it reminded him more of a Hollywood premiere than an auction.

"Your publicity campaign drew the spectators," she said. "I only hope their excitement is contagious, spreads to the bidders, and creates the frenzy you aimed for."

Quinton looked at her curiously.

Janet rushed into the ballroom. "The folding chairs haven't been delivered," she announced, agitated. "I called the rental agency and they let half our order go to local restaurants. The rest of the chairs are on their way, but that means half the bidders will be forced to stand."

"Damn!" Quinton exploded. "I knew everything was running too smoothly not to have last minute disasters!"

"I hope it's our only one," Justine said; turning to Aaron and Alex, she instructed, "Set up all the French dining chairs, Tell the auctioneer to hold those lots until last."

Quinton relaxed. "Anyone ever tell you you had great ingenuity?"

At eight o'clock, the first bidders began arriving.

Quinton, wearing a white tropical suit he had purchased for the occasion, waited at the front gate to greet them. He had hoped Helene would consent to a brief appearance, but she had locked herself in her room, refusing, according to Maria, to see anyone, even Justine, until the auction was over.

Many of those passing through the Haymes gate Quinton knew from past dealings, others from their reputations as collectors and investors. He could discern the excitement behind their professional, guarded expressions and he knew before he had welcomed the first two dozen that whatever minor doubts remained about the auction's success were groundless. It would take only the auctioneer's theatrics and the presentation of the first well-chosen items to spark the frenzy. He congratulated himself, and yet he felt curiously perturbed.

The disquietening mood lingered after the gate had been closed and he followed the last bidders around the house to the backyard. The auctioneer was just letting his gavel strike the top of the ornate dais. His elegant voice, recognized by many from the voice-overs he did on television, declared over the speaker system, "Ladies and gentlemen, let the auction begin!"

Quinton moved to the rear of the seated bidders. Justine was standing to one side with Aaron. Her beautiful face mirrored excited anticipation. The dress she had chosen to wear was emerald green; it enhanced her eyes and clung suggestively to the contours of her body. He caught her attention and winked to convey that everything was going well. She smiled, winked back, and Aaron, seeing her, turned and gave Quinton the coldest glance he had ever dared. The obvious hatred in the homosexual's eyes increased Quinton's vexation. He tried to concentrate, to pinpoint the source of his disturbance, but the hushed noise of the bidders and the excitement of the occasion made serious reflection impossible.

Alex and Janet had retreated to the cottage steps; the young couple had worked for months for today's event, but now they appeared overcome by the enormity of it. The wealth and glamour of the bidders, to them, was

something to be seen in movies and on television and
now, in actuality, had an aura of unreality.

Quinton glanced towards the closed shutters on the
top floor of the old mansion and wondered if Helene,
less sophisticated than she pretended, was watching
and was impressed. Or, if she, like himself, felt a
heaviness about her heart because her magnificent collection would soon be bartered to the highest bidders
and carried away to antique shops and homes around
the world? Quinton almost wished the old woman
would suddenly throw her shutters wide and cry down
for him to stop the madness of the auction.

The first item to go on the auction block was: "Lot
27. A French commode, signed by N. J. Marchand.
Lacquered panels framed by rococo ormolu mounts. As
you are undoubtedly aware, ladies and gentlemen, the
ebenistes began signing their work at the insistence of
the guilds around 1741. This handsome *bombe* commode has been dated between then and 1760. Who will
start the bidding?"

From the first row came an opening bid of five
thousand dollars. Immediately, an employed bidder
Quinton had placed in the second row raised the bid by
a thousand dollars. Too soon, Quinton thought. But the
bidding was picked up from several different positions.
When the auctioneer's gavel ended the bidding, the
bombe commode had brought twenty-one thousand
dollars, an unheard of price for the piece and for the
starting item of an auction. The precedent for high
bidding had been set. The bidders shifted uncomfortably in their chairs, but no one rose to leave. Quinton
signaled the auctioneer to plot a quick, cheaper sale of
the next lot; it was necessary for the bidders to realize
bargains could be had if they remained for the three
days the auction had been scheduled

Two prominent New York antique dealers were in-

terested only in bargains. As they began bidding in
collusion it was obvious they were struggling to control
prices. Quinton recognized both dealers: one's name
was Mason, a pinched-faced man in his late fifties who
was known for buying cheaply and selling for high
market prices, and the other Jackson Levin who had
been fired from one of the major galleries because of a
fraud scandal and who now operated Mason's second
shop in Greenwich Village. The two started placing
first bids, calling out low figures, each raising the other
in minimal amounts; in this way, at an ordinary auction, the other bidders became cautious and seldom
pressed the leaders.

Quinton felt himself tensing. He had known auctions
to fail because of collusion between prominent dealers.
His tension soon left him, however; the bidding frenzy
and the mere number of monied collectors made control
by any one group impossible. Mason placed a rock-
bottom bid on a Louis XV settee, Levin raised it by
twenty dollars, and then a collector, irritated by the
obvious attempt to slow down the proceedings, doubled the bid and received a polite applause from the
other bidders.

Smiling, Quinton relaxed, satisfied that Mason and
Levin would no longer attempt to control bidding. At
an ordinary auction the two dealers would have had
clout, but here they were small fish in comparison to the
wealthy collectors and dealers from Europe.

Mason, grim-faced, rose from his chair and walked
to the rear where Quinton stood. He nodded toward the
crowd, his thin lips forming a humorless smile. "You
must be pleased with yourself, my friend," he said
dryly. "You have them bidding top dollar right from
the beginning."

Quinton nodded, saying nothing. He had never liked
Mason or his partner. They were both what Helene had

referred to as antique ghouls, men who dealt in antiquities only for the love of profit.

"Can't last," the dealer murmured. "Their enthusiasm will wane. It's bargains people want at an auction."

"In this case it's quality," Quinton said.

"Their enthusiasm will wane," the dealer repeated with authority.

"I don't agree with you, Mason," Quinton told him. He had his own doubts, but he would never express them to the dealer.

"Would you care to wager on it, my friend?"

"I'm not a gambling man," Quinton answered.

Mason looked at him through slitted eyes. "I'd say you were quite the gambler. A major auction of major pieces on a godforsaken island, that's gambling." He stroked his bearded chin throughtfully. "Well, I'll stick around in the event there are some bargains. A curious collection, I'll give you that. Your publicity campaign was clever also." The word clever came out in the tone of an insult. "I've never seen so many famous collectors in one place in my life." The dealer nodded toward the front seats. "Count von Goddard isn't known for attending auctions, except, of course, for the Rothschild's. All that clever publicity about the infamous Helene Haymes must have captured his fancy."

Quinton knew that Count von Goddard was one of Mason's best customers. A collector of French antiquities, the count generally relied entirely on Mason to do his buying. The count's presence at the Haymes Auction put the dealer in an awkward position; even if he succeeded in purchasing a prized item at a bargain price he would not be able to offer it to the count now since the man would be aware of any sizable markup.

"Bargains," the dealer mumbled, "you'll kill your auction without them."

An elderly woman in the back row lifted her fan and raised the bid on a Lalique plaque to five thousand dollars. Without so much as a flutter of her false eyelashes she countered an opposing bid by an additional five hundred.

The auctioneer's gavel came down. "Sold! Your number please?"

The woman turned her fan to display the bidding number stenciled on its back.

"Good God!" Mason murmured. "I'd have sold her that plaque for under four thousand. Retail. It's insanity, sheer insanity, Armstrong! It'll never hold. The bottom will fall out of the bidding."

Quinton had had enough of Mason. "You might have sold her that plaque for four thousand," he told the dealer, "providing you'd been lucky enough to have one in stock. Then again you'd have been cheating yourself, Mason. Actually, the woman knows her Lalique. The plaque she just bought was produced in a limited edition of twenty-five. Ten of those twenty-five pieces are in museums, four were known destroyed and three you will find being sold at this auction, most likely to the same woman, possibly for even higher prices, since my appraisal for each would exceed ten thousand dollars." Quinton smiled at Mason's frozen expression; the dealer knew his expertise as an appraiser. "So you see, Mason, you have probably just missed what might be the greatest bargain of today's auction. I would suggest that you and Levin spend more time with honest bidding and less time trying to control prices." He could not help the smug expression with which he stared down at the little dealer.

Mason, spinning on his heels, marched back to his

chair and sat down, avoiding Levin who was attempting to draw his attention.

But Quinton realized there was some validity to the
dealer's complaint. He waited until he caught the auctioneer's eye and gave a prearranged signal.

"Lot 65. Figure of a goat. Hard-paste porcelain.
Meissen. Circa 1732. Who'll start the bidding?"

When the auctioneer's gavel fell on the Meissen
figurine it had been purchased for a third of its value.
Murmurs went through the crowd.

Justine glanced nervously towards Quinton. He
smiled back reassuringly. He was not required to give
further signals to the auctioneer. The man was a professional. He had the feel of the crowd. A few more lots
and he would know precisely which bidders were serious collectors and approximately how high they would
go to claim possession of the items that interested them.
He accepted his challenge of pushing them beyond their
predetermined limits. The next item was a pier table,
circa 1810 and brought a higher price than Quinton had
appraised the piece.

The tropical heat and humidity were rising. The
rattan fans with the bidders' numbers stenciled on the
backs were fluttering with greater and greater rapidity.
It was becoming difficult for the auctioneer to distinguish a bid from a mere attempt of the bidders to cool
themselves. His own furrowed brow was glistening
with sweat, the pale blue fabric of his shirt stained dark
at the armpits and about the collar.

Quinton glanced up at the sky. In another hour the
sun would be shielded from the yard by the giant
Spanish lime tree. The auctioneer's platform would
still be in sunlight, but that couldn't be helped. Turning, he signaled Alex and Janet forward. "I'm going to
call a refreshment break," he told them. "See if Maria
has everything ready."

Alex looked puzzled. "A break so soon? Won't that destroy the auctioneer's level? He's really got them going and—"

"We've got to stall for him until the sun's above the trees," Quinton explained. He nodded toward the bidders who, despite their excitement, were beginning to move restlessly in their chairs. He motioned for Janet to check with Maria. Taking Alex's arm, he told the youth, "Get some of the men to help set up the Boulle armoire on the edge of the platform during the break."

Alex's eyes widened. "You're going to put the armoire up so soon?"

Quinton smiled, "No I just want it where it can be admired, a teaser, so to speak. No serious collector is going to let a little discomfort from the heat keep him from bidding on an original Boulle."

Justine, having seen Quinton call Alex and Janet to him, stepped away from Aaron's side and came quickly forward, concern in her green eyes. "What is it?" she asked tensely. "What's wrong?"

"Nothing, darling," he assured her. "We're just going to have a refreshment break to let the bidders cool down."

"Cool down?" she echoed. "But it's going so well . . . you know best," she concluded, although her expression belied the statement. She turned and walked back to where Aaron stood watching them.

Quinton wrote a hasty note and gave it to one of the boys to take to the auctioneer. A pleased expression flooded the auctioneer's face.

"Ladies and gentlemen, I'm pleased to announce refreshments will now be served. In the shade." He wiped his brow and pointed to the bar set up near the cottage. He brought his gavel down with a bang signaling a temporary halt to the auction.

Maria, Janet and Betty, wearing her red dress and an

excited smile, emerged from the back of the house and began passing among the bidders with trays of chilled champagne. Quinton, after making certain the Boulle armoire was being placed at the best advantage on the auctioneer's platform, took the opportunity to move among the distinguished collectors and dealers.

" . . . darling, I'm green with envy," a woman was saying to her companion. "Imagine! You've just bought a writing table that actually belonged to the Queen of France!"

"And at a bargain price," her companion countered.

Mason, also passing, grumbled and moved on without acknowledging Quinton. Champagne glass in hand, he met Levin near the far corner of the house and the two put their heads together in private conversation; planning a different strategy, Quinton thought, and made a note to speak to the auctioneer about the unscrupulous pair.

Count von Goddard emerged from the crowd and placed a hand on Quinton's arm. The count was a tall man, late forties, his body kept muscular and youthful by constant exercise and diet. His antique collection was famous, his private life almost as famous because of frequent escapades that caught the attention of the press and the public. "Quinton Armstrong, isn't it?" His voice was pitched deep, resonant, his smile pleasant. "You may not remember me, but you once "

"I once appraised your collection of hard paste porcelains," Quinton interrupted. "I certainly remember, the collection and you, Count." Quinton extended his hand and shook the collector's hand firmly. "I'm pleased to see you here."

"I wouldn't have missed it for anything," the count told him. He leaned closer as if to relate a secret. "Tell me, is there any chance of . . . well, of private bidding? There's a *Sèvres* listed in the brochure that . . .

No? Well, you can't blame me for trying." The man threw back his handsome head and laughed. "I'm glad to see it's an honest auction even if it does cost me the *Sèvres*." His laughter died, but the twinkle remained in his dark eyes. "And the woman who amassed this fantastic collection, would an introduction be possible?"

Quinton expressed his regrets.

"Well, some days even a count must strike out. But do tell the remarkable lady I hold her in the highest regards." He turned as if to move away, stopped and said over his shoulder, "I also hold you in the highest regards, Mr. Armstrong. You've done a remarkable job with this auction. Should I ever feel the need to dispose of my collection you're the man I'll insist upon." The count stepped into the crowd and was engaged in conversation with another collector before Quinton could thank him.

The compliment had inflated his ego, but still something continued to nag him, something that had been with him since morning that would start to push forward in his thoughts and then evade him before realization. He scooped a glass of champagne from Maria's tray and sipped the cold liquid as he moved through the crowd seeking Justine. Neither she nor Aaron were in sight. He thought they had perhaps sought the cooler climate of the air-conditioned cottage, but before he could seek them out he was stopped by a museum curator from San Francisco. When the curator had finally wandered off, after having bemoaned the fact that Helene Haymes had made no contribution to museums, his in particular, Quinton spotted Justine speaking to Count von Goddard. He didn't know why, but he had the strange sensation she had been avoiding him since the beginning of the auction. Perhaps, he reasoned, she had feared her presence would only intensify his nervousness. He would liked to have told her that his nervousness over the success of the auction had left him after the sale of the first dozen lots. A pattern had been established. The auction would be an even greater success than he had anticipated. One need only look at the excitement, expectation and greed reflected in the faces of the bidders to confirm the auction's success.

The auctioneer appeared at Quinton's elbow. Beneath dark bushy eyebrows, his eyes expressed concern. "Let's not make the break too long," he whispered. "I don't want to lose them because of too much champagne. Champagne and caviar are very grand, but I've seen it happen before. Too much and they tighten their purse strings."

Quinton nodded his agreement. The sun was now shaded from the majority of the chairs by the branches of the giant Spanish lime tree.

The auctioneer bounded up the aisle and rapped his gavel for attention. "Ladies and gentlemen! Shall we continue the auction?"

Quinton watched the people move quickly back to their seats, an action that made their eagerness obvious. Justine, apparently at Count von Goddard's request, moved up the aisle at his side and seated herself beside him. The count was apparently attracted to her—who could blame him?—and Quinton felt a tug of jealousy mingled with the nagging sensation that had disturbed him all morning.

"Lot 78. French Empire mantel clock. Ebony lacquer and gilt," the auctioneer's voice rang out. "The *Sèvres* disc on the pendulum is a portrait of Empress Josephine commissioned by the Emperor himself for the occasion of . . ."

Convinced the auctioneer would not need him, Quinton slipped quietly around the corner of the house. He felt the need to get away from the auction, from the house, even from Justine—he needed to be alone, quiet, where he could think.

When he rounded the house he saw the crowd still choking the sidewalks. They were watching the house, and on the porch, Betty and Lucifer sat watching them with matching curiosity. He let himself out of the gate, pushed through the crowd and took the first side street, going nowhere in particular, just walking, seeking a quiet corner where he could think.

He had walked several blocks from the house when he became aware of footsteps behind him. He turned and found Betty and Lucifer following him. The girl hesitated, judging his reaction to her having followed him. "You mother's going to be angry when she misses you," he warned.

Betty smiled mischievously.

"All right, come on," Quinton told her.

Betty fell in beside him and he more or less let her steps direct him. They walked without talking, she clinging to Lucifer's collar, he lost in his thoughts.

It wasn't until they had passed through the cemetery gates that Quinton became aware of the destination to which Betty's guidance had brought them. He started to object, to retreat, but Lucifer, pulling free of Betty's restraint, darted off among the tombstones, Betty in pursuit.

Grumbling, Quinton followed.

He found Lucifer on a large flat stone, looking very docile, his head resting on crossed paws. Betty was sitting on a nearby smaller stone, watching the dog. She had picked a flower from an urn and was turning it over absently between her fingers.

"We should go," Quinton told her. "We shouldn't be here."

Betty cocked her head to one side and stared up at

him, squinting into the sunlight. "Mama and Lucifer and me, we come here all the time," she said.

Quinton, uncertain if she was lying or confused, glanced at the Doberman, and familiarity struck him. "It's from your drawing," he blurted. "It was almost exactly the same. Lucifer stretched out on the stone."

Betty giggled.

"Tell me, why did you draw a tear in Lucifer's eye?" Quinton asked. "Why did you imagine he was crying?"

"Wasn't imaginin' it," she answered. "He cries when he's sad. He's always sad when he comes here. Miss Justine, she told me not to bring him anymore." An angry expression filled her dark eyes. "I ain't goin' to play her game no more," she said unyieldingly. "It's no fun anyway. She has all the fun. She gets to dress up and wear . . ."

Lucifer gave a long, mournful howl.

"See! He's goin' to cry," Betty said, convinced.

Quinton had to admit the Doberman appeared rueful.

He glanced at the surrounding stones and realized with a sudden surge of surprise that they were in the middle of the Haymes burial tract. Some of the headstones were ancient, worn almost smooth by decades of wind and rain, but all carried the name Haymes. Quinton moved to Lucifer's side and stared down at the large stone on which he lay. The stone was almost new, but without markings. "Who's buried here, Betty?" he asked.

"Can't tell," Betty answered stubbornly.

Quinton felt a rush of adrenalin. "Who's buried here that Lucifer would weep for?" he demanded, restraining himself from shouting.

Betty sensed his sudden agitation. She saw the intense expression in his eyes and it frightened her. "I told her I wouldn't play the game no more," she fretted. "She wouldn't let me wear the wig, said I couldn't put on the makeup either. I wanted to be Miss Helene, too, but she wouldn't let me!"

Quinton staggered to the nearest headstone and sat down. "Is that who Lucifer mourns?" he asked, scarcely above a whisper. "Miss Helene? She's dead?"

Betty nodded a solemn affirmation. "I loved Miss Helene," she said, and began to whimper. "She was never mean like Miss Justine. She gave Lucifer to me, told me to look after him 'cause she was . . ."

Quinton ceased to listen.

He felt as if a devastating blow to his stomach had knocked the wind from him. Yet he no longer had the disturbing sense of something being discordant that defied identification. Everything was now suddenly extremely comprehensible. When the scope of it struck him full force tears of anguish and rage filled his eyes and blurred his vision. He rose, lurching, and started down the cemetery path.

Betty grabbed Lucifer's collar and followed at a considerable distance.

Some of the crowd, bored, had dispersed from the front of the old mansion. The auctioneer's voice continued to fill the morning air: "Two thousand, two thousand five hundred." The fall of the gavel. "Sold!"

Quinton moved around the side of the house. He halted behind the bidders, his maddened gaze sweeping the yard. Justine and Aaron were no longer where he had left them. Janet and Alex, upon seeing him return, rose from the cottage steps. Janet started to come forward, but Alex's hand on her arm restrained her. Quinton moved to the back door and entered the kitchen.

Maria saw him, read the truth behind his expression, and cried out. Ignoring her, Quinton crossed the room and pushed through the swinging doors on his way to the stairs. He knew where to find Justine, knew precisely where she and Aaron would be, where they had been many days before while he had thought them working in different areas of the house—making love in the dead Helene's bed as Justine had convinced him to do.

Maria, running beside him, grabbed at his arm. "Mr. Armstrong, don't do nothin' foolish!" she cried. "Don't do nothin' you'll be sorry for!" He pulled her hand from his arm and started up the stairs, and the distraught housekeeper, leaning against the banister, covered her face with her hands, crying, "May the good Lord forgive me, Mr. Armstrong! I wanted to tell you, I even tried once, but . . . oh, Lord! Mr. Armstrong, please, just walk 'way! She ain't worth gettin' yourself into trouble over! She's got a demon in her, always had, always tormentin' her poor mama!"

Quinton, halfway up the first flight of stairs, stopped and turned to look down at Maria. His blue eyes were now clear, dry, their expression as cold as the surface of polished stones. "Was that also a lie? Did she always know Helene was her mother?"

"Not 'til she was a grown woman," Maria admitted. "That's when she run away. Mr. Armstrong, you're a good man! Don't go up there, I beg you! Go fer the police, if you must, but don't go up there!"

Quinton continued to climb the stairs.

Outside Helene's door, he heard her laughter. Glasses touched with a clink. "We'll be rich beyond expectations, darling!" she laughed. "Now tell me it wasn't worth your jealousy! The fool did it for us! People are down there bidding in a frenzy and making us rich! rich! rich! All that lovely, lovely money!"

Quinton's hand was remarkably calm and he reached for the knob, turned it, and pushed the door open.

The side shutters had been opened and the room was bathed in the bright morning sunlight. Quinton took it all in with a wide sweep of his gaze, the dressing table with the grey wig on a form, the middle drawer open with its clutter of theatrical makeup, the silk dressing gown thrown over the back of *her* favorite bèrgere chair, the couple, Justine and Aaron, lovers, as they stood staring at him in shocked silence, champagne glasses in their hands.

Quinton was prepared for all of this. What he was not prepared for—what caused a gasp to be torn from his throat—was recognition of the man in the second bèrgere chair. "You!" he cried.

Setting his glass of champagne aside, Hal Crimmons rose from his chair. "Yes, old man, me," the reporter said calmly. "Come in, Quinton. Join our party. You are, after all, responsible for our celebration." He glanced at the pale, dazed Justine. "Pour our guest of honor a glass of champagne, my dear. We must toast him in appreciation for a job excellently done. As I told you it would be." Hal turned and flicked an ash from his brown paper cigarette into the crystal ashtray.

Quinton realized the cigarette butts he had found had been left by Hal, possibly when he had slipped into the house to meet with Justine to connive, to plan, to gloat, perhaps to laugh at his gullibility.

"In appreciation, old man," Hal said, and lifted his glass in salute.

Quinton, weakened, stumbled into a side chair. Aaron shoved a glass of champagne at him; too shocked to refuse, he clutched at the stem. The pressure of his grasp snapped the fragile glass and the bowl of champagne shattered against the floorboards at the edge of the carpet.

"Now, now, old man, you mustn't take this so

hard,'' Hal said. ''After all, with my planning and
Justine's acting and manipulation, you managed to pull
off the *coup d'etat* of the antique and auction worlds.
You'll be famous, not in the annals of crime but in the
profession at which you are such a genius.''

Quinton's head began to clear. He looked up; ignoring Hal, his gaze focused on Justine. Her color had
returned. There was a half-smile on her lips, a sparkle
in her green eyes. Her eyes mocked him, her smile a
cruel expression of her amusement. Maria's words
came back to haunt him: *People ain't always what they
seem to be on the surface, Mr. Armstrong. When the
Devil gets in 'em he can make dark patches in the soul
like rot in an apple. The surface is all shiny and you
don't know the rot's there until you bite into it.*

Justine, suddenly unable to hold his gaze any longer,
turned away.

Quinton transferred his attention to Hal.

''I see you want explanations,'' Hal said. ''Details.
Ah, the questioning mind. More champagne, Justine,
my dear. I can now afford a taste for it.'' Holding out
his glass, he went on. ''I was once Helene Haymes's
lover. Not for long. I was only a temporary diversion
between monied men. It was in Paris after the war. Just
as I told you, only of course, I wasn't thrown out of her
hotel room. I was dragged into bed and stayed there for
three days. Can you imagine my surprise when three
decades later on a vacation in Key West I meet a woman
who is an exact replica of the woman I once loved,
except, of course, for the green eyes she inherited from
her English father?''

''How long has the real Helene been dead?'' Quinton
demanded.

''Oh, only days before you received the letter
suggesting the auction. Hal answered. ''She had been a
recluse, seriously ill for a long while. Long enough for

Justine and myself to devise a scheme to prevent this old mansion from being turned into a museum. Helene selfishly wanted to do in Key West what the famous Mrs. Gardner did in Boston, make the house a museum as a tribute to her ability as a collector.''

"And the good Dr. Webb was no doubt of invaluable help to you?"

"He's old, retired, but still greedy," Hal answered. "The antiques in the sheds, the inferior pieces, were sold off to dealers in Miami to cover expenses such as the cooperative doctor, you and other sundry outlays. At an appropriate time after the auction the good doctor will sign a death certificate for the infamous Helene Haymes. But the real jewel of our scheme was you, old man. You were so predictable, so easily ensnared in the mother-daughter conflict.''

Justine glanced over her shoulder at the boasting reporter. "Don't go too far," she warned.

"And Charlotte Engels?" Quinton pressed.

"Unfortunate, most unfortunate," Hal said. "We hadn't anticipated an old friend of Helene's surfacing from her past.''

"You bastard! You threw her down those stairs! You murdered her!''

"We were running out of money, old man. We couldn't afford to appease her, not even for the few weeks required. But don't take it so hard. How long would she have lasted on the streets of New York? Her end would have been more agonizing Besides, old man, we were afraid she'd contact you again. Perhaps convince you she was telling the truth about Helene which, by the way, she was.''

Quinton rose, trembling with rage. "You made me a part of this!" he cried. "Part of murder and fraud and . . . '' He glared at Justine, "You most of all! How could anyone . . . ''

"Don't take it so hard, old man," Hal said. "Except for the girl, you have a happy ending here. You get the fame, the money. You life has been enhanced monetarily, professionally and by experience with the opposite, fiercer sex. The agonies of the heart fade. Quicker, I might add, as you grow older."

"I want to hear it from you!" Quinton shouted at Justine.

"No need to shout," Hal told him. "You discovered our little conspiracy prematurely, but you realize the auction is in progress and it's too late to stop it without also destroying your reputation. Besides, who'd believe you gullible enough not to have discovered the truth? In a few days you'll be paid your commission. You can go back to collecting *biscuit de Sèvres.*"

With a final look at Justine's cold, indifferent face, Quinton shouted, "The hell with my reputation! I won't let you get away with this!" Before anyone could make a move to stop him, he bounded through the door.

Behind him, he heard Hal shout at Justine, "Go after him! Only you can stop him! The idiot, the romantic idiot!"

Maria was still at the foot of the stairs. When she saw Quinton come rushing down the stairs, Justine in pursuit, she stepped back against the wall, crying, "Oh, Lord! Oh, Lord!"

Quinton charged through the door. The surprised security guard at the gate spun about, his hand automatically going to his holster. Quinton stopped, turned just as Justine reached the porch. Betty who had been sitting on the porch swing with Lucifer at her feet, had sprung up and come forward when she had seen Quinton run out of the door and onto the walkway. Unknowingly, she had stopped directly in Justine's path.

When Justine ran out the door she collided with

Betty, sending the screaming girl to the floor of the porch.

Lucifer sprang without warning.

Justine's scream of terror was cut off as the Doberman's teeth sank into her neck. Both dog and woman tumbled down the stairs onto the walkway. From behind Quinton, came the explosion of the guard's revolver. Lucifer rolled off Justine, and was still.

Quinton did not move. Frozen, he stared at Justine, at the pool of blood spreading from her torn throat. He was aware, but as if he was a distant observer, of Maria, Hal and Aaron appearing in the doorway, of the shouts of the crowd from the sidewalk, of the auction patrons running from around the side of the house.

The guard brushed past him and stooped over Justine's body. When he straightened, he said in a curiously dull tone, "She's dead."

Maria screamed.

Quinton forced himself to become part of the reality around him. Calmly, he turned to the crowd, and said: "The auction is over!"

Epilogue

A blazing sun rose above the Atlantic horizon, promising another hot, humid day for the Florida keys. The tide was high, depositing storm-torn kelp under the piers where by noon it would dry and permeate the air with its rotting sweetness. Last night's summer storm had left the concluding miles of the nation's longest highway shrewn with palm fronds and unripened coconuts; pools of water had collected in potholes and along inadequately drained gutters, but these would dry before the sun had climbed noticeably into the blue morning sky. From Miami came the first flight of the day bearing morning newspapers and a few locals returning from a weekend in the big city; the sun caught the airplane's wings and gave it the illusion of a silver comet descending upon the sleepy island. It was August, off season for Key West, and only a skeleton ground crew met the plane.

Less than an hour later on the gulf side of the island, the buzzer in Quinton's room at *The Pier House* brought him dripping from the shower, wrapping a towel about himself he answered the door to the room service waitress, a young woman in sloppy beach pants and a knit T-shirt, no bra beneath. Her expression was drugged, bored. "Mornin' paper's here, sir." Without even glancing at him, she deposited the tray with his coffee and orange juice on the table by the window, spread open the Miami paper, and went out, forgetting to have him sign the check.

Quinton shrugged and returned to his shower.

When he again emerged from the bathroom he was dressed for traveling: lightweight slacks, short-sleeved shirt and tie; it would be as hot and humid in New York as it was in Key West. He packed his robe, snapped his suitcase closed and placed it by the door for the bell-man. His coffee was tepid, so was the orange juice; he pushed the tray aside and opened the Miami paper to the single page devoted to Key West news. Another drug bust involving a Colombian freighter; a small boat beloning to a Key Wester had been confiscated as the go-between vessel for the freighter and land dealers. The drug traffic was estimated to be in the fifty mil-lions. Quinton skimmed down the page until he located a small paragraph: *JURY STILL OUT ON HAYMES TRIAL*. Hal Crimmons's, Aaron's and Dr. Webb's futures had yet to be decided by the jury. Dr. Webb, in failing health, was expected to be given a light sentence for his participation in the Haymes conspiracy. With no discernible expression, Quinton tossed the newspaper onto the unmade bed.

Rising, he moved to the glass door, opened it and stepped out onto the balcony.

Despite the early hour there were already a few sunworshippers stretched out on the narrow expanse of sand. From a small yacht anchored off the beach, a naked man and woman plunged into the cool gulf water for a morning swim. Their nakedness drew whistles and suggestive cries from a boat of tourists passing through the channel toward the outer reef for a day of fishing. Hidden from view of the hotel employees, a man-boy lay sleeping among the boulders separating a section of the buildings from the beach; he had lost one tennis shoe in his sleep and it bobbed about on the surf like a dead fish.

Quinton leaned thoughtfully against the railing and let his gaze sweep over the blue gulf waters and the man-made islands across the channel, and he tried to conjure up the excitement and appreciation he had felt when he had first stood on this same balcony almost a year before. Instead, he felt curiously empty. Only one year, he thought, yet he felt decades older, wiser. One year ago he had thought Key West a paradise. One year ago he had loved Justine Haymes. His love for her had died abruptly that day in Helene's room when he had learned the truth about the conspiracy, had realized he had only loved the woman she had pretended to be.

The door buzzer brought him from the balcony.

Jackson Calder was revealed by the open door. The old man ran a skeletal hand through his white hair as he stepped into the room. "I've come to drive you to the airport," he said. "Can't have you going away saying Southern hospitality isn't what it's rumored to be." He glanced down at the packed suitcase. "Ready, I see." His expression was one of disappointment.

"Yes, ready," Quinton echoed. During the past months of the pre-trial hearings and then the trial itself, he had become quite friendly with the old attorney, working with him to establish a museum for the Haymes collection on Simonton Street. Quinton took his coat from the closet and followed the old man from the room.

Jackson Calder said nothing else until they were in the car en route to the airport. "Sure you won't change your mind?" he then asked. "The Haymes Museum is going to need someone to run it. No one alive knows that collection like you, Quinton. It seems foolish to turn it over to a stranger.'' The old man glanced at him fleetingly. ''Besides, you have friends in Key West,'' he added, ''despite all the publicity this trial has generated.''

Quinton smiled and drew his gaze away from the coastline. ''I know I've made friends here, Jackson. Especially you. I want to thank you for all your legal assistance and for all the favors you've done above and beyond your professional capacity.''

''Maria and her daughter, you mean,'' the old man mused. ''Maria's established with a good family.'' He tossed his head toward the backseat. ''As for Betty Sue, there's a present for you there on the seat.''

Quinton took the cylinder wrapped in newspaper and tied with a childishly made red bow. He undid the bow, and spread out a rolled drawing.

''It's the first she's done since she was enrolled in art classes,'' the attorney said. ''Damn good, isn't it?''

The charcoal drawing was of Quinton sitting on the front porch of the Haymes house. Lucifer lay curled up beside him. Betty had not only captured her subjects, but the very essence of the house itself with its slanted porch, ornamented gingerbread carvings and even the design of the Tiffany transom window above the door. Quinton's attention was drawn to the open shutters of a front window. There, behind lace curtains, Betty had drawn the vague shapes of two women looking out. ''Yes, it's good,'' he told the attorney. He wondered if Betty's perception had been unconscious or if she had included the two ghostlike figures deliberately to express her understanding that he would long be haunted by the last two women of the Haymes bloodline. His attention was drawn by the attorney.

'' . . . can't help thinking that it's poetic justice or some such thing, all the evil things done by Helene, then Justine because of that collection of antiquities, and now with them gone the collection's going to give pleasure to a lot of people. Still, somehow it doesn't seem to balance, does it?'' The old man leaned over the steering wheel and peered through the upper windshield at the airplane coming in low above them. His foot instinctively pressed harder on the accelerator and the car picked up speed. ''Still wish you'd reconsider, Quinton. About leaving.''

Quinton rerolled Betty's drawing and returned it to its cylinder. Whether to accept the management of the Haymes Museum or not had not been an easy decision, but once made, he was firm. ''Too many ghosts,'' he murmured. Then pulling himself from his thoughts, he said with enthusiasm, ''Besides, Jackson, I've a business to reorganize. I'm still the best appraiser in the country. Even though innocent, it's going to take considerable effort to rid my reputation of being involved in a fraudulent auction. I'm going to approach it as a challenge.''

''One you'll meet and conquer, I'm sure,'' the attorney said as he turned the car into the airport. ''Then, too, there's that novel you were thinking of writing.'' He braked the car to a halt before the airline terminal. He shook Quinton's hand firmly. ''A long happy life, Quinton Armstrong.'' Then in a comic Southern drawl, he said, ''Come see us again, ya hear.''

Between the gate and the boarding platform of the airplane, Quinton paused and let his gaze sweep slowly about the island for a final time.

Later, airborne, he did not look from the window as Key West faded from view.

There are a lot more
where this one came from!

ORDER your FREE catalog of ACE paperbacks here. We have hundreds of inexpensive
books where this one came from priced from
75¢ to $2.50. Now you can read all the books
you have always wanted to at tremendous
savings. Order your *free* catalog of ACE
paperbacks now.

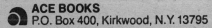

ACE BOOKS
P.O. Box 400, Kirkwood, N.Y. 13795